PHANTOM SHADOWS

IMMORTAL GUARDIANS

Dianne Duvall

WITHDRAWN

ZEBRA BOOKS
KENSINGTON PUBLISHING CORP.
http://www.kensingtonbooks.com

ZEBRA BOOKS are published by

Kensington Publishing Corp.
119 West 40th Street
New York, NY 10018

All Kensington titles, imprints and distributed lines are available at special quantity discounts for bulk purchases for sales promotion, premiums, fund-raising, educational or institutional use.

Special book excerpts or customized printings can also be created to fit specific needs. For details, write or phone the office of the Kensington Special Sales Manager: Attn. Special Sales Department. Kensington Publishing Corp., 119 West 40th Street, New York, NY 10018. Phone: 1-800-221-2647.

ISBN-13: 978-1-4201-1863-6
ISBN-10: 1-4201-1863-3

First Printing: October 2012

10 9 8 7 6 5 4 3 2 1

Printed in the United States of America

"WHAT DO YOU FEEL WHEN YOU TOUCH ME?" SHE ASKED.

"You can feel my emotions? Right now?"

"No. I have to touch you to feel them."

"So . . ."

He could see her considering it, trying to remember every time he had touched her or she had touched him. At the network. In her car. At David's. Trying to remember what she might have inadvertently revealed.

"You might have mentioned it. Given me a little warning."

"Such didn't occur to me."

More silence.

"What do you feel when you touch me?" she asked.

Bastien's attention dropped to her full lips as she licked them anxiously. "Sometimes I feel your concern. Sometimes uncertainty. Clinical detachment. Fear the first time we met."

"Well, our first meeting was rather . . . explosive."

That was putting it mildly.

"What else?"

He knew what she sought. "Sometimes my gift tells me you feel what I feel myself every time I look at you. Or think of you. Or touch you."

Her soft, smooth neck moved with a swallow. "You're attracted to me."

"Yes."

"I'm attracted to you."

"I know."

"What are we going to do about it?"

Immortal Guardians titles by Dianne Duvall

Darkness Dawns

Night Reigns

Phantom Shadows

Published by Kensington Publishing Corporation

For my family

Chapter 1

The desire to commit violence rose up within Bastien, almost irresistible in its intensity. Was this how vampires felt, he wondered, when the virus that infected them wreaked havoc in their brains and eradicated their impulse control? Because right now he would like nothing more than to plant his fist in the face of the immortal who lounged beside him.

"I hope you know what a sickeningly sappy grin you're wearing," Bastien muttered, his eyes on the students staggering about in front of the frat house across the street.

"Bite me," Richart replied as he continued to text away on his cell.

Bastien sighed. The jackass wouldn't even offer up a good fight. Bastien had been baiting him for a couple of hours now in an attempt to relieve some of the frustration spawned by Seth requiring him to have an escort. A babysitter. A guard.

"Fucking immortals," he muttered. They all wanted to kill him now that they knew he had slain one of their own almost two centuries ago. All of them but this one apparently.

"You're an immortal yourself, dumbass," the Frenchman reminded him.

Sometimes Bastien really missed the company of vampires.

Movement in the shadows north of the frat house caught his eye.

Speaking of which . . .

Bastien watched as two young couples, clearly in their cups, stumbled off the front porch and wove their way down the sidewalk. Pulsing music penetrated the house's closed windows, rumbling through the neighborhood and piercing Bastien's ears as silhouettes gyrated on the windows' curtains. The foursome argued drunkenly over which path to take to the dorm, then chose one and started down it, completely unaware of the dark predators who mirrored their every movement.

Bastien opened his mouth to give Richart the heads-up, then closed it again when he realized Richart was already returning his cell phone to his back pocket. The two stood.

When Richart reached out to touch Bastien's shoulder, Bastien dodged the contact and stepped off the edge of the roof, dropping three stories to land with only a hint of sound on the sidewalk in front of the building.

Richart appeared out of thin air beside him half a second later. "You risk discovery when you do such," he commented blandly as they set off in pursuit of the humans and their vampire shadows.

"And you don't, teleporting?"

Richart shrugged. "If they see me, they'll think me a figment of their imagination, a trick of the eye or light. If they see you, they'll think you're a jumper or some student who's drunk off his ass and come over to investigate."

True. The point was moot, however, because humans couldn't spy them in the darkness. The moon was absent, cloaked in the heavy clouds that had rolled in around sunset. And the streetlights above them had been shattered, either by vampires wanting to escape notice while they observed their prey or by students with too much time on their hands.

Bastien tuned out the human couples' inane conversation, the frat party's booming base, and the rumble of the occasional passing automobile, and zeroed in on the conversation of the vampires, inaudible to mortal ears.

The plan seemed to be to drain and dismember the men in front of the women, then torture the women, maybe keep them as toys from which the vampires could feed and extract screams for a few days until the vamps lost interest and sought new victims.

That plan changed when the men parted company from the women after a brief bout of sloppy kisses and ass-grabbing. The men staggered off down one sidewalk. The women tottered up another, their high heels clickety-clacking on the pavement.

The vampires hesitated, then followed the women.

Bastien looked at Richart. "Do you want Beavis or Butt-head?"

Richart nodded to the blond vampire. "I'll take Beavis."

The women passed in and out of pools of illumination as they walked beneath campus lights, then under the branches of ancient oak trees. They turned toward the brightly lit entrance of one of the dorms.

The vampires drew closer to their backs.

Richart touched Bastien's shoulder. The world around him went dark. A feeling of weightlessness engulfed him, not unlike that one sometimes experienced in an elevator. Then Bastien found himself standing a foot or so behind the vampires.

He frowned at Richart. Bastien may not have the aversion to teleporting that some immortals did, but he still liked to have a little warning first.

Two figures, moving so swiftly they blurred, suddenly darted around the corner of the building, swept up the women, and sped away.

"What the hell?" the brunet Bastien had labeled Butthead spouted.

"Hey, those chicks are ours!" Beavis shouted.

Bastien met Richart's glowing amber gaze. "I'll take the newbies."

Beavis and Butthead spun around.

Richart nodded. "I'll get rid of these two."

The vampires' eyes began to glow as they bared descending fangs.

Bastien took off after the new vamps and their female victims, running so swiftly that humans would not even be able to follow the movement with their eyes.

The vampires took him from Chapel Hill, North Carolina, to neighboring Durham, dodging this direction, then that, providing quite a chase.

Did they know an immortal hunted them? Or did they simply want to avoid a confrontation with the enraged vampires from whom they had snatched the women?

The vamps stopped in the deserted loading zone behind one of Duke University's buildings. Each clutched a woman. Neither human made a sound.

As Bastien halted a hairsbreadth away, he saw bite marks on both women's necks. Their hearts still beat, so neither had been drained. But the glands that had formed above the fangs the vampires had grown during their transformation had already delivered the chemical that acted like GHB, leaving the females sluggish and willing to accede to anything the vamps wanted to do to them. Tomorrow morning, if the women lived, they would have no memory of this.

The vampire closest to Bastien started violently when he realized they had company. He dropped the woman he held. "We saw 'em first."

Bastien caught the woman's blouse in a fist before she could hit the ground, then plunged his other fist into the vampire's face.

Blood spurted and bone shattered as the vampire flew backward and hit the building with enough force to crack the brick and produce a cloud of sandy mortar.

Bastien gently lowered the woman to the ground and zipped over to the vampire's gaping friend. That one tried to lock an arm around his victim and use her as a shield . . . until Bastien broke said arm and sent the screaming vamp flying through the air to form more cracks in the building's exterior.

Bastien placed the woman beside her friend and charged the vampires, guiding the battle away from the humans.

Both vampires drew weapons: hunting knives with serrated edges and bowies as long as his forearm.

Bastien drew his katanas and faced them without a qualm. He had been born two centuries ago and, at the insistence of his noble British father, had trained with a master swordsman. If that weren't enough to lend him confidence, the fact that he had trained with Seth and David, the eldest and most powerful immortals in existence, for roughly two years did.

The blond vampire swore, fear filling his glowing blue eyes. "He's an Immortal Guardian!"

Bastien thought for a moment the other one would cut and run. Then the brunet roared and dove into the fight.

Blades clashed. Wounds opened. Blood flowed.

On the vampires, that is.

Bastien remained relatively unscathed. Disarming the blond, he sheathed a sword and grabbed the blond vampire by the neck. As Bastien continued to battle the brunet, the emotions of the blond flowed into him at the behest of Bastien's gift. Malice. Chaos. Madness. He couldn't be saved. The virus that infected both vampires and immortals had been with this one too long.

Shoving the vampire back, Bastien slashed the brunet's chest, then swiftly decapitated the blond.

The brunet stilled and stared at his fallen comrade.

Bastien used his preternatural speed to disarm the second vamp and took him by the throat as well.

Richart appeared in the distance, perhaps forty yards away, turned in a circle, spotted them, then teleported to Bastien's side. "The women?" he asked.

Bastien nodded to them. "Alive, but bitten and disoriented."

Richart motioned to the vampire Bastien held. "And this one?" Richart's clothing—black pants, black shirt, long black coat (standard garb for immortals)—bore numerous wet patches that would have been obvious bloodstains on material of any other color. "Are you planning to keep him as a souvenir or what?"

Bastien scowled. "I wanted to see if he was salvageable."

If the vamp were newly turned, the madness that afflicted humans after they transformed may not have infected him yet.

"And?"

Bastien eyed the vamp with disgust. "He isn't."

"Then what are you . . . ?" Richart trailed off.

Muffled noises carried to Bastien's sensitive ears. Boots traversing grass and pavement. Several pair, each bearing a man's weight. The faint rattle of equipment.

The immortals shared a look.

Facing the corner of the building from around which the sounds approached, they both drew in deep breaths.

No cologne. No scented soap. No deodorant. No lingering hint of clothing detergent or scented fabric softener or dryer sheets. Nothing an immortal would ordinarily detect on an approaching group of humans.

The sole human-oriented scent that reached them was . . . gun oil.

Bastien frowned at Richart. Whoever approached bore the MO of a hunter. What the hell would they be hunting on a college campus? Unless . . .

"Take the women to safety," Bastien ordered too softly for humans to hear.

Richart reached the women in an instant and tossed one over each shoulder. "I shall return shortly," he promised, then vanished.

The vampire in Bastien's grasp began to struggle.

Bastien tightened his hold and waited to see who or what would come around the corner.

Had his vision not been preternaturally sharp, he would have missed the tiny mirror—barely bigger than a thumbnail—that appeared first and gave the man who held it a glimpse of Bastien and his captive.

Breath sucked in. The mirror slipped out of sight.

Something round and metal, the size of a tennis ball, bounced and jounced across the pavement toward Bastien. Light as bright as the damned sun engulfed him in a brief flash, blinding Bastien and making the vampire howl in pain.

Bastien yanked the vamp in front of him half a second before gunfire erupted, muffled by silencers. The vamp jerked and grunted. The scent of blood filled the air.

Footsteps pounded around the corner.

Because his advanced DNA made him more powerful than the vampire, Bastien's vision swiftly cleared. While the vamp continued to scrub at his eyes with one hand and clutch his chest with the other, Bastien studied the men who approached.

All were garbed like Special Ops soldiers and carried much of the related weaponry with one notable addition.

The vampire jerked when a tranquilizer dart hit him in the shoulder. His body instantly went limp and heavy.

Still using him as a shield, Bastien zeroed in on the soldier holding the tranquilizer pistol. The next time the soldier fired, Bastien moved—as swift as lightning—and caught the dart. He hurled it back at the soldier, hitting him in the throat. The man collapsed without a sound.

Another soldier fired a second tranquilizer pistol. Bastien

ducked the first dart, then caught the second and sent it back to its launcher.

All but one of the remaining soldiers opened fire with their silencer-equipped assault rifles. Bullets tore through the vampire and hit Bastien. Fire burned through his stomach and chest. Breathing became difficult as one lung collapsed.

Shit!

Dropping the vampire, Bastien sped forward, grabbed the rifle one of the downed human soldiers had dropped and fired. The remaining soldiers began to fall as bullets penetrated Kevlar or hit flesh not protected by armor.

Despite his attempts to evade the darts, Bastien felt a sharp sting in his neck. His knees weakened.

Alarm surpassing pissed off, Bastien put on a burst of speed, circled the building, and came up behind the soldiers. He grabbed the first one he met, dragged him back against his chest, and sank his fangs into the man's throat, siphoning as much blood as he could into his veins to dilute the drug he could feel steadily sapping his strength and to aid the virus in repairing his wounds.

Yanking the tranquilizer pistol from the soldier's hand, Bastien fired at the others as they turned to fight anew.

Every human fell . . . eventually. And every one of them died, either as a result of bullet wounds or being tranqed with a drug too strong for their systems to handle.

Bastien dropped the soldier he had drained.

The campus around him tilted and rolled. Staggering, he struggled to remain upright.

A loud clatter disturbed the quiet.

Bastien glanced down at the tranquilizer pistol that had fallen from his hand.

Had he meant to do that?

Noticing a dart protruding from one thigh, he yanked it out, then removed another he found in his arm.

A steady *pat pat pat* drew his gaze to the blood dripping

onto the ground at his feet. How many bullet wounds had he incurred?

Several seconds spent thinking about it yielded no numbers. He was too tired to count.

He looked at the bodies on the ground. The blood. The weapons.

Maybe somebody should clean this mess up before . . .

He frowned. Wouldn't something bad happen if this shit wasn't cleaned up?

It took a minute for him to fish his cell phone out of his pocket. His hand didn't seem to want to cooperate. Squinting down at the display, which seemed both too bright and weirdly out of focus, he tried to decide whom he should call.

He glanced at the bodies. At the phone. At the bodies. At the phone.

Oh. Right. The network.

Dr. Lipton tucked a new page in the chart on her desk and reached for her cell phone.

Just as her fingers touched it, it rang. "Melanie Lipton" she answered. Several long seconds passed without a response. "Hello?"

"Dr. Lipton?"

Her heart leapt as those deep, rich tones washed over her. Sebastien Newcombe. She'd know his voice anywhere . . . even if something about it did seem a bit off. "Yes. Bastien?"

"What are you doing here?" he asked, his words full of bewilderment.

Melanie frowned. He sounded drunk. Immortals couldn't get drunk. "What do you mean? I'm in my office at the network."

"You are?"

"Yes."

"Oh."

Melanie rose. Something was wrong.

A clatter came over the line.

"Sebastien? Are you still there?" She hurried out into the hallway.

"Yes."

"What happened?"

"I think I fell." A moment of silence passed. "Yeah, I fell."

Anxiety flooded her as she waved to one of the security officers who guarded the doors to the vampires' apartments across the hall. "Get Mr. Reordon down here," she whispered. "Now!"

The man reached for a walkie-talkie on his shoulder and began to mutter into it.

Melanie started toward the elevator at the end of the hallway. "Are you injured? Bastien?"

"Feels like it."

"How badly?"

"I don't know."

"Where are you?"

"On the ground." Bastien's words slurred.

"No, I mean . . . Look around you. What do you see?"

There was a pause. "Bodies."

Oh crap. "What else?"

A large desk rested in front of the elevator doors. A dozen men garbed in black fatigues and sporting automatic weapons stood around it. Two more, seated behind it, rose at her approach.

"Is something wrong, Doc?" Todd asked.

She nodded. "If Mr. Reordon isn't already on his way, get him down here now," she murmured. Then, louder into the phone, she said, "What else do you see?"

"Trees," Bastien muttered.

Trees? Yeah. That narrowed it down. He could be anywhere in the freaking state.

The numbers above the elevator doors lit up.

"Is anyone there with you? Another immortal perhaps?"

She had heard that he had been forbidden to go anywhere without an immortal escort.

"Um . . . I can't tell if those are vampires or immortals shriveling up over there. I think they're vampires. I killed a couple of vampires, didn't I?"

A slew of faint French erupted over the phone.

The elevator pinged. When the doors slid open, Chris Reordon—head of the East Coast division of the network of humans that aided Immortal Guardians—emerged.

"What's up?" he asked with a frown.

Melanie felt only partially relieved. Chris could send Bastien aid, but the question was: Would he? A *lot* of animosity existed between those two. Animosity that had exploded into full-blown hatred when Bastien had breached these very network headquarters only a few weeks earlier, forcing his way inside and injuring dozens of guards after . . .

Well, after Melanie had called him to let him know one of his former vampire followers had had a psychotic break. She would never forget the look in Bastien's eyes the night he had ended the young vampire's life.

Hoping personal bias wouldn't interfere in the execution of Chris's duties . . . again . . . Melanie drew in a deep breath. "Something has happened to Sebastien Newcombe."

Chris's scowl deepened. "What?"

She drew his attention to her phone. "He's been injured and . . . his words are slurred. His thoughts don't seem to be coherent. He's down and says there are bodies all around him and two of them are either vampires or immortals."

Swearing, Chris held out his hand for the phone. "Bastien? Where are you?" A growl of pure frustration followed. "On the ground *where?*"

Melanie bit her lip.

Chris's demeanor suddenly changed. "It's Chris. Is this Étienne or Richart?" He drew a pencil and small notepad from his pocket and dropped the notepad on the desk. "What?

How many?" He scribbled something down. "What side of the campus are you on? . . . Which building? . . . Okay. Take out the lights. I'll send a cleaning crew over there ASAP. Bring Bastien here. I want to talk to him."

Melanie frowned. *Talk* to him? He was injured and barely coherent.

"The holding room."

That didn't bode well.

Chris ended the call and handed her the phone.

"Why is he being put in the holding room?" she dared to ask.

Chris retrieved his own phone and began to bark orders into it.

"Mr. Reordon?" she persisted. "Why is Bastien being put in the holding room?"

Irritation swept his visage. "Because over a dozen dead humans litter the ground around him."

The guards began to grumble. They held no love or admiration for Bastien either, some of them having been injured by him personally.

"Immortals are supposed to *protect* humans, not kill them," Chris muttered as he ended the call. "Half of you come with me," he told the guards. "Todd, get two dozen more down here with full firepower. I want both the elevator and the door to the stairwell heavily guarded. Tell the men to be prepared for *anything.*"

"Yes, sir." Todd motioned to several men, indicating they should follow Chris, then reached for the walkie-talkie on his shoulder.

Chris started down the long hallway toward the holding room. Melanie hurried to keep up with him as the guards, fingers on the triggers of their weapons, fell in behind them, tense and alert.

"But . . . you don't know what the circumstances were," she broached. They wouldn't *hurt* Bastien, would they? Or deny him medical care? Because it sounded like Chris intended to chain him up and interrogate him. Again. "He's injured. What if—"

"Immortals aren't supposed to harm humans unless the humans pose a serious threat."

"Maybe these did."

He snorted. "He's immortal, Dr. Lipton. Humans can't harm him. Not seriously enough to warrant a death sentence."

She lowered her voice. "They can if they possess a certain very unique tranquilizer."

He looked at her sharply. "The odds of that are—"

"He sounded drugged."

"Not to me, he didn't."

"When you asked him where he was, he said he was on the ground!"

"That's just Bastien being Bastien. He's an ass. It's what he does."

Pounding erupted on the door to the holding room. The guards already stationed in front of it jumped and turned their weapons on it.

Chris picked up his pace.

Melanie had to jog to keep up with him.

Chris stopped before the door and swiped his key card. "New arrival," he told the guards as he punched in the security code. "Stay sharp."

A *clunk* sounded, then the door—as thick as that of a bank vault—swung open.

Inside the steel and titanium room, an immortal Melanie had never seen before waited for them, Sebastien draped over his shoulder. Around six feet tall, he boasted the raven hair and brown eyes (which still held a hint of amber glow) characteristic of all immortals save Sarah. The black clothing and long, dark coat he wore glistened in places with what she suspected was blood.

This must be Richart. As far as Melanie knew, Richart was

the only immortal currently residing in the United States who could teleport.

Aside from Seth.

"He's been drugged," Richart announced as soon as he saw them, his words softened by a French accent.

Melanie gave Chris an *I-told-you-so* look.

Lips tightening, Chris motioned to Bastien. "Put him on the cot and chain him up."

The holding room was usually reserved for vampires. Thick steel walls reinforced with several feet of concrete held in captives. Titanium chains as thick as her biceps dangled from links in the walls above a single cot. By the door, out of reach of those manacles, resided a desk.

When the immortal hesitated, Melanie spoke. "Shouldn't he be taken to the infirmary?"

"Not after killing humans." Chris denied. "Protocol states—"

"Fuck protocol," the immortal interrupted. "These were not ordinary humans. They resembled Special Ops soldiers, were heavily armed, and carried with them several tranquilizer pistols issuing the only drug that has ever proven to be effective against us. We have a serious problem on our hands." He looked to Melanie. "Where is the infirmary?"

"This way," she said. Without looking at Chris, she turned and led the way down the hallway to the sizable infirmary.

Since immortals usually moved silently, the boots clomping down the hallway behind her told her Chris and all of the guards followed as well.

At her direction, the immortal laid Bastien on an empty bed.

"Richart d'Alençon," he introduced himself with a nod.

She smiled. "Melanie Lipton." Pulling on a pair of vinyl gloves, she began to unbutton Bastien's blood-spattered shirt. "Do you know how many darts he was hit with?"

He reached into his pocket. "I found two on the ground

beside him." He showed her, then set them aside and helped her remove Bastien's clothing.

She frowned. "Two shouldn't have rendered him unconscious. Didn't it take more than that for you when you were hit?"

He nodded as he dropped Bastien's long coat to the floor. "I believe I was tranqed four times or more before I lost consciousness. Either blood loss is compounding it or he removed some darts before I arrived."

Chris stood at the foot of the bed, brow creased, arms crossed over his chest. "Why weren't any of the men left alive for questioning?"

"I don't know. I wasn't there."

"I thought you were supposed to be watching him."

Richart's eyes flared bright amber as his jaw tightened. "There were four vampires. Two remained at UNC and two headed for Duke. Bastien took the latter. I took the former. Should I have left the two at Chapel Hill to freely troll for victims in order to watch Bastien dispatch the vampires he followed?"

Still frowning, Chris said nothing.

"I caught up with Bastien just before the human soldiers arrived. The women the vamps had snatched needed to be taken to safety. I could not stay without risking their lives."

"I don't like it. The men were human. He should have been able to disarm them without killing them."

The incandescence in Richart's eyes faded a bit. "In Bastien's defense, I can tell you that in battle it is almost always kill or be killed. Considering these men were armed with the tranquilizer *and* filling him with bullets, leaving one alive may not have been an option for him."

Melanie silently applauded the immortal.

While the Frenchman stripped Bastien's shirt from him, Melanie retrieved several bags of blood from storage in the next room and set up an IV pole beside the bed.

Bastien's smooth, muscled chest and eight-pack abs were riddled with ragged holes, some of which still contained bullets.

Melanie eyed Richart as she found Bastien's vein with a needle and attached the canula. "I know they can't do anything about the drug coursing through him, but wouldn't it be better for a healer to be brought in to take care of his wounds? There are so many." She would have to remove the bullets herself if they didn't.

"David is in Egypt," he replied.

David was the second oldest immortal in existence and was a very powerful healer . . . among other things.

"Seth is somewhere in Asia, but mentioned stopping by David's place tomorrow. The only other healer in our area is Roland Warbrook. And he would rather watch Bastien die a slow, agonizing death than raise a finger to help him."

Well, Melanie had to admit, she could understand Roland's animosity. Bastien had, after all, nearly killed Roland's wife. And had tried on several occasions to kill Roland himself. After raising a vampire army to conquer the Immortal Guardians.

Bastien's past was a complicated one. And she suspected she didn't know the half of it.

"Shouldn't Dr. Whetsman be doing this?" Chris queried.

Yes, but . . . "Dr. Whetsman avoids face-to-face contact with vampires."

Richart frowned. "Bastien isn't a vampire."

"It doesn't matter. Dr. Whetsman wouldn't make that distinction, because Bastien lived amongst vampires for so long and led them in the first uprising."

"How long has this been going on?" Chris asked. He may not like Bastien, but he didn't want any of his people shirking their duties.

"Since Vince."

Vincent was one of the vampires who had followed Bastien a couple of years ago. Though he, Cliff, and Joe (two other vampires) had surrendered, hoping the network could help them, Melanie and her colleagues had found no way to stop the mental deterioration the virus caused in humans. In time, Vincent had broken, flying into a rage and injuring Dr. Whetsman and several others before Chris's men had stopped him.

"He doesn't have *any* contact with them?" Chris pressed.

"No. Only Linda and I do."

When Chris opened his mouth to say more, Melanie held up a hand. "They respond better to us."

"Because you're women," Richart offered shrewdly.

She nodded. "They're more careful around us. Protective even. The men tend to aggravate the vampires more."

"Dr. Whetsman aggravates *me* and I'm human," Chris muttered. "If he wasn't so damned brilliant, I would have fired his ass a long time ago. Hold up for a minute," he added when Melanie rolled her tray of instruments close to the bed and prepared to begin extracting bullets. "Let me go ahead and call Roland. I don't want Seth to chew me out later for not giving it a try."

Melanie looked at Richart, who shrugged, his face indicating his belief that such was a useless endeavor.

While Chris dialed, Melanie replaced the blood bag that had already emptied itself into Bastien with a full one.

"Roland. Chris Reordon. We have a man down who could use your healing skills . . . Immortal . . . Multiple bullet wounds . . . I know blood will heal those, but he's also been tranqed, so the process has been slowed significantly. The virus is too busy trying to counteract the drug to—" He looked at Richart. "Bastien." Wincing, he held the phone away from his ear.

Melanie could only make out a word here and there, but those she did were of the four letter variety.

Richart pursed his lips and whistled, eyebrows raising. His

preternaturally enhanced hearing no doubt allowed him to hear everything the reclusive, antisocial immortal growled.

Chris ended the call.

Melanie raised one eyebrow. "I'm guessing that was a no."

"You guessed right," Chris said and motioned to the unconscious immortal. "Dig in."

Grimacing at his choice of words, Melanie reached for the forceps.

A trebly version of Skillet's "Monster" broke the silence.

Richart retrieved a phone from his back pocket, glanced at the caller ID, then answered. *"Oui?"*

Melanie didn't understand anything he said after that. Her knowledge of French was pretty much restricted to yes, no, and cheese. And she wasn't sure why she knew the last one.

Richart ended the call and returned the phone to his pants. "I teleported Lisette to the scene to frighten away any curious humans before I brought Bastien here. She said your cleaning crew has arrived."

"Excellent."

"I asked her to linger until they were finished and to let me know if any soldiers should come looking for their fallen comrades."

As the two men discussed the possibility of such happening, Melanie searched for and retrieved the first bullet.

Chapter 2

"Stop beating yourself up," a male voice said.

It sounded familiar to Bastien, but he couldn't quite place it, muffled as it was. It felt as though someone had stuffed cotton in his ears.

"I can't help it," a woman responded. "I'm failing . . . everyone."

That voice was one he would always be able to identify. Dr. Melanie Lipton's warm tones wrapped around him like a soothing blanket and eased the pounding in his head. They also tempted him into cracking open his eyelids.

Bright light pierced his eyes, driving him to squeeze his lids closed again.

What the hell?

"You aren't failing anyone," the male insisted. "Look how much you've helped me and Joe."

Dr. Lipton answered with a sad laugh. "Yeah, I've really helped you."

Bastien didn't like the defeat that colored her voice. Melanie was the strongest, bravest human in the network. The *only* human gutsy enough to work with the vampires on a daily basis.

"You have," the male insisted. Cliff. One of the young

vampires who had followed him when Bastien had led the uprising against Roland and the other immortals. "I haven't had a single episode since you started administering the drug."

"You said it makes you feel sluggish."

"Hey, sluggish is better than murderous. I'm not hurting people. That's exactly what I hoped for when I came here."

"I didn't even create the drug," Melanie despaired. "I just watered down the one our enemies developed."

"And you're the only one around here who thought to try it."

"I'm sure someone else would have eventually."

Cliff snorted. "I'm not."

"Joe doesn't like it. I had to give him enough to make him sleep before we brought Bastien in here."

"I heard."

"The virus seems to be progressing more rapidly in him. He was turned eight months after you were and you aren't exhibiting nearly as much hostility as he is."

Cliff swore.

"I'm sorry," she said. "I shouldn't have said anything."

"No, it's . . . Knowing I'm not as bad off as he is, that I may not lose it as quickly as he is or as quickly as Vince did . . . It's a relief, you know? But I feel guilty as hell saying it."

"You shouldn't. It's completely understandable and Joe wouldn't hold it against you. I'm sure he would feel the same way."

Silence fell, heavy with despair.

Melanie sighed. "How are the—"

"Shh."

"What—?"

"Shhhh."

Bastien strained to hear whatever Cliff heard, but his ears still felt funny.

"Reordon's leaving. He went ahead and scheduled the meeting."

"When is it?"

"In an hour. Bastien's going to be pissed."

"Well, there's nothing I can do about it. I tried to talk Mr. Reordon into delaying it and—"

"You could try the antidote."

"No. I can't. Not without knowing all of the possible repercussions. And it may not even *be* an antidote."

"You won't know the repercussions until you try it on someone. Try it on me."

"Absolutely not. It could kill you, Cliff. Or trigger a psychotic break. One tranquilizer dart drops you—and any other vampire—like a stone. Yet it takes several to sedate an immortal. When I found a stimulant that looked like it might work, I had to multiply its strength exponentially. Any human injected with it would die instantly. It could kill the immortals, too. I don't know what it would do to a vampire or how it might affect your fragile mental state."

Bastien tried to open his eyes again. Knifelike pains pierced his cranium, eliciting a groan.

"Bastien?" Melanie queried.

A chain rattled.

"Too bright," he muttered through clenched teeth.

He heard small, sneaker-clad feet cross the room. The lights dimmed.

Sighing, he cautiously opened his eyes.

Melanie moved to stand beside his bed or cot or whatever the hell uncomfortable surface supported him. Beneath a white lab coat, she wore a baby blue University of North Carolina Tar Heels T-shirt that hugged bountiful breasts and jeans that molded themselves to full hips and shapely thighs. Her chestnut hair was pulled back into a ponytail that made her look like a college student.

"How do you feel?" she asked.

"Like someone dropped an anvil on my head."

Pretty brow furrowed, she touched his wrist to gauge his pulse and glanced over at the clock on the wall.

Her emotions flowed into him, courtesy of the gift with which Bastien had been born. So much concern. He wasn't worth it. But he devoured the sweetness of it like a piece of German chocolate pie after a long, long fast.

Relief replaced some of her concern. "Your pulse is strong."

And running faster than usual thanks to her nearness and her gentle touch.

Her eyes met his. Something skittered through her. He felt it, but wasn't sure . . .

Was it excitement or nervousness?

It must be the latter. Not that he could blame her. The first time he had met her, he had decapitated a man in front of her. They had met and spoken many times since, but how could she forget such a first impression?

Releasing his wrist, she turned and walked away. "Let me get you some more blood and a cold pack for your head."

She was through the door before he could tell her not to bother.

"Man," Cliff said when the heavy door closed behind her, "you had us worried there for a minute."

Bastien tugged his gaze away from the door and sought the vampire.

Cliff stood a few feet away, a manacle around one ankle. The chain attached to it was titanium and as big around as Bastien's forearm, keeping the young vampire from straying more than a couple of yards away from the wall behind him.

"What the hell?" When Bastien sat up, invisible sledge-hammers assaulted his brain. He pressed the heel of one hand to his forehead and held his breath until the pain eased.

The slender young man shook his head and reached up to twist one of the short dreadlocks he had recently begun to grow. "It isn't what you—"

The door opened as Dr. Lipton returned. Bastien saw several heavily armed guards posted outside the room before she closed it again.

"Who's brilliant idea was this?" he demanded and motioned to his shackled friend. "Why are we in the holding room?"

Melanie paused. "Actually, it was my idea."

He frowned. "Oh." Damned if his mind didn't go blank.

Thankfully, Cliff jumped in. "That Reordon prick ordered the guards to lock you up in here, but Dr. Lipton wouldn't let them and made them take you to the infirmary instead."

That must have gone over well.

Melanie shrugged apologetically. A blood bag in one hand and an icy gel pack in the other, she approached the gurney upon which he sat. (No wonder it was so damned uncomfortable.)

"When I heard what had happened," Cliff continued, "I wanted to go see how you were doing, but Reordon said hell no and—long story short—Dr. Lipton argued with him until they reached this compromise."

"It was the best I could do," she admitted.

Bastien took the blood and waved away the cold pack. "Thank you. I'm surprised Reordon didn't chain *me* up, too."

"He wanted to. But I needed to remove the bullets and clean your wounds. They weren't healing properly because of the drug. And Richart wouldn't hear of it."

Bastien paused. "Richart protested?" He had taken for granted that the Frenchman loathed him.as much as all of the other immortals did, and Richart really hadn't done anything to make him think otherwise.

She nodded. "He was actually quite emphatic in his defense of you. Mr. Reordon wouldn't let the fact that you had supposedly killed several humans drop until Richart pretty much made him drop it."

Bastien grunted. "I didn't *supposedly* kill them. I *did* kill them. At least, I assume I did. Isn't the drug strong enough to kill a human?"

"Yes," she confirmed.

A tinny version of Nine Inch Nails' "The Perfect Drug" filled the air.

It wasn't until Bastien reached for his back pocket that he realized the hunting clothes he wore were not his own.

Melanie fumbled with a pocket of her lab coat and withdrew his cell phone. "Your clothes were ruined. Richart loaned you those."

Okay. This was just bizarre. Why was Richart suddenly doing him so many favors?

Bastien couldn't remember the last time anyone other than Ami or Melanie had done something nice for him with no strings attached. So, what was Richart's game? What did he want?

Bastien's fingers brushed Melanie's when she handed him the phone. His heart skipped a beat at the brief contact. "Yeah?" he answered.

"It's Tanner."

Bastien hadn't seen Tanner Long since the Immortal Guardians had ended Bastien's uprising. Tanner had been one of the humans who had aided him. *The* human, he should say. Tanner had been Bastien's go-to guy. He had been invaluable, the equivalent of an immortal's Second.

And Tanner had been a friend.

Bastien had not had a friend in a very long time. Which was why he had kept his distance from Tanner ever since the Immortal Guardians had taken both into custody. Tanner was being groomed to become a Second, or personal assistant, to an immortal. If Tanner displayed any friendliness or sympathy toward Bastien, the other Seconds and members of the network would ostracize him. He didn't deserve that. Not after all he had been through.

"You there?" Tanner's voice came over the line again.

"Yeah. Just . . . surprised to hear from you."

"Changing your number and not giving me the new one will do that, asshole, but we'll discuss that later."

"How *did* you get this number?"

"Ami. Now shut up and listen. According to the Seconds' rumor mill, Reordon has called a meeting. It starts in less than an hour at David's place. And I know damned well he scheduled it for then, believing you would be unable to attend. I think he's going to condemn you for taking out the humans and, since Seth has thus far rejected every call for your execution, will push for your permanent removal from the Immortal Guardians' ranks."

Hmm. Would that be such a bad thing? Hadn't Bastien decided just a few weeks earlier that something would have to change? That the whole Immortal Guardian thing wasn't working out for him? Maybe it was time for him to move on and . . .

Well, he didn't know what. For the first couple hundred years or so of his immortal existence, he had been driven to seek revenge for his sister's murder. Once he had found his quarry, he had spent another two decades or so planning that revenge and raising his vampire army.

"Don't let him do it, man," Cliff said, his exceptional hearing allowing him to listen to the phone conversation.

"Don't let him do what?" Bastien asked.

"Don't let Reordon get you kicked out of the Immortal Guardians. You're the only one of them who gives a damn about us—about vampires. Without you fighting for us . . . what hope do we have?"

Hell.

Bastien met Melanie's gaze, saw the pleading in it.

"Don't let Mr. Reordon's prejudice keep you from taking your rightful place among the Immortal Guardians," she pleaded. "The immortals need you more than they think they do. Cliff and Joe need you, too."

Again: *Hell.*

Bastien sighed. "All right," he told Tanner. "Thanks for the heads-up. I'm on my way."

"Good."

"It'll take me a while because I'm on foot, but—"

"I'll drive you," Melanie interrupted.

"No," Bastien countered. "No, thank you," he amended. She had already come to his defense once by keeping Reordon from chaining him up. The last thing he wanted was for her to be associated with him even more. Too much unpleasantness would be directed her way.

"Yes," she retorted, raising her chin stubbornly. "I'm your doctor. You just regained consciousness and need to be monitored for the next few hours as the drug continues to wear off. You aren't going anywhere without me."

"He may not be going anywhere anyway," Cliff mentioned. "How is he going to leave the building? I doubt Reordon gave his men orders to let Bastien go."

Melanie frowned.

"Don't worry about that," Tanner said. "I'll take care of it."

Before Bastien could ask him what he meant, he hung up.

Melanie bit her lip as Bastien lowered his phone and ended the call. "If you're thinking of fighting your way out, you may want to reconsider."

Fighting his way *in* the night they had met had resulted in him being wrapped like a mummy in chains. She didn't want to see that happen again.

Bastien frowned. "Tanner said I wouldn't have to, but I don't see how—"

A *clunk* sounded as the door unlocked, then opened, pushed by Todd.

The soldier did not look happy. "I just got a call from David."

The elder immortal was warm and friendly, treating all immortals and members of the network like family, yet—at the same time—was nearly as powerful and formidable as Seth.

Todd looked at Bastien. "You're free to leave whenever you want to."

Bastien met Melanie's gaze for a moment, then eyed Todd suspiciously as if he were trying to discern if this were some sort of trick. "I am?"

Todd nodded and opened the door wide. "Mr. Reordon won't be happy about it, but . . ."

No one gainsays David, went unspoken.

Bastien shrugged. "So be it."

Melanie headed for the door. "I'll just get my keys, then we can go."

Todd scowled as she approached. "You're not going with him, are you?"

"She has to," Cliff blurted before Melanie or Bastien could say anything. "Bastien's still groggy from the drug."

Was he trying to convince Todd or Bastien, who still looked as though he wanted to protest? Melanie knew Cliff worried about his former leader.

"I'll have one of my men take him wherever he wants to go," Todd said. As Melanie passed him in the doorway, he added in a lower voice, "You shouldn't be alone with him, Dr. Lipton. It isn't safe."

Melanie glanced back in time to see Bastien's eyes flare bright amber with fury. When he opened his mouth to speak, she hurried to prevent it. "He needs to be monitored. We're still learning about this drug and its effects on immortals. I need to continue measuring his recovery time and keep an eye out for lingering side effects."

Though both Bastien and Todd frowned, neither—she was pleased to see—could find fault with her explanation.

Cliff sent her a big grin.

What are you doing, Lanie? she asked herself as she crossed the hall to her office.

What I have to.

No, you aren't. David is a healer. He can tell you anything you need to know about Bastien's recovery. So could Roland, though getting that one to cooperate would pretty much be impossible.

It wasn't really about Bastien's recovery anyway. Yes, she would like to continue monitoring him and see how long the weakness lingered. Any little thing she could learn about this drug without having to inflict it upon test subjects—namely the vampires—would help her in her attempts to combat it. But, as that little voice in her head had pointed out, David or Roland could observe Bastien for her.

Removing her lab coat, she donned the turtleneck she had discarded earlier and topped it with a sweater.

No, it wasn't about his recovery. It was . . .

She liked Bastien, damn it. She had liked him long before she had ever met him just from the things the vampires had told her about him. He may play the black sheep and be hated by his immortal brethren for past misdeeds, but he seemed to be an honorable man. A compassionate man. He wasn't the monster Chris Reordon and some of the others thought him. He just wanted to help people. Help the vampires. End the suffering of men he had considered his brothers for two centuries.

Was that so wrong?

Locating her purse, she picked it up and drew her keys from an outer pocket.

Someone needed to stand up for him. Defend him. And, though it may sound ludicrous that a man of his strength and power would need *her*, she intended to be that someone. She had more insight into his character than *anyone*.

Except, perhaps, for Ami. Bastien seemed to have a real soft spot for Amiriska.

Melanie frowned as she wondered just how soft a soft spot that was.

She headed back across the hallway.

Todd crossed his arms over his chest as Melanie approached him. "Maybe Dr. Whetsman should accompany him instead."

She raised one eyebrow. "Dr. Whetsman? Really?"

Todd grimaced and stepped aside. "Yeah, you're right."

Melanie entered the room and found Bastien standing beside the gurney. When he wavered, Cliff reached out and took his shoulder to steady him.

"Ready?" she asked.

Bastien nodded once, then gripped Cliff's arm to keep his balance.

Todd strode over to the desk, grabbed a pen and a Post-it pad, and leaned down to scribble something on it. Peeling off the top note, he turned and handed it to Melanie.

Three telephone numbers had been scrawled across it.

"The first number is Seth's. The second is Richart's. The third is mine. If anything should happen"—his gaze slid to Bastien and back—"call them in that order. Seth can teleport directly to you. If you can't reach him, Richart can probably teleport to your general area and find you. If *he* can't be reached, call me and I'll track your GPS signal and bring a small army of men."

Bastien raised one eyebrow. "A small army of men couldn't stop me last night."

Melanie sighed. Why did Bastien have to antagonize everyone every chance he could get?

Todd huffed a laugh. "Did you or did you not have to be carried in here?"

Melanie hoped that would end the exchange.

It didn't. True to form, Bastien spoke in a taunting voice. "Not before I killed every human that was gunning for me."

Todd's jaw tightened.

"Enough," Melanie said, throwing up her hands. "If you two want to continue duking it out verbally later, then feel free. Right now we need to get going. Bastien has someplace he needs to be." She turned a stern look on Bastien. "Don't you?"

Some of the tension in his face eased as the corners of his lips twitched. "I suppose I do." He glanced at Cliff, then down at the manacle around Cliff's ankle. "What about Cliff?"

"Todd, would you please release Cliff and escort him back to his apartment?"

The soldier nodded, his countenance relaxing. "Yes, ma'am."

"Thank you." Melanie looked to Bastien. "Shall we?"

She noticed he didn't nod this time and wondered how bad the lingering headache and dizziness were.

Bastien clasped Cliff's arm and pulled him into a man hug. "Thanks for watching over me."

"Any time, man. You've been doing the same for me for years."

Bastien strolled over to the door, bumping Todd hard with his shoulder as he passed.

Melanie shook her head and followed him out of the room. She was beginning to suspect Bastien would have had a hard time fitting in with the immortals even if he *hadn't* killed one of their own and injured dozens of their human assistants at the network.

In the hallway, the guards' close scrutiny unnerved her.

Bastien seemed utterly unaffected by it. He also exhibited none of the weakness he had demonstrated in the holding room. Not until they were alone inside the elevator with the doors closed, traveling upward.

Staggering, he threw out a hand and leaned against the wall.

Melanie grabbed his other arm to steady him.

He closed his eyes for a moment, then opened them and looked down at her. "You're irritated."

She shrugged. "You don't exactly make it easy for them to like you."

"I don't care if they like me."

"Don't you?"

"No."

"Why?"

"Why should I? They judged me and condemned me before they even knew me."

"Well, you have to admit your past is a little . . . dark."

He emitted a humorless laugh. "And my present isn't?"

Melanie didn't know what to say to that.

When the elevator *pinged*, letting them know the five-story climb to the ground floor was over, Bastien straightened. Melanie's pulse jumped when he removed her hand from his arm and gave it a squeeze before releasing her.

The doors opened.

Melanie swallowed.

John Wendleck, head of security at the network, waited for them in the lobby with at least two dozen men. "Dr. Lipton," he said with a nod of his head.

"Hi, John." She had known him ever since she had come to work for the network right out of medical school and had tried numerous times to coax him into calling her Melanie or Lanie. But he insisted on calling her by her title, telling her merrily that she had earned it.

Well, he wasn't merry now. He was all business.

Melanie stepped off the elevator, Bastien beside her.

Before Bastien could muscle his way through the guards or do something else to rile them, she asked, "Did Todd by any chance call you?"

"He did. These men"—he motioned to the soldiers standing at attention behind him, fingers on the triggers of their automatic weapons—"are going to accompany you wherever you choose to take Mr. Newcombe."

Not a good idea. Bastien was bound to say or do something to set them off and she really didn't want to end up digging more bullets out of him.

"I'mmmmm pretty sure my Chevy Volt won't hold this many," she commented.

Beside her, Bastien laughed. It was the first time she had heard him do so, the deep rumble warming her insides like hot cocoa.

John's lips twitched. "I'm sure it won't," he agreed. "Two men will ride with you. The others will follow in separate vehicles."

"That really isn't necessary—"

"I believe it is. You're an important member of our family." Chris worked hard to make the network feel like a family. "We just want to make sure nothing happens to you." His eyes shot Bastien a warning.

Bastien stiffened. "I didn't harm her when I breeched the network. What reason would I have for harming her now?"

"You threatened her life and forced her to allow you access to Vincent."

Guilt rose up inside Melanie, souring her stomach. Bastien had done no such thing, but had told Chris he had when interrogated. To protect her. Melanie had freely and willingly aided Bastien in seeing Vince that last time. But Bastien had feared she would lose her job and all credibility if she admitted as much.

"That was then. This is now," Bastien gritted.

"I have no way of knowing what motivates you from one moment to the next," John spoke evenly. "If you mean her no harm, you shouldn't object to the added security."

Melanie could have sworn she actually heard Bastien's teeth grind together.

"So be it," he said again and headed for the back doors.

The tension in her Chevy as they left the network was about a twenty-one on a scale of one to ten. Bastien sat beside Melanie in the passenger seat, large and powerful even when not in motion. Two soldiers sat in the backseat, automatic weapons in hand.

"I'm going to have to ask you to take your fingers off the triggers, gentlemen," Bastien said after several long minutes, his gaze on the darkened scenery that zipped past outside his window. "There are a lot of bumps in North Carolina's roads that could precipitate an accidental discharge."

In the rearview mirror, Lanie saw the men exchange smug glances.

"If it happens, it happens," one drawled.

Bastien continued to stare out the window. "If you should accidentally shoot me, I'll merely break your arms and all of your fingers to prevent such stupidity from happening a second time," he said blandly. "But if you accidentally shoot *Dr. Lipton*, I'll rip your throats out so swiftly you'll bleed to death before the men in the vehicles behind us even realize something has gone wrong. Just something for you to consider."

Again the men exchanged a look, this one neither smug nor confident. Both shifted, removing their fingers from the triggers she assumed.

"A wise decision," Bastien commented.

Thanks to an unusual amount of traffic on the road, they were late arriving at David's sprawling one-story estate.

Bastien opened and exited his door before Melanie could remove the key from the ignition. Grabbing her purse, she reached for the door handle only to have it slide from her grasp as Bastien opened the door for her.

He held out a hand.

Surprised, she took it and exited the car. "Thank you." Her

pulse picked up, doing jumping jacks as though she were a girl out on her first date.

Nodding, he released her hand and eyed the soldiers clambering out of the back. "Your services are no longer needed. A number of immortals and their Seconds are inside. I'm sure they can keep my violent impulses in check." .

"Our orders are to stay close until Dr. Lipton leaves your company," one said, then met Melanie's exasperated gaze. "We'll be out here if you need us."

She doubted they would listen if she tried to send them on their way, so she nodded and headed for David's front door.

David maintained an open-door policy in all of his residences. Anyone with the access code—human, *gifted one*, or immortal—was welcome to enter and make him- or herself at home no matter the hour.

Bastien guided Melanie up to the front door with a hand on the small of her back. If anyone asked, he would say he did so to provoke the soldiers currently glaring holes in him. But he really just wanted to touch her again.

When he had taken her hand and helped her from the vehicle . . . the emotions that had flooded him where they had touched had taken his breath away. Excitement. Attraction. A touch of shyness. All of the things he felt himself when he looked at her. At Melanie.

He only allowed himself to speak her first name in his thoughts, hoping verbal formality would help him remember to keep his distance.

Bastien punched the code into the electronic keypad beside the door.

The high-tech security system wasn't for David's benefit. The second eldest immortal in existence was incredibly powerful. He could hear the approach of even the quietest vampires long before they reached his door and dispatch them if necessary. The Seconds and human employees of the network, however, could not. Nor could younger immortals. Not to the extent that David could. And David wished to keep those he considered family safe.

Melanie entered the house before Bastien, her scent enchanting him. She didn't wear perfume. No doubt her close work with the vampires had taught her that *any* strong fragrance—no matter how sweet—could offend rather than please.

Male voices filled the house with a constant hum. The meeting must not have begun yet, because the bits and pieces of conversation Bastien picked up were fairly frivolous.

The living room ahead of them was empty. But the dining room to the left bustled with activity.

A table long enough to seat twenty-four dominated the space. David sat at one end, thin dreadlocks drawn back from his face and falling down to his hips. At his elbow, Darnell spoke softly to him, asking if they shouldn't try one more time to convince Ami to leave the country.

Bastien may not like Darnell, may have even wanted to shove the Second's smoothly shaven head through the wall a time or two, but he had to give the man credit for watching over Ami and putting her safety above everything else.

Ami and Marcus were just taking their seats on David's other side. Ami seemed oblivious to Darnell's comments, but Marcus listened closely as he drew his wife closer and wrapped a possessive arm around her narrow shoulders.

Roland and Sarah sat beside Darnell. Bastien still felt nothing but animosity whenever he encountered the nearly millennium-old immortal. Old habits were hard to break, and the hatred Bastien had nursed in his heart for Roland had lasted two hundred years.

Sarah smiled at Ami and engaged her in conversation. If Bastien hadn't already liked the newly transformed immortal before, he would now just for befriending Ami. Ami had endured so much pain, so much torture since her arrival in their world . . .

She deserved as much kindness as she could find.

The other immortals stationed in the area filled most of the remaining seats: Lisette d'Alençon and her twin brothers, Richart and Étienne, all roughly Bastien's age of two centuries. Their Seconds: Tracy, Sheldon, and Cameron. Yuri and Stanislov. Bastien knew little of those two immortals, nor of their Seconds, who were also present. Ethan, an American immortal barely a century old, and Edward, a Brit like himself, were present, too.

Chris Reordon circled the table, distributing more of his precious files and handing out friendly comments with each.

Melanie strode forward. Bastien followed.

With the exception of Ami—who viewed all doctors and scientists with a fear that bordered on absolute terror—those present greeted Melanie with smiles that morphed into scowls and tight-lipped rejection when their gazes shifted to Bastien.

Fuck you, too.

The frowns on Lisette's and Étienne's faces deepened, telling him they were once more prying into his thoughts and didn't like what they heard.

What did he care? He didn't need their friendship or acceptance. He didn't need anything from them at all.

"What the hell are *you* doing here?" Chris demanded.

"I'll escort him out," Roland said, a malicious smile lighting his features as he rose.

Sarah placed a hand on his arm. "No, you won't. There will be *no* fighting between you two tonight."

Roland hesitated. Usually Sarah could coax the dour immortal into doing almost anything, but restraining his impulse to kill Bastien may be beyond even her capabilities. Roland would never forget that Bastien had once fractured her skull.

Bastien sent Sarah a smile. "Hello, sweetheart. How's the head?"

Melanie gave him a reproving look.

Hell. He couldn't seem to help himself.

Roland's eyes flashed bright amber. His jaw clenched with fury.

Sarah's grip tightened on his arm as she visibly restrained him now. Offering Bastien a sweet smile, she said, "My head's just fine, thank you. How's your ass?"

There was a moment of stunned silence, then Lisette and her brothers all burst into laughter. The other immortals joined in, as did the Seconds.

Roland glanced at his wife, caught the playful wink she sent him, and relaxed, retaking his chair.

Judging by the confusion on Melanie's face when she looked up at him, she hadn't heard the whole story.

Shrugging sheepishly, he explained, "Sarah stabbed me in the ass."

She blinked. "She did?"

He nodded and, catching Sarah's eye, tipped an imaginary hat to her.

Sarah grinned and shrugged as if to say, *I had to do something*.

When the laughter died down, Chris said, "I still want to know what he's doing here."

"Sebastien is here at my invitation," David told him, which was news to Bastien. "We need him here if we're going to fully understand what happened last night."

As usual, Chris balked. "How are we supposed to trust him to tell us the truth?"

David sighed heavily. "I can read his thoughts, Chris. As can Lisette and Étienne. *And* Seth when he arrives. We've been over this before."

When Chris opened his mouth to continue bitching and moaning, David raised a hand. "Think wisely before you question my decisions in the future. I'm growing tired of having to explain myself. To you or to anyone else."

Chris clamped his mouth shut and immediately wiped all expression from his face.

David may be kindhearted, but it was still exceedingly unwise to piss him off.

Richart rose and drew out the empty chair beside him, motioning to Dr. Lipton.

Melanie smiled and seated herself, offering him a muted thank you.

Bastien took the chair on the other side of her, cursing the jealousy he felt slither through him. Richart wasn't interested in Melanie. He had his mysterious human lover.

Yet the other immortal's attention still rankled.

And it shouldn't, Bastien reminded himself. Melanie wasn't his and would never *be* his.

Her shoulder brushed his arm as she swiveled to loop her purse's strap over the back of her chair. "Sorry," she murmured.

Bastien nodded, but said nothing. She was nervous. His gift syphoned her emotions with each tiny brush against him and told him sitting at a table with so many ultra-powerful beings . . . Well, it didn't frighten her exactly. But she wasn't comfortable.

Bastien leaned down and whispered in her ear, "We're all just like Cliff, Joe, and Vincent, only without the madness."

She pursed her lips and looked pointedly at Roland.

Bastien couldn't help but grin. "Okay, I'll give you that one."

She smiled back, eyes twinkling as some of the stiffness left her shoulders.

He supposed it *could* be a tad intimidating, being surrounded by men and women who could read your thoughts, teleport, move things with their minds, heal with their hands, and more. He was just so accustomed to it that it hadn't occurred to him that it might take some getting used to.

The faint tones of "Mack the Knife" sounded. At the other end of the table, Sarah drew out her cell phone. "Hello?"

"It's Seth," came the immortal leader's response. "Just calling ahead."

She smiled, as did every immortal present. "Thank you."

While she returned her phone to her pocket, the Immortal Guardians' leader materialized beside the empty chair at the end of the table opposite the one David occupied.

Sarah had only been with the immortals for a couple of years or thereabouts and still jumped whenever Seth or Richart suddenly appeared in the room, so Seth had taken to calling ahead to warn her.

Returning her smile, Seth seated himself in the empty chair.

Chris handed him a file folder, reluctantly handed a couple more to Bastien and Melanie, then seated himself.

Seth opened the file and perused its contents.

The front door opened.

Bastien glanced over his shoulder and was surprised to see Tanner enter.

"Sorry I'm late," Tanner said, crossing swiftly to the table and taking one of the last two seats.

"No problem," Seth responded. "Glad you could make it, Tanner."

Tanner took the file folder Chris handed him and opened it to glance at the papers within. Though his blond hair was windblown, he still looked like an accountant as he reached up to adjust his glasses.

What was he doing here? Was he already one of the immortals' Seconds?

Bastien's gaze slid to the surly immortal whispering in Sarah's ear. *Hell.* Seth wasn't going to assign him to Roland, was he? Roland was notorious for scaring the crap out of any Second sent to serve him, which was why Seth had allowed him to go without one all of these centuries.

Or perhaps Tanner had been assigned to Marcus? Was Ami no longer going to serve as Marcus's Second now that they had married?

That would actually be a relief. She had come too close to death too many times since being assigned to that volatile immortal.

Seth closed the file and folded his hands atop it. "So, tell us what happened last night, Sebastien."

Surprised that he had been asked directly, Bastien complied.

Every brow present furrowed as his words floated around the table.

"You couldn't have spared even one?" Chris asked. Leave it to him to ignore everything except the deaths of the humans. Hell, if Bastien had let every human soldier live, Chris no doubt would have *still* found fault with his actions.

"Not without risking capture myself."

Richart nodded. "It's true. He was barely conscious when I found him, with two darts on the ground beside him. By the time I got him to the network, he was out cold."

"How are you feeling, Sebastien?" Seth queried softly.

Bastien fought the urge to squirm, uncomfortable with the concern in the elder's voice. He had yet to figure out why Seth gave a damn about him. "I'm fine."

Seth's gaze shifted to Melanie. "Dr. Lipton?"

Melanie sent Bastien an apologetic look. "He's still a little groggy and hasn't yet fully regained his strength. I understand he's roughly the same age as the d'Alençons, so—based on the time it took *them* to recover when they were hit—I'd say he should recover fully during the next few hours. Certainly by dawn."

Seth nodded. "I assume you'd like to observe him while he does so?"

"Yes, if that's all right."

"Of course. We rely on your medical expertise in matters

such as this and know you need to gather as much information as you can." The words, as well as the warning look that accompanied them, seemed to be directed at Bastien.

Bastien scowled. The bastard had better not be reading his thoughts again.

Of course I'm reading your thoughts, Seth said. *As is David. And most likely Étienne and Lisette. How else can we reassure the others that you are sincere in your claims?*

"These men . . . these soldiers . . . weren't out to kill," Richart continued. "They were out to capture and would have done so had Bastien left any standing. Perhaps if I had returned sooner, we could have taken one or more alive. But alone, Bastien had no choice but to protect himself."

"This is *so* bad," Darnell muttered.

Several heads nodded.

"Chris," David spoke, "have you succeeded in tracking down your missing contacts?"

Chris shook his head. "No. There's no trace of them at all, or of their families. Nothing to tell me where they may have gone or where they were taken or if they're dead or alive. Or that they ever *were*. It's as if they never existed."

Bastien may frequently think about dismembering Chris, but he couldn't help but sympathize with him over this. Reordon had spent years cultivating contacts in the various government agencies that were swathed in secrecy. Years tapping those contacts for information and enlisting their aid whenever the Immortal Guardians needed it. When those contacts had mysteriously disappeared a few weeks ago . . .

It didn't take much of an imagination to guess what had happened to them. The Immortal Guardians' new enemy had gotten his hands on them. And the blame for it—all of what they were currently dealing with—could be laid squarely at Bastien's feet. *He* had inadvertently set all of this into motion when he had begun his quest for revenge a lifetime ago.

"Any luck finding new contacts?" Seth queried.

Chris shook his head. "Some. But it's slow going. I don't know who exactly we're dealing with, who we're fighting, who has the power and influence needed to wipe the slate clean the way they did, so I have to be even *more* careful when approaching potential aids. There are a handful who escaped scrutiny and survived the sweep only because I hadn't yet called upon them to act. I couldn't then and can't now because they're still working their way up the ranks and aren't yet in a position to find out what I need them to."

"Any word on who this Emrys prick is?" Marcus broached, his voice tight with hostility.

It was a hostility shared by all those familiar with Ami's past: Bastien, David, Darnell, Chris, and Seth. Melanie, too, he imagined, since she had been allowed into the loop.

Emrys had been one of the bastards responsible for Ami's capture a few years ago, as well as the months of torture she had endured afterward. Bastien didn't know how Emrys had escaped Seth's and David's wrath when they had rescued Ami, and hoped like hell he wouldn't again. If *anyone* needed to pay for past sins, Emrys did. Preferably with blood.

"I'm getting closer, but still can't say definitively."

"Did you find out how he was connected to Keegan?" Bastien asked.

Fucking Montrose Keegan. Bastien wished he had never worked with the man. How the hell had Montrose known Emrys?

"They went to college together and were in the same fraternity, but appear to have parted company once they graduated," Chris said and motioned to the file in front of Bastien. "Keegan pursued a teaching career. Emrys went to work in the military's bioweapons program. Everything I could dig up tells me they lost contact and didn't speak again until Montrose looked him up during the vampire king's reign."

"Is Emrys still military?" Sarah asked.

"I don't know. All of the intel on him stops approximately four years ago. There's no mention of him retiring or being discharged from the army. Nor is he on any active duty lists or stationed on any known bases. We know he reappeared briefly in Texas a couple of years ago. But I still haven't been able to ascertain whether the facility he surfaced in was military or mercenary. And there's a big void in his history between his army days and his days at the facility. I'm still digging, but . . . as I said, it's taking time."

"Just be careful," Ami pleaded softly. "I don't want you falling into their hands. I don't want you disappearing like the others."

"May I say something?" Melanie asked, looking around the table tentatively.

"Of course, Dr. Lipton," David said.

"While I was waiting for Bastien to regain consciousness, I had Linda examine the darts Richart found and it appears the dosage of the drug they deliver has increased substantially." She looked up at Bastien. "That's why it didn't take as many darts to fell you as it did Richart, Étienne, and Lisette."

"Same drug, but more powerful?" Darnell said. "Emrys *must* have been behind this attack. He's the one who gave Dennis the drug."

Bastien wished he would have killed Dennis—the self-proclaimed vampire king who had led the last uprising—when he had first met him over a decade ago. He simply hadn't perceived how crazy the bastard was. Or would become.

"And who else would know the original drug wasn't powerful enough?" Darnell continued. "Only someone who had interacted directly with Montrose Keegan and had access to his notes and those damned movies Dennis made of the battles. As far as we know, Keegan didn't talk to anyone else."

"As far as we know," Roland reiterated.

Chris shook his head. "I don't know who he could have

talked to. Anyone else would have had him committed if he had started rambling about vampires and immortals."

"It's worth looking into," Bastien said, seeing where Roland was going and reluctantly agreeing. "When I worked with Montrose, he worked alone. I'm certain of it. Even when I pressured him to speed up his research. But I was sane."

"That's debatable," Roland muttered.

Bastien ignored him. "Dennis wasn't. If Montrose feared him even more than he did me—"

"He did," Ami spoke up. "When Dennis took me to Keegan's lab"—she swallowed as if just saying the word resurrected fears that threatened to choke her—"Montrose was terrified of him. And there was blood. Old blood. On some of the papers I rifled through looking for a weapon. And on the walls. I don't know what happened down there, but . . ." She shook her head. "Montrose was visibly shaking while Dennis talked to him. He was terrified of him."

Marcus drew Ami closer and kissed the top of her head.

Bastien nodded. "If Dennis was pressuring Montrose to find a drug that would incapacitate us or at least weaken us enough to defeat, I'm sure he was issuing more frightening ultimatums than I did. Montrose may have taken his plea for aid to others besides Emrys."

Chris retrieved a small spiral notebook and a number two pencil from his jacket pocket. Flipping the notebook open, he began to scribble notes. "I'll look into other med school chums. Hell, I'll look into *all* of his old school chums, both those he kept in contact with and those he didn't."

Sarah pointed to Chris's notebook. "You might want to check out the professors he studied with while pursuing his doctorate." Until Roland had turned her, Sarah had been a music theory professor at University of North Carolina at Chapel Hill. "His students, too. Particularly any grad students with whom he worked closely."

Nodding, Chris continued to write.

"Did he have any family?" Darnell asked.

Bastien shook his head. "Just his brother Casey. Casey said their parents were killed in a car accident almost a decade ago. It's why Montrose was so protective of him."

"What about grandparents?" Sheldon asked.

Tracey snorted. "How the hell would grandparents fit into the equation?"

Sheldon shrugged. "Money? I don't know."

Chris kept writing. "I already looked into that. The grand-parents are dead. Both sides of the family."

"What about girlfriends?" Sarah suggested.

Étienne scoffed. "Who the hell would date Montrose Keegan?"

"Hey," Sarah retorted, "some women choose brains over brawn."

He tossed her a flirty grin. *"You* didn't. But if you're of a mind to . . . have I by any chance mentioned that at university I—" Étienne's file folder flew up and hit him in the face a moment before his chair was telekinetically yanked out from under him, landing him on his ass.

Even Bastien had to laugh.

Grabbing the chair with a curse, Étienne regained his feet and once more seated himself beside his siblings. "Are you going to do this every time we have a meeting?"

"Are you going to flirt with her every time we have a meet-ing?" Roland ground out.

Étienne muttered something in French.

The chuckles quieted.

Seth leaned back in his chair. "All right. Now that we know a little more about the attack on Bastien last night, let us discuss how to address this latest threat while Chris pur-sues his leads."

Chapter 3

Melanie listened quietly as their words flowed. She had never been privy to an Immortal Guardians' meeting before and was surprised by the teasing banter the powerful men and women shared.

She hadn't expected that. Even Seth and David smiled.

While the talk continued, Melanie wondered if meetings like this had even been necessary before Bastien had sought his revenge. Vampires may have launched occasional uprisings over the millennia, but none had been anywhere near as successful as his.

Or the subsequent uprising led by Montrose Keegan and the vampire king.

This really was a first for the immortals. The network, too. Without knowing the extent of the enemy they faced—who Emrys was, how many men he commanded in his shadow army, and what his ultimate goal may be aside from getting his hands on Ami again—she didn't know how they would combat this threat. How could they even know what kind of attack the immortals would face next? The threat seemed to constantly evolve. As did the drug the enemy used. The *only* drug that affected immortals.

One by one, the immortals and their Seconds bounced

ideas off each other that mostly entailed heightened security protocols.

Having a swift antidote to the drug would be a tremendous help if not an outright game changer, but Melanie had yet to test the one she had concocted. Had not even told them she may have found one. How could she when she didn't know how to test it without significant risk?

"I think we should bring the vampires into the loop," Bastien announced abruptly.

All conversation ceased.

"What?" Darnell asked as though he questioned what he had heard.

Melanie certainly did.

"I think we should bring the vampires into the loop, maybe even enlist their aid," Bastien repeated.

Dead silence filled the room, so thick one could practically swim in it.

"Are you insane?" Chris demanded incredulously.

"Chris," Seth warned.

Perhaps, like Melanie, he was growing tired of the hostility the network's leader continually directed at Bastien. There must be more to it than Bastien's breaching network headquarters.

Melanie touched Bastien's arm. A *zing* of electricity zipped through her as it always did when she touched him. Or when he touched her.

His warm, brown eyes lowered to meet hers.

"Do you mean Cliff and Joe?" she asked.

He shook his head. "They're already in the loop."

Melanie felt Chris's accusing gaze before he spoke. "Have you been discussing classified information with the vampires, Dr. Lipton?"

Trepidation claimed her. Chris Reordon could and would fire her if he thought she had circumvented the rules. And she feared what he might do to the vampires if he found out just how much they knew of the inner workings of the network.

Technically, it wasn't her fault—Cliff and Joe knowing so much they weren't supposed to. But she didn't think that would matter to Chris, who fiercely fought any threat to those who worked for him or to those for whom he worked.

"Answer me, Dr. Lipton. If you've been sharing information—"

"Leave her alone, Reordon," Bastien snarled. *"I'm* the one who has been talking to Cliff and Joe."

Chris turned to Seth and motioned furiously to Bastien. "You see? *This* is why I tried to prevent him from visiting the vampires at the network, why I didn't want him on the premises."

"Yes, and look how well *that* worked out for you," Bastien drawled.

Chris shot him a fulminating glare.

Melanie kicked Bastien under the table, then caught her breath. What the hell was she doing?

Bastien looked down at her, face full of surprise for a few heart-stopping seconds.

Melanie waited for a caustic comment.

Instead, the corners of his lips twitched before he looked away.

She heaved a silent sigh of relief and told her heart to stop pounding. Bastien was irresistibly handsome when he almost smiled.

Seth held up a hand. "Neither Bastien nor Dr. Lipton has betrayed the network, Chris."

"Then how—"

"The vampires have hearing that is almost as sensitive as ours. They hear things while in their apartments, in the labs, and in the other areas they are allowed to frequent. Not that it matters. They never leave the building and neither possesses telepathic abilities, so who are they going to tell?"

Chris actually seemed to think about that as he turned back to Melanie. "You should have told me they could hear us."

"To be honest," she replied, "it never occurred to me that you didn't know."

He nodded. "You're right, of course. I *should* have known and should have taken that into consideration."

Melanie hoped he didn't plan to soundproof everything at the network now. The restrictive lives the vampires led sometimes bored the pants off them. And Joe had once confided that listening to all of the "bullshit goings-on" at the network was a bit like watching a soap opera.

Would Janet finally agree to go out with Charles? Would Kevin get the promotion for which he and Sam competed? When would Tara tell Jack she's pregnant?

Tune in tomorrow to find out.

Bastien shifted in his seat.

Realizing she was still holding his arm, Melanie flushed and withdrew her hand.

At David's end of the table, Ami leaned forward. "Bastien, if you weren't talking about Cliff and Joe, then what did you mean when you said we should bring the vampires into the loop? What vampires?"

"All of them."

Melanie had to admit she could understand the *What the hell?* looks sent his way.

Darnell said, "You're kidding, right?"

"There was no way those soldiers could have known whether they were hunting an immortal or a vampire," Bastien said.

Tanner nodded. "No way they could have kept up with the chase from UNC to Duke at the speeds Bastien and the vamps traveled either. They had to have been waiting, hidden somewhere at Duke, hoping one or the other would happen to come along."

Bastien didn't seem pleased by the other man's input,

though Tanner had made a good point. Melanie wondered why. Cliff and Joe had mentioned Tanner nearly as often as they had Bastien and seemed to think the two men were good friends.

Chris began to scribble in his notebook again. "Did you make a phone call before you left to pursue the vamps, Bastien?"

"Who the hell would I call?"

"He didn't," Seth answered for him.

"What about you, Richart?"

"No. I took care of the vampires left behind, followed Bastien's trail long enough to discern the others were leading him toward Duke, then teleported to the campus to search for them."

Chris stopped writing.

Darnell leaned back in his chair and crossed his arms over his chest. "Montrose Keegan told the vampire king to have his vamps stake out all of the garages with tow trucks and wait for an immortal to call for a cleanup. If Keegan told Emrys that college campuses are prime vampire hunting grounds, he may have done the same thing, just divided his soldiers amongst a few of the campuses and . . . waited."

"Or *all* of the campuses," Lisette added. "We don't know how many men this Emrys commands."

Bastien leaned forward and rested his elbows on the table. "Those men could have had no idea who would've made an appearance last night: a vampire or an immortal."

Seth nodded. "The odds were greater of it being a vampire."

Melanie looked up at Bastien. "Would they even know how to tell the difference between vampires and immortals?"

Vampires were humans who had been infected with the virus. Immortals were *gifted ones*—men and women born with extremely advanced DNA—who had been infected. That DNA, whose source remained a mystery, not only lent immortals special gifts, it gave them all certain similarities in appearance: namely black hair and brown eyes. Only Sarah had brown hair and hazel eyes, a result of the *gifted ones'* DNA being diluted with human DNA over so many millennia.

"No," Bastien responded, meeting her gaze. "Keegan only knew there were genetic differences, that immortals' DNA is different." Yet again, he had said *immortals'* DNA rather than *our* DNA. "He wasn't aware of the physical characteristics immortals share. Even vampires seem to be unaware of those. Hell, I wouldn't have noticed it myself if Sarah hadn't pointed it out to me. Vampires don't survive encounters with immortals often enough to compare notes."

Melanie considered the consequences of Emrys's capturing a vampire. She had read the files on Ami, knew the gruesome details of her capture and subsequent torture. Their *study* of her.

They had justified the inhumane treatment in their notes by insisting they *must* study her in such fashion in order to protect themselves from a possible alien invasion. But no doctor would consider what they did to her merely studying her.

Melanie *studied* the vampires who lived at the network. She carefully scrutinized their blood, examined tissue samples, searched their DNA for anything dormant that could be stimulated to act as the immortals' DNA did and protect humans infected with the virus from the brain damage it caused. She routinely ran tests—CT scans, MRIs, and more—to seek the same. But all of this was done with the express permission of the vampires. And none of it harmed them.

Ami had basically been dissected while she was still alive. They had cut her, burned her, removed fingers and toes, even entire organs . . . all while she lived, while she was alert, without anesthesia and with a complete disregard for the agony they inflicted. If her body did not have astounding regenerative capabilities, she would be dead.

And Ami had approached them in peace.

Melanie doubted Emrys and his crew would show any vampires they managed to corral more regard or handle them with more care than they had Ami. Particularly since, unlike Ami, there were plenty of other vampires around to torture, making them expendable.

"Emrys could learn almost everything he needs to know about you—your strengths and weaknesses—if he got his hands on a vampire," she murmured. "I'm sure any doctors he employed would be utterly ruthless in their study."

Bastien nodded. "Because he was too afraid to work with vampires when I knew him, there was much Montrose still didn't know. But Emrys clearly doesn't have such fears. He also may have the balls to go public with whatever he learns without worrying about facing the scorn or disbelief Montrose feared. That's why we need to keep the vampires out of his hands."

"By befriending them?" Roland asked dryly. "Hunting and destroying them will keep them out of Emrys's hands just as efficiently."

The other immortals all nodded.

"No, it won't," Bastien insisted. "There are too many of them. And you can't divide your attention between hunting vampires and hunting Emrys's men. Immortals are already stretched too thin because vampires continue to flock to this part of the country."

"And whose fault is that?" Marcus queried.

"Marcus," Ami stated softly, "Bastien was there for us when the vampire king took me. At least listen to what he has to say."

The eight-century-old immortal frowned down at his wife. Seconds later, his eyes began to glow faintly and a decidedly *not* irritated look entered them. A slow smile slid across his features. "You don't play fair," he told her.

She grinned. "I know."

Shaking his head, he motioned for Bastien to continue.

"The only way we can possibly succeed in keeping the vampires out of Emrys's clutches is by bringing them into the loop and warning them that humans armed with this drug are now hunting them. Word of mouth is what keeps luring them here in the first place. They've heard about the uprisings and want to see what's going on firsthand. Word of mouth can also warn them of the new threat and work to our advantage."

"Have you never heard the saying *the enemy of my enemy is my friend*?" Roland drawled.

Bastien's lips tightened. "We all have. That's precisely my point. If we can convince the vampires that they have a *new* enemy—one the two of us share—who poses an even greater threat to them than we do, then perhaps we can work together to defeat Emrys. For whatever reason, the vampires today are more willing to band together."

"Again, I think we know whose fault that is," Roland drawled.

"Why not use that to our advantage?" Bastien persisted. Melanie silently applauded him for not rising to the bait. "Why not have them band together and work *with* us instead of against us? Find a way to make it worth their while?"

Roland emitted a bark of laughter. "If you think I'm going to work with vampires, you're out of your bloody mind. And I'm sure as hell not going to let Sarah work with them."

Sarah's eyebrows flew up. "I'm sorry. Did you say you're not going to *let* me?"

He cleared his throat. "I meant I'm sure as hell not going to let *them* work with *you*."

"Shouldn't that be my decision?"

He smiled. "Only if you agree with me, sweetling."

Sarah laughed and shook her head. "You're impossible."

"I know."

"Roland made a good point," Marcus threw in. "How do

you know the vampires won't side with Emrys against us? It's too great a risk."

"They stand to lose as much as we do if Emrys gets his hands on them," Bastien insisted.

"The vampire king didn't think so," David stated. "Emrys promised him an army if he would capture and hand over Ami. I'm sure there are many vampires out there who would leap at such an offer. And many others who might leap at less. Their mental instability does not leave them with the best judgment."

"So we convince them the offer is bullshit," Bastien persisted. "Tell them Emrys is the one who killed the vampire king. That we were only able to defeat the king's army because Emrys got there before us and destroyed most of them. Make *us* seem like the lesser of two evils and make the point so clearly that even a complete psychopath can see it."

Us? Melanie stared at him. That was a slip.

In the silence that followed, Tanner cleared his throat. "It worked before."

Seth turned his attention on the blond. "Elaborate."

"The vampires who served under Bastien feared him."

That surprised Melanie. Not because she doubted Bastien was capable of inspiring fear. He had frightened *her* a bit the first time she had met him in person and had *no* trouble in the intimidation department. But Cliff and Joe spoke so highly of him. Vince had, too.

"Most of them did anyway," Tanner qualified. "It was the only way Bastien could control those who were starting to lose it mentally. He had strict rules. And the vampires feared what he might do to them if they disobeyed those rules." He held up a hand when Roland started to speak. "Yes, some of them broke the rules anyway, but a majority of them didn't or else there would have been a hell of a lot more Missing Person reports." He looked to Chris. "Am I right?"

Melanie wondered just how much it galled Chris to nod his agreement.

"My point is," Tanner continued, "the vampires considered Bastien the lesser of two evils. They knew they had a greater chance of survival with him than if they were on their own. And they knew that defeating the immortals would increase their safety. If they think Emrys and his soldiers—or whoever the hell he commands—pose a greater threat to them than you do, they'll get the word out to the other vamps and the more stable ones may work with you to defeat him and help keep the others out of his hands."

Richart studied Tanner curiously. "How can you be certain the vampires will listen to us?"

"They're vampires," Tanner said. "You can't be certain of anything with them. But, as you know, enough listened to Bastien that he was able to not only raise, but successfully maintain a vampire army for the first time in history. And word went global."

"You must be a charismatic bastard," Yuri droned, scrutinizing Bastien as though he were some peculiar new insect species.

"He is," Melanie said. Honestly she didn't know why that would surprise any of them. "Charismatic, that is."

Richart turned narrowed eyes on Bastien. "I don't see it."

Melanie rolled her own. "Well, if any of you had bothered to visit the vampires living at the network, you *would*. Spend any time at all talking with them and you'll see just how much they respect Bastien and how much they like him."

"Dr. Lipton," Bastien protested.

"What?" she said. "It's true. Even Vince liked and respected you and Vince was already descending into madness when he surrendered."

"You knew that?" Bastien asked.

"Not at first. But now that I know the more subtle signs . . . yes. I can see that the brain damage the virus causes was progressing more rapidly in him." She looked around the table. "Even when they're succumbing to madness, what the vampires experience during lucid moments can alter their behavior. I interacted with Vincent daily. Spoke with him. Made him feel less like a vampire or lab subject and more like an ordinary guy. He liked me. He trusted me. And when those swift psychotic breaks would come upon him with no warning, he didn't hurt me. He *never* hurt me. Anyone else who happened to be in the room . . ." She shrugged. "But not me. Because he trusted me."

Lisette pursed her lips. "I *have* noticed that the vampires who travel in groups no longer seem to prey upon each other as they have in previous centuries."

"The vampire king did," Ami corrected. "I saw him tear into his followers with a machete."

Stanislov grimaced. "And Yuri, Bastien, and I all saw the mess he left behind."

Sarah wrinkled her nose in disgust. "Yes, but the vampire king was crazy as a bedbug. He wasn't descending *into* madness. He was already there. I seriously doubt he gave a rat's ass about his followers. If he considered them expendable when he was lucid . . ."

Étienne shook his head. "Isn't all of this moot? Even if we actually considered embarking upon this *befriend the vampire* plan, it would be impossible to implement. Vampires *hate* immortals. They would never listen to us if we attempted to converse with them and coax them into . . . I don't know . . . joining forces with us. And, though they might have listened to Bastien the vampire leader, they certainly won't listen to Bastien the Deceiver, as he is now known. They despise him as much as or more than they do *us*. Where does that leave us?"

"They don't have to like you to listen to you," Tanner insisted. "Most of the vampires in Bastien's army *hated* my ass."

"I find that hard to believe," Lisette said with a glance at his ass and a flirtatious wink.

Melanie grinned when Tanner seemed to lose his train of thought for a moment while he stared at the lovely French immortal.

Étienne nudged him.

"What? Oh." Tanner smiled. "Right. Anyway, ah, the vampires in Bastien's army hated me, but none of them ever tried to hurt me."

"They knew I would destroy them if they did," Bastien said blandly.

"That's part of it," Tanner acknowledged. "But I think it was also because we were on the same side, working against common enemies."

Melanie's interest increased. This confirmed her own hypothesis about the vampires' subconscious holding on to what they felt in lucid moments even when the madness directed their other actions.

Richart shook his head. "Even if we could sway some of the vampires to our side and get them to warn the other vamps to beware of Emrys and stay away from his men, such would require us to let the vampires live and continue to prey upon humans. I don't think any of us here can in good conscience allow that."

Melanie thought furiously. "You could continue to destroy those who have already succumbed to the insanity and only recruit the youngest vampires. Maybe offer them bagged blood so they wouldn't feel the need to attack humans."

"Such would put a strain on our resources," Seth said.

True. The bagged blood that immortals utilized was donated by members of the network and their families. It was one of the reasons immortals were so strict about only eating organic foods. (The other reason, of course, being pure stubbornness. After eating nothing but organic foods for hundreds if not thousands of years, most simply refused to change their diets.) The virus repaired even the most minute damage done to the body, using blood to do so, and immortals wished to reduce their need as much as possible so they wouldn't have to seek alternative sources.

"You could do what Bastien did," Tanner suggested. "Assign them pedophiles to feed upon."

Melanie had heard about that. Rather brilliant thinking, in her opinion. Bastien had lacked a steady supply of bagged blood, so he had enlisted Tanner's aid to track down pedophiles through a little cyber sleuthing and ordered his vampire followers to feed upon *them*.

"We lack the resources necessary to ensure they don't stray from their diet," Seth responded.

David nodded. "Though his army feared and respected him, Bastien was still unable to keep some of his followers from killing the pedophiles' families."

"Drug them," Melanie blurted.

All heads turned her way.

"What?" Bastien asked.

"Drug them," she repeated. "I've been experimenting with Cliff and Joe—" She broke off, realizing what she had just said and hurriedly caught Ami's eye. "Not the way you're thinking, Amiriska. I promise you: Everything I do with them is with their consent."

Marcus tightened his arm around Ami, whose brow remained furrowed with doubt.

Vowing to choose her words more carefully in the future, Melanie continued. "What I meant to say is, I've been working with Cliff and Joe, monitoring the effects of various doses of the tranquilizer. And my"—not experiment—"research has given me real hope that regular injections of a low dose can help suppress the vampires' violent impulses. It leaves them sluggish . . . and they don't like that part of it . . . but they have far fewer outbursts and maintain control better. I realize it's a temporary fix, but it might be something you can use to your advantage if you decide to go through with this."

Leaning back against his chair, Bastien touched her arm beneath the table. "The drug really helps them?"

Pulse picking up, she nodded. "Yes."

"Emrys used it to gain the vampire king's cooperation," Seth mentioned.

"He did?" Melanie asked. "How?"

"Every time the vampire king flew into a rage, Emrys tranqed him. If he managed to hit him with the dart before the vampire gave the rage free reign, it seemed to stop it in its tracks . . . or at least left the vamp too tired to do anything about it. If the vampire king was already destroying everything around him, the drug stopped him and, again, left him too tired to continue acting on impulse."

Hope rose. If the drug could work on someone as insane as the vampire king, perhaps she would have more time to find a cure for Cliff and Joe.

"Then that's the answer," Tanner said, his handsome face lit with triumph. "If you can suppress their impulses with drugs, you can control whom they feed upon."

"My entire army consisted of men who were lucid when I recruited them and desired help," Bastien said. "They didn't *want* to become monsters. They didn't *want* to prey upon the innocent."

"But they did," Roland said.

"Yes. Some of them. Because I had no way of curbing their madness. Dr. Lipton does. If this drug works as she says it does, we can seek out those few who can still benefit from it, recruit them if you will, and have them spread the word to other vampires themselves."

"I still don't like it," Roland said.

Many of the others nodded.

Melanie cleared her throat. "With all due respect, the only ones at this table who are qualified to make this decision are Seth, David, and Bastien."

Bastien's head snapped around. His hand tightened on her arm.

The others all stared at her as if she had just shouted, "Peacocks like Pumpernickel!"

"I beg your pardon?" Richart said finally.

Étienne nodded. "Seth and David I could understand. But what makes Bastien so special?"

More than they knew, but she didn't say that. "Seth, David, and Bastien are the only ones who regularly visit and interact with the vampires at the network."

Bastien looked at Seth and David with surprise. "You visit Cliff and Joe?"

Seth inclined his head. "Yes."

"Vincent, too, when he still lived," David added.

"Why?" Bastien asked.

The other immortals seemed interested in knowing the answer to that one, too.

"Because they asked for our help," Seth said simply, "and, by doing so, joined our cause."

"We take care of our own," David said, "regardless of their origins."

Seth nodded. "We also hoped to extend the vampires' lucid moments by trying to heal the brain damage the virus has wrought." Both elders were extremely powerful healers, powerful enough to reattach severed limbs, if necessary.

Bastien returned his attention to Melanie. "Is it working?"

"Not as well as we had hoped," she admitted with some reluctance. She suspected Seth and David knew as much. As long as they had lived, they must have tried such before. "The vampires do remain lucid for longer periods after Seth and David's visits. But the healings only *slow* the progression of the virus, they don't cure it or reverse the damage done."

"David," Seth said, eyeing the immortal at the other end of the long table, "what are your thoughts on Bastien's proposed alliance?"

Silence reigned as everyone waited to hear what the immortal would say.

"Most of the immortals at this table are too young to remember times in the past when humans have banded together to hunt us," David began. "Roland, you have an inkling of what such is like thanks to your fiancée's deception a few hundred years ago."

Roland's countenance darkened. "I do."

"Bitch," Sarah muttered.

Roland barked out a laugh, then wrapped an arm around his wife and pressed a kiss to her hair.

Every person in the room stared. Even after two years, it was still a shock to see him smile and express affection.

"Vampires in the past may not have had the Internet vampires today adore so much," David continued, "but word still managed to spread throughout the countryside that both vamps and immortals were being hunted by humans. And, as Dr. Lipton said, what the vampires learned when they were lucid lingered somewhere in the backs of their minds, so that even when the madness struck they exhibited more caution."

Melanie nodded. "I think the fact that even the maddest vampires continue to use blades instead of guns when they fight immortals or hunt their prey is an indication that anything concerning their safety tends to linger when everything else falls away. They know they shouldn't attract undue attention and take measures to avoid doing so, whether they do it consciously or not."

David nodded. "Which is why I think Bastien may be right. I think we should find a way to turn this in our favor. These are new times with new troubles and, perhaps, new opportunities. The rules have changed. We should change accordingly." He looked at Bastien. "Lie to the vampires. Let them believe Emrys is the real reason the vampire king and his followers fell. That he's an even greater threat to vampires than we are."

Seth drew Bastien's gaze. "Find those who want our aid and offer it to them."

"And those who don't?" Bastien asked.

"Must be destroyed as usual. They will continue to kill

innocents otherwise and are the most likely to fall for any bullshit Emrys or his men may feed them."

Roland leaned forward. "You trust Bastien to do this? To meet with and conspire with vampires? Again?"

Seth met Roland's gaze. "I trust you *all* to do this."

Roland's lips tightened. "I won't risk Sarah's safety by pausing to chat with vampires who most likely are only interested in severing our heads."

Sarah leaned away enough to look up at him. "If you aren't worried about your own safety, sweetie, then don't worry about mine. I'm as strong as you are, remember, and just as unlikely to be caught off guard."

"We shall discuss this later."

"No, we won't. If Seth and David think this is worth a try, then we should do it. They've been dealing with this crap a lot longer than we have. I trust their judgment, and you should, too."

Scowling, he pulled her back against his side.

"I have a concern," Lisette said, glancing from Seth to David and back. "Bastien's followers were still able to deceive him despite his gift, convincing him to believe they followed his every order when they did not. Such could be true of any immortal who is not telepathic."

"David and I will have no difficulty discerning who truly wishes our aid," Seth murmured. "Nor will you or Étienne. Richart and I will have to make ourselves available to the rest of you. If any of you find a vampire who appears to be amenable to joining our cause, call me and I will teleport to you and read his thoughts. Or call Richart and he will teleport Lisette or Étienne to you to do the same."

Only Tanner seemed satisfied with the plan.

"If you encounter Emrys's shadow army and are tranqed," Seth cautioned, "immediately move as far away as fast as you can and call your Second before you pass out. Do not try to capture the humans at your own expense."

"This would all be far easier if we had an antidote to the tranquilizer," Roland pointed out, looking at Melanie. "Have you devised one yet?"

Melanie's heart flipped over nervously. She had, but . . . "We're still working on it." From the corner of her eye, she saw Bastien glance at her, but avoided his gaze. For some reason it was hardest to lie to him.

"As I said," Seth instructed, "if you're drugged, though it goes against your every instinct, leave the battlefield, call your Second, and secure your own safety."

That did not go over well at all. Every man and woman present was trained to fight to the death if necessary, not to flee.

Guilt suffused Melanie. She could spare them what they no doubt considered such an indignity if she could just gather enough courage to test the damned drug she had manufactured to combat the tranquilizer.

Seth looked at David. "Anything else?"

David shook his head.

"That will be all for now."

Chairs scooted back as immortals and their Seconds rose. All gave both Bastien and Tanner a wide birth.

Melanie didn't have time to draw any conclusions before the room around her blurred and she abruptly found herself standing in the middle of a field with Bastien, Seth, and Tanner.

Seth released the two mens' shoulders and looked at Melanie with some surprise. "My apologies, Dr. Lipton. I didn't realize Bastien was touching you or I would have waited to teleport him."

"Oh." That was what teleportation felt like? Cool.

Wintery wind buffeted her. A full moon illuminated the clearing enough for her to see a dirt drive overgrown with weeds and several large holes in the ground that looked as though dirt had erupted from them.

"Where are we?"

"My lair," Bastien answered, dropping his hand from her arm. (Had his fingers lingered for a moment?) "Or what remains of it."

The lair that had housed his vampire army?

Melanie surveyed the area again, unable to see beyond the dark trees that formed a small amphitheater around them. If Seth hadn't meant to teleport her . . . "Should I leave?" She didn't know where she would go, but . . .

"No," Seth said. "I didn't mean you weren't welcome. I only wished to apologize for teleporting you without first warning you."

"Apology accepted."

Tanner held his hand out to her. "I'm Tanner Long, by the way." He was an attractive man, perhaps in his midthirties and dressed in slacks and a dress shirt. His short blond hair really stood out against the darkness characteristic of the immortals. His wire-rimmed glasses also set him apart physically. He sort of looked like a banker or an accountant. Maybe a professor.

A *hot* professor, Linda would likely say before singing "Teach Me Tonight."

Melanie shook his hand. "Melanie Lipton. Nice to meet you."

"Nice to meet you, too. This is the first opportunity I've had to thank you for everything you've done for Vince, Cliff, and Joe. I think some of the immortals and humans at the network have been fighting vampires for so long that they've become numb to their plight. You haven't."

That meant a lot to her. "I wish I could have done more for Vince."

"You tried to help him when no one else, save Bastien, would. He appreciated it, believe me."

"Thank you."

Bastien's gaze swung from Melanie to Tanner, then shifted to Seth. "So why are we here?"

"I didn't want to tell you in front of the others that I've

chosen Tanner to be your Second. I thought you might say something stupid like—"

"I don't need a Second," Bastien protested.

"That," Seth finished.

Tanner examined Bastien thoughtfully. "You needed a Second when you were working with the vampires."

"That was different."

"Not really."

Seth held up a hand to forestall whatever Bastien intended to say. "If you want to execute your duties as an Immortal Guardian without a babysitter, as you put it, you need a Second."

"No, I don't."

Tanner frowned and propped his hands on his hips. "I thought you were happy with my work."

"I was."

"If you're worried that I won't be able to fight by your side, you can relax. The network's been training me for almost two years now."

"It isn't that."

"Then what is it?"

Melanie was curious to know that herself. She would've thought Bastien would be happy with the arrangement.

"If you become my Second, you will be ostracized at the very least and—"

Tanner laughed. "Hell. Is *that* what's worrying you? That I won't be accepted by the other Seconds? This isn't high school, Bastien. I don't give a rat's ass who likes me and who doesn't."

Chapter 4

Bastien stiffened. While he didn't appreciate his concerns being so easily dismissed, he thought Tanner wasn't seeing the full picture. "You're right. This isn't high school. It isn't a popularity contest that means nothing in the greater scheme of things. It's life or death. If the other Seconds don't accept you, you won't be able to count on them to back you when you need them." He looked at Seth. "Tell him."

Seth shook his head. "They'll back him or they'll answer to Chris Reordon."

"Who would love nothing more than to see me fall. I'm sure he would feel the same way about anyone he considered my ally."

Melanie spoke. "If that were true, I wouldn't have a job."

Bastien stared at her. "What?"

"Who do you think pushed Mr. Reordon to allow you more frequent visits with Cliff and Joe?"

"Seth."

"Actually," Seth said, "it was Dr. Lipton. I merely offered my approval."

"And Richart and I *both* refused to let Mr. Reordon chain you up in the holding room," she said. "He may not have liked it, but he didn't fire me."

Bastien still didn't understand why Richart had stood up for him. Or Dr. Lipton for that matter.

As for Tanner . . .

Bastien glanced uneasily at Melanie. He would really rather not do this in front of her, but didn't see any way to avoid it. Seth wasn't going to leave this unresolved.

"Look," Bastien told the only man he had truly considered a friend in many, many years, "the last decade has been beyond fucked up for you. What happened to your son was horrible enough." Tanner's boy had been kidnapped and murdered by a pedophile, whom Bastien had himself tracked down and punished . . . very slowly. "Then you got tangled up in my folly and lived every day surrounded by vampires who apparently wanted you dead whenever I wasn't around."

"Vampires who aided me in my quest to get every fucking pedophile off the street."

"I'm just saying this is a chance for you to have something better. If you serve as my Second, people will give you shit every time you turn around. You don't need that."

"Sure I do," Tanner retorted with a grin. "Kinda makes life interesting, don't you think?"

Bastien stared at him a moment, then shook his head. "All right, you crazy bastard. I was trying to help your sorry ass, but if you're determined to be miserable . . ."

"Misery loves company," Tanner quipped.

Bastien, Seth, and Melanie all rolled their eyes.

"Now that that's settled, Tanner can move into David's place." Seth tilted his head to one side and seemed to listen for a moment. "I'll take him there now so he can get settled."

Him? "Aren't we all going back?"

"No. I think it would be best to let David's place clear out a bit before you return."

"Don't want to taint them with my presence?"

"No. Just trying to save David's new furniture. The paint is still drying from the scuffle that arose at the last meeting we held. And the new furniture hasn't even been around long enough to gather dust. I don't want to risk your opening that mouth of yours and saying something asinine that will give the others an excuse to kick your ass again."

"It isn't my fault if they can dish it out, but can't take it," Bastien said.

"Something you might try to keep in mind," Seth added, "is that David doesn't *have* to open his home to immortals, their Seconds, and members of the network. He does it because he knows how lonely this existence can be and wants to provide us all with a family that we can turn to for company, for comfort, hell, just for fun. Family that we *won't* have to watch age and die. I didn't ask him to mentor you. He offered. When everyone else called for your execution, David welcomed you into his family. The least you could do is refrain from instigating altercations that reduce his home to something that looks like a tornado hit it."

Damn. Seth really knew how to make a man feel like a teenager being upbraided by a parent. As old as Bastien was, that was quite an accomplishment.

Bastien refused to duck his head and say, "Yes, sir." He hadn't asked for any of this.

He would, however, see if he couldn't restrict his acerbic commenting to the training room where less damage would be done if a fight ensued.

"The others should leave to begin the night's hunt shortly. I'll ask Richart to come for you then." Seth met Melanie's gaze. "Are you warm enough, Dr. Lipton?"

She smiled. "I'm fine, thank you."

Seth returned his attention to Bastien. "You have company."

Bastien looked at Melanie.

"Not her," Seth said with exasperation. "A handful of vampires are headed this way. You'll hear them momentarily." He reached out and touched Tanner's shoulder.

"Wait!"

"What?"

Bastien stared at him. "What are you doing? Aren't you going to take Dr. Lipton with you?"

"No. I want her to continue monitoring you."

"While I'm fighting vampires?" Bastien asked incredulously.

"She's been trained." Seth looked at Melanie, who nodded she was okay with it.

Then Seth and Tanner disappeared.

Bastien couldn't believe it. He turned to Melanie. "What did he mean you've been trained?"

She shrugged sheepishly. "I can kick ass."

She said it with such reluctance that Bastien felt a rush of amusement. His lips twitched as he fought a smile.

"What?" she demanded with a frown. "You think I can't?" She crossed her arms in a defensive pose that only drew his attention to her lovely breasts.

"No, it's just . . ." *Eyes up.* "You looked so chagrined when you said it, like someone admitting they'd just farted or something."

She laughed and lowered her arms. "It just felt weird to say it. I've never been comfortable tooting my own horn."

Something as simple as her smile should *not* make his heart race and his body react in unsuitable ways. It really shouldn't.

But it did. It also cast a spell that made it impossible for him to avoid smiling back.

This was not good.

The sounds of several bodies approaching through the trees reached his sensitive ears. Five vampires ambled in their direction. They were still a couple of miles away and seemed to be in no hurry. The scent of blood—several types—accompanied them. They must be fresh from feeding.

Very odd. The insanity that infused vampires was usually

accompanied by extreme paranoia that prevented them from getting along. Even the vampires who had banded together under Bastien's rule had only refrained from attacking each other over the least provocation because they feared what Bastien would do to them. He hadn't lied when he had told the others that vampires had to fear you to follow you. Like the vampire king, Bastien had had to make an example of a few before that fear had solidified. He hadn't done so with a machete. But it had nevertheless been unpleasant.

"What is it?" Melanie asked. She had the loveliest brown eyes.

Keep your head in the game!

"Five vampires, fresh from feeding."

And damned if it didn't sound like an ordinary bunch of guys out killing time until the next movie started at the nearest theater.

This could potentially be interesting.

He would've looked forward to the confrontation if he weren't concerned for Melanie's safety. "What kind of training are we talking here?" he asked. "Self-defense?" He needed to know just how vulnerable she would be when the vampires attacked. He'd like to think they wouldn't, that he would luck out and find new allies on his first night searching, but vampires *always* attacked. If they didn't, they were plotting something.

"Self-defense," she confirmed. "Martial arts. Weapons. Speaking of which, I'll need to borrow a few. I don't usually carry when I'm at work, because Mr. Reordon doesn't want Cliff and Joe to get their hands on them." Expression brightening, she reached into her back pocket and pulled out what looked like three EpiPens, but were—he assumed—auto-injectors packing the tranquilizer. "Except for these."

Bastien considered them thoughtfully. Three auto-injectors. Five vampires. He could work with those numbers. Perhaps he could begin to forge ties with the vampires tonight after all.

"I tell you what . . ." He drew his katanas and gave them a twirl. "Do you know how to use these?"

"Of course." Her pragmatic response, utterly devoid of boasts, convinced him she spoke the truth. Richart's Second crowed about his skills all the time, but Bastien had yet to see the boy win a single sparring match.

"Then I'll trade you these for those."

Melanie eyed his weapons. "I'd rather have the daggers."

Smiling, Bastien returned the katanas to their sheaths and drew a dagger from the loops sewn into the lining of his coat.

Melanie offered him the auto-injectors with a sly smile. "You work fast."

His pulse picked up.

When he didn't respond, she motioned to the forest. "Already planning to recruit?"

He shrugged and studied the auto-injectors. Melanie was just too irresistible at the moment. "No point in waiting, really. How do these work?"

"Remove the red cap, press the tip against their skin, and hold it for three seconds."

Bastien removed all of the red caps. "Three seconds is a long time."

He could cross a football field from end zone to end zone in three seconds.

"I know. But usually auto-injectors take ten seconds to deliver a full dose. I cut it down as much as I could."

He nodded and handed her another dagger. Then another. And another.

Each one she tucked into a different pocket.

The vampires were close enough to catch Bastien and Melanie's conversation now.

He caught Melanie's attention, touched his ear, then motioned to the forest on the east side of the clearing.

"It was the vampire king's fault," he said, beginning his performance. "He should never have believed the lies."

She nodded. "He'd be alive today if he hadn't. He *and* his army."

The vampires stopped moving. Their voices hushed.

"It's the old sleight-of-hand trick," he went on. "Keep the vampires' attention focused on the immortals—"

"And they'll never see the new enemy coming," Melanie finished, her soft, warm voice filled with regret.

"Vampires as a whole will be as easily extinguished as the vampire king and his army. Immortals, too."

A nearly silent conversation began among their audience.

"Most vampires think the *Immortal Guardians* quelled the king's uprising."

"Some know the truth. But not enough. The immortals never would have achieved victory if so many of the vampire king's followers had not already been destroyed," Bastien lied.

"Well, now that vampires no longer have a leader, I don't know how to warn them."

Foliage rustled as the vampires put on a burst of speed and raced for the clearing.

Bastien moved to stand in front of Melanie, then cursed when she took two steps to the side and frowned up at him.

Reddish leaves already loosened by the cool weather burst from the bushes on the east side of the clearing and tumbled to the ground like candy from a piñata.

Dirt rose and fell in a cloud as the vampires skidded to a halt and faced them, all in a line, hands at their sides as if they were gunslingers preparing for a showdown.

Rather slovenly gunslingers.

Sans guns.

The vamps ranged in size from Melanie's height—roughly five foot five—to nearly Bastien's height of six feet and possessed the standard rangy, never-lifted-a-weight-in-their-lives build undisguised by baggy jeans. The blond wore a leather jacket he had probably filched from one of his victims. His auburn-haired friend wore a Carolina Panthers sweatshirt. The third vamp, whose short, raven hair was slicked back with what looked like an entire can of Murray's Pomade, wore all black. Black pleather pants. Black dress shirt. Black pleather tie. Black belt. Shiny black loafers. Bastien couldn't decide exactly what look the vamp had been going for, but he'd missed it whatever it was.

The other two vamps, who Bastien surmised had not been vamps for very long, wore matching Tar Heels sweatshirts.

Three of the vamps, the ones whose eyes were already glowing and whose fangs were exposed, were splattered with blood. The other two weren't.

"Who the hell are you?" the blood-speckled blond in the leather jacket demanded.

"Yeah," the vamp with auburn hair seconded. "What are you doing here?"

Bastien made a show of looking around. "If I'm not mistaken—and I'm not—this isn't your property, so I have every right to be here."

"Answer the question, asshole," the blond said and took what Bastien assumed was supposed to be a menacing step forward.

"I'm here for the same reason you are. This place means something to me." He let his fangs descend.

"He's a vampire like us," one of the Tar Heel vamps murmured.

"I don't know," the other muttered. "The woman is human. Doesn't one of the Immortal Guardians have a female Second?"

The vamps all tensed.

"Are you Roland?" the blond demanded.

Bastien sighed and looked at Melanie. "Why do so many vampires think Roland is the only man infected with the virus who has a human consort?"

"Consort?" she repeated with an intriguing amount of interest. "Am I your consort then?"

"Don't tempt me." Seriously. The mere suggestion sent erotic images writhing through his brain and he needed to keep his head clear at the moment.

Later though . . .

No. Not even later. Melanie was off-limits.

"What's a consort?" the Murray's man asked.

Bastien turned back to the vamps. "Why are *you* here?"

The blond raised his chin. "I lived here once. I was one of Bastien's soldiers."

"No, you weren't." Bastien had never seen the little snot before.

"Was, too," he retorted in a petulant singsong. "I wasn't a grunt either. I was his second in command."

"No, you weren't," Bastien repeated.

"How the hell do you know?" The vamp blurted, his face broadcasting his frustration.

"Because I'm Bastien, dumbass."

Melanie sighed loudly and sent Bastien a look that said, *Really? This is how you try to gain their cooperation?*

Inwardly, Bastien shrugged. He'd tried. But he had always had a low threshold for bullshit. Particularly when that bullshit was doled out with a great big steaming pile of arrogance.

The blond shot forward in a blur, but stopped short before the others could do more than tense to follow. His expression stunned, he stared down at the dagger sticking out of his chest.

The dagger Melanie had thrown.

Bastien turned to Melanie. "And this would be *your* method of forging an alliance?"

She grimaced. "Sorry. Instinct."

Once more fighting the urge to laugh—the two of them were really botching this—Bastien leaped forward.

* * *

While Melanie cursed herself for reacting too quickly, Bastien sped forward and plowed into the blond like an NFL linebacker. Without slowing, he caught the Panthers fan, too, and took them both down. The three slammed to the ground, dirt and winter brown foliage spraying up from the small crater they formed. Bastien reared back and hit the two vamps with the auto-injectors just as the other three vampires shot forward.

Melanie threw two daggers. One hit the vampire with the slicked back hair in the chest. The other hit one of the Tar Heels in the biceps. Both jerked to a halt and reached up to yank the blades out, giving Bastien enough time to deliver the full doses to the vampires he straddled.

The other Tar Heel kept going, streaking past Bastien and the others toward Melanie.

Fear sliced through her. She hurled another dagger, but the vamp dodged it, letting it fly past and land in the neck of the vamp with the slicked-back hair.

Down to her last two daggers, Melanie began to walk backward as she swung the blades in front of her. Mortals couldn't combat a vampire's strength. Nor could they match a vampire's speed. The best chance they had was to try to anticipate where the vampire would strike and swing to deflect the blow long before the vamp actually made it. Melanie had always been good at guessing the next move. And vampires *did* tend to underestimate any mortals who challenged them, toying with them first before they attacked in earnest.

At the last minute, Melanie dropped to the ground. A breeze combed through her hair as the vampire sailed overhead.

Heart pounding, she jumped to her feet and faced the vampire as he hit the ground and spun around.

His face mottled with anger. His hands closed into fists. His blue eyes began to glow as brightly as the moon above them. Lips curling into a sneer, he drew a butterfly knife from his back pocket, fanned it open with a flourish, and gripped the handles.

Melanie balanced her weight lightly on the balls of her feet, gripped her daggers, and waited.

The vampire blurred.

Swiveling to the side, Melanie swung both blades and stepped back.

A sharp pain stung her thigh. Again raising her weapons, she watched the vampire halt and stare down at the two long rips in his sweatshirt. One tore the material open from the middle of his chest to his hip. The other opened his side and lower back. The edges of both swiftly turned crimson, the stain spreading beneath each opening.

Jaw clenching, he charged forward.

Melanie again dropped to the ground. This time the vampire tripped on her, his foot lodging painfully in her ribs, then flew several yards to land in an ignominious heap.

Not too bright, this one.

Melanie rose and fought the urge to clutch her sore ribs. Another lesson she had learned when training was to never tip off her opponents to a weakness. Show them an injury and they would exploit it.

Rustles and thumps sounded behind her. She wanted desperately to peek and see how Bastien was faring, but didn't dare take her eyes from the vampire stumbling to his feet and facing her. Dirt clung to the wet ruby patches on his clothes. His hair stood up on one side.

Growling in fury, he lunged in her direction, then froze, his gaze going over her shoulder.

A body brushed up against Melanie's back.

Jumping, she spun around and swung one of the daggers.

Bastien caught her wrist before the blade could sink into his throat. "It's all right. It's just me."

Relief rushed through her. "Make a sound next time. Or say

my name. *Something.* I thought you were one of the other vampires."

"I realize that now. My mistake. I've never fought alongside a human before." He pointed at the vampire, who was easing back a step. "You," he pronounced in an authoritative tone. "Stay where you are. We need to talk and if you run away you won't escape. You'll just piss me off." His expression darkened. "And you do *not* want to piss me off."

The vampire blanched and swallowed audibly.

Melanie looked behind Bastien at the others. The blond, the Panthers fan, and the other Tar Heel were unconscious on the ground, successfully tranqed by the auto-injectors. The vamp in black with the slicked back hair was rapidly shriveling up as the virus that infected him devoured him from the inside out in a frantic bid to continue living. He could have survived the knife to the chest. It had hit near his shoulder. But the throat . . . Her borrowed dagger had severed the carotid artery.

Vampires weren't like immortals. Immortals wouldn't die from blood loss alone. If the blood loss was extreme enough, the immortal would slip into a sort of stasis or hibernation until another blood source came along. Vampires like this one, however, simply bled out, dying before the virus could repair the damage.

Melanie stared. She had never killed anyone before. Had never even imagined doing so, even while undergoing her training. It left a sick feeling in her stomach. A heaviness in her chest.

Bastien's hand on her wrist loosened, sliding up to her biceps to brush up and down in a gentle caress.

She looked up, met his gaze. "It was an accident."

"I know."

"I didn't mean to kill him. The second dagger was supposed to hit that one." She motioned to the sole upright vampire, who glanced around frantically, seeking some avenue of escape.

"I know," Bastien murmured softly, then maneuvered her around so her back was to the others. "What about your leg? How deep is the wound?"

She glanced down. The blue jean material clinging to her left thigh had parted in a clean slice about half a foot long. Shifting the dagger in her left hand to join that in her right, she poked the wound. "It's shallow. I don't think I even need stitches."

Bastien suddenly pointed in the vamp's direction. "Boy, do *not* make me chase you."

The vampire, who must have been about to bolt, went still, eyes wide.

"You're sure you're okay?" Bastien asked Melanie, his voice much softer.

She nodded.

"Why aren't the others shriveling up?" the vampire blurted. Melanie could almost hear his nerves jangling.

"They aren't dead," Bastien told him and held up the used auto-injectors. "They're drugged."

"Drugs don't work on us," the vampire countered. "I used to be hooked on Ketamine. Now it doesn't do shit to me."

"This," Bastien told him, again drawing his attention to the auto-injectors, "will."

"Bullshit."

"Have you ever seen a dead vampire *not* disintegrate?"

"No," he admitted. "But I haven't seen very many dead vampires."

Melanie eyed the vamp. Could they have lucked out and actually found a newly turned one so soon? "How long have you been infected?"

"Since Spring Break." Less than a year then. "I went to Acapulco, got high, passed out on the beach, and woke up like this." His gaze, still luminescent blue, strayed to his companions.

"Listen for their pulse, if it will make you feel better," Melanie suggested.

All were silent for a long moment.

"They really are still alive," he said. "But they're out? They're unconscious?"

"Yes."

He started forward.

Bastien reached out, touched Melanie's hip, and eased her behind him.

She tried to resist—she could take care of herself—but Bastien got his way through sheer strength, keeping himself between her and the vampire at all times as the boy went to stand over his friends.

All but growling with frustration, Melanie poked Bastien in the ribs.

A bark of startled laughter escaped him when she inadvertently hit a ticklish spot. He quickly cut it off and frowned down at her.

Raising up the daggers she still held in one hand, she pushed him away with the other. "I don't think he's stupid enough to try to hurt me," she said dryly. "Are you . . . what's your name?"

The vampire stopped next to the blond. "Stuart." Without answering her first question, he crouched down and started rifling through the pockets of the blond's leather jacket.

Bastien grumbled something she couldn't hear under his breath. Truth be told, she wouldn't mind being in his arms under other circumstances.

Stuart made a sound of discovery and withdrew an iPod and what appeared to be Bose earbuds from the blond's pocket. Rising, he wrapped the cord around and around the iPod, then tucked both into his back pocket.

"He won't remember any of this?" Stuart asked, his eyes on the blond.

"No," Bastien answered.

A second later, Stuart drew his foot back and kicked the blond hard in the head. "Asshole. Takin' my shit." A second kick followed.

"I take it you two weren't close," Bastien drawled.

"Hell, no. But if there's one thing we vampires learned from . . ." he motioned to Bastien ". . . well, from you, it's that there's strength in numbers. *Dick* here was the strongest among us and seemed to be doing pretty well, so I joined him."

Lovely, Bastien thought. The immortals were going to enjoy holding *this* over his head.

"So . . ." Stuart said, easing back a step and clapping his hands together. "I guess I'll just be going now."

"Nice try." Bastien drawled and motioned to a pile of dirt that bordered a crater in the soil, a remnant of the last battle fought here. A battle he had missed, damn it. It may have turned out differently had he not. "Park it."

Face grim, Stuart perched awkwardly on the soil. "It's damp."

"I care. Now pay attention. We have something to discuss." Bastien untucked his shirt and began to tear a long strip from the hem like someone trying to pare away an apple's skin in one long piece.

"Is it what we heard you talking about before we reached the clearing?"

"Yes. We've a new enemy."

"The Immortal Guardians do?"

"Both of us—vampires *and* immortals—do. One bent on destroying us all so he can usurp our power."

"Yeah. Right."

"What are you doing?" Melanie asked, watching him curiously.

Bastien knelt before her. "Remember what I said, Stuart.

Don't make me chase you." Taking the long strip of cloth, Bastien began to wind it snugly around and around Melanie's thigh where the vamp had cut her.

She braced a hand on his shoulder. "Thank you."

Bastien completely lost his train of thought as warmth flowed into him at the sweet contact. He heard her pulse leap at his touch. Felt her breath catch as though it were his own.

"Our new enemy developed the sedative, Stuart," she said.

"And yet, you're using it."

"I didn't get my hands on the drug," she said, "until it was used against vampires and immortals during the vampire king's uprising."

Bastien tied a knot in the makeshift bandage. "The enemy's name is Emrys and he runs a mercenary group." Rising, he glanced at the vamp. "At least we think it's mercenary and not military."

Stuart frowned. "What, you mean like Blackwater?"

"Yes, but think smaller and more elite. Only those who need to know are even aware of this shadow army's existence. It's so secretive we haven't been able to ascertain its name or location, only that of the leader."

"We wouldn't have even known that," Melanie said, "if he hadn't duped the vampire king."

Stuart looked doubtful, but at least he was listening.

Bastien hadn't really anticipated accomplishing this much when he had proposed his plan. He and Melanie had really lucked out.

Of course, there *were* a lot more recently turned vampires in the area, thanks to the vampire king. Near the end, he had told his followers to turn others at will, and his soldiers had taken that order and run with it. Chris Reordon was *still* sorting through all of the Missing Person reports that had inundated the police and sheriff's departments in North Carolina and surrounding states.

"Was this before or *after* you killed the king?" Stuart asked with an abundance of sarcasm.

Bastien stood too close to Melanie. Every time their arms brushed, he was struck by little shocks of her emotions, many of which revolved around *his* sorry ass. "Before. What do you think weakened the king's ranks enough for us to destroy them?"

Stuart frowned.

"This mercenary—Emrys—promised the vampire king power, an army . . . everything the king desired basically . . . in exchange for the capture of one of us. The vampire king trusted him and was taken down with the drug, many of his followers with him."

Sure it was a fabrication. Well, not the deal part, but the Emrys taking down the vampire king part. That had been pure Immortal Guardian handiwork accomplished with the aid of Reordon and his network.

And a butt-load of Napalm-B.

"So they want one of you guys?" Stuart asked, a speculative gleam entering his eye.

"They want you, too," Melanie said in that soft, genuine voice of hers. "We don't know what their aim is. I assume they want to study you, possibly expose you to the public."

"What's so wrong with going public?"

Bastien snorted. "Nothing if you invest your money in repeating pump-action crossbow manufacturing. Because as soon as word breaks, an ass-load of religious fanatics, hunting aficionados, and horror movie fans are going to come after us. *All* of us. But, since vampires are the ones who actively prey upon humans, they'll come after *you* first."

"Shit."

"Precisely."

"It isn't just that," Melanie said. "This man and those he commands are butchers. We've seen their handiwork. They may promise you wealth and power and anything else they think you desire, but they will use the drug when you least expect it. It may be at your first meeting. Or at your fifth or fiftieth, when they feel you're no longer useful to them. They think you're an expendable animal. And when they have you at their mercy, they will torture you."

Bastien nodded. "When I say they want to study you, I don't mean they want to take your blood pressure or ask you to turn your head and cough. They'll torture your ass. The pain and discomfort you experienced during your transformation will be as minor as a paper cut in comparison."

Stuart swore.

Bastien tensed when the boy jumped up and began to pace.

"So what you're saying is I'm screwed. This mercenary fuck wants me and every other vampire dead and so do you immortals."

"No, we don't. You'd be an empty pile of clothing like Murray's man over there if that were true. The immortals are looking for vampires with whom we can form an alliance of sorts."

"Bullshit."

Melanie caught Stuart's eye. "This isn't the first time an immortal has approached a vampire with an offer of aid. You wouldn't be in this clearing tonight if you hadn't heard that Bastien had done so in the past."

"Yeah," Stuart said, voice high with anxiety, "because he thought he was a vampire!"

"But that's a good thing," she insisted. "He lived with vampires for two centuries. He knows what you're going through. *I* know what you're going through. Two vampires have already joined our fight. Had they not, I wouldn't have been able to alter the drug so that it only *sedates* and doesn't kill vampires."

Stuart stopped short. "Really?"

"The two were members of my army," Bastien said, "who

had the foresight to surrender and ask the Immortal Guardians for help rather than continuing to fight once I was taken."

"Once you were taken?" Stuart repeated. "Like as a prisoner?"

Bastien shrugged. "I had spent too many years wrongly blaming immortals for something they didn't do to go willingly. And, yet—as you can see—they didn't harm me. They won't harm you either if you help us."

"Help you how?"

"We need someone to help us spread the word to the other vampires, impress upon them the importance of avoiding capture by Emrys and his soldiers. I narrowly escaped capture myself, and you know I'm much stronger than you are."

"Yeah. You wish."

The words had scarcely left Stuart's lips before Bastien flew to his side and lifted him two or three feet off the ground with a hand at his throat.

Eyes bulging, Stuart clawed at Bastien's hand with both of his own to no avail. His face mottled. His legs kicked.

Melanie cleared her throat. "Um . . . Bastien."

Opening his fingers, he let the vampire drop to the ground. "As I said, I'm much stronger than you."

Stuart coughed and gasped. Climbing to his feet, he glowered at Bastien.

Melanie ambled over to join them.

Bastien clutched Stuart's arm. "Do you kill when you feed?"

"Yes," he responded defiantly.

The emotions flowing into Bastien told him otherwise. Stuart was all boast and no bite.

Releasing him, Bastien stepped back.

"What do I have to do if I join you?" the vamp asked.

"Vampires from all over the globe have been pouring into North Carolina since tales of my uprising leaked, so we know you use a method to communicate that goes beyond word of mouth or congregating at the local pub."

Stuart rubbed his neck. "There are . . . places on the Internet where a lot of us like to hang out."

"We'll need a list of those."

Stuart shook his head. "I don't know, man. I need to think about it."

"Not if you want to live."

"So, if I say no, you'll kill me?"

"If you aren't with us, you're against us."

"There's more," Melanie said, issuing Bastien a frown. "You've been a vampire long enough to notice that older vampires are less than stable mentally."

Stuart's gaze strayed to the blond.

"The mental deterioration is a result of brain damage that increases every day you're infected with the virus. You may be fine now. But you'll begin to have psychotic episodes in the next year or so. Before then, twisted fantasies will disrupt your thoughts. Disturbing impulses that will become harder and harder to deny."

Stuart eyed Bastien. "You have that?"

"No. Immortals don't have to battle the insanity vampires do."

"Why?"

"I can't tell you that."

"Stuart, the two vampires I told you about . . . We're working with them to find a way to prevent that and to reverse the damage, to find a treatment so being infected won't result in an automatic mental decline. We want to *help* vampires."

"Then why kill us?"

"You leave us little choice," Bastien said. "If there were a rabid dog in your neighborhood, would you let it run around attacking at will, or would you put it down?"

"We're trying to spare you both fates," Melanie explained. "But, we can't impress upon you strongly enough that either of those—a descent into madness or death at the hands of an immortal—would be preferable to the fate you would meet if you were captured by Emrys and his army."

"They're humans. I just don't see—"

"They have pistols that will sedate you and any other vampire in seconds," Bastien reminded him. "These are mercenaries armed with automatic weapons. You won't be able to stand against them. I barely escaped myself."

Stuart still looked uncertain. "I have to think about it."

"I'll give you until tomorrow night."

Stuart shook his head. "What if I need more time? I mean . . . I don't know."

Bastien took the boy's arm again and felt only fear. No malice. Or triumph. Or anything that might indicate deception. "Three nights," Bastien conceded. It *was* a hell of a decision. "Meet me here at midnight or I'll assume you've opted not to join us and will hunt you down. And Stuart . . ."

"Yeah?"

"If I have to hunt you down, there won't be any talking when I find you. We clear?"

"Yeah." Stuart took a step back. Then another. Seconds later he vanished into the foliage and Bastien heard him rushing away as fast as he could.

He turned to face Melanie and found her studying him, her pretty face impassive.

"You *can* kick ass," he praised, both impressed and puzzled by the fact that she had held her own so well against a vampire.

"Yes." With a tip of her chin, she indicated the trees through which Stuart had departed. "You're really going to let him go?"

"Yes."

"You can't do that, Bastien."

He should *not* like the sound of his name on her lips so much. "He can't spread the word if I don't."

"But he said he's killed."

"He was lying."

"You don't know that with any certainty, not without one of the telepaths confirming it."

"I know it with *some* certainty."

"How?"

"Don't you know about my gift?"

"No. Why? What is it?"

"I'm an empath."

She stared at him in silence for so long he began to feel a bit self-conscious. "You can feel other people's emotions?" she asked finally.

"Yes. And Stuart's told me he was lying to try to save his ass."

Again she stared at him.

"What?" he asked when the silence stretched.

"You can feel my emotions? Right now?"

"No. I have to touch you to feel them."

"So . . ."

He could see her considering it, trying to remember every time he had touched her or she had touched him. At the network. In her car. At David's. Trying to remember what she might have inadvertently revealed.

"You might have mentioned it. Given me a little warning."

"Such didn't occur to me."

More silence.

"What do you feel when you touch me?" she asked.

Bastien's attention dropped to her full lips as she licked them anxiously. "Sometimes I feel your concern. Sometimes uncertainty. Clinical detachment. Fear the first time we met."

"Well, our first meeting was rather . . . explosive."

That was putting it mildly.

"What else?"

He knew what she sought. "Sometimes my gift tells me

you feel what I feel myself every time I look at you. Or think
of you. Or touch you."

Her soft, smooth neck moved with a swallow. "You're attracted to me."

"Yes."

"I'm attracted to you."

"I know."

"What are we going to do about it?"

"Nothing."

"You're not going to give me a reason?"

"If you need one, I'm not looking to enter into a relationship just now." He wasn't sure how much longer he would be
with the immortals. He would only be able to tolerate so
much crap before he would have to move on to avoid killing
someone. And, for all he knew, if he *did* move on, they might
hunt him down and finally execute him for killing Ewen. Why
the hell would he bring a woman into his life now?

"Blunt," she said. "I can respect that."

"I'm too old to play games."

"Some men are never too old to play games."

"The same could be said of some women."

"That's true, though I wish I could say otherwise." Sighing,
she looked around the clearing, then down at the daggers in
her hand. She held them out to him.

His fingers brushed hers when he took the weapons, allowing him to feel her emotions. No embarrassment. Mainly
frustration and disappointment.

He felt a healthy dose of that himself.

Some men were only interested in physical beauty. Bastien
needed a brain to go along with that. Without wit and intelli-
gence to intrigue him, after two hundred years a hot body just
became the same old same old to the extreme. And *no* sex
was better than sex with someone who bored him.

Melanie would *never* bore him. She was smart and funny
and so damned sexy . . .

"Did you feel anything else when you touched me?" she asked.

"Irritation," he mentioned. Thinking of her aggravation with him during the meeting, he smiled. "Which reminds me . . . You kicked me."

She shrugged, lips tilting up just a bit. "You were being an ass. Didn't anyone ever tell you *you can catch more flies with honey*?"

"Sure. But who wants to catch flies?"

She laughed. "You're impossible."

"So everyone keeps telling me, but in far less pleasant terms."

Melanie's Chevy Volt suddenly appeared in the clearing. Richart stood next to it with his hand on the hood.

She jumped, then looked at Bastien. "Doesn't it startle you when he does that?"

"It did at first, but I've spent so much time around him lately that it no longer phases me."

Richart lifted his hand off the car, took a step, then sank to his knees.

Bastien zipped over and caught him before he could fall forward and hit the ground face-first. "What is it? Have you been tranqed?"

"No." Richart gripped Bastien's arm and used it as leverage to gain his feet. "I've never teleported a car before and was curious to see if I could do it."

Bastien released him as soon as he stood, but prepared to throw a hand out as the Frenchman swayed.

Beige grasses and weeds crackled and crunched as Melanie joined them. "Does teleporting weaken you?"

"Teleporting cars does, apparently."

"What about people?"

Bastien could see her slipping into her physician mode. Odd that even when she was clinical and impersonal he found her utterly alluring.

"Not if I only teleport one person at a time."

"Do you need blood afterward?"

He sent her a flirtatious smile. "Are you offering?"

Bastien's fist slammed into Richart's jaw.

Richart's head snapped back. Blood sprayed from his lips. Melanie gasped.

Bastien stared. He really hadn't meant to do that. Hadn't he just told Melanie he didn't want a relationship with her? Behaving like a jealous moron wouldn't go very far in helping him convince her of that.

Richart staggered back against the car and raised a hand to cup his cracked jaw. "What the hell, man?"

Bastien risked a glance at Melanie, then swore.

Though her eyes were wide, the look in them was too knowing.

"Dr. Lipton is under my protection."

Richart leaned over and spat blood. "I wasn't going to bite her, you horse's ass! It was a joke!"

A harmless joke that every immortal on the planet, himself included, had probably spouted dozens of times. Except tonight it had sent a storm of jealousy thundering through him. "Well, it wasn't funny."

Richart grunted as his jaw began to heal. "If you'd just told me you wanted her for yourself, I wouldn't have opened my mouth. Asshole."

"He doesn't want me for himself," Melanie said. "He isn't looking for a relationship."

"It doesn't matter if he's looking," Richart grumbled. "He's found one. The two of you can't take your eyes off each other. And in the rare moments you do, you usually touch."

"What?" Bastien said the same time Melanie did.

Was she as appalled that her feelings were so transparent as he was?

"Don't worry." Richart drew out a handkerchief and wiped

his crimson lips. "I doubt anyone else has noticed. Bastien is usually too busy pissing them all off."

"He doesn't piss you off?" Melanie asked.

"Other than just now"—Richart glared at Bastien—"no. I've spent enough time in his company that I've become immune to his bullshit." He tucked the stained cloth away. "We'll have to either drop by my place or return to the network because *now* I need blood."

"The network," Bastien chose. "I want to run our plan by Cliff and Joe and seek their advice. And we need to drop these guys"—he motioned to the unconscious vampires— "off in the holding room."

Chapter 5

Once at the network, Bastien and Melanie helped Richart chain the vamps up in the holding room and notified Chris. Then they accompanied Richart to the infirmary, where he drained a couple of bags of blood. As he finished the second one, "Monster" imbued the stark, hospital-like environment with a bit of life.

Richart pulled out his phone, looked at the caller ID, and donned the dopey smile Bastien had come to think of as *her* smile. "Excuse me." He turned away and took the call. "Hi." His voice always softened when he spoke to his mystery lover.

"Hi," Bastien heard her say, her voice a little flat. He didn't know if Richart was so smitten that he forgot Bastien could hear both sides of the conversation or if Richart simply trusted Bastien not to run to Chris with any information he overheard, but the immortal rarely sought privacy during the calls unless their talk turned amorous. "Am I interrupting anything?"

"Not at all."

"You aren't fighting vampires?" she asked, a teasing lilt entering her voice.

"No. No vampires," Richart said with a light laugh. "How are you feeling?"

"Not that great. That's actually why I was calling. I wanted to let you know I'm playing hooky from work again. I think I may have done too much too fast. My fever went back up today and I pretty much feel like crap."

"I'm sorry, darling. Can I bring you anything? Some soup, perhaps?"

Melanie looked at Bastien.

"His girlfriend," he murmured. "She's fighting that flu that's been going around."

Melanie grimaced in sympathy. "It's a nasty one. The network employees who have come down with it have been missing up to two weeks of work and come back noticeably thinner."

"Are you sure there's nothing I can do?" Richart asked.

Melanie spoke up. "Orange juice and club soda."

Richart turned around. "What?"

"Take her some orange juice and mix it with club soda. It will help settle her stomach and give her some vitamin C at the same time."

Richart nodded. "Thank you."

"And crackers," Bastien added. "Saltines." He had heard Sarah mention that crackers had helped curb her nausea during her transformation. She hadn't had the flu, but . . . nausea was nausea, wasn't it?

Richart's face reflected his surprise at Bastien's input. "Thank you."

Bastien consulted his watch. "If you're going to get her the organic stuff, you need to go now. Whole Foods closes in fifteen minutes."

"Right," Richart acknowledged, then spoke into the phone. "I'm going to pick up a few things at the store, then come by, if that's all right."

"You know it is," she said. "But I don't want you to go to any trouble for me, Richart. You have enough on your plate."

"It's no trouble, sweetheart. Try to get some rest. I shall be there shortly."

Melanie couldn't help but be curious about the woman who had stolen the French Immortal Guardian's heart. Everything about him softened when he spoke to her. His voice. His features. His body language. He clearly adored her.

Richart tucked his phone away. "Well. This is awkward. Dr. Lipton . . ." He paused. "Let me think how to word this . . ."

Bastien rolled his eyes. "He isn't supposed to leave me unsupervised and wants your discretion."

"Oh." Really? Bastien was supposed to be watched *every* minute? "Yes, of course." She wondered how much of that was distrust on Seth's part and how much was wanting a bit of protection for the heavily disliked newcomer. Did Seth and David worry that one of the other immortals might try to avenge Ewen's death?

Richart pulled his handkerchief from his pocket and wiped his face, then tucked it away and combed his fingers through his hair. "How do I look?"

Melanie grinned. "Very handsome."

Bastien eyed Richart balefully. "If you ask me to check your breath, I'm going to hit you again."

Richart flipped him off with a grin and vanished into thin air.

Melanie looked up at Bastien. "I know, as a doctor and a researcher, I should find a more clinical way to say this, but that is *so* cool."

He laughed. "Yes, it is."

Dr. Whetsman entered the room, his attention on an open file cradled in his hands. Raising his gaze, he caught sight of them, blanched and—without breaking stride—made a sharp U-turn and strode right back out.

"Who the hell was that?" Bastien grumbled.

"Dr. Whetsman."

His countenance darkened. "The prick who scratched your face when Vince had his last break?"

"Yes," Melanie said, stunned that he even remembered her mentioning it. So much had happened since then. And she had only mentioned it the one time when they were facing Vince as he struggled for lucidity.

Bastien's eyes flashed amber. A growl rumbled forth from his muscled throat.

When he took a step after the retreating doctor, Melanie grabbed his arm. "Whoa there, tiger. Leave him alone."

"He hit you."

"He scratched me while he screamed like a little girl and ran away from a crazed vampire."

His expression changed from fury to amusement to one of self-loathing. "Oh, hell. I forgot you were wounded." Bending, he scooped her up in his arms and carried her over to an exam table.

Melanie gasped. "What are you . . . ?"

He seated her on it, then began to unwind the bandage he had applied.

"Bastien, you don't have to . . ." She broke off when he took one of his daggers and applied it to her jeans. Her snug jeans. Which became something very close to Daisy Dukes on one side as he swiftly and efficiently cut away her pant leg above her injury.

"What are you thinking?" he asked, voice light with curiosity. "Your emotions are all over the place."

It really was disconcerting that he could know what she felt anytime he wanted to simply by reaching out and touching her. The only thing worse would be his being able to read her thoughts.

"Just off the top of my head?" she said. "I'm glad I shaved my legs last night."

He grinned. "What else?"

"I like you touching me, even though the cut is stinging like crazy."

His eyes began to glow. "I thought we weren't going to go there."

"I'm a grown woman. I can go wherever I want to go."

"Why would you *want* to go there?" His tone was pure puzzlement.

"I don't know," she answered honestly. Anyone who spent five minutes in his company knew he was something of a mess, still trying to find his way in his new life. Still battling the bitterness of the past. Reluctant to trust after being deceived by—oh—about a hundred of his closest friends.

"There's just something about you," she said finally, "that . . . lures me."

Bastien pilfered first-aid supplies from nearby drawers and cabinets.

Melanie sucked in a pained breath as he disinfected the cut. It felt as though he were holding a blow torch to her skin.

"Sorry," he said, his eyes losing some of their glow as his brow furrowed.

She nodded, blinking back tears. Crap, it hurt. But it didn't halt her body's response when he leaned down and blew on her thigh in an attempt to squelch the fire.

Giving in to temptation, she reached out and combed her fingers through his dark locks.

She had never dated a man with long hair before. Bastien's fell past his shoulders in a sleek midnight curtain.

It was so soft. She hadn't expected that. More often than not when men let their hair grow long it looked frizzy, split-endy, or just plain greasy and in need of a wash. Bastien's appeared as smooth and shiny as that of the models in shampoo commercials. Smoother and shinier than *Melanie's*, making her wish she had found a better conditioner or used a curling iron or *something* to make her brown locks less blah. She was always just so tired when she got home in the morning. Even two extra minutes spent combing a conditioner through her hair in the shower seemed like too much work.

Bastien's breath halted the moment her fingers sank into his raven tresses. His eyes flared bright amber again. His lids lowered.

Melanie combed his hair back on one side, let it fall forward in graceful waves. Heart pounding, she buried *both* hands in his hair—so thick—and slid her fingers, nails clipped short to accommodate her work at the computer, along his scalp.

A growl, more like the rumbling purr a leopard might make, arose deep in his throat.

Her pulse spiked.

Bastien braced his hands on the edge of the exam table, gripping it tightly.

"What are you doing, Dr. Lipton?" he asked hoarsely.

"Melanie," she corrected, heart pounding so hard she was sure Cliff and Joe must hear it in their apartments across the hall.

"What are you doing, Melanie?"

She repeated the action. "Whatever feels good," she whispered.

That drew a groan from him. Leaning forward, he rested his forehead on her shoulder.

She waited for him to turn his head and nuzzle her neck, maybe take a little bite. But he didn't. He increased the pressure of his forehead on her shoulder, pressed her back the tiniest bit, the battle raging within him palpable.

"I need you to not do that," he said, voice low.

"Why?"

"Because every time you touch me I feel how much you want me and it makes me want you even more."

Her blood heated. "I don't have a problem with that," she murmured.

Bastien groaned and did turn his head, then pressed his lips to her throat. "You should." He lifted his head, stared at her with those incredible, luminescent eyes. So bright. So beautiful. So full of desire.

Mere inches separated them.

He raised one hand, cupped her cheek, smoothed his thumb across her skin.

Melanie had never wanted a man to kiss her more.

He shifted, leaned closer, touched his lips to hers.

Her breath caught.

"I can feel everything *you* feel," he whispered.

"Is that the only reason you're kissing me?"

His head moved from side to side in a barely discernible shake. "You don't know how much I wish it were." His lips again closed on hers, firmer, hungrier.

Melanie hummed in pleasure as fire licked its way through her veins. His tongue met hers, stroked, enticed. So hot she thought she might melt onto the table.

Abruptly, he broke the contact and again braced both hands on the table, rested his forehead on her shoulder.

"We can't do this," he said gruffly. "I've made a lot of mistakes in my long life, Melanie. A *lot*. And, knowing me, I'll make many more. I don't want you to be one of them."

"What makes you think I'd be a mistake?" She couldn't change his mind if she didn't know his train of thought.

He straightened suddenly, shoulders stiff, eyes lowered, though not enough that she couldn't still see their glow. Bastien may do his damnedest to appear cold and indifferent, but his eyes reflected the strong emotions that whipped through him.

"I won't do this." He spoke not another word as he finished cleaning and dressing her wound.

Melanie was impressed by the quality of his work. "You're good." She tested the dressing. "Have you studied medicine?"

"Formally, no," he answered, tossing the discarded makeshift bandage and other trash into the can marked hazardous waste.

"But I long ago grew tired of butchering myself every time I had to remove chunks of lead, shards of glass, blades long and short, and once, a wooden stake nearly the width of your wrist. So I purchased a library full of medical textbooks that have helped me improve my first aid skills."

"Did you understand what Montrose Keegan was doing then? His research?"

"Some. In the beginning, I read all of his notes and paid close attention to his experiments. But destroying Roland and maintaining control of an army of men who were rapidly losing their grips on reality was . . ."

"A full-time job?"

"Yes. How do you feel? Do you require pain medication?"

"For this?" she scoffed. "No."

When she had first begun her training, she had been so freaking sore all over that she had walked like a century-old human. Hunched over. Bitching and moaning with every step she took. (The last part wasn't necessarily characteristic of an old woman. But for some reason it had helped her to complain about it.)

She had taken no pain relievers for it though. Her trainers had emphasized the importance of becoming accustomed to pain so that if she ever engaged in battle, the pain of any wounds she might incur wouldn't totally freak her out.

Mission accomplished. She thought she had held her own rather well tonight.

"By the way, are the vampires you hunt usually so chatty?" she asked.

He laughed, some of the tension in his body easing. "No. Many are boastful or make scathing comments until I strike the first blow. Stuart was something of a surprise. He must be like Cliff. The madness must be progressing more slowly in him, otherwise he would have run off or stayed and fought without listening to a word we said."

"I hope he can be trusted."

"I do, too."

"I guess we'll find out in three nights. Can I go with you to meet him?"

"Hell, no! It could be a trap."

"All the more reason to have an extra set of hands—"

"Not gonna happen."

She could see he wouldn't budge. "Fine. At least call me and let me know you're on the way to meet him in case it *is* an ambush."

The tension in his face eased. "That I can do. Now, I'd like to go ahead and speak with Cliff before Richart returns so I'll bid you good night."

Melanie stared up at him. "I don't suppose I could talk you into *kissing* me good night, could I?"

She thought he would refuse. So, when he cupped her face in his large hands, ducked his head, and captured her lips in a fiery hot, tongue-tangling kiss . . .

Well, she lost the ability to think and speak coherently and could only feel.

His eyes blazed brightly when he raised his head. "Good night, Melanie."

He was through the door before she could find her voice.

Melanie was still thinking about that kiss three nights later while she was supposed to be focusing on the results of Joe's latest MRI. Though the lab boasted no windows, she knew by the clock that the sun had just set. Bastien would be rising and preparing for the night's hunt.

Was he still thinking about the kiss, too? Did he regret it? Because she hadn't seen or spoken to him since.

"Hello." As though her thoughts had conjured him, he spoke behind her.

Breath catching, she whipped around. "Hi." His black cargo pants, long-sleeved T-shirt, and coat were clean and outlined his tall, handsome form to perfection. Beside him, Richart nodded to her, then disappeared.

Neither she nor Bastien spoke for a long moment as his gaze roved her like a pair of hands.

"So," she said when he made no move to give her a hello kiss, "tonight's the night, huh? You're meeting with Stuart later?"

He nodded. "I thought I'd come see Cliff first."

Cliff. Not her. She would've been more disappointed if his eyes weren't glowing faintly with desire.

"Of course." Melanie slid off her stool and led Bastien not to Cliff's apartment, but to her office. Swiping the key card in her pocket, she typed in her personal security code, waited for the beep, and opened the door. "Just a minute." Grabbing the white lab coat draped over her office chair, she slid her right arm into the appropriate sleeve.

Bastien stepped up behind her, took the coat, and held it for her while she donned it. His hands lingered on her shoulders.

"That isn't fair," she whispered, heart racing. He could feel her every emotion, while she remained in the dark.

"I missed you, too," he admitted. "And want nothing more than to pull you into my arms and see if you taste as good as I remember."

Smiling, she turned around.

His normally somber expression was as tender as Richart's was when Richart spoke with his girlfriend. He brushed her cheek with his fingers. "Unfortunately, the matter I need to discuss with Cliff is one of some urgency."

"I understand." Heartened by his admission, she crossed to a cabinet, keyed it open, and removed three syringes filled with the sedative. When she turned toward the door, she found Bastien frowning at her. "After what happened with Vince, I always keep some on me when I'm with Cliff or Joe in case one should have a psychotic break. I don't want to see either of them brought under control with multiple gunshot wounds."

"Have you had to use them?"

She hesitated. "Once."

His eyes flared. "When?"

"Last week. On Joe. He—"

"Why didn't you tell me?"

She didn't want to say, but thought he deserved the truth. "He was so ashamed afterward, Bastien. And he didn't hurt me. He tried to grab one of the guards and . . . I was afraid you might . . ."

"Do to him what I did to Vince?"

"Yes."

His lips tightened.

Well . . . he had asked. Melanie strode past him and led the way to Cliff's apartment. Cliff was sunk in the cushions of a black leather sofa, feet propped on the coffee table, reading a science fiction novel when they entered.

Melanie smiled at the guard outside the door as she closed it behind them.

"Did you two want privacy?" she asked belatedly.

Bastien shook his head. "I didn't really want to talk to Cliff."

"Nice to see you, too," Cliff said sunnily as he rose and joined them.

"I don't understand."

"I wanted to talk to *you*," Bastien explained, "and knew we would not be overheard in here."

Melanie frowned. If Bastien were about to go into some long-winded explanation of why he didn't want her to hit on him anymore . . .

Her thoughts halted. Wait. Had she been hitting on him? She had never been the aggressor in a relationship before.

And there was that word again: Relationship.

"What's up?" she asked as casually as she could.

"I sensed you lied and wanted to know why," Bastien said.

Cliff's gaze swung back and forth between them as he eyed them with interest.

"When?"

"At the meeting. When you said you had no antidote to the tranquilizer."

Oh crap. "What makes you think I lied?" she bluffed.

"I was touching you and felt your guilt."

Damn it! "You know, that's *really* annoying."

"Tell me about it," Cliff quipped.

Bastien shot him a quick glare and once more met Melanie's gaze. "Have you found a way to counteract the drug?"

She opened her mouth to respond.

Bastien reached out and touched her face. "Have you?"

Crap! He'd know if she lied.

"The fact that you hesitate tells me you have. Why are you keeping it from the immortals?"

She sighed. "You're an immortal, too, Bastien. The faster you come to grips with that—"

"What? The faster they'll all welcome me into the fold and love me like a brother? Not going to happen. Please answer my questions."

Cliff cleared his throat. "She thinks she's found an antidote, but is afraid to test it on anyone because it might be too stressful on their heart. Make it beat fast enough to stop it or something like that."

Melanie growled. "I told you that in confidence!"

"I know. But if this thing works, it will help Bastien."

Bastien lowered his hand, brushing her arm and hip on the way down. "Tell me."

She sighed. "It's a stimulant. One so strong I wouldn't use it on a comatose elephant."

"Sounds like it's just what we need. What's the problem?"

Melanie thought that was fairly obvious. "If you were undead like the vampire mythology suggests, I wouldn't worry. But you aren't. Your heart beats. The virus infecting you can heal a lot of damage, but it requires the circulation of blood to do so. If this antidote, this stimulant, is strong enough that—like the tranquilizer—the virus can't counteract it, then instead of just waking you from the tranquilizer, it could cause ventricular fibrillation. Your heart could begin to beat so fast that it would *stop* beating and quiver instead, no longer circulating the blood through your body and your brain."

Cliff looked at Bastien. "I tried to get her to test it on me. Hell, I'm *already* brain damaged, so I figured I didn't have much to lose. But she wouldn't."

Bastien popped Cliff on the back of the head.

"Ow! What the hell?"

"You're here to *prevent* or at least slow down the mental deterioration, not speed it up."

Thank goodness she wasn't the only one who understood that.

"Thank you," Bastien said.

She nodded.

"So, this stimulant needs more work? More testing?"

"Yes." She just didn't know how she was going to do it.

"How would it be delivered? Once we're hit with the darts, we don't have much time to react before we pass out."

"I've put it in auto-injectors similar to the ones you used the other night."

"I don't know that that's the best option. A hypodermic might be faster and easier to handle. You said it's similar to the ones I used, but not identical."

"Yes."

"Could I see one? I may not know much about the chemical itself, but I can at least let you know if you'll need an easier delivery system."

"Sure. I'll go get one."

Melanie had only made three of them. She took one from the lab and left the other two behind in a locked cabinet.

When she returned to Cliff's apartment, he and Bastien were conversing rather vehemently in that way of theirs that was inaudible to human ears. Which was a trip, because it looked like they would be shouting if they were truly alone.

She hoped Bastien was convincing Cliff to stop pressuring her to test the drug on him. She just couldn't and wouldn't do it.

All conversation ceased when she entered. Closing the door, she approached Bastien with the auto-injector.

He turned it over and over in his hands, then flipped the lid off. "Could we carry it without the lid? It would slow us down less. And my motor skills were a little sluggish after I was tranqed."

"The lid is a safety release. You need to keep it on until you use it."

"Is it like adrenaline? Do you have to administer it in the leg?"

"No. Like the tranquilizer, it can be administered anywhere."

"And you just push it against your skin and hold it for three seconds?"

She shook her head. "Ten seconds."

"Ten seconds is too long. We'll either be fighting vampires who move about in fractions of seconds or humans firing automatic weapons. Could you cut that time in half?"

"We don't know how the virus will react to delivering too much too quickly."

A faint tap broke the silence that ensued. Melanie glanced down and realized Bastien had dropped the lid to the auto-injector. He followed her gaze. "Oh. Sorry about that."

She smiled. "I got it." Melanie bent down to pick it up. A tingle of foreboding scuttled down her spine, a warning that came too late.

Cliff leapt forward.

Melanie gasped as he wrapped his arms around her in a vicelike grip, yanked her back against him, and flew backward across the room, putting the sofa between them and Bastien.

"Cliff?" She struggled to free herself.

His hold tightening, he eased back several more steps.

Oh shit. Was Cliff having an episode? He hadn't had one yet, so she hadn't been expecting it.

Bastien turned to face them.

"It's okay!" Melanie blurted, terrified he would attack Cliff. "I—"

She tucked a shaking hand in her pocket the same time Bastien reached into his own and drew out the hypodermics containing the tranquilizer that should have been in her hand by now.

He had taken them? When? "What are you . . . ?"

Placing all three plastic needle guards in his mouth, he pulled them off with his teeth and spat them on the floor.

"Bastien . . ."

Drawing his arm back he shoved the needles into his neck and depressed the plungers.

"What the hell are you doing? Are you crazy?" she demanded shrilly.

"We have to see if this"—he held up the possible antidote—"is going to work."

Alarm shot to the surface as she realized what was happening. Cliff wasn't having a psychotic break. Bastien was testing the damned serum.

"You can't do this!" She intensified her struggles, but found them ineffective when pitted against a vampire who already held her immobile. "Cliff, don't let him do this. Please!"

"It's his choice, Dr. Lipton."

Bastien swayed as the triple dose of tranquilizer went to work.

"It could kill him!"

Cliff said nothing.

"Bastien, please! Don't do this."

Bastien staggered back a step and nearly lost his balance. Raising the auto-injector with the antidote, he shoved it into his neck on the side opposite the needle marks.

Panic seized Melanie, robbing her of the ability to move, to struggle, to call out. She couldn't seem to do anything but watch in horror as each second passed.

One. Two. Three. Four.

Bastien tipped to one side and started to fall over, but caught himself by tripping over to the sofa and bracing a hand against it.

Nine. Ten.

Releasing the auto-injector, he let it fall to the floor.

"Well?" Cliff asked, all of the worry she couldn't see in his face there in his voice.

"I don't think it's working." He closed his eyes. "All I feel is the tranquilizer weighing me down." His words slowed and slurred.

Melanie hadn't expected this. She hadn't considered that there might be *no* reaction. That it wouldn't do a damned thing.

She patted Cliff's arm. "You can let me go now."

Giving her shoulders a soft squeeze, he released his hold and stepped back. "I'm sorry. Bastien asked for my help. After all he's done for me, I couldn't say no even though it scared the hell out of me."

She nodded and started forward.

Bastien's knees buckled.

Cliff leapt over the sofa and caught him. Looping one of Bastien's arms around his shoulders, Cliff guided him around to sit on the sofa.

"You don't feel anything at all?" Melanie asked.

He shook his head. "Do you have any more?"

"Bastien—"

"Get it. Maybe the dose isn't strong enough."

He leaned forward, braced his elbows on his knees, and let his head droop.

A thousand thoughts racing through her mind, Melanie left the apartment and dashed across the hall to the lab.

"Everything okay, Doc?" one of the guards outside Cliff's room called out behind her as she swiped her card and entered the security code with trembling fingers.

"Yes."

"Are you sure? Because you look a little . . ."

The buzz sounded.

Melanie threw the door open and hurriedly retrieved the other two auto-injectors.

It hadn't worked. The stimulant hadn't worked. Why hadn't it worked? She hadn't been exaggerating when she had said she wouldn't use it on a comatose elephant. Any human injected with it would die. Quickly.

But Bastien had felt nothing.

Closing her door, she walked swiftly to Cliff's apartment.

"Rattled," the guard said.

"What?" she asked absently.

"You look a little rattled. Are you sure—?"

"I'm fine." She forced a smile. "It's just been one of those days. Nights."

His expression remained doubtful. "Well, we're here if you need us."

"Thank you, Mark. I appreciate that."

Once inside the apartment, she closed the door and circled the sofa. "Any change?"

Cliff shook his head.

Bastien raised his head and held out his hand.

When Melanie started to remove the cap for him, he stayed her.

"I have to be able to do it myself."

She handed him the auto-injector.

His fingers were clumsy as he removed the green cap, then pushed the auto-injector into his thigh and held it for ten seconds.

Melanie held her breath.

"Anything?" Cliff asked.

"I think so." He held out his hand. "Give me another one."

"You need to give that one more time. It could—"

"I won't have more time in a fight. Give me another one."

She handed him the last one.

He had no difficulty uncapping this one.

Despite her concern, she felt a twinge of hope.

He pressed this one into his thigh, too. Held it for ten seconds.

He was right. Ten seconds was too long. Now that she had a better idea of what dosage she should use—an insanely strong dosage—she could cut that time in half.

Bastien tossed the auto-injector on the coffee table and stood. "Okay. It's getting better. I don't feel so sluggish now." Nudging Melanie aside, he stepped away from the sofa and started meandering around the room.

After all of the anxiety that had riddled her over testing the new drug, she couldn't help but find this a bit anticlimactic.

No sooner had the thought crossed her mind than Cliff blurred and shot across the room, tackling Bastien and slamming him into the far wall.

Melanie's heart stopped.

Bastien grunted, then flew into motion.

As Melanie watched, eyes wide, mouth gaping, artwork crashed to the floor, along with piles of drywall. The warring vampire and immortal were indistinguishable as they zigzagged with astonishing speed around the living room, smashing furniture and trashing the apartment to a chorus of grunts, thuds, and curses.

Melanie looked around frantically for some way to stop this. She couldn't alert the guards. Though, if this racket continued, she wouldn't have to. As much as they loathed Bastien, they would probably just yank her out of the way and open fire, not caring who they hit or how many times they hit them. And Melanie didn't want either man hurt.

She jumped out of the way when the sofa splintered.

Had the vampires been allowed fully functional kitchens (too many sharp *and* blunt objects that could be used as weapons), she would've gone old school, grabbed a frying pan, and knocked some sense into the two. Aside from that . . .

Her gaze fell upon the bar stools. The vampires were allowed snacks and cereal and the makings for sandwiches, as well as a bar at which they could eat them.

Melanie ducked as the battling duo flew past overhead. Racing over to the bar, she picked up a stool—wooden with a black padded seat—and headed for the center of the room. The next time the writhing, growling, nebulous mass neared her, she concentrated on anticipating their direction and swung. Hard.

Thud! The seat went flying as the wooden stool broke apart, leaving one long leg in her hand.

Bastien slowed to a halt, bent over, and grabbed his head. "Ahh! Shit, that hurt!"

Cliff halted, too, then ducked as Melanie swung the last leg. "Wait! Don't stake me!"

"Get back, Cliff," she warned, heart racing, hands clutching the wooden leg so tightly she was surprised splinters didn't break off and pierce her skin. "Just stay back."

She eased between the two men, her back to Bastien.

Cliff's eyes glowed bright amber. Holding out his hands in a *take it easy* gesture, he retreated. "Don't hit me. I'm not crazed."

She shook her head, not taking her eyes off him. "Your eyes are glowing." She would have to swing as soon as he blurred. And as close as he was, she still might not be able to hit him.

"If my eyes are glowing, it's because I'm having fun."

"I bet you are."

"Not like that. Not like you're thinking. This is the most exercise I've had since you performed all of those strength and endurance tests on me a couple of years ago. It just felt good to be active again."

"Active? You attacked Bastien!"

"I told him to," Bastien spoke behind her.

She risked looking at him over her shoulder. A large red lump graced the center of his forehead. "What?"

"I told him to attack me."

She lowered the wooden leg and stared at him. The lump in his forehead darkened with a bruise, then began to heal and fade. The fear that had sent adrenaline coursing through Melanie's veins turned to icy fury. "You *what?*" she roared.

Uncertainty furrowing his brow, Bastien looked at Cliff. "Should I tell her again?"

"I wouldn't," the vampire advised and wisely took another step backward.

Bastien met her gaze. "I needed to know if I could hold my own in a fight after using the antidote. If my breathing would be affected or my heart . . . how long it would take to regain my strength and speed."

Unbelievable! Melanie threw the wooden leg down. "So you planned all of this?"

"Yes," Bastien answered.

"Both of you."

"Yes."

"Without consulting me."

He shared another look with Cliff. "Yes."

"Well, next time send me a fucking memo first!" Melanie

shouted, incensed. Here she stood, shaking, thinking Cliff had experienced one of the sudden violent episodes that had begun to afflict Joe, that Bastien would hurt him or even destroy him, or that Cliff would hurt or destroy Bastien while he was still weakened from the drug . . . and the two men in question looked like a couple of kids who had been wrestling on the floor in front of the TV while watching Saturday morning cartoons!

Cliff's eyes widened.

"What?" she growled.

"Nothing," he said quickly. "I've just . . . never heard you drop the F-bomb before."

"Well get used to it because now that I'll be spending more time with *him*"—she jerked a thumb in Bastien's direction—"you'll probably be hearing it a lot more."

"Now wait a minute," Bastien said, all levity fleeing. "I thought we agreed we wouldn't see each oth—"

"You just blew any chance you had of ditching me by injecting yourself three times with an experimental drug I thought would kill you," she snapped. "Now I have to monitor your ass for at *least* twenty-four hours. So congratulations! You're stuck with me!"

Chapter 6

Bastien really should be more upset about being *stuck* with Melanie than he was—which was not at all—but, damn it, he liked her. And with her face flushed with fury, her chest rising and falling with quick breaths beneath her long-sleeved shirt, and every word emerging a shout . . .

"She's hot when she's pissed, isn't she?" Cliff asked in a voice too soft for her to hear.

Bastien flung daggers at him with his eyes. "Watch it."

"Oh, please. As if you weren't already thinking it yourself."

"That doesn't mean I want *you* thinking it," he grumbled.

"And *that*," Melanie said, pointing at the two of them, "stops right now. No more whispering. No more secrets."

"Sorry," Cliff said sheepishly. "Bastien was just saying he thinks you're hot when you're pissed."

Bastien swore.

"I don't care what he—" Melanie began, then cut her own rant short. Her face went blank with surprise. "What?"

"Cliff—" Bastien warned too late.

Cliff was already saying with a broad I'm-lovin'-this grin, "He thinks you're hot when you're angry."

She squinted her eyes at Bastien as though trying to peer into his thoughts.

"What?" he bluffed. "You can't take this guy's word for anything. He's insane."

Cliff laughed. "You can't use that excuse yet, dude."

Melanie frowned. "Don't joke about that."

Cliff shrugged. "If I don't joke about it, I'll . . ."

"What?" Bastien posed. "Go crazy?"

Both men grinned.

Melanie rolled her eyes. "You're impossible. *Both* of you."

The door buzzed, then opened. Several of the guards out in the hallway peered inside.

"Everything okay, Doc?" one with short blond hair asked, face full of suspicion as he took in the damage.

"Everything's fine, Mark. Just . . . a little experiment."

Bastien scowled at the man. "It took you *this* long to check on her?"

Granted, he wouldn't have wanted an interruption earlier. Such would have no doubt resulted in both Bastien and Cliff being riddled with bullet holes and Melanie could have been caught in the crossfire. But if Joe or Cliff had had a psychotic break and attacked Melanie, a response this slow would not have saved her. She could have been drained before they even punched in the security code.

Mark stiffened. "Look, we hear all kinds of weird shit coming from these rooms. It's hard to determine what's harmless and what might be a problem."

"Then don't waste time guessing. As soon as you hear something that might signify violence, open the damned door and see what's going on. Cliff and Joe may be annoyed by the intrusion, but both understand the necessity of it."

Cliff nodded.

Bastien knew from his visits that Cliff's biggest fear now was that he might lose it and hurt Melanie. He hadn't had any violent outbursts thus far, but none knew when those might begin.

And Bastien was finding it harder and harder to read Joe. As his madness had progressed, he had withdrawn into himself, rarely interacting anymore with Cliff, keeping his distance from Bastien and Melanie.

Bastien would never have asked Joe's aid in tonight's experiment for just that reason.

Mark looked at Cliff. Bastien was surprised there didn't seem to be any animosity in his expression. The security staff here at the network apparently liked the vampires in residence a hell of a lot more than they did Bastien.

"The invasion of privacy is annoying," Cliff said, "but I would rather deal with that than risk your not being here if I . . . if something happens and Dr. Lipton needs you."

Mark nodded, his gaze full of both respect and compassion.

Good guy. Bastien almost regretted having broken both of the man's arms and giving him a concussion a few weeks ago.

The security team withdrew and closed the door.

"I'm surprised Chris didn't tell them to barge in at every little sound," Bastien told Melanie.

"He did," she admitted. "I asked them to back off. I thought the constant interruptions were increasing the stress Vince, Joe, and Cliff were feeling too much." Looking around at the debris that surrounded them, she sighed. "I'm not cleaning this up."

Cliff laughed. "I'll do it. I've been bored as hell lately. It'll give me something to do."

Stepping over what was left of the coffee table, a shredded sofa cushion, and—Ah, hell. Was that the flat-screen TV?— Melanie crossed to Cliff and drew him into a hug.

Cliff wrapped his arms around her and hugged her back. The two seemed close.

Melanie drew back and reached up to tweak one of Cliff's dreadlocks. "Are you sure you're okay?"

He smiled. "I'm fine."

"The fighting didn't . . ."

"Spark a flare of insanity? No. It actually felt good. Like a release."

"Hmm." Stepping back, she nearly tripped over more crap on the floor.

Bastien darted forward and grabbed her arm to steady her.

"Thanks," she said. And he felt the spark of attraction that whipped through her and sped her pulse at his touch despite her fading irritation. "I wonder if sparring might help Joe?"

Bastien and Cliff both turned toward the wall bordering Joe's apartment when his voice floated through it.

"He's willing to give it a try," Bastien told her. "But only if he spars with me. He doesn't want to risk sparring with Cliff."

He didn't have to state the obvious: Bastien was the only one of the two who would be able to stop him if the fight triggered an episode and Joe attacked in earnest.

"Seth and David might be willing to spar with him, too," she said.

Joe nixed that one in short order. *Hell, no. I don't like those guys.*

Bastien shook his head. "Joe doesn't feel comfortable around them."

The other vampire didn't trust them. The violent outbursts may not be too bad yet, but the paranoia had kicked in fully. Joe told Bastien through the wall that he was afraid the two powerful healers were making his madness worse instead of trying to heal him when they visited. *They're trying to steal my thoughts. Taking my memories. Planting new ones. Fake ones.*

Bastien eyed Cliff. "Is that what *you* think?"

Regret colored his youthful features. "No. But I *am* uncomfortable around them."

Melanie bit her lip. "I'm sorry, Cliff. I'd ask them not to come anymore, but their healing sessions are helping you."

No they're not! Joe practically screeched in the next room. *They're just fucking with us!*

A sick feeling sank into Sebastien's gut. Joe was farther gone than he had realized.

He met Cliff's somber gaze. "How long has Joe . . . felt this way?" he asked, trying to word it in a way Joe might not fully grasp.

"A while."

Melanie looked back and forth between them. "What way? What's he saying?"

He felt her concern spike.

"Perhaps Seth and David should only treat Cliff from now on," he suggested.

She stared up at him for a long moment.

He mouthed, *Later.*

She nodded. "All right. I'll see what I can do."

A dark pall blanketed them.

"Well . . ." she said, and Bastien felt her need to lighten the atmosphere and raise Cliff's spirits once more. "Cliff, why don't I go get my laptop and you and I can order you some cool new furniture and a new flat-screen TV while Bastien cleans up this mess?"

As Bastien started to protest, Cliff laughed and said, "Sounds good to me."

Closing his mouth, Bastien bent and picked up half a sofa arm.

"You're quiet tonight," Richart commented.

Melanie glanced at the French immortal sitting on her left.

He was fiddling with his cell phone, perhaps checking for messages from his lady love.

She looked to her right.

Bastien said nothing, just stared down at the mostly deserted college campus below.

The three of them sat on Davis Library's roof, feet dangling over the edge. Not the front. The front was too well lit. They sat instead on one side, facing away from UNC's campus-lighting corridor, in the shadows cast by trees that blocked the campus lights.

Melanie had been serious when she had told Bastien he was stuck with her. For millennia, immortals had believed no drug would affect them and had acted accordingly. In other words, with no concern for anything someone might try to dose them with. They thought themselves utterly impervious.

Emrys had demonstrated they were not with the tranquilizer he had manufactured to immobilize Ami during his torture and experimentation. But instead of viewing this as something of a wake-up call and thinking there might be *other* drugs out there now that could affect them, they seemed to assume Emrys's sedative was the only one.

Melanie had proven them wrong again when the stimulant she had concocted had worked earlier tonight. Yet Bastien had *still* objected to her joining him and Richart on tonight's hunt. He thought that, since he hadn't keeled over from the stimulant when he had injected himself with it, he was fine. That there could be no lasting damage. No delayed side effects.

Melanie, however, wanted to be sure and had insisted.

When even Richart had expressed some doubt concerning the wisdom of her hunting with them, Melanie had dared to call Seth, who had backed her without hesitation.

Perhaps Bastien's continued silence was a demonstration of his anger at her having gone over his head.

Hmm. Maybe Seth was one of the reasons Bastien was having such a hard time integrating himself into the Immortal Guardians' ranks. The other immortals had always deferred to Seth and obeyed his will. He was the oldest among them and, thus, had more experience dealing with the challenges immortals and *gifted ones* had to face. He was also the most powerful immortal among them, able to kick *anyone's* ass. Two, three, a dozen at a time. Though Melanie had heard that there was a pool going—had been for centuries—over who would win in a fight between Seth and David.

Melanie doubted anyone would ever know the answer to that one because the two men reputedly never argued.

"What's wrong?" Richart continued. "Someone hurt your dainty feelings earlier?"

Again Bastien said nothing.

"Pouting because Seth now thinks you need *two* babysitters?" the handsome Frenchman taunted.

Nothing.

"Maybe your tussle with your vampire friend damaged your vocal chords."

"Perhaps I'm just weary from my *tussle* with your girlfriend," Bastien drawled.

Richart's head snapped around. His eyes flashed a bright amber as his body tensed.

"Who do you think would win in a fight between Seth and David?" Melanie blurted. The two sat so close on either side of her that their arms brushed hers. She really didn't want to be wedged between them when they broke into a brawl.

Richart frowned. "What?"

"Who do you think would win? Seth or David? I was thinking about tossing some money into the pool." Not really, but who cared? The diversion seemed to be distracting Richart from whatever violence he had been contemplating.

"Seth," Bastien said.

"Why?" Melanie pressed.

"Because I've seen him lose his temper."

Richart's eyes lost their glow and returned to a light brown. "You have?"

Bastien nodded, his gaze still searching the slumbering campus.

"What happened? What set him off?" Melanie asked. She

had never heard of the Immortal Guardians' leader losing control.

"I attacked Ami."

"Merde!"

"What?"

Bastien glanced at her briefly from the corner of his eye. "It was an accident."

Richart snorted. "You don't *accidentally* attack someone."

"I thought she was an immortal coming up behind me and just . . . reacted."

Melanie was a little surprised he offered an explanation. Was it for her benefit? "So, what happened?" she asked.

"Seth lost it and . . ."

"What?" Richart pressed.

Bastien shook his head. "His castle nearly came crashing down around us. I've never seen such an exhibition of power. And the thing is . . . I think he was holding back. I think that was just a tiny hint of what he can really do."

Richart muttered something in French.

"I really thought he was going to destroy me that night," Bastien went on. "I still don't know why he didn't."

Melanie looked at Richart. He seemed pretty impressed.

"You've never seen Seth lose his temper?" she asked.

"No. Never."

Bastien made a sound of amusement. "Trust me. You don't want to."

Silence enfolded them once more.

Melanie swung her legs like Popper Knockers, bumping her combat boots together. Before leaving the network, she had donned the hunting gear Seconds normally sported: black cargo pants, black shirt, black sweater over the shirt to accommodate the weather, 9mms in shoulder holsters, knives in sheaths on her thighs.

A long, dark coat covered all and staved off some of the winter chill. Her fingers stiffened, however, as the cold breeze buffeted her, stronger up here on the roof than down at street level. If she didn't think it would freak the men out or send the wrong message (wrong to Richart), she would stick her hands in each man's pocket to warm them.

One of the coolest things she'd learned about immortals was that they could regulate their body temperature. Even in icy, below zero temperatures, they could remain toasty warm. If both men threw off their coats and stripped down to their underwear in these frigid temperatures, steam would rise off their skin.

"So this is what vampire hunting entails?" she asked. "This is what you guys do? You just sit around and pick at each other while you wait for vampires to come along?" It was kind of dull. She couldn't seem to keep herself from fidgeting like a small child forced to sit through an unusually long church service in an itchy wool suit. She just wasn't accustomed to being idle. It was beginning to get on her nerves.

And her nerves were already stretched taut from sitting so close to Bastien. Though her nose was numb from the cold, she could smell his unique scent and wanted nothing more than to pounce on him and rip his clothes off.

Bastien swore softly and moved a few inches away from her so they no longer touched.

Richart gave him a knowing look and returned his phone to his pocket. "We possess extraordinary hearing. If we sit quietly, we can hear for miles. Our sense of smell is the same. Should a vampire attack and attempt to feed anywhere on campus, we will hear it and smell it, so we don't have to patrol, as it were."

"So I was right? You really do just sit here and irritate each other until something happens?"

"He's being kind," Bastien said. "We usually walk the campus, searching it visually and widening the area we hear or smell, but want to play it safe tonight."

"Because I'm here."

"Yes. If or when vampires make an appearance tonight, we can leave you up here where it's safe and take them out below."

The arrogance! "I told you I can kick ass. Didn't our little encounter with Stuart and company demonstrate that?"

Richart eyed her speculatively. "You helped Bastien defeat them?"

"Yes." They hadn't told him much about the battle itself. They had simply told him they'd found a potential recruit in Stuart. Richart had then teleported the unconscious vamps to the holding room, but they had ended up being too far gone. "I thought I held my own very well."

Richart questioned Bastien silently with his eyes.

"She did," Bastien confirmed, frowning at Melanie. "You never did tell me how you came to be trained. You're a doctor, not a Second."

"Oh, please. I work with vampires every day. Do you really think Mr. Reordon would've given me access to Vince, Cliff, and Joe if I hadn't undergone the same training a Second does? Mr. Reordon wanted to make damned sure I could protect myself if the vampires ever attacked me."

"Cliff had no difficulty capturing you tonight," Bastien pointed out with a frown. "You were completely at his mercy."

Melanie frowned. "That's because I wasn't on guard. *You* were there, giving me a false sense of security."

"That really was bad form, Bastien," Richart criticized.

"And don't think I'll fall for that crap again," Melanie warned. "I managed to stop your scuffle, didn't I? *Without* the tranquilizer."

Richart chuckled. "I really wish I could've seen that one. You don't know how many times I've wanted to knock him in the head myself since Seth foisted him on me."

Melanie laughed. "I completely understand."

Bastien's scowl deepened. "What is it you Americans say—that's so funny I forgot to laugh?"

"Wow," she commented. "I haven't heard that one in years."

"Showing your age there, old man," Richart goaded.

"We're damned near the same age, dimwit."

"In years. Not in spirit."

Melanie grinned. This was much better.

Both men abruptly turned their heads to the north.

Melanie instinctively followed their gaze, but saw nothing. Richart and Bastien stood.

When Melanie did the same, Bastien took her arm and carefully steered her away from the edge. Both men had been rather astonished by her total lack of acrophobia. Since her father had worked as a high-rise window washer, she assumed the absence of a fear of heights ran in the family.

The immortals seemed to keep an ear tuned to whatever had caught their attention.

"What is it? Is it . . . rats?" She caught herself before saying vamps, unsure if the vampires would be able to hear them.

Bastien's lips quirked. "Yes."

"How many?"

He held up a hand and touched his middle finger to his thumb.

Melanie thought back to the hand signals she had had to memorize during her training. Eight. That was a large number to find trolling for victims together. There was no telling how many humans the vampire king and his followers had transformed, but . . . with so many turning up so frequently, the numbers had to be off the charts.

Bastien and Richart both did a quick weapons check.

"We shall return shortly," Bastien told her.

Richart reached out to touch Bastien's shoulder.

Oh, hell no. Melanie leapt forward. Her fingers closed around Bastien's arm just as Richart teleported him.

The world darkened. That bizarre feeling of weightlessness suffused her. Then her feet were touching pavement on the sidewalk near the Physical Sciences building.

Melanie wasn't sure what Richart said next, but suspected it was a string of French swear words.

"Don't do that!" he snapped in English.

She offered him a hasty apology. "I'm sorry. I didn't want you to leave me behind."

"We were leaving you behind for a reason!"

"Hey." Bastien stepped forward, eyes flashing. "Don't speak to her like that."

Richart scowled. "Look, I'm just saying if she's going to be joining us—"

"She isn't."

"Shut up," Melanie and Richart both said.

Bastien clamped his lips shut.

"As I was saying," Richart began again, "if you're going to be joining us we need to set some ground rules."

Melanie nodded. "I get it. But don't you think we should do that later? Don't we have more pressing issues to deal with right now?" She pointed behind them, where eight vampires—eyes glowing blue, green, silver, and amber—had stopped short and stood gaping.

"Immortal Guardians," one sneered.

One by one, the vampires bared their fangs.

Richart looked at Bastien. "You're the one who wants to make friends. How do you want to do this?"

Bastien considered the vampires.

A couple of them started to growl.

Melanie choked back a laugh. The sound was intended to intimidate, but . . .

When immortals made that deep rumbling sound in the backs of their throats, it brought to mind large, ferocious animals preparing to attack.

These guys reminded her of Tom from the Tom & Jerry cartoons she grew up watching, when Tom would try to roar

like a lion and instead sounded like the little kitty cat he was:
Raaor, pfft, pfft.

One of the vamps took a step forward. The others followed suit.

Just as they began to blur, Melanie said, "Hey, do any of you guys know Stuart?"

Their forms solidified. Surprise and confusion colored their features as they looked at each other, then back at her.

"Stuart?" a blond with glowing sea-green eyes repeated.

She nodded. "About this tall." She held one hand several inches above her own head. "Thin build. Dirty blond hair. Big Tar Heels fan."

"Dude," one said. "They know Stuart."

"They don't know him," the first speaker said. "They *killed* him!"

Melanie gaped. How the hell had they jumped to *that* conclusion?

The vampires leapt forward.

Bastien and Richart armed themselves with auto-injectors and raced to meet them.

Melanie drew her 9mms, already equipped with silencers. As a human, she would never be able to hold a vampire still for the three seconds it took the auto-injector to deliver the tranquilizer, so she had no choice but to wield the deadlier weapons.

Both immortals grabbed vampires and injected them, using the vamps they held as shields to fend off the attacks of the others.

So many figures were darting about, their forms hazy and indistinct with speed, that Melanie had some difficulty determining friend from foe. Darkness hampered her vision further. Had their eyes not glowed, Melanie would have feared hitting Richart or Bastien if she fired her weapon.

Three seconds seemed an eternity.

The fact that Richart and Bastien protected themselves with vampire shields seemed to concern the vampires not at all. Only one held back. The others fought with what she thought was true madness, doing their damnedest to cut through their friends to reach the immortals.

The hesitant one, with a sudden burst of inspiration, sped around to attack Bastien's back.

Melanie fired three times, body shots that would slow the vampire down without killing him.

As the vamp dropped to the ground, another ceased trying to carve his way through the vampire Richart was tranqing and turned to Melanie.

His blue eyes flashed. His lips pulled back in a fang-flashing snarl.

Melanie's pulse raced. Her breath quickened. Fear filled her as the vampire shot toward her.

She stumbled backward, firing repeatedly, following her instincts, and aiming where she thought the vamp would go each time he ducked and swerved to avoid the heavy bullets.

He jerked and slowed as she scored one hit after another.

Bastien dropped the vampire he held, drew his katanas, and blurred.

Melanie didn't know what he did to the vamp so intent on reaching her. It happened too quickly for her to see. His body landed several yards away and began to rapidly deteriorate as the virus went to work devouring him from the inside.

Richart dropped his vamp and tore into the three besieging him. Bastien planted himself in front of Melanie and took out any vamp who headed her way.

Even so, she emptied the clips of her 9mms. The vampires fought like rabid dogs. No training. No thought. Only a manic desire to kill and rend and bite and tear.

It shook her.

These vampires were not like the ones they had encountered

at Bastien's lair. These had been infected long enough for the madness to take complete control of them. As it did now.

The battle was quick. It was violent. It left her quaking like a leaf caught in hurricane force winds.

All movement ceased.

White puffs formed in front of Melanie's lips as warm air met cold. Her breath came quickly, as though she had been sprinting.

Bastien turned and met her gaze. "Are you all right?"

She nodded. "My hands are shaking."

Sheathing his swords, he drew closer and examined her thoroughly with his luminescent gaze. "You aren't injured?"

"Not so much as a scratch. You?"

"The same."

They looked at Richart.

"Stupid bastards," Richart said, scowling down at the vamp he had tranqed. That one now deteriorated like the others they'd destroyed. "They cut right through him."

"Not stupid," Bastien corrected. "Insane."

Melanie returned her 9mms to their holsters and struggled to still her quivering limbs. At least she hadn't killed anyone this time.

"Are you sure you're all right?" Bastien asked again, moving closer. His black coat glistened like satin where vampire blood had sprayed and spattered it.

She nodded, wondering if he would have held her to comfort her if he weren't so bloody.

"You did well," he praised. "You remind me of Ami. You seem to anticipate the vampires' movements very well."

Being compared to Ami was a huge compliment, and one she didn't deserve. Ami fought nearly on the same level as the immortals. With guns *and* blades. No other Second could best her. Some *immortals* couldn't even best her, though none would admit it. "That's because—"

Something hit Melanie in the chest. She frowned. Neither Bastien nor Richart had moved as far as she could tell. And, even if they had, why would either of them strike her in the chest?

She glanced down and saw a small tear in her shirt in the vicinity of her heart. Around and beneath it, a wet stain began to spread.

Melanie raised a heavy hand to touch the stain and stared at the blood that painted her fingers. Looking up, she fought for breath as pain crashed through her. "Bastien?"

Horror froze Bastien as he met Melanie's gaze.

The scent of her blood surrounded him as the stain on her shirt spread with alarming speed.

Another hole appeared in her chest a few inches from the first.

She blinked and staggered back a step.

"Sniper!" Bastien wrapped his arms around her and turned his back to the shooter.

Her knees buckled.

A bullet hit him in the back, passed through his body, and entered Melanie.

Swearing, Bastien lifted her into his arms and raced for the shadows, ducking around the corner of the nearest building. "Melanie?"

She didn't answer.

He looked down. Her eyes were closed, her face devoid of color. Panicked, he listened for a heartbeat. Weak. Thready. Her breath came in faint wheezes.

"Richart." He didn't shout the name. He whispered it, fear rendering him nearly mute. A fear he hadn't experienced in two centuries. Fear *Seth* had not inspired the night Bastien had thought Seth was going to destroy him.

Richart arrived in a blur. "How is she?"

Bastien carefully deposited Melanie in the Frenchman's arms. "Take her to David. If he isn't home, find Seth or Roland."

Richart nodded. "The shooters—"

"I'll handle the shooters. Now hurry. And when you return, don't let them see you teleport. We don't know if they saw you do it earlier and they may not be aware of our individual gifts yet."

Richart cradled Melanie close and issued a short nod. "Don't do anything stupid."

Darkness bled into Bastien's heart, robbing him of any emotion save rage. "I'll do what I have to."

Uttering a final epithet, Richart vanished.

The faint squawk of a walkie-talkie met Bastien's ears. The men who whispered confirmation of a hit, of a target taken out, thought he couldn't hear them. But he could. And every word hardened his resolve to make the bastards pay for hurting Melanie.

There were a lot of them. They must have been in position for hours. Snipers on the roofs. Foot soldiers on the ground, hidden in alcoves, behind shrubs, in fucking Dumpsters, ready to pounce. Trained not to move, not to make a sound until their quarry arrived.

Sheer dumb luck was all that had kept Bastien, Melanie, and Richart from teleporting to one of the many buildings that boasted snipers on the roofs. The same luck that had landed the snipers behind structures that impeded the immortals' view of them.

While the soldiers consulted each other, seeking any sighting of the paranormal beings they hunted, Bastien scaled the side of the building behind him with all of the speed and dexterity of Spiderman.

With the stealthy tread of a cat, he found the first soldiers.

Two. Fatigues. Hair covered in skull caps. Faces blackened. They knelt with weapons poised on the raised cement edging. Dark duffel bags full of ammo, more weapons, and heavy restraints rested—zippers open—on either side of them, ready to be pillaged. The soldier on the left bore an assault rifle. The soldier on the right bore a tranquilizer rifle. Both men remained tense, eyes pressed to the scopes as they slowly searched the shadows for their victim . . . and their executioner.

Bastien's gaze went to the assault rifle bearer. Was this the one? Was this the fuck who had shot Melanie? Who had hurt her? Who could've . . . might have killed her?

He struck without warning. Grabbing the protruding butts of their weapons, Bastien yanked hard, slamming the scopes into their eyes and knocking them onto their backs. His hands closed on their throats before a sound of pain could escape them, crushing their tracheae and shutting off their air.

The humans writhed in pain, kicking the heels of their boots against the roof and clawing at their throats. Their eyes widened as they slowly began to suffocate. One determined bastard reached toward his bag of toys. Bastien stepped on his wrist and crushed the bones. Snatching the walkie-talkie from the dead man's shoulder, he depressed the button and whistled sharply.

Echoes of his whistle sounded throughout the campus, some close, some distant, alerting him to the location of every mercenary intent on capturing him.

"What the hell was that?" a voice hissed over the walkie-talkie.

Adopting an American accent, Bastien whispered with false urgency, "I see 'em. I see 'em. They're moving toward Kenan Stadium. Holy shit they're fast!"

A flurry of movement sounded as soldiers readjusted their positions in an attempt to glimpse the supposedly fleeing beings.

"Maintain position! Maintain position!" came the order in a rough whisper yell. "Who the hell was that? Was that Charlie?"

Bastien dropped the walkie-talkie.

"No, sir. It wasn't me."

"Well, whoever it was, shut the fuck up! And for fuck's sake everyone stop moving! They'll hear us!"

Too late.

Bastien backed toward the center of the roof, then raced for the edge. Over he went, flying through the air he didn't know how many yards to land on the next.

He couldn't land silently when traveling at such velocities, but it didn't matter. He was on the soldiers crouched there before they could finish spinning around. Snapping their necks, he leapt to the roof of the next building. Two more swore and swung around. One fired a tranquilizer dart at him. Bastien caught it and flung it back at the bastard, who dropped like a stone. The other released a shout cut short when Bastien snapped his neck. Still moving, Bastien increased his speed and leapt to the next roof. Two more down. Then the next. Three on that one.

On the next, he skidded to a halt. The barrel of one of the men's rifles was still warm. The acrid scent of gunshot residue lingered on the man's hands.

In that instant, Bastien understood more fully than he ever had the psychotic episodes that gripped vampires, the fury that engulfed them and took control of their bodies in a millisecond.

This was the one who had shot Melanie.

Bastien snapped the other soldier's neck without any conscious thought. All of his attention focused on Melanie's shooter.

This man had caused her pain. So *he* would feel pain.

Bastien knocked the man's weapon aside with one hand and clamped the other around his throat, lifting him until his feet dangled two feet off the ground.

Within the soldier's wide, fear-filled eyes, Bastien could

see the reflection of his own, burning bright amber. He bared his fangs in a snarl.

The soldier whimpered and wet his pants.

Ripping the walkie-talkie from the man's shoulder, Bastien threw it halfway to the damned football stadium.

"You shot my woman," he growled.

If the man's eyes could get any wider, they did. His fingers clawed at Bastien's hand as he struggled for breath.

"You're going to die slowly."

One of the man's hands dropped.

Something sharp pierced Bastien's chest. He looked down. The dumb fuck had stabbed him with a tactical knife.

He met the soldier's gaze and noted the gleam of triumph in them. "You don't actually think that hurts me, do you?" he drawled.

The soldier's fear returned, so strong Bastien could smell it.

Curling the fingers of his free hand around the soldier's, Bastien slowly withdrew the knife without so much as a wince, confiscated it, and held it up. "You're going to regret that."

Chapter 7

Ami was parked at her computer in David's study when a commotion arose in the living room.

Other than her, the ground floor should have been empty. Darnell was downstairs training half a dozen Seconds. Étienne was down in one of the basement's guest rooms, showering off the blood that had coated him when he had come up against five vampires, none of whom had apparently been interested in making friends.

The immortal had not been pleased.

Ami feared such confrontations, drawn out and made more dangerous by Bastien's plan to seek an alliance, would not endear him to the immortals. His brethren already pretty much hated him. Some outright resented the fact that he still drew breath when Ewen didn't.

But Ami knew him better than they did. Yes, he had made some mistakes. Some pretty *big* mistakes, but his intentions had been good.

The road to hell is paved with good intentions.

Marcus had spouted that the other night when she had tried to defend Bastien.

She knew it rankled her husband that she cared for Bastien. But Bastien had been kind to her. He had been a kindred spirit in the early days of their acquaintance, housed not entirely of his own free will at Seth's castle, facing a new life, surrounded by new people, with nothing but an unknown future and a messed up past for company.

During those first few weeks, while she had recovered from the torture she had endured at Emrys's hands, she had formed a bond with Bastien that was as unbreakable as those she had formed with Seth, David, and Darnell.

Heavy boots tromped down the hallway.

She rose from the lovely desk David had purchased for her. "Where's David?"

Richart stepped into the doorway, Dr. Lipton's unconscious form cradled in his arms. Melanie's head drooped over his arm, her hair falling in a mahogany curtain to his waist. The front of her shirt bore three holes and was completely saturated with blood, some of which trailed over his hand and dripped onto the floor. One slender arm swung limply as he ceased moving.

"He isn't here." Ami hurried forward. "Chechenko nearly lost his leg tonight, so David had to go to Virginia to heal him."

"What about Seth?"

She took out her cell phone and dialed.

The sounds of battle came over the line. Metal clashing. Men howling in pain.

"What's up, sweetheart?" Seth asked.

"Dr. Lipton has been injured."

"I'm afraid I have my hands full here. You'll have to—" He grunted, swore, then continued. "You'll have to call Roland or take her to the network."

"Okay."

"Keep me posted though."

"I will."

She ended the call. "You'll have to take her to Roland."

Richart swore. "I don't know where the paranoid bastard lives!"

Ami leaned out into the hallway. "Darnell!"

Boots pounded up the stairs from the basement.

Darnell burst into the hallway, the six trainees fast on his heels. "What's wrong?" His eyes widened when he caught sight of Dr. Lipton. "Oh, shit. How bad?"

"Fatal," Richart said.

The Seconds all stared somberly.

"David and Seth have their hands full," Ami told him. "Do you know where Roland lives?"

"No." He reached into a back pocket and drew out his cell phone. "He'll have to come here."

Richart shook his head. "Have him meet us at the network. She won't live long enough for him to get here. Hopefully, the doctors there will be able to keep her alive until he arrives."

He vanished in the next instant.

Ami heard some of the trainees gasp. "You call Roland. I'll call Chris."

Bastien pitched the last soldier off the roof. The man's vocal chords had been crushed, so he couldn't alert any campus stragglers with screams as he plunged to his death.

The snipers were all dead. Now it was time to tackle the soldiers on the ground.

Withdrawing his cell, he dialed Chris.

"Reordon!" the human barked impatiently.

"I need a cleanup crew," he said and leapt to the dense green lawn below.

"Bastien? What the fuck is going on? Richart just showed up here with Dr. Lipton."

"Why the hell is he there? Why isn't David healing her?"

"He can't. Seth can't either. They're both busy elsewhere.

The medical team is working on her and Roland is on his way. Now tell me—"

"Ask Bastien where I should meet him," Richart said in the background.

Knowing now that there was a strong chance Melanie would not make it, Bastien felt an icy calm settle over him. "Tell him to teleport to Peabody Hall. I'm at Fetzer Hall now and am about to sweep through the soldiers between us like a fucking tidal wave."

"Damn it, we need some of those men left alive to—"

"All you're getting are corpses. When you send the cleanup crew, send a fucking bus."

Disconnecting the call, Bastien sped through the darkness toward the first cluster of soldiers.

Chaos infected the remaining soldiers' ranks as one after another after another ceased communicating over the walkie-talkies. Panicked, unable to spot their attacker even with night vision goggles, they ignored their commander's orders to maintain radio silence and begged for help, alerting Bastien to all of their positions.

He took out three of a cluster of six in two seconds. The others tried to fire their weapons and retreat at the same time. Shots muffled by top-of-the-line suppressors filled the night, unheard by anyone but Bastien and Richart if he had appeared as instructed.

Bastien didn't flinch as bullets struck him. Drawing his katanas, he cut the throats of two men, then disarmed the last. Dropping a sword, Bastien yanked the last man forward, sank his fangs into the prick's neck, and drained him.

Dropping the body, Bastien retrieved his sword and raced for the next cluster. Already his wounds were healing. But he would have continued even if they hadn't.

These bastards had killed Melanie. By the time this night was over, not one of them would ever draw breath again.

* * *

Richart delayed returning to UNC. Roland's home was half an hour away from the network by car. The Frenchman had seen the doubt on the network doctors' faces when asked if they could sustain Dr. Lipton for that long. Their best hope, therefore, was for Roland to meet Richart at some halfway point with which Richart was familiar.

Richart paced the agreed upon parking lot impatiently.

The tires of Roland's black Fisker Karma squealed as he turned into the lot without slowing and slammed on the brakes.

Both front doors flew open. Roland and Sarah hopped out.

"We must hurry," Richart urged, crossing the brief distance between them and clasping Roland's shoulder. "I can't take you both."

Sarah nodded. "I know. Go ahead. I'll meet you at the network. Be safe, sweetie."

"Always," Roland said.

Then Richart teleported him directly to the network's OR.

Judging by the frantic activity taking place there, Dr. Lipton had not yet expired. Richart would take that news with him to UNC and hope it would appease Bastien's wrath.

But first, he had a stop to make.

Étienne d'Alençon knew his brother as well as he knew himself.

The twins were like those sometimes mentioned on the news with a strange combination of awe and skepticism. If Richart's arm was broken, Étienne felt an ache in his own. If Étienne's leg was shattered, Richart felt the agonizing pain in his own.

Not the most convenient connection to have, considering

the two brothers hunted and fought vampires for a living and were injured damned near every night. But they were used to it.

While Richart didn't possess the telepathy Étienne and their sister Lisette did, Étienne could often sense when his brother was troubled without reading his thoughts because of the close connection they shared.

Which is what had happened a few minutes ago when Richart had teleported to David's home.

Hands braced on the shower wall, warm water sluicing down over his hair and rinsing the blood from his battered body, Étienne had felt his brother's presence and raised his head.

Thanks to his acute hearing, the voices of Richart, Ami, and Darnell had reached him easily. Dr. Lipton had been fatally wounded by the sounds of it.

What the hell had she been doing hunting vampires with them?

No matter.

Something else was agitating his brother.

What is it? he had asked his brother mentally in French.

How soon can you be ready to go? had come his response even as he continued speaking with the others.

A minute. Maybe two. How soon do you need me? He hadn't asked for what. It didn't matter.

Get dressed. I don't want to alarm the others, but . . . I may need help reining in Bastien when I return to UNC.

Étienne had frowned. *What do you mean, reining him in? You'll see when we get there. I must go.*

Étienne had lost the connection when his brother had teleported away.

Swearing, Étienne lathered and rinsed his body at preternatural speeds, then shut off the shower.

David kept a ready supply of new clothing for immortals and their Seconds that rivaled one might find in a depart-

ment store. So many men and women tromped in and out of
the elder immortal's home (which really did feel like home
to many of them), often coming straight from battle, their
clothing torn or bloodstained. David liked to be prepared
and enjoyed providing his *family* with anything they might
need or that might make them more comfortable, including
spare bedrooms and the aforementioned clothing.

Étienne pillaged the wardrobe in the guest room he had
been using more and more often of late, pulling out cargo
pants, a long-sleeved T-shirt, boxers, and socks. All black.

He didn't know if David and Darnell had caught on yet, but
ever since the immortals in the area had learned that this
Emrys prick was itching to get his hands on Ami, they had
begun to spend more of their free time here to ensure her
safety.

Not that David couldn't protect her singlehandedly. She
just seemed so small and fragile, despite her astonishing ability to kick vampire ass.

And she could kick some serious vampire ass. Étienne had
only seen her in action once, but he would never forget it.

Besides he liked it here. His Second, Cameron, had fallen
hard for a woman recently and spent every minute he could
with her. The house he and Cam inhabited just felt so damned
empty now. Since Ami and Marcus had moved in, David's
house was constantly bustling, always entertaining, never
boring.

Never lonely.

Dressing in short order, Étienne added his comfy, but battered boots, then packed on the weapons.

I may need help reining in Bastien when I return to UNC.

What the hell did that mean?

Ready for whatever his brother needed him to do, Étienne
scaled the stairs to the ground floor.

Ami and Darnell spoke in tense sentences in David's study.
It sounded like Dr. Lipton wasn't going to make it. Étienne

didn't really know her, but would mourn her passing never-theless. She had helped him and the other immortals during the vampire king's uprising. And, as David often said, she didn't have to be immortal to be a member of their extended family.

"Seth needs to tell Roland to cut the shit and let Richart know where he lives," Étienne pronounced as he passed through the doorway into the study. Roland was fanatical about ensuring no one knew where he lived. Had he not been so paranoid and antisocial, Richart could have tele-ported directly to his home and Dr. Lipton would have been healed by now.

"I'm pretty sure he will after this," Darnell said.

Ami agreed. "Richart is meeting Roland at a halfway point so he can teleport him the rest of the way to the network, but even then he may be too late."

The two were huddled around Darnell's phone.

"One of the nurses on call is giving us live updates," Ami explained.

Étienne made himself comfortable in one of the chairs across from David's massive desk. A copy of the latest Stephen King novel rested atop the gleaming surface, a page near the middle marked with a Stephen King bookmark.

David was a big fan of the horror writer.

Darnell swore. "She's crashing."

Richart appeared, the front of his coat and shirt saturated with blood.

How much of that, Étienne wondered as he rose, was vam-pire blood and how much was Dr. Lipton's?

His brother met his gaze. "Ready?"

"Oui."

Richart touched his shoulder.

Étienne knew that most immortals and Seconds found teleporting uncomfortable and disorienting. He'd been tele-porting with his brother, however, since Richart had first discovered he could do it as a very young boy, so it didn't disturb him in the least.

They appeared in the shadows of UNC Chapel Hill's Peabody Hall.

Étienne—like all of the other immortals who were stationed in the area—was well acquainted with the quiet campus.

The stench of blood and death and fear that traveled on the wind tonight staggered him.

Holy hell. What had happened here?

A quick examination of his brother's thoughts revealed that Richart had only aided in killing a party of vampires.

But eight destroyed vampires wouldn't create this stench.

Something moved behind them.

Étienne and Richart both swung around, ready to attack.

Bastien stepped from the deeper darkness, eyes glowing, hair loose and disheveled and sticky with blood. Nearly every inch of him was coated with the liquid. His face was crimson with it. His expression was as feral as the most insane vampire Étienne had ever fought. And his thoughts . . .

Étienne drew his swords and motioned for Richart to step back.

Richart grabbed his arm. "What are you doing?"

"Seth and David made a mistake. I don't know how or why but . . . somehow they missed it."

"Missed what?"

"Bastien isn't immortal. He's vampire."

"No, brother. He's immortal."

Étienne shook his head. "You can't read his thoughts. There's nothing there but chaos and bloodlust and violence."

Bastien emitted a low warning growl. Étienne wasn't even sure Bastien knew whom he faced.

"Stand down, Étienne," Richart enjoined. "He isn't maddened. Not the way you think."

"Bullshit."

"Look deeper into his thoughts. He cares for Dr. Lipton.

More than he will admit even to himself. He fears he has lost her. That the mercenaries have killed her."

What?

Étienne did as his brother advised and delved deeper into Bastien's thoughts. Normally he would have had a hard time doing so. Bastien was one of those unique immortals who could sometimes protect his thoughts from telepaths. But the doors he usually erected were down, sundered by the white hot rage that teemed within him. And there beneath it all was what Richart had seen without Étienne's gift: burgeoning love for Dr. Lipton.

The other immortals thought Bastien visited the network on a nearly daily basis to calm the vampires, but Melanie (as Bastien thought of her) was just as great a lure to him. Her kindness. Her patience with Cliff and Joe. The way she seemed to look at Bastien as a man and not the monster everyone else thought him.

Étienne lowered his weapons and looked at his twin.

He didn't know what to think of it. He *loathed* Bastien. Not only had the blackguard started all of the shit they were dealing with now by pitting a fucking vampire army against them and employing Montrose Keegan, he had killed Ewen. Both Étienne and Richart had been friends with the Scottish immortal.

Richart spoke to Bastien as though the latter were a wild horse he sought to calm. "What happened here?"

"Is she dead?" Bastien growled.

"Not yet," Richart responded, then Étienne heard his brother curse silently.

"Not *yet?*" Bastien choked out. "She can't be saved?"

Richart had been right. Not madness. Fear and grief.

Bastien's hands tightened around the hilts of his swords.

Étienne braced himself to fight the immortal, should he choose to attack the messenger.

"I meant no," Richart corrected swiftly. "Roland is with her."

Some of the tension in Bastien's shoulders eased. The threat seemed to pass.

Étienne risked taking his eyes off the dangerously wound immortal long enough to glance around. He could see several bodies in the distance, shoved up against the wall of the next building behind some shrubs.

"That's why I was late," Richart continued. "I met Roland at a halfway point and teleported him the rest of the way."

Bastien swallowed. "Thank you."

"What happened here?" Étienne interrupted. Judging by the smell, those bodies were only the tip of the proverbial iceberg. "What did you do?"

"Nothing they didn't deserve," Bastien replied darkly.

Étienne remembered Bastien claiming the vampires had had to fear him to follow him. Seeing him now, he had no problem understanding why the vamps had been afraid of their former leader. "How many were there?"

"I lost count."

"Did you leave none of them alive?"

"Not one."

"Chris won't like it."

"I don't give a flying fuck what Chris does or doesn't like." Bastien turned to Richart. "Take me to Melanie."

Did Chris Reordon know Bastien had a thing for his top researcher? Étienne would think Chris would have limited Bastien's visits to the network if he had.

"I can't," Richart refused bravely. "Not until the cleanup crew arrives."

"They'll—"

Richart held up a hand to halt the coming argument. "You've left a trail of bodies from here to Fetzer Hall. I don't want any innocents to stumble upon them and have to be dealt with. We stay until the cleanup crew arrives."

Jaw clenching, Bastien nodded.

Richart frowned as Bastien staggered backward and leaned against the brick exterior of Peabody Hall. "Are you injured?"

Bastien closed his eyes. "It's nothing."

The hum of an engine drew their attention to a chartered bus rumbling up South Columbus Street.

Richart stared. "Chris took you seriously. He actually sent a bus."

"They'll need it," Bastien said, sounding so weary now Étienne began to look for tranquilizer darts. The despised immortal appeared ready to pass out at any moment.

The bus slowed and pulled into the drive between Peabody and Sitterson Hall.

Bastien straightened. "This will go faster if we retrieve the bodies for them." Wiping his weapons on the cleaner inside of his coat, he sheathed them. "I'll get the ones on the roofs. You get the ones on the ground."

As Bastien sped away, Étienne shared a look with Richart.

"Had we gotten here earlier, that would not have gone nearly so well." Richart nodded at the men stepping off the bus. "It would be best, perhaps, to warn them what they will face."

Étienne nodded. "I'd encourage them to stay the hell away from Bastien, too."

Turns out the latter wouldn't be too difficult.

The humans who had just disembarked yelped and leapt out of the way as two men dressed in Special Ops uniforms plummeted from the sky and hit the pavement beside the bus with a sickening thump.

"Holy shit!" one of them uttered.

Just what Étienne had been thinking.

Bastien's method of "retrieving" the bodies from the roof apparently entailed scaling the building, grabbing the bodies, and hurling them at the bus.

Richart sighed. "This is going to be a very long night."

* * *

It took the full might of Étienne and his brother to hold Bastien back when they reached the network. Roland had healed Melanie's wounds, but not before she had lost way too much blood. And not before her heart had stopped beating.

The doctors and nurses at the network were still with her, giving her blood, monitoring her vitals, and praying the cerebral hypoxia that resulted from cardiac arrest had not injured her brain. Before leaving, Roland had told Étienne that brain damage was difficult to detect and harder to heal. Only Seth and David could do it, and some damage exceeded even their abilities.

Bastien was beside himself.

Chris adamantly refused to allow the volatile immortal in the OR.

One of Dr. Lipton's colleagues—Linda—convinced Chris to let Bastien wait in Cliff's apartment with both Cliff and Joe for company. Chris would have vetoed that, too, if he hadn't had two immortals (and didn't Étienne feel so lucky to be one of them) on hand to guard the vamps and their former leader.

Étienne stood just inside the door of Cliff's apartment. Richart had taken Cliff up on the offer of a chair and sat nearby.

Bastien sat on a sofa they'd had to retrieve from Joe's apartment because Bastien and Cliff had evidently obliterated all of Cliff's furniture earlier.

The vampires, Cliff and Joe, sat on either side of him. All three leaned forward, elbows on their knees. Bastien dropped his head into his hands, his usual *bite me* attitude gone.

Cliff, the young African-American vampire, absently twisted his short dreadlocks, not giving the Frenchmen much thought, his concern all for his former leader.

Joe, the vampire on Bastien's other side, glared at the "intruders," blue eyes glowing faintly, unkempt blond hair a mass of uncounterfeited bedhead. Of the two vamps, *this* was the one to watch. Étienne didn't have to delve too deeply into Joe's thoughts to know Joe was fighting tooth and nail to keep the madness at bay. And he was losing the battle.

This was Étienne's first encounter with the vampires . . . if one omitted the night they had surrendered to Seth. Or been captured, as Joe's burgeoning madness now convinced him.

Étienne kept his eyes on Joe, his hands resting loosely on the hilts of his weapons.

His mind he devoted to listening to Bastien's mental podcast. And what he heard frankly shocked him. There was much inside that thick skull that Étienne had not expected to see. Or hear.

It pissed him off, because now he was going to have to rethink his opinion of the prick.

I never should have injected myself with the damned antidote.

Bastien kept his ears tuned to Melanie's heartbeat and monitored the conversations of the men and women who worked on her and watched over her.

Roland had come and gone. Melanie's wounds had been healed. Her chest was once more pristine. But she wasn't conscious. And Roland had been unable to determine if she had suffered brain damage when her heart had ceased pumping oxygen to her brain before his arrival.

If I hadn't injected myself with the damned antidote, she wouldn't have felt the need to monitor me.

Bastien's heart clenched when he heard Linda sniff back tears in the OR.

He should have made Richart teleport Melanie back here at the first sign of trouble. Or should have at least had Richart teleport her back up to the library's roof when she had hitched a ride down with them. Then she wouldn't have been in the direct line of fire.

Hell, he should have just stayed away from her completely tonight.

But they had needed to know if the antidote would work. The immortals needed that in their arsenal if they were going to defeat Emrys and his mercenaries.

Melanie had been too afraid to test it on any of the others, so he hadn't seen any other option. No one would have missed Bastien if it had killed *him*. And Melanie had been stressing over not being able to tell anyone she might have found the answer.

He combed his fingers through his hair, rubbed eyes that felt as though someone had thrown sand into them.

Once he had tested the damned drug, he should have left before she could insist on hunting with him or before Seth could back her. Reordon wouldn't have stopped him. Bastien would've been the one in danger. Reordon would *love* to see him perish. And if he destroyed himself, so much the better.

As long as Richart hadn't known where Bastien was, he couldn't have teleported Melanie to him. Seth wasn't omniscient. He didn't know where everyone was all of the time. Bastien could have just laid low for twenty-four hours, dropped by the network so Melanie could see he was okay and that the drug had no lingering side effects, then gone on with the hunting and recruiting.

Then she wouldn't be lying in there on a fucking table . . . possibly . . .

His throat thickened.

Every time he had come to see Cliff and Joe she had greeted him with a smile.

He combed his fingers through his hair. *She* was the reason he was able to visit Cliff and Joe as often as he did.

He remembered the first time he had seen her.

Bodies had littered the floor between them, broken but still breathing.

She had been down on the floor, arms covering her head protectively as she waited for the violence to end. Then her arms had fallen away, she had raised her head, and . . .

It had been like the sappiest chick flick ever made where the hero looked at the heroine and shit went all slow motion because she was *The One* and he knew it. The thump of his boots hitting the industrial-strength vinyl flooring had echoed through the hallway as he had approached her.

She had stood her ground, beautiful brown eyes wide.

The woman had courage. A lot of it.

He had crowded her intentionally as she had let him into Vincent's room, wanting to touch her and feel her emotions. Sure there had been fear. Concern for the guards he had taken down. But she had not feared *him* so much as she had the situation.

And once he had seen Vincent . . .

He didn't know why, but her being there had helped him through that.

Don't tell them you called me, he had advised her. *You don't want to be linked to me in any way. You were in the wrong place at the wrong time. That's all. I threatened you and forced you to open the door for me. You feared for your life.*

She hadn't liked it, had tried to protest. But the guards had come and . . .

For days afterward, every time he had returned to the network he had felt her guilt, her regret that she had not stood up for him and defended him, her determination to never make that mistake again. What a balm that had been, soothing the wounds that had plagued him for over two centuries.

He should have ignored it.

He should have avoided visiting the network when he knew she was working instead of scheduling his damned visits so they would coincide with the time she spent with the vampires.

Perhaps she wouldn't have cared then. Perhaps, like the rest of them, she wouldn't have given a crap if the drug harmed him and wouldn't have insisted on monitoring him.

This was all his fault.

"Seth would remind you of free will," Étienne said from his position by the door.

Bastien drew his hands down his face and straightened. "What?"

The Frenchman looked uncomfortable. "Free will," he repeated. "Dr. Lipton chose to accompany you of her own free will."

Richart looked over at his brother. "She insisted, actually."

Ordinarily, Bastien would have kicked Étienne's ass for reading thoughts that were none of his business, but he was too damned tired. He hadn't mentioned it to the others, but he had been tranqed again while bringing Melanie's shooters to justice.

Étienne swore.

Richart frowned. "What?"

"He's been tranqed."

"Damn it!" Bastien snapped. "Stay out of my head!"

Cliff straightened. "You were drugged again?"

"Maybe *they* did it," Joe said, his accusing gaze never straying from the twin immortals.

Bastien patted the boy's shoulder. "It wasn't them, Joe. It was the soldiers."

"The network soldiers," Joe spat.

"No. It was the mercenaries I told you about. The network soldiers are helping us fight them."

Cliff spoke up again. "You need to have one of the doctors examine you."

"I'm fine."

"You've been dosed three times tonight. First with the

tranquilizer. Next with an experimental stimulant Dr. Lipton thought would kill you. Then again with the sedative. You should go see Linda."

Bastien shook his head.

He didn't know Linda. He didn't *want* to know Linda.

"She's awake," Étienne said.

"Linda?" Of course she was. Bastien could hear her weeping.

"No, Isaac Newton. Dr. Lipton. And she's all right. There's no brain damage."

Bastien's heart began to pound. "How do you know?"

"Because she's thinking of you."

Chapter 8

Melanie opened her eyes.

The bland walls of the OR swam into focus. Machines she had used to monitor numerous patients in the past hummed and beeped.

Where was Bastien?

She glanced around.

Linda sat beside her, her nose and cheeks blotchy pink, her eyes red-rimmed. She turned away and pulled a tissue from a box on the bedside tray.

Melanie looked beyond her. Dr. Whetsman stood across the room, his back to her, writing something in a patient file. Two more members of the medical staff bustled about, cleaning up the mess tending . . . *her* . . . had left behind?

Where was Bastien? Hadn't they been at UNC together?

Yes. Richart had been there, too. They had taken out a handful of vampires and then . . .

Someone had shot her in the chest.

The little line on one of the machines began to jump up and down faster.

Had mercenaries gotten him? Neither Bastien nor Richart had been aware of the soldiers' presence prior to them shooting her. Had the soldiers shot the immortals, too? Tranqed them? With none of the antidote on hand to combat the drug's effects . . .

"Where's Bastien?"

Linda let out a surprised gasp and spun around. "Lanie?"

"Where is he?"

So much fear darkened her friend's gaze. "Do you know what day it is?"

"Yes. It's Friday night. Or Saturday morning, depending on the time."

"Saturday morning. And the date?"

"It's the . . ." Hell, what was the date? "The fifteenth."

"Do you know how old you are?"

"Old enough not to want to voice it."

Linda burst into watery laughter, then lunged forward and hugged her. "Thank goodness. We were afraid . . ."

"What?"

"You crashed. Your heart stopped and we couldn't get it going again . . . We bagged you and kept up chest compressions until Roland got here, but we didn't know what or how much damage may have been done before he arrived and healed you."

Crap. They had feared she had suffered brain damage? "I'm fine, honey." She patted Linda's back. What had happened to—

Shouting erupted in the hallway. Then gunshots. More shouting.

The doors to the OR flew open, one of them knocking the crap out of Dr. Whetsman, who dropped unconscious to the floor.

Linda bolted upright and spun around.

Melanie leaned to one side and looked past her.

Bastien stood just inside the doors, blood spilling from one-two-three-*four* gunshot wounds in his torso, the gaze he pinned on her frantic.

Richart materialized beside him. "You crazy bastard! I

would have teleported you here if you had just given me a chance!"

Bastien didn't appear to hear him. He crossed to Melanie's side. His long hair was sticky with congealing blood. His face looked like he had wiped it clean, then dragged his hands through his crimson hair and touched his face, staining it again. His neck was red. His clothes clung to him damply. Everywhere. He looked as if someone had dunked him in a vat of blood.

Linda rose and backed away slowly. She had expressed to Melanie several times concern over Bastien's trustworthiness.

"Are you . . . all right?" he asked, hands clenching as if he wanted to reach out and touch her but held himself back.

"I'm fine." Her gaze dropped to his wounds. "Are *you?*"

He nodded, the tense muscles in his face relaxing into almost a smile. "I'm good."

She raised one eyebrow. "I heard gunshots."

"The damned guards posted outside Cliff's apartment didn't want to let me pass."

Étienne appeared in the doorway. "You stupid bastard! Why didn't you just let Richart teleport you?"

Melanie raised one eyebrow and gave Bastien a slight smile. "Still acting, *then* thinking?"

He grinned. "What would Reordon's guards do if I didn't liven things up around here periodically and keep them on their toes?"

Linda bent and checked on Dr. Whetsman.

"How is he?" Melanie asked.

"He's fine," she said and left him on the floor. Neither of them cared much for the man. He was a brilliant physician, but knew it and made damned sure everyone else knew it, too.

When Melanie started to sit up, Bastien slipped an arm around her back to help her.

She would have told him she didn't require the aid, but she liked it. She positively tingled whenever he touched her. It didn't even have to be flesh against flesh to start her heart racing.

His eyes began to glow, reminding her he could feel her emotions.

"That really isn't fair, you know," she protested, removing the pulse monitor so the spike in her heartbeat wouldn't be noticed by any of the humans present. Not that many remained. Those who did sidled out of the room as soon as they could manage it.

He shrugged. "True, but since the advantage is mine, you won't hear me complaining about it."

She had to laugh as she took stock of her body. Other than suffering a bit of weakness, she felt surprisingly normal. "This is amazing. I can't believe I was shot in the chest and—what—a couple of hours later feel almost normal."

"Thrice," Bastien said, face darkening.

"What?"

"You were shot thrice in the chest."

Three times? Hell. She only remembered the first one. "How did—"

"Richart brought Roland to you."

She frowned. "That's what Linda said, but . . . You mean, *the* Roland?"

"Yes."

"Roland Warbrook?"

"Yes."

"And he just . . . touched me with his hands—"

Bastien's eyes flared brightly. Was he jealous?

"—and now I'm fine?" she finished.

"We had to give you blood," Linda threw in.

Bastien nodded. "Roland can heal your wounds, but he can't replace the blood you lost."

"Well, technically, he can," Richart corrected. "He could have transfused you with his own blood, but you lost so much that—had he done so—the virus would have inundated your system and you would have been transformed."

Knowing she had come so close to dying was frightening.

Her gaze strayed to Bastien's chest. "Did the soldiers shoot you, too, or are all of those from the guards here?"

"I took a few from the soldiers."

Étienne drew her attention. "And he was tranqed again."

She looked at Bastien. "How many times?"

"Three or four. I think."

He had been unconscious for hours the last time he had been tranqed. Without the antidote . . .

"How long have I been out?" she asked. She shouldn't have lost a lot of time if Roland healed her swiftly. No wonder Linda had feared she'd suffered brain damage.

"Not long," Bastien said, increasing her confusion. "I didn't lose consciousness this time. I was tired afterward. A little woozy, perhaps—"

"Insane, perhaps," Étienne muttered.

"But I think the antidote you've concocted may do more than we thought. It didn't just alleviate the weakness *after* I had been tranqed. It seemed to have a preventative effect as well and acted as a buffer when I was tranqed again later, keeping me from feeling the full effects."

"That's . . ."

"Fantastic," he said, his praise warming her.

"Yes. But it's also worrisome. I didn't expect it to do that, so I have to wonder what else it might do that I didn't anticipate."

He shrugged off her concern. "It worked perfectly. I feel a bit tired, but otherwise am myself."

Étienne raised his eyebrows. "What you did at UNC is normal for you?"

Uh-oh. "What did you do?" Melanie asked.

Bastien shot the Frenchman a warning glare. "Only what needed to be done."

"Could you be a little more specific?"

"No."

When no more was forthcoming, Melanie shook her head. "I'm going to hear about it eventually." She pushed the covers back, revealing a standard hospital gown that covered her to her knees. "If not from the network rumor mill than from Cliff or Joe. Those guys hear everything around here. If Mr. Reordon bitches about it—and I'm guessing from the looks you're getting from the d'Alençons that he will—then Cliff and Joe will hear it."

Bastien shifted his weight from one foot to the other, glanced at the French immortals, and looked for all the world like a little boy not wanting to cop to hitting a baseball through the window. "I . . . brought your shooter to justice."

"Thank you." She had no problem with his killing the man who would've succeeded in killing *her* had Roland not been available to aid her. That shooter had known nothing of Roland and his healing ability. So when he had shot her, he had meant for her to die. "Was there just the one?"

Bastien had been attacked by a dozen or more last night. A lone gunman seemed odd. Unless Emrys's operation was smaller than they had guessed.

"No. There were others," Bastien said, seeming to steel himself.

"How many?"

"I lost count."

She eyed his bloody clothing. What exactly had he done?

"I killed them," he stated.

"All of them?"

She let that sink in as he stood stoically before her.

Did he think she would condemn him? This was war. She knew well what this group was capable of, what they would do if they got their hands on any of the immortals or on Ami. Clearly they believed human Seconds, which they must have thought her, were expendable.

Bastien looked so grim.

If the others weren't here, she'd put her arms around him and comfort him. It wasn't as if he enjoyed the killing.

"He did tonight," Étienne said darkly.

Bastien frowned at him. "Who did what?"

"Because they hurt me," she said.

Bastien's expression darkened as his gaze ping-ponged between them. "Stop reading her thoughts."

You would defend him?

The unfamiliar voice in her head startled her. *Yes. Wouldn't you?*

I saw the bodies.

I assume you've also seen his thoughts.

A look of unease passed over the immortal's attractive face.

When Bastien took a menacing step toward Étienne, Melanie swung her legs over the side of the bed and leaned forward to snag Bastien's hand.

He glanced back.

She met Étienne's gaze squarely. *You've seen his thoughts?* she repeated.

Yes.

Did he kill for the hell of it? Did he kill for the fun of it? Or did he kill them because they tried to kill me?

Bastien gave her fingers a gentle squeeze. "Dr. Lipton?"

Étienne sighed. "You may as well drop the formality. One, I've heard your thoughts and know your concern for her extends beyond that of a work colleague. And two, I've *seen* your thoughts and keep coming across her naked."

Richart tried without success to choke back a laugh. "Nothing to say?"

A muscle in Bastien's cheek jumped. "I'm debating over whether or not I should kick Étienne's ass for seeing Melanie naked."

Richart burst into laughter.

"It wasn't real! It was fantasy!" his brother protested.

"I don't care. She was naked."

Melanie felt heat bloom in her cheeks and didn't know why the hell she should feel embarrassed. It wasn't as if she really *were* naked. As Étienne had said, they were talking about fantasies he had seen in Bastien's head.

How hot was it that Bastien was picturing her naked?

I was naked in his thoughts? she asked, unsure if Étienne was still tuning in.

A lot.

And we were doing . . . ?

Things that would make you blush even more than you are now.

I don't suppose you could show me, could you?

It doesn't work that way.

Damn.

His lips twitched.

Bastien tugged her hand. "I can't hear what he's saying to you. Should I kick his ass?"

"As if you could," Étienne murmured.

"No." Melanie said, "It's fine."

All three immortals suddenly looked at the ceiling.

"What is it?"

"Reordon," Bastien grunted.

"And he's pissed," Richart said needlessly.

If Bastien had once more plowed through Chris's guards, she was surprised it had taken Chris this long to join them.

She looked to the twins. "He'll chain Bastien up."

Étienne frowned. Easing farther into the room, he closed the door behind him. "For being shot by the guards?"

Surprised, Melanie stood and stared up at Bastien. "You didn't hurt any of them?"

He shrugged and watched her carefully. "I was in a hurry. Perhaps next time."

She smiled and shook her head.

Richart turned to his brother. "It's true. Chris will order the guards to restrain him and chain him up."

"But he didn't hurt anyone."

"He didn't hurt anyone the night he was drugged either. Not here, anyway. He was unconscious when I brought him in, but Chris wanted to restrain him in the holding room."

Étienne's brow creased as he swore and glared at Bastien. "I can't believe you've put me in a position where I'll actually have to defend your sorry ass."

Bastien's lips compressed in a tight smile. "You don't hear me asking for your help, do you?"

Melanie tightened her fingers around his in warning. *"I'll ask for it."* When Bastien started to protest, she held up her free hand to shut him up. "Can you two buy us some time?"

At most, she thought one or the other of them might keep the guards at bay long enough to convince Mr. Reordon that Bastien had indeed left his men unharmed. Maybe offer a token protest when Bastien was escorted to the holding room or tranqed or shot. So she was shocked when Richart strode toward them. "I'll teleport him out of here."

She held on to Bastien's hand. "Where he goes, I go."

"That's what we thought," the brothers said simultaneously.

Richart motioned to their entwined hands. "It's easier for me to take you one at a time. I'll take Bastien first, then immediately return for you, Dr. Lipton."

"Melanie."

"As you wish, Melanie."

"Where are we?" Bastien asked when he and Richart appeared inside a house.

"My home. I'll return in a moment."

Bastien clutched his arm. "You should leave her there."

"I should," Richart agreed. "But I gave her my word."

As soon as Bastien released him, the other immortal vanished.

When he reappeared, Melanie was with him.

She grinned up at Bastien. "That is so awesome."

Try though he might, he couldn't prevent himself from returning her smile. Not because he thought it was cool, too. (It was the only perk to having to hunt with Richart nightly.) But because he found her smile so enchanting and irresistible. So utterly free of guile.

Richart let out a piercing whistle.

Bastien heard a thud sound in some distant room.

"Damn it!" a male they couldn't see shouted. "I told you not to do that! You scared the crap out of me!" It must be Sheldon.

Bastien met Richart's gaze. "Have you told him he doesn't have to shout for you to hear him?"

"Several times." He seemed amused rather than annoyed by his new Second's slow learning curve.

Melanie aimed her smile up at Richart. "I'm dying to know how you do that."

"It's easy. I just purse my lips and blow."

Laughing, she shoved him. "Not the whistling. The teleporting."

Richart, no more immune to her charm and goodness than Bastien was, grinned down at her. "I wouldn't mind knowing that myself."

"Really? Could I by any chance talk you into letting me run a few tests? I'd love to do an MRI while you teleport and see what lights up."

Richart's smile faltered beneath a look of supreme unease. Immortals tended to be nearly as uncomfortable around doctors—on the doctors' territory at least—as Ami was. And Ami still broke out in a cold sweat if she had to go anywhere near the network.

Melanie touched Richart's forearm, resurrecting Bastien's jealousy. "Just think about it."

His stance relaxing, the Frenchman nodded. "I will." He motioned to the living room around them—modern, with more clutter than Bastien was accustomed to seeing since most immortals were neat freaks. David's place, despite the heavy traffic it saw, was usually immaculately clean and tidy. "Please make yourself at home. The kitchen is through there. Bastien, there is blood in the modified meat compartment in the refrigerator. There's a bathroom just down the hall. There are four guest rooms on this floor and four more in the basement. If you need anything, don't hesitate to ask Sheldon."

How long did he think they would be here?

"Oh, and Bastien . . ." His words turned brittle. "Tread carefully with my Second. Mistreat him in any way and you will answer to me."

Bastien had lived with vampires with vicious mentalities and violent tempers that could explode at any moment for two centuries. He was confident he could best the other immortal in a fight, but frankly had no interest in doing so. Richart had just done him a solid. Bastien may be the asshole others thought him, but he didn't forget things like that.

"I don't abuse children."

Giving him an abrupt nod, Richart vanished.

Silence descended upon the room.

"So," Melanie said.

Bastien raised one eyebrow. "So?"

"You picture me naked?"

He had hoped she had forgotten about that—damn Étienne and his prying—but, since she hadn't, he saw no reason to deny it. "Yes, I do." He didn't feel any embarrassment. He was a man with healthy sexual appetites and she was a very appealing woman. He did experience some confusion, however, when she exhibited no anger over the admission.

She didn't call him a swine or a dog or whatever animal women currently called men who did something inappropriate. She merely eyed him speculatively, making him feel as if she were trying to imagine *him* naked, then said, "I should warn you that I probably won't live up to your expectations."

Every muscle in his body tightened. He swallowed. Hard. "What?"

"I'm going to go out on a limb and guess that I don't look nearly as good naked as you think I do."

"I seriously doubt that."

"I'm just saying . . . I didn't exercise regularly until I underwent training by the network and . . . I've lost weight since then and . . ."

"And?"

She pursed her lips. "Even though I'm in shape now, certain body parts aren't what I would like them to be."

He was quiet for a moment. "I'm sorry. I don't know how to respond to that."

She grinned. "You don't have to respond at all. I just wanted to make sure you knew that clothing can hide a lot of flaws."

Said the flawless woman who made his body harden even when she tried to convince him she was unattractive. Or that she wasn't as attractive as he might imagine. Or . . .

Actually he wasn't sure. "I'm certain you're just being overly critical of yourself."

She tilted her head to one side. "Could be. The media does condition women to believe they should look a certain way. But, just to be on the safe side, you might want to imagine me with smaller breasts when you fantasize about me."

Again he remained silent for a moment. "Could I just say that this is the most peculiar conversation I've ever had?"

She laughed. "Why?"

"Well, for one thing, you seem convinced that I am laboring under certain delusions concerning your appearance. I'm not."

"My breasts aren't this big. I'm wearing a push-up bra."

"I know."

The look of surprise on her face was too adorable. "What?"

"I know you're wearing a push-up bra."

Now she was silent. "If you tell me you have two gifts and that one of them is X-ray vision, I'm going to have to hurt you."

He laughed. "I don't have X-ray vision. But, as you know, all of our senses are heightened. I can hear the faint rustle of the padding that humans can't. And your breasts don't move the way they would in a bra without the padding."

"Wow. You guys really notice the little details, huh?"

"With you, yes."

A teasing smile curved her lips. "So you stare at my breasts?"

"Yes," he said, returning her smile, and shook his head in bafflement. "And for some reason, admitting that makes me feel like a naughty schoolboy caught peeking up his teacher's skirt."

"Cool."

Again he laughed.

"So what's the other reason?"

He tried to recall what they had been talking about but now could only think of her breasts.

Her smile widened into a grin. "The other reason this is the oddest conversation you've ever had," she prodded.

Ah. "You seem to believe I'm going to see you naked at some point in the future. That's never going to happen."

"Says you."

He grinned. "Are you trying to make me laugh again?"

"Yes."

"Why?"

"Because you don't seem to laugh very often. And I like it when you laugh. It makes me happy."

Hell. He was in *so* much trouble. There was only so much a man could withstand.

"I like you, Sebastien."

"I don't know why," he murmured.

"I see what the others don't."

Once more, he found himself at a loss for words, because the desperation with which he wanted her to see something good in him—something he could never seem to find himself—was terrifying.

"Now, I know you don't like to be touched," she began.

What nit told her that? his inner voice screamed.

"But brace yourself." She took a step closer. "Because I'm going to give you a hug."

He stiffened.

Don't let her touch you! Not now! Not after that weird-ass conversation that left you fixated on her body and feeling all soft and mushy inside because she likes to see you laugh!

Stepping closer, she slipped her arms around his waist, pressed the front of her delectable body to the front of his, leaned her weight into him, and rested her cheek on his chest.

He closed his eyes. It felt wonderful. *She* felt wonderful.

Though he willed himself not to give in to temptation, he found himself wrapping his arms around her slight form and holding her tight.

"Thank you for saving my life tonight," she said softly.

"I didn't. Richart and Roland did."

She shook her head. "I remember what you did now. You put yourself between me and the shooter."

"It made no difference. The bullet just went through me and hit you anyway."

"For all you know, he may have been aiming that third bullet at my head. When you stepped between us, you blocked his view and he couldn't do anything but a body shot. Then you whisked me to safety behind the building."

He hadn't thought of that, but knew it to be standard practice. How many times had he heard Darnell tell the Seconds he trained to hit the body first to disable, then follow up with a head shot?

The idea left him cold.

But not cold enough to keep him from getting hard at the feel of her. The scent of her. The sheer seduction of her.

How he wanted to let his hands wander down and see if that hospital gown gaped in the back the way some did.

"Okay, I'm going to say something now and don't want you to take offense," she said then, voice changing.

"Okay," he agreed warily.

"Ewwww. Gross. I forgot you were covered with blood." She leaned back. Sure enough, her face and hair were now sticky with some of the gore that coated his clothing. And the hospital gown looked as if someone had dipped a sponge in red paint and dabbed it repeatedly.

"Sorry." He reached under his coat and into one of his back pockets to draw out a pristinely clean white kerchief.

Gently clasping her chin with his thumb and forefinger, he wiped the blood from her cheeks and nose and forehead.

Her brown eyes stared up at him so intently he felt her gaze like a touch.

"There," he murmured when her face was clean, and stuffed the kerchief back in his pocket.

Her gaze didn't waver. "You know what?" she said, voice equally hushed. "Screw it. In for a penny, in for a pound."

Reaching up, she clasped his face in both hands and drew his lips down to meet hers.

Electricity seized him, sizzling his blood and stiffening every muscle in his body.

She tasted as good as she looked. As good as she smelled. So good no force on Earth could have kept him from deepening the kiss. Teasing her lips apart, he slipped his tongue inside to seek hers.

Melanie thought if her heart pounded any harder it might burst right out of her chest.

The man could *kiss*.

Heat consumed her as his soft, warm lips moved against hers. And when his tongue stole inside . . .

She rose onto her toes and slid her arms around his neck. Their bodies came into alignment, breasts to chest, abs to abs, hips to hips. His erection strained against his zipper. His strong arms locked around her and pressed her so close she almost couldn't breathe.

Bastien had fantasized about her naked form, imagined what she looked like. Well, Melanie hadn't had to imagine. She had seen Bastien naked when she had tended his wounds after he was drugged. Every firm, delectable inch of him from that gorgeous mane of hair, down muscle and sinew, to his large feet.

She had wanted to know Bastien the man for weeks. Now she wanted to know his body. Wanted to taste and touch and—

One of his big hands slid down and cupped her ass over the gown, grinding her against him.

Her breath caught. Sparks shot through her.

"Dude, did you hear me? I said stop—*Whoa!*"

Melanie cursed the interruption when Bastien relinquished her lips and glared over her head at Richart's Second.

"Oh, sorry. I didn't know you had Jenna with—*Holy crap! It's you!*"

Jenna? That must be the name of Richart's girlfriend.

Melanie raised her head.

Bastien's eyes glowed a vibrant amber, the passion in them swiftly replaced by irritation.

Sighing—talk about spoiling the moment—she unglued her front from Bastien's and turned to face the intruder.

The man who stood gaping at them was unusually young for a Second. He had attended the meeting at David's, but she hadn't paid that much attention to him because she had been so distracted by Bastien.

As she studied Sheldon's smooth face and red hair, she

guessed he was no more than twenty years old. Most—if not all—other Seconds were over twenty-five. She had once heard Chris say he liked to make sure his recruits had made it past the I'm-going-to-party-my-ass-off-and-go-wild-now-that-I'm-out-of-my-parents'-house phase and were ready to get down to business. Immortals needed their Seconds to be on call and ready to rush to their aid and fight, if necessary, twenty-four hours a day. If the Seconds were drunk off their asses from partying with their friends, they could get their immortals *killed* instead of helping them.

And there was also the matter of discretion. Seconds were forbidden to speak of their profession to *anyone*. (Melanie didn't know what Chris did to those who spilled the beans and didn't *want* to know.) Seconds who spent their weekends partying could not be counted on to keep their mouths shut. And those young enough to still succumb to peer pressure would be more likely to brag about their cool gig in order to get attention or to increase their chances of getting laid.

So Sheldon was a real rarity.

Richart's Second stared at Bastien for what felt like five minutes. "Um . . . would you excuse me for a moment?" Taking three slow steps backward, he leaned out into the hallway. *"Richart?"* The bellow vibrated with nervous tension.

Behind her, Bastien sighed heavily. "You don't have to shout. If he were standing outside on the lawn, he could hear you whisper."

"Oh. Right." A moment passed. "Richart?" he said in a normal voice.

Melanie tried not to laugh. "He isn't here."

"Oh." He cleared his throat. "So. Did he, ah . . ." His gaze returned to Bastien. "Did you . . . force him to bring you here?"

"Oh, for shit's sake!" Bastien snapped. "No!"

She did laugh then. She couldn't help it. "I assume you're Sheldon?"

"Yes, ma'am."

"I'm Dr. Lipton." She held out her hand. "You can call me Melanie."

Much to her surprise, Sheldon strode forward and clasped her hand. "Nice to meet you, Melanie."

Bastien moved to her side. "You can call her Dr. Lipton."

She expected the young Second to fall victim to Bastien's stern warning and acquiesce.

Instead, he said, "So . . . *Melanie* . . . what brings you to our humble home?"

"I was wounded earlier tonight by some of Emrys's soldiers."

"Son of a bitch!" He frowned at Bastien. "Did you get 'em?"

"All of them," he answered, some of the harshness leaving his expression.

"Good."

There was more to Sheldon than met the eye. "That's why Richart brought us here. He knew Mr. Reordon would go on a rampage and want to lock Bastien up for not leaving any of them alive."

Sheldon tilted his head to one side as he studied Bastien. "Well, you did kinda deviate from the plan. The whole point was to catch some of them and interrogate them. But I get why you killed them instead. I would've offed the fuckers, too." He nodded to Melanie. "How are you doing? Do you need anything? Should I get the med kit? I aced field medicine during my training, so if you—"

"I'm fine, thank you. Roland healed me."

"Roland Warbrook?"

"Yes."

"Wow. You really have a knack for making friends with antisocial bastards, don't you?"

Bastien's lips curled up. "Yes, she does."

Sheldon clapped his hands together. "Well, I assume Richart will be back once things cool down. What can I do for you in the meantime?" He eyed Bastien. "No offense, dude, but you look like shit. You need some blood?"

"I do actually."

"Follow me." He led the way out of the living room and into a spacious kitchen. "Melanie, can I fix you something to eat? I suck as a cook, but can warm you up some of the vegetarian pot pie Richart made earlier."

"No, thank you."

He crossed to the refrigerator, opened it, and bent down to retrieve bags of blood from the meat compartment. He handed them to Bastien. "Are you sure? It's better than it sounds. I mean, I thought any pot pie that was all organic and didn't contain meat would taste like whale snot, but the shit is delicious."

Melanie laughed. She could sort of see why Richart was willing to put up with Sheldon. "I don't—"

"You should eat something," Bastien interrupted. "We both should. It's been a long night. And it may not be over yet. We don't know what's going to happen once Chris burns Seth's ears with his interpretation of what went down."

She nodded. "You're right. Thank you, Sheldon. We'd appreciate it."

"My pleasure. Would you guys like to shower and change first?"

Melanie glanced down at her now-sticky hospital gown. "I'd love to, but I don't have anything to change into." Anything in Richart's size would swallow her.

"No problem. One of the guest rooms is reserved for Richart's sister. Lisette doesn't stay the day often, but she keeps several changes of clothes here for when she does. I don't think she'd mind you borrowing something."

Lisette was close to her size, so Melanie fervently hoped she'd find something that would fit. She wasn't sure how much the back of her hospital gown exposed, but it felt pretty breezy back there. And, while she wouldn't mind Bastien catching a glimpse of her butt, she would rather not flash Sheldon.

"If you're sure . . ."

He led them out of the kitchen. "I'm sure. Lisette's great. Let me show you to the guest rooms." Stopping, Sheldon turned around and eyed them speculatively. "Or guest *room*. Are you guys together? Because when I walked in on you a minute ago, you were—"

"No."

Sheldon's eyebrows rose at Bastien's clipped response.

"It was a momentary . . . digression."

Now Melanie raised her eyebrows. "Says you."

Bastien smiled. "Would you stop saying that?"

"No."

"Why?"

"Because it makes you smile."

Sheldon started walking again. "Momentary digression, my ass," he mumbled.

"I can hear you," Bastien reminded him.

"I know." Sheldon guided them to guest bedrooms that were next to each other. "I'll be back in a minute with some clothes, Melanie."

Once the Second was gone, Bastien stared down at her in silence.

He was thinking again. Or, she should say, he was thinking *too much* again. She could almost see the thoughts swirling around behind those gorgeous brown eyes and knew what he would say before he said it.

"About what happened . . ."

Yep. She had figured he was obsessing over that. Poor guy. The immortals had really done a number on him, convincing him he was the evil monster they seemed to think him. Now he probably thought kissing her would taint her somehow. She was going to have to do something about that. She just needed a little time to decide what.

"I assume you mean the kiss?" she asked innocently.

"Yes."

"The warm, wet, pulse-racing, make-me-want-to-strip-you-naked-and-rub-every-inch-of-my-body-against-yours kiss?"

His eyes flared, an involuntary reflection of his arousal. "That's the one."

"What about it?"

"It shouldn't happen again."

"You didn't like it?" Okay, teasing him was mean, but she couldn't resist.

"You know I did," he admitted, voice deepening in a way that sent a sensual shiver through her. "If my eyes didn't clue you in, I'm sure other body parts did."

"Very impressively," she agreed.

"Even so, it wouldn't be a good idea."

"You've said something similar before."

"I meant it. I care about you, Melanie. A lot. And . . . I don't want to sound condescending . . . I just don't think you understand how bad things will get for you if you're associated with me romantically. We're not just talking dirty looks or snide comments. We're talking the possible destruction of your career. Chris Reordon doesn't trust me and never will. Give him even the tiniest reason and he will lock me up. We're here right now because he wants to chain me up in the holding room."

And she would really like to know why Chris hated Bastien so much. Her boss was usually a levelheaded guy. Friendly. There if you needed anything. But with Bastien . . . it just seemed personal.

"I'm not worried about that."

"You should be." He said it with such concern. "Your work at the network is invaluable. If anyone can find a cure for this virus or a method of preventing or treating the damage it causes in humans, you can."

That was both an incredible compliment and a heavy burden to bear. So much expectation . . . If she failed them . . . "Look, don't put me on a pedestal, Bastien."

"Don't underestimate yourself, Melanie. You're too important. And you like your job, don't you?"

"Absolutely." And she knew how rare that was. So many people were stuck in jobs they hated, working with people they didn't like. There may be a lot of pressure involved with her job, but she enjoyed it and liked most of the people she worked with (Dr. Whetsman was the exception).

"Being with me will jeopardize all of that," Bastien continued. "Right now, you have the highest level clearance at the network and access to any and all information you need. If word gets out that you and I . . . If anyone suspects you might have tender feelings for me, that clearance will be revoked. You will no longer be trusted at the network and they will shut you out. I wouldn't even put it past Chris to deny you further access to Cliff and Joe."

Okay. That got her attention. Would Chris really do that? Would he take it so far? Let his dislike of Bastien flow over onto her?

Even if it did, wouldn't the importance of her research tie his hands?

"Trust is everything, Melanie. You don't want to lose theirs and have your every decision countermanded, your every motivation questioned. Such becomes tiresome very quickly."

Something to ponder, true. But Melanie wasn't willing to give up what Bastien made her feel for a few negative what-ifs. She felt certain she could find a way around any obstacle Chris might throw in their path.

"So no more kissing?" she asked slowly.

The look that crossed his face was a mixture of relief and regret. "Yes."

"Okay." Rising onto her toes, she leaned into him and captured those silken lips with her own.

No one tasted better than Sebastien. No one kissed better. And he may think kissing her a bad idea, but he didn't pull away.

He wound his arms around her waist even as she slid hers up around his neck.

Melanie pushed him back into the wall and leaned into his large, firm, muscular form.

Bastien groaned. "You're making this very hard for me."

She grinned and rubbed her hips against his. "That's sort of the whole point."

He smiled. "You aren't going to give up, are you?"

She stared up at him, at his glowing eyes, his face so relaxed with that handsome half smile. "No," she said somberly. "I haven't felt this way in a long time, Bastien."

His smile slowly faded. "Nor have I."

"I'm not going to refrain from exploring what's happening between us because others may not approve. It's too important."

He stroked her hair. "You're so fearless. I wish I could be, too."

She raised an eyebrow. "You are. You went up against I-don't-know-how-many soldiers on your own tonight."

"For you."

"Well . . ." She drew a hand down to his chest. "When it comes to us, I want you to follow your feelings, not do what you think is best for me. If you don't want to kiss me because you aren't interested—"

"You know I am," he said gruffly.

"Then stop thinking and act."

"There will be consequences."

"We'll deal with those as they arise." She couldn't help but notice he wasn't pushing her away. "So, are we going to do this?"

"Dude, I say go for it," Sheldon said as he strolled down the hall toward them. "Melanie is smokin' hot and you're . . . you."

As Melanie reluctantly moved away from Bastien, whose arms she was happy to note were a little slow to release her, Sheldon held out a pile of folded clothes.

She took them. "Thank you."

He nodded and sized the two of them up. "I can hold off on warming up the pot pie if you guys want to have sex. Just let me know so I can put in my earbuds and blast Disturbed in case one of you is a screamer." He looked pointedly at Bastien.

Melanie laughed.

Bastien scowled. "How has Richart not killed you yet?"

"That's what his brother and sister keep asking."

"And Ami," Bastien added with an evil grin.

Anxiety instantly darkened Sheldon's face. "Really? Has she said something to you? Is she coming for me? She isn't coming for me, is she?"

Wow. He seemed genuinely afraid of Ami. Did he know what she was? That she was different? Or was it something else Melanie hadn't heard about?

"I don't know," Bastien said slowly. "I suppose it depends in part on my treatment during our stay here. Ami and I are close friends, you know."

Sheldon swallowed. "Seriously?"

"Yes."

Melanie started to wonder why Bastien wasn't worried about Ami being associated with him, then realized he didn't have to. Seth would kill anyone who treated Ami badly.

Sheldon forced a laugh and clapped Bastien on the shoulder. "Dude, I was totally joshing you about the screaming thing. You want me to hold off on the pot pie? 'Cause I don't mind."

"No." Bastien sent Melanie a rueful smile. "Go ahead and heat it up. We'll join you shortly."

"Yes, sir. And, if you change your mind, don't worry about it. I'll keep it warm for you." After giving Melanie a grinning thumbs-up, he hurried down the hallway and out of sight.

Bastien shook his head. "That boy is strange."

Melanie smiled. "But I can see why Richart likes him."

"And why Ami doesn't."

Melanie laughed.

Bastien moved closer, bent his head, and touched his lips to hers in a brief caress. "Shall I meet you out here in ten minutes?"

His touch sent her slowing pulse racing again. "Make it fifteen. It takes me awhile to comb my hair out when it's wet."

"Take your time. I'll be here when you're ready."

She smiled and stole another kiss. "So will I."

Chapter 9

"Sir?"

Emrys turned away from greeting his guests, noted the soldier's grim expression, and clenched his teeth. Holding up a hand to stay the soldier's words, he faced his guests once more and donned a false smile. "This will only take a moment. If you'll head into my office, I'll join you shortly."

Nodding, they entered his office.

Emrys reached in, grabbed the doorknob, and pulled the door closed. "What is it?" he murmured to the soldier.

"We've lost contact with Team Viper."

"Damn it. I told you to maintain radio silence in the field. The squawk of a radio or the vibration of a cell phone is guaranteed to give away your positions."

"Yes, sir. We have not attempted to contact any of the groups in the field. But they were ordered to contact *us* at the top of every hour, either with a few clicks over the radio or with a phone call, asking one of a dozen predetermined, totally inane questions that anyone with preternatural hearing would assume came from one of the students on campus. Team Viper has done neither for two hours. They've gone silent."

"All of them?"

"Yes, sir. Should we try to raise them on the radio? Call one of their cell phones?"

"No. Send Black Mambo to UNC. Full stealth mode." He started to turn away, paused, and reconsidered. "Where's Team Taipan?"

"NCCU, sir. They just checked in."

"Have them meet Black Mambo at UNC."

"Yes, sir."

Emrys entered his office and closed the door behind him. "Gentlemen, thank you for meeting with me." He motioned to the chairs facing his desk. "Please, have a seat and make yourselves comfortable."

"How have you been?" Donald asked, taking the seat on the right as Nelson seated himself on the left. "I haven't heard from you since . . . the incident."

Emrys ground his teeth again, but made damn sure he kept his smile as he circled the desk and seated himself behind it.

Donald hadn't seen him since Emrys had been dishonorably discharged from the military.

"I've been good. I've been busy."

Donald nodded. "I was surprised to hear who my competition was."

Yeah, I bet you were, Emrys thought. Donald had retired from the military a year after Emrys had been forced out. But Donald had been given a going away party. Donald had been asked to stay. Donald had turned down a promotion.

Then Donald had done the same thing Emrys had: gone into the professional army business. More money. Less risk to himself. And, let's face it, as Emrys's son frequently said, mercenaries kicked ass.

Nelson was Donald's right-hand man. Emrys had never met him before today and didn't know if Nelson was looking down his nose at Emrys because he had heard about *the incident* or if he was just an arrogant dick because he and Donald had found greater success than Emrys had.

No thanks to the Immortal Guardians. Emrys was convinced now that those were the bastards who had stolen Amiriska, though what they wanted with the alien bitch he couldn't guess.

While only a handful knew what he had been doing in his central Texas facility, the loss his company had suffered as a result of the immortals' raid had been a big one. And the lies told to cover up the research he had been hired to conduct had severely damaged his credibility.

All of that, however, was about to change.

"As was I," Emrys said at last.

"I heard you ran into some trouble two or three years ago. This is a tricky business, is it not?"

Just keep smiling. You need this asshole's money. "It certainly is. But things are looking very good for me right now."

Donald exchanged a skeptical look with Nelson. "Are they?"

"How so?" Nelson asked.

"What we're about to discuss doesn't leave this room," Emrys warned.

"All right," Donald verbalized as both nodded.

"I've recently discovered something that will make me a very wealthy man. I might even go so far as to say one of the wealthiest men in the world. And, if you play your cards right, you can join me in my triumph."

"What, did you sleep with the lotto girl?" Nelson joked.

Emrys shook his head, his smile genuine now. "Something even better."

"What are we talking here?" Donald asked. "Weapons? Bioweapons? Drones? Software?"

"I've discovered the means of creating what every nation and rebel army on the planet wants: the ultimate supersoldier."

Donald snorted. "Shit. We already have supersoldiers: men

who don't give a rat's ass who they kill as long as they get paid to do it. It doesn't get any better than that."

"Oh, but it does." Leaning forward, Emrys planted his elbows on his desk. "I'm not talking about *psychological* supersoldiers. I'm talking about *physical* supersoldiers. An army of men who are faster and stronger than anyone else on the planet. Men who can heal from any wound inflicted upon them in minutes. An army of men who will spark bidding wars throughout the world, because *everyone* is going to want them on their side."

He had their interest now. Again the two shared a look, this one both dubious and intrigued.

Nelson spoke. "If you're talking about steroids or—"

"Steroids don't make you heal spontaneously when shot. They don't enable you to see in the dark without night vision goggles either."

"What the hell does?"

"Before I show you, I want to know one thing: If I can deliver what I promise, I want our companies to merge. I have the product. You have the capital and the connections."

Nelson opened his mouth.

Donald placed a hand on his arm. "If you can deliver what you've described . . . we'll get you the money you need. It will be a joint venture."

"We have a verbal agreement then?"

"We do."

Emrys rose. "Then I suggest you come with me."

Bastien watched Melanie wolf down the pot pie and felt guilty that he hadn't offered her food earlier. "I'm sorry." He took another bite of the tasty dish.

Sheldon hadn't lied. The shit was good. Richart was an excellent cook.

What was it with the Immortal Guardians? Wasn't there *anything* they didn't do well?

"For what?" Melanie asked between bites.

They were ensconced in Richart's cozy dining room. Melanie sat at the head of the table, which was about half the length of David's, with Bastien on her left.

"I didn't think to ask if you had dined before you went hunting with Richart and I."

She waved her fork. "Don't worry about it. To be honest, I forgot. I do that sometimes." She sipped her tea. "I get busy, get distracted, go hours without looking at the clock, and just forget to eat."

"And today was busier and more distracting than most, I would imagine."

She laughed. "Yes, it was." She scooped a small brown square onto her fork. "If this pot pie doesn't contain meat, what do you suppose these little things are?"

He smiled. She must not be a health food nut like the immortals. "Tofu."

Her face lit with surprise. *"This* is tofu?"

He nodded.

"I thought tofu tasted like feet. This is delicious."

He laughed. "I imagine anything can taste like feet if it isn't seasoned properly." He sipped his own tea, took another bite of pot pie, and watched her do the same.

When was the last time he had shared a meal with a woman?

As best as he could recall, he had not done so since his transformation. Everything after that had been about survival and avenging his sister Cat's death.

And helping his fellow vampires.

Inwardly he cursed. He'd been with the immortals for almost two years now and still thought of himself as a vampire on most days.

Melanie grinned. "Which is why I've never invited you to dinner. I can't cook worth a crap."

As Bastien took another drink, he studied her over the rim of his glass. "You considered asking me to dinner?" He lowered the glass to the table. "Before . . . all of this, I mean?"

She nodded and moved the vegetables around with her fork, eyes on her plate. "I liked talking with you when you came to visit Cliff and Joe."

He had, too. And, though it shamed him to admit it, he had looked forward to seeing Melanie more than his friends. And not just because she was prettier. "I enjoyed it, too."

She looked up with a smile. "I probably would have gotten up the nerve to ask you out eventually. I assume you guys are allowed to date?"

Were they? "Richart does."

She nodded. "And tonight he saved me from having to comb the Internet for a recipe I could actually follow that might satisfy you."

He smiled. "Cheese and crackers would satisfy me as long as you were my dining companion."

Melanie reached over and rested a hand on his forearm. "That's so sweet."

Bastien took her hand in his and stroked her fingers. "If you say that in front of the immortals, they'll swear you're delusional."

She shrugged. "That's just because they don't know you like I do."

If she thought him sweet, then she didn't know him as well as *they* did. And part of him hoped she never would. He didn't want her to see that side of him.

"Should we consider this a date then?" he teased.

She smiled. "The first of many, I hope."

Hope had long since abandoned Bastien. "I can't resist asking . . . how am I doing?"

She squeezed his hand. "Very well. I freely admit I'm smitten. Isn't that a word someone from your era would use?"

"It is." And *he* was beyond smitten.

They tucked into their meal again, hands still clasped.

"I'm curious about something," he said after awhile, almost afraid to break the silence it was so pleasant.

She raised her brows in question.

"How did you come to work for the network? I've never learned how exactly they go about recruiting members."

"They didn't so much recruit me as find me," she said. "My freshman year in college, my roommate was killed in our dorm room."

Considering how prevalent violence was in society, he didn't know why that surprised him as much as it did. "I'm sorry. Were you harmed?"

"No. It happened while I was out cramming with my study group. I found her body when I returned to our room."

"Were you close?"

"Not really. She pretty much annoyed the crap out of me, always blasting music and bringing guys over to screw while I was trying to study my ass off so I could keep my academic scholarship. I was the nerd to her party girl, I guess you could say. She had moments when she wasn't the worst roommate in the world. Not nearly as many as I would've liked, but . . ." She shook her head. "Irritating or not, I would never have wished that on her."

"Of course not."

"Usually the cops look first at the boyfriend, but she hadn't been seeing any one guy exclusively. MPDC ruled me out quickly because everyone in my study group alibied me. Detectives asked me to submit a DNA sample, though, so they could run it against the DNA the crime scene unit collected, exclude me and Dana, and see what they were left with. When I did, all hell broke loose. They said there was something up with my DNA, that they had found something in it that didn't make sense or didn't belong."

Bastien tightened his hold on her hand. "Are you a *gifted one*, Melanie?"

She nodded. "They wanted me to go to the hospital so they could run some tests. I was freaking out, thinking I had some sort of incurable genetic disease or something."

"I'll bet."

"Then two men showed up and introduced themselves as Chris Reordon and Seth. All of the medical personnel got these weird blank looks on their faces, turned, and filed out of the room."

"Seth erased their memory of you?"

"Yes. And Mr. Reordon took care of the physical evidence, both that collected by the police and any mention of it in their computers. I still don't know how he did that."

"He may be an asshole, but I've heard he can work wonders."

"He did. They explained what I was, why I was different and, when I mentioned I was interested in studying medicine, Mr. Reordon asked me if I'd like a job. I said, hell yes. The network took over paying my college tuition and . . . the rest is history."

Bastien wondered if Chris's knowing her so long would be a plus or a minus now that she wished to pursue her attraction to him. Would Chris feel betrayed and be all the more pissed? Or would he be less inclined to extend his distrust of Bastien to include her?

"What is your gift?" he asked curiously. He hadn't noticed anything during the time they had spent together.

She wrinkled her nose. "Precognition that's really too weak to benefit me. Sometimes I know the phone is going to ring before it rings. Or that a package will be delivered. Or just when and where to swing a bar stool to break up a fight between a hardheaded immortal and his vampire friend."

He smiled. No wonder she was so good at anticipating vampires' moves.

"Sometimes I'll get an . . . uneasy feeling . . . when something bad is about to happen. I felt it the night my parents were killed in an accident. I felt it the day Vincent had his last break. I felt it the night Dana was killed."

He mulled that over while he finished the last few bites of pot pie. The younger the immortal, the weaker his or her gift. Seth said it was a result of the *gifted ones'* bloodline being diluted many times over with that of ordinary humans. Sarah hadn't even realized she *had* a gift, which was actually a little bit similar to Melanie's. Sarah's dreams were prophetic, just not literally so. According to what he'd heard at David's, there were always symbols that needed to be deciphered. If, say, she and Roland were about to face a life and death situation, Sarah didn't see it unfold in her dreams as it would happen in the days that followed. Instead she dreamed about tornadoes or some shit.

"Did you feel any uneasiness before we went hunting tonight?"

She hesitated. "Yes."

"Why didn't you say something?"

"I thought it was nerves. And concern. I was worried about you and excited about spending time with you and nervous about hunting vampires for the first time . . ."

He was such an ass. Melanie had an internal shit's-about-to-happen warning system and he was jumping up and down inside because she had been excited about spending time with him.

"I also wasn't sure how to bring up the whole *I'm a gifted one* thing," she continued. "I didn't want it to seem like . . ." She gave an embarrassed laugh and started to withdraw her hand.

Bastien didn't let her. "Tell me." He could feel her reluctance to tell him and wanted to know what was causing the flush to creep up her neck.

She sighed. "I knew you were aware of my attraction to you and didn't want it to seem like I was . . . I don't know, trying to make myself seem more appealing to you, like I was saying, 'Hey, you should totally date me because I can be transformed,' or something."

That's right. She *could* be transformed. If he actually thought she could fall in love with him and that she could do so without facing pretty damned dismal consequences, he would be bouncing off the walls right now.

"Have you . . . thought about being transformed?" *Subtle.*

She nodded. "Down the line sometime. I'm not really ready to give up the sun." She smiled ruefully. "Or my favorite foods. That sounds pathetic, I know, but there you have it. I know all of you immortals only eat organic, and most of my favorite foods and snacks are anything but."

"Well, I hate to tell you this, but those favorite foods won't taste the same to you after your transformation."

She frowned. "They won't? Why?"

He motioned to his nose and his eyes. "Our sense of smell and our vision aren't the only senses that were heightened during our transformation. Our sense of taste was, too."

Cool. "Then my favorite foods will be even yummier."

"A hundred years ago, I would've said yes. But now . . . We can taste every individual ingredient." He nodded at the pot pie. "I can taste every spice and every vegetable in this pie and tell you in what proportions they were used."

Melanie may not be able to judge the proportions, but she could taste many of those flavors, too. "And . . . ?"

He gave her an apologetic smile. "And I can taste the difference between vanilla and synthetic vanillin. Or the difference between an organic chocolate bar made with seventy-three percent cacao and one of the chocolate bars I've seen you eat that contains twenty-five percent cacao and makes up the difference with vegetable oil and artificial flavoring. It's as obvious as the difference in taste between turkey and tofurky would be to you."

Melanie stared at him. "Are you telling me that all of my favorite foods are going to taste like crap after I'm transformed?"

"Not the organic ones."

"I don't eat organic!"

He motioned to the pie. "That's organic. You like the taste of that, don't you?"

"Yes, but . . ." Crestfallen, she said, "That sucks."

"Not as much as you might think. I heard Sarah say making the switch isn't as hard today as it would've been forty years ago because there's an organic version of most of her favorite snacks. And, on the up side, you gain near immortality and never age or get sick again."

"Which is why I'll probably ask to be transformed at some point in the future. Just not now." She winked. "I like junk food too much."

He laughed.

Squeezing his hand, she sobered. "Listen. Since we're spending more time together, and considering my near-death experience earlier, I feel like I should tell you that if something should happen to me—"

"It won't. I won't let it."

Lowering her fork, she covered their clasped hands. "Let me finish."

He nodded, silently vowing to do everything he could to keep her out of danger in the future.

"If anything should happen to me, if I'm fatally wounded and the network can't save me and no immortal healers can be reached, I want to be transformed."

Her trust and her confidence that he would see that her wishes were carried out flowed into him via his gift, making his heart pound. "You're sure?"

"I'm sure." Her lips tilted up in a small smile. "I may love junk food, but I don't love it enough that I think life isn't worth living without it. And I can still enjoy the sun from a distance. I may not be able to go out and frolic in it—"

He smiled, enjoying the image her words evoked.

"—but I can leave the blinds and curtains open as long as I don't sit directly in the sunbeams."

He nodded and squeezed her hand. "As you wish."

"Thank you."

"I'm honored that you've chosen to confide in me."

For some reason that pleased her, which pleased him.

When Melanie leaned toward him, he met her halfway for a tender kiss.

"Are you kidding me?"

Melanie jumped at the sound of Richart's irate voice.

Bastien swore silently. That was the bad thing about teleporters. You couldn't anticipate their arrival because there was no approach to hear.

"I'm busting my ass trying to keep Chris from figuratively hanging you—he would do it literally if it were possible—and you're here having a romantic dinner for two?" Sighing, Richart raked a hand through his hair, drew out a chair, and sat down. "Hell, I don't blame you. Is there any pot pie left?"

"I don't know," Bastien said. "Sheldon prepared it."

Richart let out a piercing whistle.

A thud sounded somewhere deep in the house. "Damn it! Don't do that!" Sheldon shouted. "You scared the crap out of me!"

Richart grinned. "I love Seconds."

Melanie laughed.

Even Bastien had to smile as Sheldon stomped into the room, rubbing one elbow. "Dude, the next time you invite Satan to dinner, give me a little warning first."

Bastien flipped him off.

Richart looked up at his Second. "Is there any pot pie left?"

"Yeah. You want me to heat you up some? You look beat."

"Wrap it up and I'll take it with me. We're expected at David's. I can heat and eat it there."

"Sure thing." Sheldon headed into the kitchen.

"No luck swaying Reordon?" Bastien asked.

Richart shook his head. "As I said, he would hang you if he could. Or at least kick your ass. In fact, I think if the man were a *gifted one*, he would ask to be transformed just so he *could* kick your ass."

Melanie patted Bastien's hand, her sympathy with *him*.

Damn, that felt good. And how odd was it that Richart's sympathy seemed to be with him, too?

"You aren't going soft on me, are you?" Bastien asked.

"Hell, no. I just have more important things on my mind than mocking you."

Melanie's brow furrowed. "Jenna isn't feeling any better?"

Richart straightened in his chair, his countenance darkening. "Where did you hear that name?"

Bastien released Melanie's hand and leaned forward, resting an arm across the table in front of her in a gesture meant to remind Richart he would have a fight on his hands if he threatened Melanie in any way. "Watch your tone."

Melanie didn't appear worried. "Sheldon let it slip."

Richart swore and rolled his eyes. "The boy is entertaining but sometimes can be a real pain in the ass."

Sheldon walked back in, carrying a cloth lunch bag Bastien assumed was full of Richart's meal. "Says you," he retorted and winked at Melanie.

Bastien bristled. Damn it. Why was every man on the planet suddenly flirting with her?

Richart took the lunch bag and gave his Second a reproving glare.

"What?" Sheldon said. "It was an honest mistake. A tall guy with black hair, your build, and dressed like you was shoving his tongue down a woman's throat in our living room. I drew the obvious conclusion."

Sighing, Richart transferred his attention to Bastien and nodded toward Melanie. "You know this isn't going to go over well, right?

"Such has occurred to me, yes. As long as the fallout only falls on me, I can handle it."

"And if it doesn't?"

Bastien gave him a tight smile. "Then I'll handle it in a whole different manner."

Melanie sighed. "Don't encourage him, Richart." She rose. "And both of you need to remember one thing: I'm a grown woman and can take care of myself. If someone has a problem with my feelings for Bastien and thinks I shouldn't get involved with him because *they* don't like him, they can kiss my merry mortal ass."

Sheldon burst out laughing, moved forward, and held up a hand.

Melanie high-fived him and gave Bastien a truly appealing *so-there* look. "Now, I believe Richart mentioned something about us being expected at David's."

They opted to drive to David's. Richart had teleported so many times in recent hours that he said his batteries were running low, which Melanie took to mean he would have to consume more blood if he kept it up.

His was a fascinating gift.

Richart took the wheel with Sheldon in the passenger seat that Melanie had refused so she could sit in the back with Bastien.

Both immortals seemed preoccupied.

Melanie leaned against Bastien and toyed with one of his hands while Sheldon bobbed his head to Skillet.

It was a nice drive. Melanie had been raised in the city. The apartment had been small and cramped. No yard. No fresh air. Constant noise. When she had moved to North Carolina, she had had to sleep with the television on every night because she was so unaccustomed to the quiet.

She loved it here now, though. Sure it sucked that Walmart and gas stations were about the only things open past midnight. But the fresh air . . . the clear skies so full of stars . . . the scenery . . .

As if on cue, the headlights illuminated two deer grazing by the side of the road.

Bastien draped an arm around her.

She looked up and found him smiling down at her.

"I like this moment in time," she said.

"So do I," he admitted, curling his fingers around hers where she played with them.

Richart turned onto the long drive to David's home, pulled up behind a shiny black Prius parked at the end of it, and cut the engine. Skillet stopped midsentence.

Melanie didn't want to go in. Chris was probably already inside ranting and calling for Bastien's head on a platter, and she really didn't have the patience for it tonight.

Bastien and Richart must not want to go in either, because neither immortal moved. They did, however, share a weighty look in the rearview mirror.

"What is it?" she asked.

"It's too quiet," Bastien said.

Richart nodded.

All cocky kid-itude drained from Sheldon, who drew two 10mms. "Out here or in there?"

Richart nodded at the house. "In there."

A buzz sounded as someone's cell phone vibrated. Bastien leaned forward and drew his phone from a back pocket. He looked at the screen. His brows drew down.

Altering the angle of the phone, he showed Melanie the text from Darnell:

Come in, sit down, and keep your mouth shut.

You do NOT want to piss David off tonight.

Had something happened to upset David? Or was he beginning to tire of championing Bastien when Bastien did so little to ingratiate himself with the other immortals?

Melanie hoped it wasn't the latter.

Bastien held up the phone for Richart and Sheldon to see. Richart's face showed no expression when he met Bastien's gaze. Sheldon looked nervous as hell.

Melanie didn't know what to expect when the four of them exited the car and entered the home.

Inside was a replay of the last meeting she had attended with all of the same players at the table, except . . . no one spoke.

At the head of the table, David reclined in his chair, his weight leaning on the right elbow he'd propped on the table. His dark, handsome face was set in stone. Unlike the others, whose appearances showed the effects of a night of hunting, his black, long-sleeved shirt was clean and dry, his beautiful dreadlocks neatly confined in a thick ponytail that fell beyond the seat of his chair.

Darnell sat to one side of him, his eyes and face reinforcing his command to sit down and shut up.

Everyone remained utterly silent as Melanie, Bastien, Richart (who had opted to leave his dinner in the car), and Sheldon approached the table and took the four empty seats beside Étienne.

Seth's chair remained unoccupied.

Darnell took out his cell phone, moved his thumb across it, then put it back in his pocket.

"Mack the Knife" began to play.

Across from Melanie, Sarah drew out her cell phone and held it to her ear. "Hello? . . . Okay. Thanks."

Seth appeared before Sarah finished putting her phone away.

Melanie thought it sweet of him to warn her each time he teleported.

Seth nodded to all present, started for his seat, then paused. His gaze traveled around the table, then zeroed in on David. "What happened?"

David hesitated. "I took out one of the groups blocking UN aid workers from bringing food to the Somalians."

David had been in Somalia earlier? There must be another immortal who could teleport somewhere on the planet.

"Good job. Anyone help you?"

"No."

Seth studied him closely. "And?"

David scowled. "I lost my damn arm."

Melanie's mouth fell open as her gaze went to his broad shoulders and muscled arms. Plural.

Frowning, Seth crossed to David's side. "The left?"

"Yes."

"You reattached it?"

David's jaw worked. "Mostly. A lot of damage was done by the explosion that took it."

It may seem morbid, but Melanie wished heartily that she could have witnessed that. Not the explosion, of course. But the reattachment. She would love to know how such could be accomplished with just his gift and his hand.

David's warm brown eyes met hers. "Maybe next time."

Horrified that he had read her thoughts, she felt heat rush into her face.

No need to fret, his voice spoke kindly in her mind. *I know your reasons. And there are many in this room who aren't physicians, but have the same curiosity.*

Thank you. I'm so sorry you were injured.

He nodded.

Seth wrapped his long fingers around David's left wrist and lifted the arm to shoulder's height.

A muscle jumped in David's cheek as he grunted and stiffened. His eyes flashed amber.

Seth touched David's shoulder with his other hand, which—beneath Melanie's fascinated gaze—began to glow. Down the arm Seth trailed his hand, his touch gentle.

David's breath soughed out in a relieved sigh. The tightness left his face. The tension that had wrapped those present in a cocoon of discomfort eased.

The pain David had inadvertently been broadcasting had felt to Melanie and the others like displeasure.

The glow faded from Seth's hand as he removed it. "Better?"

David rotated his arm experimentally. "Much. Thank you."

Seth patted his shoulder, then strode down the table to take his seat.

Roland cleared his throat. "I could have helped you with that."

David shook his head. "You're still healing from the wounds you incurred while hunting vampires, then healing Dr. Lipton."

Sarah's head snapped around. "You said you were fine."

Roland shifted. "I *am* fine . . . for the most part."

"You can't do that, Roland."

"I didn't want to worry you."

Her eyes narrowed as she stared up at him. "Am I going to have to start strip searching you to check for wounds every night, or will you tell me the truth from now on?"

"I would prefer the first option."

Chuckles rounded the table.

Sarah punched Roland hard in the shoulder.

"Ow! That hurts a lot more now that you're immortal, you know."

Her lips twitched. "I know."

Seth took his seat. "All right. Let's get this over with. Darnell told me you're pissed about something, Chris. I assume whatever it is involves Bastien. But before we get to that . . ." He glanced at each of the immortals present. "Any vampire recruitments yet?"

Heads shook.

Bastien leaned forward. "I may have succeeded in recruiting one. I was supposed to have met him tonight, but forgot when Dr. Lipton was injured. I'll see if he shows tomorrow."

"Good work. Make sure Richart accompanies you in case the vamps plan another ambush." He held up a hand when Chris opened his mouth. "Dr. Lipton, I'm sorry you were injured tonight. I trust your presence here means you are well now?"

"Yes. Roland healed me." She met Roland's gaze. "Thank you."

He gave a short nod. "You're welcome."

Sarah smiled and leaned into him.

"You weren't bitten, were you?" Seth went on.

"No. One of Emrys's men shot me."

"Three times," Bastien added, voice tight. "And there were two shooters. They waited until they saw us destroy the vamps we were hunting, then zeroed in on Melanie in the aftermath."

Yuri and Stanislov swore.

Richart leaned forward. "There were thirty-six total concealed on the campus. On the rooftops. In alcoves. Behind bushes. We were there for some time before the vamps arrived, and the soldiers did nothing to give away their presence."

Yuri grunted. "They were armed with the drug?"

"Yes."

"How many were you able to capture?"

Richart glanced at Bastien. "None."

Here it comes, Melanie thought.

Chris leaned back in his chair and crossed his arms over his chest. "Bastien killed them all."

"Where were you?" Yuri asked Richart. "I thought the two of you hunted together. Did you aid him?"

Richart shook his head. "Dr. Lipton's wounds were fatal. I teleported her here to see if David was present, then to the network so the doctors could work on her until I could locate Roland."

"Roland," Seth said, "Take Richart to your home first thing tomorrow night. I won't have someone dying because he doesn't know where you live."

Roland gave an abrupt nod.

Stanlislov eyed Bastien. "So while Richart took Dr. Lipton to safety, you killed all of the soldiers?"

"All of them," Bastien confirmed. "When they shot Dr. Lipton, they weren't shooting to wound. They were shooting to kill. Any of them who saw us fight the vampires knew she was neither immortal nor vampire, but they shot to kill anyway. The bastards deserved to die."

Looks were exchanged all around.

Étienne cleared his throat. "I have no problem with that."

"Nor I," Lisette added.

"Nor I," Richart said.

"Seriously?" Chris demanded. "We needed the intel those men could have provided. Marcus, you more than anyone ought to understand how important it is that we find and destroy Emrys. Any one of those men could have helped us accomplish that."

Marcus's brow furrowed. "I understand your anger, Bastien. But there are others you should have taken into consideration. Emrys will do anything to get his hands on Ami. And tonight we had a real opportunity to obtain the information we need to locate him and end this once and for all."

Bastien swore. "You're right. I fucked up. I'm sorry, Ami."

"It's okay, Sebastien."

"No, it isn't," Marcus countered.

"He's right," Bastien agreed. "I wasn't thinking."

"You *never* think," Chris accused.

When no one came to Bastien's defense, Melanie said, "He was thinking when he devised the plan to enlist vampires' aid in defeating Emrys. He was thinking when he came damned close to recruiting a vampire just hours later."

Bastien squeezed her arm under the table. A warning not to speak up for him? Well, screw that.

Chris raised his eyebrows. "We don't even know if that vampire is trustworthy. He could arrange an ambush. Or run scared. Or offer to help and prove no aid at all because he's too deranged. Those soldiers, on the other hand, we *know* could have helped us. They have to report to *some* commanding officer. Any one of the telepaths here could have withdrawn that information from their minds and we would have known the location of Emrys's outfit and possibly Emrys himself."

"And any one of those soldiers could have drugged Bastien while he was disabling and restraining the one or two or ten men that would have satisfied you," Melanie again defended Bastien, who squeezed the hell out of her hand. "We had no idea they were there until they shot me."

"If he had time to kill them, he had time to knock them out," Chris maintained.

"I agree," Marcus said.

Seth turned to Bastien. "He has a point. Next time maim and disarm them. Don't kill them."

Bastien nodded, face grim.

Melanie felt guilty because he wouldn't be in this position if she hadn't been shot. And he looked as if he were mentally kicking himself in the ass.

"I think Bastien should be removed from duty," Chris announced. "I don't think he should be allowed to hunt anymore. And I want him banned from network premises forthwith."

The pronouncement spawned many looks of surprise, but no protests.

Melanie's temper roused. "You can't do that. Cliff and Joe need him."

"He should have thought of that before he plowed through my men again."

Seth groaned. "Damn it, Sebastien. What did you do this time?"

"They wouldn't let me see Dr. Lipton," Bastien bit out. "And if Richart hadn't come to my defense, Chris would have had me chained up in the holding room as soon as we arrived at the network."

Melanie gaped at Chris. "You tried to chain him up again?"

"Yes," he said unrepentantly.

"For what?"

"He killed all of those human soldiers in a fit of rage. I wasn't going to take the chance that he would harm my men."

Stanislov looked around. "I don't see how one action would necessarily follow the other."

Richart nodded. "I objected. I thought Chris overreacted."

Melanie looked around the table. "Okay. Maybe everyone else here already knows the answer to this or maybe they're just too polite to ask. Or maybe they just don't give a damn. But I have to know . . ." She returned her gaze to Chris. "Why do you have such a bug up your butt about Sebastien?"

A few of the immortals—namely the French immortals—coughed to cover laughs.

Bastien's head jerked around. "Melanie—"

"No. I want to know."

Chris's brows drew down. "Melanie?" he repeated, catching Bastien's more casual address.

"Well?" she persisted. "Why do you dislike him so much? I understand why Roland, Sarah, and Marcus do. Bastien tried to kill them. And I know why *they* do." She motioned to the other immortals present. "They're pissed because he killed their friend Ewen." She paused. "And, by the way, while you're busy hating and condemning him for that, you might ask yourselves why David and Seth aren't. They're the wisest men in this room and neither one of them seem to have a problem with Bastien."

Seth held up a finger.

"Except for his mouth," she amended.

Seth smiled and dropped his hand. "Thank you."

"I mean, did it ever occur to any of you that there might be a reason for that? That maybe Bastien killed Ewen in self-defense? That maybe Ewen mistook Bastien for a vampire and attacked him, leaving him no choice but to fight to the death?"

"How did you know that?" Bastien demanded and looked at Seth. "Did you tell her that? I told you to stay out of my head."

"I didn't tell her."

Again Bastien asked Melanie, "How did you know that?"

She shrugged. "What other reason would you have to kill him?"

"Because Bastien's a prick?" Roland suggested.

Melanie rolled her eyes. "You're biased."

"And you aren't?" he posed.

Étienne's eyes widened. *"Merde.* It's true. Ewen attacked him."

Marcus straightened. "Bastien must have given him reason."

"He was draining a woman," Lisette said.

"Stay out of my head," Bastien growled at the French siblings.

"Then Ewen was in the right," Marcus proclaimed.

Chris nodded. "He can't be trusted."

"Bullshit!" Tanner blurted. "Bastien doesn't kill anyone who doesn't deserve it."

"His vampire followers did," Chris said.

"Vince, Cliff, and Joe didn't," Melanie denied.

Tanner nodded. "And Bastien had no way of knowing about the ones who did."

"If he couldn't control them, he should have killed them."

"You're just pissed because he managed to get past you and all of your men and kidnap Sarah, taking her right out from under your noses."

Heavy silence took the room.

Really? Was that it? Was that the bug, so to speak?

Melanie studied Chris's reddening face and decided, yes, that was definitely the bug.

"Actually," Bastien said slowly, "he's pissed because, while I stole Sarah right out from under his nose, I broke that nose and shattered several bones in his face, knocking him unconscious before he could get off a single shot or give a shout out to warn the rest of his men."

Ooh. That was . . . That was not good.

Chris's face turned positively purple.

Sarah cleared her throat. "If it helps, I didn't see Bastien coming either."

Darnell grinned. "Yeah, but you managed to shoot him twice and stab him in the ass."

Laughter erupted.

Seth held his hands up. "All right. All right. Settle down. We're all glad Sarah stabbed Bastien in the ass."

More chuckles.

"Chris," Seth commanded, "you're just going to have to get over Bastien hitting you in the face, because it's interfering in your work. Follow Sarah's example and move on. As for the network . . . tell your men to give Bastien some space and he'll stop kicking their asses. I want Cliff and Joe to continue to have access to him. They're doing us a favor and pretty much voluntarily incarcerated themselves to do it. They need the break and whatever happiness and contentment he can bring them."

Though that didn't go over well, Chris made no objections. It was Seth. How could one oppose his edicts?

Seth turned to Bastien. "Bastien, I need you to do your part as well. Stop antagonizing everyone and show a little more patience if you run into interference at the network. Instead of injuring the men who work there and who help us, pick up your phone and give me or David a call. If you can't reach us, call Richart. He wisely teleported you out of there tonight before the situation could escalate. If necessary, he can do so again."

Bastien nodded.

"David, have you anything to add?"

David said nothing for a moment, his handsome ebony face thoughtful. Melanie had never encountered anyone with such dark skin before. It was beautiful. As flawless as a supermodel's. Yet somehow remained masculine.

"Everyone here must be mindful of the situation that brought us here tonight," he said in his deep, honeyed voice. "Though Richart, Bastien, and Dr. Lipton were at UNC for quite some time, they were unaware of the soldiers' presence until those soldiers made their presence known. I wonder, Chris, if the network might provide the immortals and their Seconds with some kind of thermal imaging binoculars or scopes that would allow them to see the heat signatures of soldiers who may otherwise escape their notice upon initial inspection."

Chris reached into his jacket and drew out one of his ever-present notebooks and a short, stubby pencil. "Done."

Melanie had seen him scribbling in similar notebooks so often she wondered if he didn't have a roomful of them somewhere.

As Chris made notes on the memo pad, he raised his eyes and met Bastien's. "Would that have helped you tonight?"

Melanie held her breath.

Chris could have asked Richart instead and avoided conversing with his *nemesis*. Was this a sort of peace offering?

"Before tonight I wouldn't have thought such necessary," Bastien replied slowly, "but, yes. Thermal imaging would have revealed at least a few of them. Those who were concealed by shadows and foliage even *our* eyes couldn't penetrate."

Richart nodded. "When I returned to UNC, I was surprised to see just how many had escaped our attention."

"Good." Chris made a few more notes. "Something else to have in our arsenal then. I'll have them in the hands of every immortal and every Second in North Carolina, South Carolina, Virginia, and West Virginia by nightfall tomorrow. We don't know how much territory these guys are covering."

Maybe this *was* a truce. That would be such a relief.

Melanie patted Bastien's knee under the table.

Bastien caught her hand and held it against his thigh.

"Stay alert," Seth commanded. "This is the second time they've managed to surprise us. Let us ensure it doesn't happen again."

Chapter 10

As the meeting concluded, Bastien released Melanie's hand and rose.

Beside them, Richart vanished as Melanie scooted her chair back and stood.

Tanner circled the table. "Do you want me to accompany you tomorrow night when you meet with the vamp?"

"No. I'd rather you stay here." Where it was safe. And where he could rub elbows with David and Darnell. Those two could befriend a badger. If *they* liked Tanner, they would do their damnedest to ensure everyone else did, too.

Just look how they were constantly pushing Bastien on the others.

"Only if you call me before and after your meeting."

"Of course."

Tanner clapped him on the shoulder, then headed into the kitchen.

As the other attendees left the table and milled around, some dropping onto the living room sofas and others venturing downstairs, Sheldon sidled up to Bastien. "So." He cleared his throat and looked around furtively. "I thought I'd hang around here today. See what's doin'."

Bastien glanced at Melanie, who shrugged. "And you're telling me this . . . why?"

He dropped his voice to a whisper. "Richart's going to spend the day with you-know-who, so I thought you might like to have the house to yourselves." Dangling a set of keys in front of Bastien, Sheldon looked from Melanie to Bastien and waggled his eyebrows.

Bastien took the keys. "You do realize everyone in this house just heard you."

Oops written all over his face, Sheldon turned around and jumped when he saw everyone staring at him.

Lisette raised one eyebrow.

"What I meant to say was . . . Richart needs his car back. Gas it up before you drop it off."

Bastien sighed. "Smooth. Don't worry, everyone, I'm just going to give Dr. Lipton a ride back to the network."

All returned to their conversations.

Melanie waved good-bye and followed him out to the car.

Bastien opened the passenger's door for her, waited for her to get settled, then closed it and strode around to the driver's side. Neither spoke as he started the engine and left David's estate behind them.

Minutes passed.

Melanie leaned closer and glanced at the instrument panel, then shifted back to her side.

A few minutes later, she did the same.

"Checking my speed?" he asked, wondering what drew her interest.

She shook her head. "Watching the odometer. We're about six miles away from David's, right?"

"Yes."

"Good. Now we can talk without any of them hearing us. Are you really taking me to the network?"

He had intended to but . . . "Do you *want* me to take you to the network?"

"No." Short. Simple. Sweet.

And just what he wanted to hear. "Do you want me to take you home?"

"I don't know. Sheldon did go to all the trouble of coming up with that *grrreat* cover story so we could have Richart's house to ourselves."

Bastien smiled. "Sorry about that. Sheldon has shown me the benefits of thinking before one speaks."

She laughed. "And yet I like him."

"Yeah. I can see why Richart hasn't killed him yet."

"If you'd like, we could go to my place. I should warn you, though, that I'm not the tidiest person in the world. At the office? Yes. At home? No."

We. Bastien's attention zoomed in on the word. "I think I'll head to Richart's house, if that's okay with you. After the night we've had, I'd prefer the added security it offers."

"True. Richart's it is."

Melanie was a little surprised when Bastien capitulated so easily. She had expected him to embark upon yet another verbal dissertation on the many hazards of dating him.

Her eyes narrowed. He didn't intend for them to go their separate ways at Richart's, did he?

She wouldn't put it past him. He seemed determined not to cast a pall over her with his presence. She didn't think he had even realized that some of the immortals—definitely Richart, possibly his siblings—were starting to soften toward him.

At least, she thought they were.

The ride to Richart's home was a comfortable one. Instead of worrying about what would or wouldn't happen once they reached it, Melanie asked Bastien what exactly had happened on the night he had kidnapped Sarah and ended up laughing herself silly when he told the tale.

She was sure it hadn't been funny at the time, but Sarah

really had done her darnedest to thwart him and escape. Bastien had been so shocked and baffled by her actions. Melanie had to applaud him for his patience. *And* for not holding a grudge. He made the whole kidnapping sound like a Three Stooges skit.

They were both still chuckling when he parked in Richart's driveway, got out, and guided her up to the front door.

Upon stepping inside, Melanie was surprised to find Richart waiting for them.

"Finally!" he said. "I forgot to give you the code for the alarm system and your phone is off."

Bastien stared at him. "You trust me with your security code?"

"No. I'll change it tomorrow. Right now, I don't care. I'm eager to get back to Jenna. So, here." He handed Bastien a sticky note. "Make yourselves at home."

As soon as the tacky paper stuck to Bastien's finger, Richart disappeared.

Bastien looked at Melanie as silence surrounded them.

Seconds later, they were in each other's arms, bodies straining against each other, lips melding in a searing kiss, sticky note sticking to who-knew-what.

Melanie rose up onto her toes, wrapped her arms around his neck and clung tightly.

Bastien ravaged her lips, his kiss fierce and demanding, his hands . . .

Anticipation seared her as he slid his hands over her back and up her sides, his fingers grazing the sides of her breasts.

He raised his head. When his eyes met hers, they glowed brighter than she had ever seen them. "Wait," he murmured, voice hoarse.

Melanie dropped back onto her heels, wanting to scream.

"No, it isn't what you're thinking."

He must have felt the twinge of disappointment and

frustration that had struck her. She had assumed he was going to try to dissuade her one last time.

"I don't want to stop. I just want to slow down a little." He shook his head. "I've been fantasizing about this for too long. I don't want to rush it. I want to savor it."

Melanie's heart raced as she nodded. "Savoring sounds good."

He smiled. Such a tender smile. His face relaxed, looking youthful and utterly irresistible.

Reaching up, she touched his stubbled cheek.

Who else ever saw him this way?

Bastien captured her lips once more. When his tongue delivered a tantalizing stroke, she parted her lips and drew him in.

Some of the urgency may have been tempered, but there was no less passion. Fire heated Melanie's blood as he drew her close, pressed every inch of her front to every inch of his.

Bastien's body heated as Melanie buried her hands in his hair, her fingers grazing his scalp. He wanted to go slow. He really did. But he could feel everything she felt.

When he slid one hand up to caress her breast, he felt the sharp arousal that darted through her. When he drew a circle around her tight nipple with his thumb, then pinched the sensitive peak, he felt the shock of electricity that shook her and shortened her breath. When he trailed his lips down her throat over her shirt and closed them over her nipple through the soft cotton cloth . . .

Bastien groaned. There were definite perks to his gift. And being able to feel exactly what pleased her had to be the best one.

Melanie moaned. Bastien's mouth was so warm and wet and he knew exactly how to use it to rekindle the desperate need that had claimed her earlier. Her breath shortened. Sliding her leg up the outside of his thigh beneath his coat, she hooked her knee over his hip and ground her core against the hard bulge behind his zipper.

His hand tightened on her breast. His lips sucked harder. He gripped her hip with his free hand, then cupped her ass and urged her to rock against him. "Wrap your legs around me."

Melanie didn't hesitate. Jumping up, she wrapped both legs around him.

He turned and pressed her up against the nearest wall. "Perhaps I was mistaken," he said, eyes blazing down at her as he thrust against her. "Fast and hard has its merits, too."

Melanie nodded, pleasure consuming her despite the material that separated them. "Fast and hard is good."

Their surroundings blurred. A second later, they were in the bedroom Melanie had used earlier. Bastien kicked the door closed. "Take off my coat," he ordered.

Melanie hurried to peel it off his broad shoulders.

"Now my shirt." He lowered her feet to the floor.

She was already on it, hands shaking with need as he nibbled her throat and continued to fondle and tease her breasts.

Warm, tan skin stretched taut over muscle drew her heated gaze and demanded her touch. Leaning forward, she drew her tongue across one masculine nipple.

She felt a tug, looked down and saw bare skin from her waist up. No sweater. No shirt. No bra. "How did you do that?"

"I'm immortal."

"Cool."

"If you liked that . . ."

Lifting her, he crossed to the bed and laid her atop the covers.

He blurred as Melanie felt another tug. She looked down . . . and her boots, socks, pants, belt, and panties were all gone.

She grinned. "I like this. Now do you."

Laughing, he blurred for a split second, then stood naked before her.

Melanie laughed with delight and pulled him down atop her.

Bastien captured her lips once more, consuming them as their limbs tangled and teased. Flames scorched her with every touch. Every stroke of his tongue. Every caress of his fingers as they slid down her stomach to brush her clitoris.

She gasped.

"You're already wet for me."

She nodded, head falling back.

Bastien parted her legs with a knee and settled his lower body between them. She was so beautiful. So passionate. As eager to please him as he was to please her. She slipped a hand between them and curled her delicate fingers around his heavy erection.

He hissed in a breath as she squeezed and stroked, inciting a riot within him even as he did the same to her. When she guided him to her entrance, he forced out a gravelly protest.

"I want to taste you first."

"Taste me later. I want you inside me."

He wasted no time, plunging in to the hilt, groaning at the feel of her tight, moist warmth.

She caught her breath. Moaned. Writhed beneath him as he had imagined her doing too many times to count since he had met her.

"So good," she murmured, gripping his ass and urging him on as he withdrew and thrust again and again.

Melanie gazed up at him. Bastien's hair tumbled down and caressed her already sensitive flesh as he moved against her. Those eyes . . . She couldn't look away from them as he reached between them and stroked her with his fingers in time with his thrusts.

A climax rippled through her, stealing her breath, splintering her thoughts. Bastien stiffened above her and shouted her name.

Sheer ecstasy.

As the last tingles faded, he lowered his forehead to hers.

Melanie wrapped her arms around him and hugged him close, loving the feel of his big, muscled body on hers, though he supported the bulk of his weight with his forearms.

As his breathing evened, Bastien titled his head, touched his lips to hers in a profoundly tender kiss, then drew back and smiled down at her.

He was so beautiful. So perfect.

And she loved to see him smile.

She loved to *make* him smile.

She grinned up at him.

His eyes narrowed with amusement-laced suspicion. "What are you thinking?"

"I was thinking immortal speed isn't just a plus on the battlefield. You stripped me naked in only a couple of seconds."

"I can do more than *that* in a couple of seconds."

"Really?" She couldn't imagine what.

He winked, then blurred.

A second climax drove through her, catching her totally off guard. She thought she may have even screamed with it, gripping the sheets with fists as her body convulsed over and over again.

When she opened her eyes, Bastien was grinning down at her as if he had never moved.

Melanie stared up at him in amazement. She didn't even know what he had done—it had happened so fast—but her heart raced madly and . . . she didn't think she had ever come so hard in her life.

"What the hell was that?" she panted.

He laughed. "Another benefit of being an immortal."

That was one hell of a benefit.

He left her long enough to turn the overhead light off, then hastened back to bed. Reaching down, he pulled the covers over them both and drew her close.

Quiet enfolded them as they lay in the dark. Weariness snuck up on Melanie and weighed her down. Though she was tempted to try anyway, she thought she would have been too tired to do anything other than lie there like a limp noodle if they made love again.

Almost dying was apparently exhausting . . . and continued to mess with her head in slow moments like this.

What must Bastien have thought earlier tonight when she had basically voiced a living will?

"Do you think I'm paranoid?" she asked softly.

"No." He seemed as disinclined to move as she was. She didn't think she had ever seen him so relaxed and content.

"You don't think I overreacted when I told you I want to be transformed if anything else happens to me?"

"No. I think you were being smart and practical. Shit happens in this business. Even in the hallowed halls of the network."

"Yes, but most of the shit that happens at the network is instigated by you."

He chuckled, the rare sound of it trickling through her and relaxing her like wine. "True." Another moment passed. "Times are changing though. You might consider making your wishes known to Seth and Chris. Someone at the network needs to know in case I'm not around and something foul goes down."

"Linda knows."

"Good. She seems like good people."

Melanie smiled. "She is." She was pretty damn courageous, too. Linda had been scared as hell when Vince, Cliff, and Joe had taken up residence in the network, but she had sucked it up and worked with them until she had lost that fear.

Unlike Dr. Whetsman and certain other colleagues.

Melanie guided her mind away from the job. She didn't want to think of work when she had Bastien snuggled up with her. All she wanted to think about was how good it felt to have his large, warm, muscled form pressed against hers.

Well, that and . . .

"Go ahead. Ask me," he murmured.

"Ask you what?"

"The question I imagine you've been wanting to ask ever since the meeting."

"Are you sure you aren't telepathic?"

He grunted. "I wish I were. It would take all of the guess-work out of dealing with people."

"True."

"So go ahead and ask me."

"Who was the woman?"

"The one Ewen caught me draining?"

Melanie nodded as lethargy stole upon her. She shared Tanner's belief that Bastien wouldn't kill anyone who hadn't done something seriously wrong. So what had the woman done? What had she been to him?

"She was a madam . . . of sorts. There were a lot of home-less children and poor children in what the ton would think of as the seedier parts of London. Always hungry. Working at a ridiculously young age to help put food in their mouths and on the family's table."

"I'm guessing there were no child labor laws back then."

"No. Though a few fought for them." He sighed. "Pe-dophiles are not new in our society. They were present in my youth and long before that. This particular woman catered to that sort of clientele, stealing, conning, or buying children and selling them into prostitution."

Melanie didn't understand people like that. People who seemed to have no conscience. "How did you find out about her?"

"There was a boy. He had been earning just enough to stay alive working as a chimney sweep when he stumbled upon a temporary resting place I had chosen after I stayed out too late to make it back to the apartment Blaise and I used to share. Blaise was dead then, recently destroyed by Roland and I was . . . lost. First my sister. Then my best friend. I had had to give up the rest of my family when I was transformed. So I had no one."

Melanie gave him a squeeze.

"Anyway, this boy stumbled upon my hiding place and . . . He looked so damned skinny and hungry. And he was such a proud boy. I offered him a job, gave him some busy work so he wouldn't think he was a charity case. You might say he was my first Second." He shrugged. "I really just wanted to give him a warm place to stay, three squares a day. And his chatter filled the silence." He sighed. "I don't know. There might have been a little 'I could have had a son like him if I hadn't been turned' mixed in there, too. It doesn't really matter because he didn't come home one day. And by the time I found him he was dead."

"The woman . . . ?"

"Mistook him for fair game and sold him to the man who killed him."

"So you . . ."

"Killed them both . . . and everyone associated with the woman. Her employees. Her other customers. I saved her for last. Unfortunately, Ewen came along just as I finished draining her."

"He must not have been a telepath or he would have seen the reason you killed her."

"I don't know what his gift was. I only know he didn't give me a chance to explain and nearly destroyed me before I finally managed to destroy *him*. I didn't have a ready supply of blood then, so it took me three days to recover."

"You should tell the others."

"Do you really think knowing their friend died because he made an error in judgment will make his loss less painful or me more popular?"

"I suppose not." She yawned.

Bastien brushed his hand over her hair. "It's been a long night. See if you can't get some rest."

Melanie gave him a quick kiss and closed her eyes.

If he said anything else, she didn't hear it. Sleep claimed her too quickly.

As Chris promised, a network employee delivered two thermal vision scopes—one for Bastien and one for Richart—and one pair of thermal vision goggles for Sheldon just before dusk.

Bastien liked the scope. So did Richart when he teleported home soon after. It fit in their pockets, and they could take it out and peer through it without altering the vision in both eyes. Call him old-fashioned, but he didn't want to completely abandon his super-sharp immortal vision in favor of high-tech whatever.

Bastien took Melanie home once the sun set. She had a small place out in the country that reminded him of the tiny frame house Sarah had been renting when Roland had met her.

He suspected she was as obsessively neat as the immortals because the clutter he found there was minute at best. Mail scattered on the coffee table. A couple of dishes soaking in the kitchen sink. A jacket tossed on a chair.

Unable to resist, Bastien followed her into the bathroom and made love with her in the shower. It was so good it terrified him. With every touch, every look, every minute they spent together, he could feel the bond between them strengthening.

While she dressed for work, he meandered around and snooped freely. There were only two framed photographs in her small home. The couple pictured in them, their arms around each other in one and looped around Melanie in the other, must have been her parents. They looked happy in a way Bastien's aristocratic parents never had.

Melanie's furniture was mismatched. Some, he thought,

had probably belonged to her parents. Some were purchases of her own. The atmosphere was warm. Homey. Welcoming. He wanted to sprawl on her beat-up couch, prop his feet on the coffee table, and just soak it and her in.

But duty called them both. So he took her to the network, left her with a kiss, and met Richart at UNC.

"You're doing it again."

"What?" Bastien looked over at Richart as the Frenchman held his thermal scope up to his right eye and scanned UNC's campus for the fiftieth time from their position on the roof of Davis Library. "I'm doing what?"

"Mooning."

Bastien snorted. "Last time I checked, my ass was still in my pants."

"Not the drop your drawers and bend over mooning. The sighing as you fantasize about Melanie mooning."

"Bollocks."

"You're infatuated with her. At the very least."

Bastien thought about denying it, but . . . "Can you blame me?"

"No. But your distraction with her last night may have contributed to your not noticing the soldiers earlier."

"So what was your excuse?"

He sighed. "I was distracted by Jenna." He gave Bastien a rueful smile. "We're a pair, are we not? Two hundred years old and behaving like we're each caught up in a first crush."

Bastien shrugged. "For me it sort of is. I've never felt like this before."

Richart stared at him. "Never?"

"No time, really. When I wasn't fighting other vampires who had succumbed entirely to the madness and avoiding fights with you immortals, I was hunting Roland."

"I didn't realize you fought vampires when you lived among them."

"Hard to avoid. Sometimes they did the craziest shit. And

I don't mean crazy wild. I mean crazy demented. I knew some of them weren't right. It just took me awhile to realize that they *all* eventually weren't right."

Richart grunted and looked at his watch. "Time to meet Stuart."

"Already?" Maybe he *had* been mooning. He hadn't noticed the passage of time. Bastien took out his cell phone and dialed as promised.

"Yeah?" Tanner answered.

"We're heading over to meet Stuart."

"Okay. Let me know if you need me."

"Will do."

Ending the call, he dialed again.

"Hello?"

Lowering his voice to a sleazy, rusty whisper, he said, "What are you wearing?"

Melanie's laughter danced over the line. "Chuck Taylors and nothing else."

Bastien smiled. "I wish."

Beside him Richart chuckled.

"Are you heading over to meet Stuart now?" she asked.

"Yes."

"Be careful."

"I will."

"And call me afterward to let me know you're okay."

"I will."

Richart gave the campus one last thermal once-over as Bastien put away his phone. "How does it feel to have people worrying about you?"

"Strange."

"But good, right?"

Bastien nodded.

Richart put away the scope. "All right. Let's do this."

Bastien kept his eyes open while Richart teleported them

to the site of his old lair, ready to fight if Stuart had betrayed them.

What he saw the instant they materialized filled him with rage.

Stuart had returned. And he had not returned alone.

While Stuart stood off to one side, looking as somber and itchy as a drug addict in need of a fix, nine vampires staggered around the center of the clearing.

Raucous laughter silenced wildlife. The scents of alcohol, stale sweat, and urine befouled the air. The dumbasses were talking loud and saying nothing, acting drunk even though the liquor they swilled had no effect on them, courtesy of the virus. Bastien's gaze flashed amber as it narrowed on the loudest, who laughed and turned in a half circle as he whizzed on what remained of Bastien's property.

On some level, Bastien knew this was no longer his home. Though he still owned the land, this chapter in his life had ended.

But damned if that kid pissing on the winter brown landscape with such glee didn't feel downright disrespectful.

Stuart's eyes widened when he sighted Bastien and Richart. Wrapping his arms around his middle, he hunched into his jacket and edged farther away from the others. Anxiety pinched his features. And Bastien got the distinct impression the boy wanted to say something.

The whizzer, dick still in hand, turned and saw them. "Hey," he called the others' attention to them. "Where the fuck did you guys come from?"

Bastien ground his teeth together and offered him a smile. It was not a nice one. "I would say your mother's bed, but . . . I've seen your mother."

Richart turned slowly to look at him and raised his eyebrows.

Bastien didn't care. The little prick was pissing on what used to be his home.

A moment of silence passed, then the other eight men burst into guffaws.

"Ooh! Burn!"

"He thinks your mom's too ugly to fuck!"

The whizzer's eyes flashed a dazzling greenish blue.

Bastien nodded to him. "If you're wise, you'll put your wee willy away now."

"Why? Is it turning you on? You want to suck it?" the whizzer asked snidely and gave his friends an ain't-I-clever grin.

"Perhaps I wasn't clear. If you want to *keep* your wee willy, you will put it away."

Something in his voice or appearance must have registered on some lone firing neuron, because the asswipe tucked himself away and zipped up. "What's it to you anyway?" he asked. "Who the fuck are you?"

"Yeah," another added. "And what's with all the black? What are you guys—Immortal Guardian wannabes or something?"

Richart never cracked a smile. "Or something."

Bastien cocked his head to one side. "As for who I am: I'm the man upon whose property you are currently trespassing."

"Bullshit. That would mean you're Bastien."

Which meant the little prick had known whose territory he had just desecrated. "Give the man a cigar."

The whizzer exchanged glances with his buddies.

"So . . . what? He's Roland?" one asked, peering at Richart

"I thought Bastien and Roland ran around with some human bitch," another said.

Richart looked askance at Bastien. "You know, I'm beginning to feel a bit testy that you and Roland are so revered amongst the vampire population, yet my name remains unknown."

Bastien glared at the whizzer. "If they don't know your name, they can't piss on your lawn."

"Good point."

"Wait," yet another vamp said. "You really *are* Bastien? For real?"

The whizzer's incandescent eyes narrowed. "You're Bastien the Betrayer?"

"My, aren't you quick?"

As one, the other men's eyes flashed.

"Kick his fucking ass!" the whizzer shouted.

Their forms blurred.

Bastien drew his katanas.

Richart vanished, then reappeared in front of the rushing vampires, swords extended to either side.

Two heads leapt from the bodies that carried them. As they tumbled to the cold ground, Richart spun and stabbed two more vamps through the heart.

The remaining vampires reached Bastien en masse.

Bastien focused on the whizzer, disarming him while deftly fending off the others' clumsy attack.

These vamps, like those last night, lacked the training he had attempted to instill in his own vampire followers and boasted none of the training the vampire king had driven home in his. There was a lot of exuberance and power, but no control or direction. One even overextended himself and stabbed one of his cohorts.

The bumbling buffoons didn't appear to have ever fought together as a unit. That was somewhat comforting as it meant the vamps they were dealing with now were just random roving bands rather than a new army gathering.

These were also members of the digital generation and had no notion of what real battle was like, carrying what Bastien liked to think of as vanity weapons that they thought were cool but proved utterly useless when fighting immortals. Bowies with elaborately carved handles and animals painted on the damned blades. Shiny butcher knives that looked like they would be more at home on a cooking show or in a horror movie. A flashy hunting knife with a ridiculous blade shaped like a dragon of all things. And one weapon that Bastien could've sworn was a fillet knife.

What did they do, buy all of their blades on one of those cable shopping networks?

While Bastien opened the whizzer's veins, a couple of the vamps belatedly noticed their two headless companions and the pair Richart was carving up. Halting their attack, they gaped at Richart.

As his opponents gasped out final breaths, Richart smiled a Grim Reaper kind of smile and vanished.

The vampires near Bastien looked around frantically.

Using the distraction to his advantage, Bastien took out the two fighting him with ease. Both were slavering like rabid dogs, so focused on their desire to kill and bite and tear that they didn't even seem to register what was happening around them. Both were clearly too far gone to be helped or recruited.

Their bodies sank to the ground and began to shrivel up.

Bastien sheathed one of his swords and grabbed the arm of the distracted vamp closest to him as Richart appeared beside the other. The vampire's emotions infiltrated Bastien like acid. Fear. Violence. Rage. Hatred. No remorse. No grief for his friends. Nothing remotely positive.

When the vamp belatedly swung his butcher knife, Bastien knocked it aside and cut the vamp's carotid and femoral arteries. The vampire stumbled backward, tripped over one of the bodies, and fell.

The last vamp standing leapt away from Richart and swung bowies at Bastien.

Bastien deflected several blows, grew bored, and struck in earnest. The blade in one of the vamp's hands broke. Bastien hit the other with such force that the vamp yelped, dropped the blade, and gripped his hand with a grimace of pain. Bastien grabbed him by the shoulder. Emotions flooded him, so sick and twisted he felt almost physically ill from it. Shoving the vamp away, Bastien cut his throat.

Blood spattered his face.

Bastien sighed and swiped his sleeve across it.

The vampire fruitlessly tried to stave off the inevitable, sank to his knees, and keeled over.

Bastien cleaned his blade on the guy's Dead Kennedys T-shirt, then turned to Stuart.

Stuart's eyes were almost as big as his face. Spinning around, he bolted into the trees.

Richart vanished and appeared in front of the vamp, who dropped several F-bombs as he rebounded off the immortal.

"I wasn't with them," he blurted as he rubbed his forehead and turned to face Bastien. "I mean, they weren't with me."

Bastien strolled over to join them. "Who were they, then?"

Richart removed a handkerchief from an inner pocket of his coat and began to wipe the blood from his blades.

"I don't know," Stuart said, his expression frantic. "You weren't here last night—"

"Something came up."

"Or someone," Richart muttered.

Bastien nodded. "We had to take care of some of those human mercenaries we told you about."

Stuart looked back and forth between them. "At Duke?"

"No. UNC. Why?" Stuart wasn't already in cahoots with Emrys, was he?

"There were some humans at Duke last night. They looked like SWAT or military or some shit. They were dressed in dark fatigues and were armed out the ass."

Bastien looked at Richart. "You *saw* them or you heard a rumor?"

"I saw them. I was there with this guy I hang out with. Another vampire. We fed on—"

Richart scowled.

"I mean we, ah . . ."

"Just go on," Bastien instructed.

"We fed on these two guys who were geêking out over some phone app on their way to the parking lot, but we didn't kill them. I swear."

"Just tell us about the men you saw."

"We propped the dweebs against their car and were leaving when all of a sudden Paul jerked a couple of times and stopped walking. Someone fucking shot him, man. And they must have hit an artery or something because blood started gushing from his chest. Then his eyes rolled around in his head and he just sort of collapsed, like his legs stopped working, and I saw a dart sticking out of his neck. Guys in dark fatigues rushed out from behind the closest building and . . ." He shook his head. "I took off running."

"You left . . . Paul, was it?"

"Paul was already starting to shrivel up. I didn't stick around to see if it was the bullets or the dart that killed him. I was scared."

At least the mercenaries hadn't been able to take one alive. By the time the virus had finished fighting for survival, there wouldn't have been anything left of the body that had formerly housed it to study. "So you got away?"

"Yeah, but not before the fuckers hit me with one of those darts." Reaching into his pocket, he drew out a dart that looked identical to the ones that had incapacitated Bastien a couple of nights earlier.

Richart took a step forward. "If you were hit with this dart, how did you get away?"

Stuart shook his head. "I don't know."

Bastien gripped the boy's arm.

"Dude. What are you—?"

"Just tell us how you got away."

"I don't know," he insisted, eyes straying to the swords Richart had not yet sheathed. "It must not have knocked me out instantly. Maybe because I wasn't bleeding out like Paul was. Or maybe I was at full speed when it hit me and just managed to get far enough away before I passed out that they couldn't find me, 'cause the last thing I remember is haulin' ass to get out of there. Then I woke up at sunset in a damn garden shed in someone's backyard not far from campus."

Bastien met Richart's doubtful gaze. "According to my gift, he's telling the truth. He doesn't remember."

"What gift?" Stuart asked.

"I can feel your emotions," Bastien said.

Stuart swallowed and pulled away. "Really?"

"Yes." He looked at Richart. "He seems to be telling the truth."

Richart's brow remained furrowed as he motioned to the decomposing corpses. "So, who were those vamps?"

"I don't know. They just showed up while I was waiting to see if Bastien would come tonight. I didn't want to stick around—I could tell those guys were real manic motherfuckers—but . . . I don't want to end up like that. Paul and I don't . . . didn't kill the people we fed on. Those guys—the ones you destroyed— did. And liked it. They were bragging about the chicks they fucked up earlier before you arrived. That and talking some crap about kicking your ass for betraying all vampires."

Richart put away his swords. "So you've decided to take Bastien up on his offer? You're willing to join forces with the Immortal Guardians?"

"You guys aren't gonna kill me, are you?"

"No," Bastien promised. He didn't add, *not unless you give us reason to*.

"Then . . . yeah. Those guys last night . . . I-I think they would've done what you said they would if they caught me. I think they would have tortured me. I think they would have used me as a lab rat. You . . . you guys aren't gonna do that, right?"

"No," Bastien said. "The vampires who have already joined us periodically donate blood and undergo CT scans and other routine medical tests because they want to help our doctors and scientists find a cure for the virus or a way to treat it. We would appreciate it if you would do the same, but we won't require it."

Stuart nodded, a nervous, jerky movement. "Yeah. Sure. I can . . . I can donate blood and stuff. I did that once when my ex's sorority sponsored a blood drive."

"Excellent. Then we have an accord." Bastien offered him his hand.

Stuart hesitated only a moment, then grasped it. Richart shook his hand next while Bastien retrieved his phone and dialed.

"Melanie?"

"Hi. How'd it go? Are you okay?"

His pulse jumped. Yeah. He was falling in love with her. And Richart knew it, damn it, because the other immortal could hear Bastien's heart racing. "It went well. We're bringing in a recruit. Stuart agreed to join us."

"Great! I'll tell Mr. Reordon."

"Where should Richart bring him?"

Stuart took a step forward. "You're coming, too, right?"

"Richart will come back for me."

"No. I don't want to go unless you go, too."

Bastien looked to Richart. "Can you take us both?"

Richart eyed the jittery vamp and must have drawn the same conclusion Bastien had. "Yes."

"Richart is going to bring us both."

"Okay. Why not bring him to my office. He might be more comfortable if it's just us at first."

"Thank you. We'll do that."

"Okay. See you soon. And, Stuart, I know you're listening, so . . . I just wanted to say I'm looking forward to seeing you again."

Stuart looked flabbergasted. "Um. Okay. Thanks."

"Bye, Bastien."

Bastien ended the call.

Stuart shifted his weight from one foot to the other. "Was that the chick I fought the other night?"

"Yes."

"Wow. She seems really nice."

"She is," Bastien confirmed.

Richart swore. "I just remembered Lisette is patrolling Duke tonight."

"Who's Lisette?" Stuart asked.

"His sister," Bastien explained, then told Richart, "You should warn her."

Richart nodded, already dialing his cell. More epithets. "Straight to voice mail. I'm going to pop over there and make sure she's all right."

"No problem. Come back for me if you need me."

Richart vanished.

Stuart gaped. "Dude, that is *awesome*! Are y'all gonna teach me how to do that?"

Bastien shook his head. "That particular skill is one with which you must be born, I'm afraid."

"That bites."

"Yes, it does."

Chapter 11

Melanie had feared relations between her and Chris would be strained after she embarrassed him at the meeting, but he behaved the same way he always had: all business, but cordial.

As soon as Bastien hung up, she called Chris to warn him their first new vampire recruit was on his way. Activity exploded on Sublevel 5. Dr. Whetsman ducked into the stairwell and skedaddled upstairs, the wuss. Additional guards disembarked from the elevator.

Standing in the doorway of her office, Melanie watched Chris consult Todd beside the desk positioned near the elevator doors.

Linda stepped into the doorway of the lab next door. "I kinda feel sorry for the vampire. All these guys and guns . . . Hell, they're even making *me* a little nervous. Can you imagine how *he's* going to feel?"

"Hmm. You have a point." Melanie dodged elbows and weapons and big, masculine bodies as she headed up the hallway toward her boss. "Mr. Reordon?"

He turned around. "Yes?"

"Bastien couldn't say anything in front of the vampire, but I got the impression the guy's pretty nervous. I think seeing this"—she motioned to the hard-looking guards armed with automatic weapons that clogged the hallway—"might freak him out."

Chris took in the foreboding men around them. "Where did Bastien say Richart was going to teleport him in?"

"I suggested my office. I thought it would be more welcoming than the lab."

He nodded. "I won't take the men off the floor, but I'll keep most of them out of sight. What's the plan?"

That was a relief. "I thought I would just introduce myself, let him get acclimated a bit, then show him to Vincent's apartment."

Chris had had it refurbished after Vince had been destroyed. Melanie wasn't sure why. At the time, the chances of finding another vampire willing to live there had seemed astronomically low.

"I'll spread the men out on the floor, take the OR, the break room, Linda's office, the labs, and the stairwell and only leave a few visible in the hallway."

"Sounds good. I'll let you know when Stuart is settled."

"Stuart?"

"That's the new recruit's name."

He nodded and turned back to Todd.

As she walked back to her office, a sheet of paper slipped from beneath Cliff's door and slid across the hallway.

Melanie picked it up, turned it over, and read Cliff's neat handwriting:

You need to sedate Joe. He's ranting again. And if the new vampire hears some of the things Joe is saying, I guarantee you he'll try to bolt.

"What is it?" Linda asked, joining her and peering curiously at the note.

Melanie showed it to her.

Linda patted her shoulder. "I'll take care of it."

"Thanks."

The rest of the conversation was spoken with the sign language both women had learned when they had realized the vampires could hear *everything*, all the way up to the ground floor.

Give him the low dose, enough to calm him, but not enough to knock him out, Melanie signed.

Okay.

Melanie understood the relief on Linda's face. Both women preferred administering the lower dose to knocking the vampires out with a full one. The latter left the vamps fuzzy-headed when they awoke.

Be careful, Melanie added. *If he's headed for another break, he may not understand. Have a couple of the guards handy . . . just in case.*

I will.

Melanie ducked between two guards.

"Hi, Doc."

"Hey, Doc."

She waved and darted back into her office, closing the door behind her. Richart could teleport them in at any minute and she didn't want the new vamp to see the growing army in the hallway. He would hear their heartbeats once he arrived. That was unavoidable. But with any luck, he would think at least some of those were the heartbeats of regular employees like herself.

Minutes passed. Sublevel 5 quieted.

Biting her lip, Melanie consulted her watch. What was taking so long? Had Bastien anticipated Chris's actions and decided to give them a little more time to prepare?

Rustling sounded behind her.

Melanie spun around, startled by the three males who stood there despite having expected them. "I see why Seth calls ahead to warn Sarah."

"Sorry it took so long," Bastien said.

She noted the damp patches on his and Richart's clothing,

the red speckles and streaks on their faces. "Did something happen?"

The vampire sandwiched between them bore no stains on his clothing, so their fight must have been with someone else.

"There were other vamps at the rendezvous site," Richart explained.

Bastien nodded, brows drawn down into a V. "Pissing on my property," he grumbled.

Ooh. Very unwise. She glanced at Stuart, wondering why Bastien hadn't pummeled him for bringing such disrespectful companions with him.

Stuart gave his head a vigorous shake and held up both hands. "I didn't know 'em. They just happened to be there, checking out Bastien's legendary lair."

"Ah." She drew closer to Bastien and patted his arm. "I assume you kicked their asses?"

He shrugged. "The madness had progressed too far in all of them. They were beyond our help, so we destroyed them."

"And enjoyed it a little too much, I'm guessing."

He smiled. "Just with the pisser."

Melanie laughed.

Stuart's fascinated gaze skipped back and forth between them. "Dude, you're dating a human? Y'all can do that?"

Bastien's handsome face grew uneasy.

Melanie shook her head. Hopefully, in time, he would stop worrying about the detrimental effects their relationship might have on her life and career. "Yes, we're dating. And the jury is still out on whether or not it's acceptable because Bastien has a bit of a checkered past." She held her hand out with a smile. "I didn't formally introduce myself the other night. I'm Dr. Melanie Lipton. It's nice to meet you, Stuart."

* * *

Bastien knew Melanie didn't want him to put her on a pedestal, but he practically threw her up there when she smiled at Stuart and offered him her small, pale hand.

Damn, he liked her. Okay, loved her. That tingly, sappy, I-just-want-to-hold-her feeling warming him like brandy *must* be love. She was just so brave. And smart. And beautiful. Willing to put her own safety at risk to aid others. Welcoming another vampire into her territory and attempting to put him at ease.

Stuart took her hand and shook it with care. "Yes, ma'am. I'm sorry I cut you."

"Don't worry about it. Welcome to the network."

"Thank you."

"I head the viral research we're doing here and frequently work with the other vampires. There are two currently in residence—Cliff and Joe."

Welcome, Stuart, Bastien heard Cliff say. *I'm Cliff. It'll be nice to have another vampire to hang around with.*

Stuart looked toward the hallway. "You're one of the vampires?"

Yes. I know you're probably scared . . .

Melanie caught Bastien's gaze. "Is Cliff talking to him?"

"Yes."

I sure as hell was. But you can relax. Dr. Lipton is great. So are Linda and some of the others we work with. And you don't have to constantly be on your guard here, worrying about humans discovering what you are, or vampires attacking you, or wondering if you'll find a safe place to rest during the day. You made the right decision.

"How do I know you're not an immortal just saying that to get me to drop my guard?" Stuart asked, his face reflecting both suspicion and hope.

Well for one thing, immortals are powerful enough that they don't need *to coax you into letting down your guard. They*

*can overpower you and do whatever it is you think they might
do with very little effort. For another, I was one of Bastien's
followers. I surrendered the night of the final battle with the
immortals at his lair and have been living here ever since. But
you'll learn all of this and more eventually.*

"What about the other one? Where is he?"

Bastien caught Melanie's gaze. "Where's Joe?"

She bit her lip and looked uneasy. "I think he's resting."

Had she had to sedate Joe? Had he had a break? Or had she
worried what Joe might say to Stuart?

I'm here, Joe said, voice low and emotionless. He had
definitely been drugged. *The virus is fucking with my head
today. Listen to Cliff. He isn't as far gone as I am. I think . . .
I think I'm not seeing things clearly right now. Cliff is.*

Stuart sobered. He turned to Melanie. "Can you help us?"

"I hope so, Stuart. That's why I'm glad you're here. The
more I learn and the more insight you and other vampires can
provide me with, the closer we'll get to finding a method of
preventing the madness."

Stuart nodded. "What can I do?"

"For now? If you aren't averse to it, I'd like to take a small
sample of your blood, then we can get you settled in your new
apartment."

Stuart looked at Bastien. "It's . . . it's really an apartment?
It's not a cell?"

This isn't a prison, Stuart. We live well here, Cliff said. *We
each have our own apartment with whatever furnishings and
electronic gadgets we want, though our phone and Internet
activity is monitored for safety's sake.*

Bastien smiled and nodded as Stuart's eyes widened.

"So . . . I get my own place?"

Melanie smiled. "Yes. We want you to be comfortable and,
more important, happy here."

Stuart looked stunned. "I've never had my own apartment
before. Or my own room. I always had to share . . . with my

brothers or with a dorm mate. *Man*, I had some sucky dorm mates."

Melanie laughed. "Well, let's hurry and do your blood work so you can get settled."

Stuart gave her an enthusiastic nod.

Bastien touched her arm as she started to turn away. "We should get back to hunting. Stuart said something went down at Duke last night, so every immortal needs to be out there trying to find Emrys and his men before they find more vampires."

Her brow creased with worry as she tilted her head back to meet his gaze. "Okay. Be careful."

"I will." He started to move away.

She held on to his arm and tapped her lips with her index finger. "Kiss?"

Bastien might be mistaken, but he was pretty sure the heat stealing up his neck as he looked at the others was a blush.

Stuart snickered. Richart grinned and crossed his arms over his chest.

Full of aw-shucks, Bastien bent and pressed his lips to Melanie's. Drawing back, he decided she tasted too good not to go back for seconds and proceeded to kiss the stuffing out of her.

"Okay, sport." Richart grasped the neck of Bastien's coat and gave it a yank, forcing them apart. "You can come back for more later." He smiled at Melanie, whose eyes were bright and cheeks were flushed. "Always a pleasure."

Then Bastien and Richart were being buffeted by a strong wintery wind atop Perkins Library at Duke University.

Richart may as well have dumped Bastien in a cold shower.

Lisette's slender figure stepped from the shadows. She did not look pleased to see them. "I told you I was fine."

The frown on her lovely face dissolved as her gaze dropped to the very obvious bulge in Bastien's pants. "Is that for me? Because I will admit to having a fondness for bad boys."

Bastien sighed. Some nights the headaches spawned by living with immortals seemed far worse than those vampires could provoke.

Stuart *loved* his apartment.

Sitting at the desk in her office, Melanie smiled as she made several notations in the chart she had begun for him. He had been so eager to see "his new place" that she had relented and taken him there first.

He had been astounded by the size and room he'd been afforded. While he had sat on the sofa and ogled the large flat-screen TV, cushy furniture, and assorted electronic playthings, she had drawn blood, measured his blood pressure, taken his temperature, and done all of the usual things doctors and nurses did to humans who went in for a physical.

Everything showed normal for a vampire.

Tomorrow she would elicit a verbal history from him. Find out what, if any, illnesses he had suffered before his transformation, how long he had been transformed, *how* he had been transformed, and how he had lived since. What he ate. How often he fed. From whom he fed.

He seemed nice, albeit cautious. She was looking forward to working with him and thought Cliff would enjoy the company now that Joe had fewer lucid moments.

So, as she stared down at his chart, she couldn't understand why she felt . . . unnerved? Was that what she was feeling?

After those kisses Bastien had delivered, she should be floating several inches above the floor, eagerly anticipating the next.

Instead, she fidgeted in her seat and kept feeling almost as if someone were standing in the corner, watching her. Twice she'd caught herself gnawing on the inside of her cheek, a nervous habit that tended to resurface whenever she was troubled.

Melanie set her pen down and looked around her office again. Nothing out of place. No spooky shadows drew her eyes to corners. She had been having a hard time reading lately (and was too stubborn to admit she might need reading glasses—she was too young, damn it!), so she'd installed the highest-wattage bulbs she could find overhead. All was as bright as a sunny afternoon outdoors. Her peace lilies and bamboo plants thrived and provided cheerful color. As did her kitten calendar.

Tiny ripples of foreboding nipped at her feet like waves at a beach.

What was it? Was it Bastien? Had something happened to him?

Reaching for the phone, she dialed his cell.

"Hello?"

"Hi. It's me."

"Hi. Is Stuart settled in?"

"Yes. He even met Mr. Reordon, who was surprisingly friendly."

"Good."

"Is everything okay there?"

"Yes. It's been quiet as hell actually. Why? What's wrong?"

"Nothing."

"No, really. What's wrong? I can hear it in your voice. Something's troubling you."

She sighed. "I just . . . feel sort of like I did before those soldiers shot me and . . . everything's fine here, so I thought you might be in trouble or something. I don't know. I feel stupid now for bothering you."

"First, you aren't bothering me."

"He was mooning over you again," Richart said in the background.

Melanie laughed. "Hi, Richart."

"Ignore him," Bastien implored. "Second, are you having a premonition?"

"Dr. Lipton is a *gifted one?*" she heard Lisette ask.

"Hi, Lisette," Melanie said.

"Would a little privacy be too much to ask?" Bastien demanded.

"*Oui,*" Lisette retorted. "Hello, Dr. Lipton. Are you a *gifted one?*"

"Yes."

"*Merveilleuse!*"

"That does it." A moment passed. A breeze came over the line. "Okay. Talk quickly before they find me. I'm on the other side of campus."

Though Melanie smiled, that low hum of danger continued to strum through her.

"What's going on?" Bastien continued, his warm voice full of concern.

How could the others not see the good in him?

"Nothing. Everything is quiet here. I just feel . . . anxious . . . like something is going to happen. Are you sure there aren't any soldiers there? Could they be hiding again?"

"No soldiers. We've been teleporting from campus to campus, checking them out with the thermal vision scopes Chris gave us. We've checked every roof, every alcove, every damn tree and shrubbery, and have only encountered civilians. We haven't even come across any vampires. I don't know if word got out about what happened at Duke and they're lying low or what."

"Well . . . maybe it's nothing. Maybe I'm just tired."

"Trust your instincts. If—"

A thunderous *boom* drowned out whatever Bastien said next. The room around Melanie shook so violently she dropped the phone and had to grab hold of her desk to keep from falling to the floor. Pieces of sheetrock dropped like stones from the ceiling as cracks formed in the walls.

Heart racing, Melanie scrambled to pick up the phone. "Bastien?"

"Melanie? What happened?"

"Something's wrong! I think—"

Another *boom*. The room quaked, rocked her from side to side, and tossed her to the floor. She rolled over and got to her hands and knees.

What the hell could rock a building that extended five stories underground?

The room plunged into darkness. Dimmer reserve lighting flared to life. Alarms blared.

"Code red! Code red!" Mr. Reordon shouted over the building's intercom system.

Oh crap. That was the call to evacuate via the underground tunnel. Were they under attack?

Melanie saw the phone she'd dropped a few feet away and scrambled over to pick it up.

Broken. Great.

Thunder rumbled almost constantly above, created by explosions, not weather.

Melanie clambered to her feet and staggered across the vibrating floor toward the door. A form appeared in front of her.

Screaming, she rebounded off Bastien's chest as he and Richart teleported into her office.

Bastien caught her by the arms and steadied her. "It's okay. It's okay. What's going on?"

"I don't know."

He and Richart looked toward the ceiling, then met each other's gaze.

"I'll get Lisette." Richart vanished.

"What is it? What's happening?" Melanie shouted over the noise.

"The fucking mercenaries are attacking! They're blowing the place to hell!"

"What? How did they—"

"Stuart," Bastien said, his expression darkening.

Richart and Lisette appeared. Richart vanished again as Bastien ushered Melanie out into the hallway.

Guards urged the other network employees toward the far end of the hallway. Already at the dead end, Todd fiddled with something in his hand, yelled, "Fire in the hole!" and detonated a charge, blowing a huge, jagged opening in the wall and revealing a cement escape tunnel.

"Lanie!"

Melanie turned and saw one of the guards steering Linda past.

"I'm fine. Keep going!"

She nodded, face pinched with fear, and was soon swallowed by the mass of men and women flowing toward Todd.

Bastien curled an arm around Melanie's shoulders and cut a path across the stream of moving bodies, leading Melanie to the door of Stuart's apartment. "Open it," he ordered grimly.

Hands shaking, she fumbled for her security card. *Déjà vu.* Swiping the card, she entered the code as Lisette stepped up behind them.

Bastien threw the heavy steel door open as though it were hollowed-out plywood.

Stuart stood across the living room. Eyes wide, he backed away as Bastien and Lisette stalked toward him. "I didn't do it! I swear! I didn't lead them here!"

"Then how the hell did they find us?" Bastien demanded.

"I don't know! I don't know!"

"Wait." Lisette halted Bastien. "He's telling the truth. He has no memory of interacting with the mercenaries."

"He *wouldn't* if he let them drug him afterward."

Lisette's eyes narrowed. Her eyes glowed brighter.

Stuart winced and gripped his head. "Ahh! What are you doing?"

"Your memories are still there. The drug has merely hidden them from you. I intend to find them."

Melanie bit her lip as Stuart tugged his hair, his face creased with pain.

The building continued to shake with blasts. Pieces of the ceiling fell like snow.

Was it true? Had Stuart betrayed them? Had he made a deal with the soldiers, then let them drug him?

"How could he have told them where we are?" she asked. "He has no way of communicating with them. No phone. No walkie-talkie."

"I don't know," Bastien said. Face set in stone, he watched the vamp writhe as Lisette riffled through his thoughts. "But he found a way."

"You said you searched him before you brought him here."

"I must have missed something. Anything yet?" he asked Lisette.

"No. There's nothing between his running from the mercenaries and his waking up in the shed."

"There must be *something*! Because they sure as hell didn't follow us from my lair. We teleported!"

"There's a chip," Richart spoke behind Melanie.

She spun around. "What?"

Clothing torn, rumpled, and stained with blood, he nodded at the vamp, who abruptly stopped moaning. "I heard the mercenaries talking. There's a chip implanted just beneath the skin."

"Where? I didn't see anything when I examined him."

"Under his hair at the base of his skull."

Eyes wide, Stuart reached up to touch the back of his head.

Bastien palmed a dagger and strode toward him.

Stuart shook his head frantically. "Bullshit!" His voice rose an octave as he scrambled backward, bumped into a wall, and skidded sideways. "That's bullshit! I didn't help them!"

"It's true," Richart said. "He didn't get away when they tranqed him. He passed out. They implanted the chip, then stuck him in the garden shed so he would think he *did* get away. All they had to do then was wait for us to take the bait."

Melanie jumped when Bastien suddenly shot forward in a blur and caught Stuart. He overpowered the boy's struggles with ease. Lisette crossed to the duo and took the dagger from Bastien.

When she ran her fingers through the vamp's dark hair, then angled the dagger to remove the chip, Melanie looked away from the kid's fear-filled face.

Richart dialed his cell phone and swore. "Why is Seth so fucking hard to reach?"

"Because so many need him," his sister replied drolly as the building shook again.

Stuart howled.

Richart shoved his phone back in his pocket. "I already teleported Étienne in. He's trying to hold down the fort on the ground until there are enough of us to start a counter-assault. They've got fucking shoulder-fired missiles up there. Grenades. Too many mercenaries to count. Lisette, help Chris evacuate the mortals."

"Hell no!" She handed Bastien his bloody dagger and the chip she'd removed, then zipped over to her brother's side. "I'm going with you."

Richart nodded and gripped her arm.

Melanie threw out her hands. "Wait!"

They hesitated.

"In my office. In my desk. Bottom right drawer. Auto-injectors with the tranquilizer antidote Bastien tested. They have green caps. I upped the dose, so you should only need one each. Take one for Étienne, too."

Richart nodded. The two vanished.

Bastien drew his phone out and strode toward Melanie. Face pale, she stared up at him with wide brown eyes.

Her heart raced. Her hands shook. But she didn't bolt. Her courage both impressed and terrified him. He wanted her on her way out of the damned building with her colleagues.

Taking her hand, he headed for her office, checking out the hallway as he did. No infiltration down here thus far.

"Would you please get me one of the auto-injectors?" he asked.

She nodded and hurried over to her desk.

Richart and Lisette had already come and gone, leaving the drawer cracked open.

Bastien stayed in the doorway and dialed two numbers. Seth didn't answer. David did.

"Yes?"

"The network is under attack."

David swore foully. "By vampires or humans? Darnell!"

"Humans. The mercenaries are here in force with heavy-duty weaponry. Shoulder-fired missiles are pounding the hell out of the building. So are grenades. We need all hands."

David relayed the information to his Second, who began to make calls in the background.

Bastien could hear automatic weapons firing on the first and second sublevels, so those two floors must have already been infiltrated by soldiers. Mortal network employees continued to walk, limp, or drag each other past the doorway. Lisette, Richart, and Étienne began to wreak havoc among the mercenaries' ranks, eliciting satisfying screams.

Melanie handed Bastien an auto-injector, then returned to her desk.

"Help is on the way," the elder immortal told him.

Bastien thought furiously. "David."

"Yes?"

"We need Ami here."

"Are you out of your mind?"

"Look, I know—"

"Forget it!" David ended the call.

Swearing, Bastien dialed another number. The scent of blood grew stronger as casualties from the upper floors entered the hallway and trekked past.

He glanced over at Melanie and did a double take when he saw her loading up with weapons. 9mms. Extra clips. Tranquilizer darts. Daggers. *Shit!* No way in hell was he letting her fight!

She met his gaze. "Bastien, you know how badly Emrys wants to get his hands on Ami. Why do you—"

"Hi, Bastien," Ami answered in a cheerful voice. Darnell must not have contacted her.

"Hi, Ami. I need to talk to Marcus for a moment."

"What's wrong?" she asked, voice sobering.

"Just let me talk to Marcus for a minute, please."

"Okay. Marcus, honey, he wants to talk to you."

Marcus answered, his voice as cold as his wife's was warm. "What?"

"I'm at the network with Richart, Lisette, and Étienne. Emrys's soldiers are attacking."

"How many?"

"All of them by the sounds of it."

"I'm on my way."

"Marcus! I was thinking . . . We have a chance to end this here and now, but I need you to listen to me. Okay? Will you listen to me?"

"All right. Go ahead."

"You need to bring Ami here."

Marcus hung up.

Growling, Bastien dialed Ami's number again.

"Fuck you!" Marcus snarled into the phone.

"We can use her gift to get these bastards!" Bastien shouted. "To get Emrys! You want him dead, don't you? You want to find him and make him pay for what he did to Ami? *I* sure as hell do!"

Steely silence.

"Look, I'll find Richart and have him teleport both of you

to Sublevel 5. The fighting hasn't reached here yet. All Ami has to do is stand here and absorb all of the energy signatures she can so if any of these assholes get away she can trace them back to the source and we can napalm their asses, or better yet, turn them over to Seth and David."

Ami had done the same once before. She said every living creature possessed a unique energy signature. Once Ami was in close proximity to that individual, she could locate that signature again, tracking it like a homing beacon. If even *one* soldier got away, he could lead them back to Emrys.

Marcus's inner struggle was palpable, his tension carrying over the line.

"You can remain by her side every second," Bastien promised. "If it looks like the mercenaries are going to get down this far, have Richart teleport her to safety. This is our best chance, Marcus. I don't want those fuckers to get their hands on her again. Or on Sarah or Lisette. Or any immortal, for that matter."

Melanie stared at him, face grim.

Bastien couldn't read what she was thinking and wished she were close enough to touch. Did she think him as crazy as the others to risk Ami's safety? Did she think him uncaring?

"I'll ask Ami what she wants to—"

"I'm in," Ami said before Marcus could finish. "He was kind of yelling, so I heard enough to figure out the plan."

"Darling, it's too dangerous."

"I'm doing it. Bastien, send Richart."

The call ended.

Bastien pocketed his phone. "Go ahead and say it. I'm a bastard."

Melanie shook her head. "It's brilliant. I'm just afraid for her."

Relieved, he yanked her to him and hugged her close. Her fear stole into him. "Lisette!"

What? I'm busy taking out a Hummer.

Tell Richart to go pick up Marcus.

He's fetching Roland and Sarah. I'll tell him when he gets back.

Across the hall, Stuart stepped into the doorway of his apartment. The collar of his shirt bore a red stain from the wound Bastien had inflicted. Brow furrowed, he watched the humans hurry past as debris and dust fell from the ceiling. He shifted his weight, met Bastien's gaze.

"Cliff," Bastien said.

I'm here, Cliff answered through his door. *How bad is it, because it sounds fucking cataclysmic.*

"It's bad."

Chris Reordon exited the stairway at the end of the corridor, the arm of an injured guard looped over one shoulder.

Dr. Lipton's okay? Cliff asked.

"For now." His gaze returned to Stuart. "Cliff, you up for a fight?"

Hell, yes, man. Let me out and I'll help you kick some serious ass.

Me, too, Joe said. *I'm a little out of it from the drug, but I can hold my own against humans.*

Bastien set Melanie away from him and urged her out into the hallway. "You have to go now."

"No. I'm staying. I can fight."

Above the employees' heads, through the dust and shit falling from the ceiling, he caught Chris's gaze as Chris half carried, half dragged the guard forward. "Don't argue with me, Melanie. You're human."

"So are they!"

He didn't have time for this. He wanted her safe and didn't want to risk her being taken and tortured for information. "If you insist on staying, help Chris evacuate the wounded. But I need you to stay down here."

She nodded.

"Promise me."

"All right. I promise. Be careful."

He gave her arms a squeeze, then zipped through the

throng to Chris's side. "Étienne and Lisette are up on the ground," he shouted so the human could hear him over the explosions that grew louder and closer as parts of the structure gave way above them. "David will be here any minute. Richart is fetching Roland, Sarah, Marcus, and Ami." Bastien took the injured guard from him, swept him over to Melanie, then returned in a blink.

Chris stared at him in disbelief. "Why the hell is he bringing Ami here?"

"We have a plan! I'll fill you in later!" He motioned down the hallway. "Right now you need to let the vampires out to play!"

"Now I *know* you're crazy!"

"They want to help! And we need all the help we can get! It's going to take all of us immortals to handle the human firepower. We need the vamps to keep the damned building from collapsing until the rest of you can evacuate! Let them out! I'll take full responsibility!"

"Which doesn't mean shit! Because once Seth hears you put Ami in danger, he's going to kill you!"

Probably. But . . . "What other choice do we have?"

"You'd better be right!" Chris headed for the vampires' apartments. As he passed Stuart, Chris pointed at him and said, "You're dead, motherfucker!"

Bastien shook his head. "He didn't know they were tracking him!"

Stuart followed them to Cliff's apartment. "You won't kill me if I help, right? You aren't going to let those guys capture me again, are you? I mean, I can help, right?"

"Yes," Bastien answered while Chris swiped a card and entered the security code. "Help the humans get their wounded to the tunnel."

Stuart did as ordered. Racing to the stairwell, he grabbed a wounded network employee two others were struggling to support, looped him carefully over one shoulder and raced over to the ragged tunnel entrance to pass him off to Todd.

Cliff's door opened. Cliff stood there, brown eyes already glowing amber. "I can help up on the ground."

Bastien shook his head. "I don't want to risk your being tranqed."

Chris moved on to unlock Joe's door.

Joe stepped into the hallway, eyes glowing a vibrant blue.

"Help with the evacuation," Bastien ordered and it felt almost like old times. These were *his* men. Members of *his* army. "Check the upper floors. See if anyone is trapped. Get everyone out you can."

Nodding, the two took off down the hallway, their forms blurring with speed. The stairwell was packed. So they forced the doors of the disabled elevator open and leapt up the shaft.

"They'd better damned well keep their fangs out of my people!" Chris shouted.

"They will!" At least he hoped they would. *Cliff* would. But Bastien wasn't so sure about Joe.

Stuart raced past with a whimpering woman in his arms. Bastien couldn't tell if it were pain or fear of the vampire that instigated the sounds.

Across the hall, Melanie applied a pressure bandage to a guard's arm to stanch the blood gushing from his wound.

Bastien drew his katanas. "I'm heading up!"

Melanie raised her head and met his gaze. It seemed a thousand words, all unspoken, passed between them in that moment.

She nodded.

Bastien raced for the elevator shaft. There were four bodies in the elevator. Bastien didn't know if the drop had killed them or the explosion that had snapped the cables.

Half of the ceiling of the elevator was gone. Bastien leapt up through the hole. Far above him, he saw stars twinkling in a sky that was beginning to lighten as dawn approached. Emrys had timed his attack well.

Three ropes suddenly fell through the open doorway to

Sublevel 2. Soldiers garbed in black camo followed, sliding smoothly down, intent on taking the rest of the building.

Bastien grabbed the ropes and yanked with all of his preternatural strength.

The grappling hooks held. The ropes didn't, snapping where they bent over the edge of Sublevel 2's floor. The men shouted as they free-fell toward Bastien.

Bastien dropped the ropes and met them with his swords, his blades ensuring they would die if the fall didn't kill them.

As their bodies hit the elevator, he leapt up, catapulting from level to level until he reached the ground floor.

Most of the building above ground had been demolished. Only fragments of walls stood, pillars among piles of rubble.

Emrys's troops surrounded the place. Military Humvees. Sisu XA-180 armored personnel carriers with mounted 12.7-mm machine guns. Soldiers with shoulder-fired missiles. Grenades. The usual automatic weapons.

Smoke and dust and debris hovered like fog and stung Bastien's eyes. Lisette was on top of one of the Sisus, firing the mounted machine gun while she fed on the soldier who had previously manned it and used him as a shield.

Richart was doing his Grim Reaper thing, appearing and disappearing amid the soldiers, picking them off before they even knew he was there, throwing them into a panic. Étienne swept a circle around the crumpled building's perimeter, a constant blur, fatally wounding every soldier he passed. The soldiers began to shoot each other as they tried to stay ahead of him and failed.

Bright light blinded Bastien. He shielded his eyes and glanced up in time to see a door gunner lean out of one of two Black Hawk helicopters that hovered overhead and drop a grenade.

With lightning speed, Bastien caught the grenade and lobbed it back.

Panicked shouting ensued.

Soldiers dove out just as the vehicle exploded.

Bastien smiled. This was going to be fun.

Chapter 12

"The sun will be up in a few," Roland murmured.

Lounging on the sofa, feet propped on the coffee table, with Sarah curled up against his side, he soaked in her warmth like a sponge. Savored her scent. Listened to the familiar thumping of her heart.

He would never grow tired of moments like this. And, now that she was immortal, he looked forward to enjoying thousands upon thousands of them.

"Already?" she posed with a yawn.

Nietzsche rumbled and purred like a Harley as Sarah stroked his back and watched the news. The ornery feline had done his best to wedge himself between them, then given up, and settled for sprawling across them both.

"Mm-hmm. Want to shower and head for bed?" Both still wore their hunting togs, sans bloodstains since they hadn't encountered a single vampire tonight. Their weapons were scattered around his feet on the coffee table.

Tilting her head back, Sarah smiled up at him. "You gonna wash my back?"

He brushed his lips against her forehead. "Among other things."

Her heartbeat picked up. "I like the sound of that."

He dipped his head and did what he'd been dying to do ever since they had settled here on the sofa half an hour ago: tasted those luscious lips and listened to her pulse begin to race as her slender arms curled around his neck.

Damn, he loved her.

"Ahem."

Roland grabbed a dagger from the coffee table and let it fly.

Richart ducked, barely evading it. "Damn it!"

"I told you to call before you came here," Roland growled. He hadn't wanted the immortal to know where he lived in the first place and sure as hell didn't want the man to think he could drop in whenever he wanted to.

"I didn't have time!" Richart snapped. "The network is under attack."

Roland and Sarah rose, dislodging a disgruntled Nietzsche. "What?" they demanded in unison.

"Emrys's men are blitzing the place," Richart said while they donned their weapons. "Large force. Heavy artillery. I don't know how the hell this isn't going to make the news. The civvies are being evacuated through the tunnel, those who haven't already been killed."

Sarah finished fastening her last holster. "Ready."

Richart drew something out of his pocket. "Here." He held out two cylindrical objects that looked like big plastic pens with green tops. Roland and Sarah each took one.

"What are they?" she asked.

"The antidote Bastien tested. If you get tranqed, use this to counteract it."

Roland tucked his away. "Let's go."

Marcus broke out in a cold sweat as he watched Ami pack on the weapons. "Please rethink this." He didn't want her to risk falling into Emrys's hands. Didn't want to find out what being at those people's mercy again might do to her.

"I have to."

"No, you don't. It's too risky. And you know damn well Seth would *not* want you anywhere near that place." Marcus had tried without success to reach the immortal leader at least ten times in the seconds or minutes that had passed since Bastien had called.

"Bastien is right. We haven't been able to locate Emrys or his base through any means we've tried. This may be our only chance. If I can get close enough to his men, I can memorize as many signatures as I can and . . ." She looked up as she tied the bottom of one of her Glock 18 holsters to her thigh. "I know I can lead you all to them. I did it before with the vampire king. I can do it now."

Marcus knelt in front of her. Brushing her hands aside, he finished tying the holster for her, then tied the other. When he finished, he leaned his face into her stomach and wrapped his arms around her hips. "I can't lose you, Ami. I can't."

He heard her swallow, and wondered if her throat had as big a lump lodged in it as his did.

Her fingers tunneled through his hair and held him close. "You won't lose me." She pressed her lips to the top of his head. "A handful of immortals will be there to protect me."

"Such has been the case before. Look how that ended."

She rested her cheek on his hair. "We'll be fine. Maybe you can kick some ass while we're there. Won't you enjoy that?"

He chuckled and shook his head.

She stiffened, then relaxed. "Hi, Richart."

Marcus sighed. Rising, he turned to face the other immortal. "You'll take us both at once or you won't take us at all. I'm not letting Ami out of my sight."

Richart nodded and held something out to him. "The antidote. Use it like an EpiPen if you're hit with a dart."

Marcus nodded and tucked it into one of his many pockets. "Ready?"

He nodded and wrapped an arm around Ami.

Richart reached forward and touched their shoulders.

Melanie was helping another injured guard down the hallway when Richart, Marcus, and Ami appeared in a corner near the entrance of the escape tunnel.

Ami's face was pale, but set with determination. After a quick look to take in the damage, she closed her eyes and stood very still.

Beside her, Marcus loomed protectively, weapons in hand, face dark. Melanie thought that if anyone so much as sneezed, Marcus would be on them in an instant.

Melanie helped the wounded man through the jagged hole in the wall and turned back to aid more. It was like a war zone. Explosions frequently rumbled in the distance or rocked the building. A cloud of dust hovered in the hallway, tickling her lungs and leaving her eyes gritty. The network's headquarters was huge and employed hundreds of men and women from dozens and dozens of occupations. Doctors. Nurses. Accountants. Lawyers. Hackers. Internet monitors. Translators. Actors. Weapons trainers. Martial arts trainers. Electronics geniuses. Cooks. Linguists. Repairmen.

The names of the dead had been dropped by the wounded as they made their way to her and asked for aid. And more were dying. She could tell by the grim expressions on the faces of Cliff, Joe, and Stuart as they rescued those they could.

Marcus's eyes widened as a blur sped toward them from the elevator shaft. Raising his weapons, he stepped in front of Ami.

Melanie reached over and placed a hand on his arm. "Wait."

He scowled at her. "Is that—?"

Cliff halted in front of them. An elderly woman, skinny as a rail, was cradled in his arms. Her hair a tangled mess dragged from a formerly neat chignon, she stared at Melanie with round, blue eyes.

"Ma'am? Are you hurt?" Melanie asked.

The woman shook her head. "The ceiling collapsed. I was trapped and couldn't move until this young man freed me. I told him I could walk, but—"

Cliff lowered the woman to her feet. "I said I could walk faster."

The woman nodded, her expression slack with amazement. "He could."

Cliff took a step back, sent Marcus a cautious glance. Then, nodding to Melanie, he took off back toward the elevators.

Melanie guided the older woman through the hole, asked one of the guards forming a relay line in the tunnel to help her, and turned to face Marcus.

Just as she had anticipated, the immortal's face was full of disapproval.

"They let the vampires out?"

"In case you hadn't noticed, the vampires are helping us. The immortals are fighting the soldiers above ground and are doing their damnedest to keep them from demolishing the whole building. The vampires are working on the inside, taking out the soldiers they encounter and rescuing all of the network employees they can."

As if on cue, another blurred form shot toward them through the throng. Joe halted, a man draped over his shoulder. The vampire eyed Marcus impassively as he lowered the man's feet to the floor.

The man straightened, brushed at the dust on his torn suit, and squinted up at Joe. "Thank you."

Joe turned luminescent blue eyes on Melanie. "He isn't injured."

The man shook his head. "I'm fine. A few bruises is all. I just can't see shit without my glasses." Eyelids nearly touching, he peered around them. "Where are we?"

"Sublevel 5," Melanie told him. She motioned to another of the guards in the tunnel. "This man will help you evacuate. Thank you, Joe," she added with a smile for the vampire.

"Yes," the man said over his shoulder. "Thank you, Joe."

Melanie had no idea if the man knew he had been saved by a vampire rather than an immortal.

Joe nodded and raced away.

Marcus muttered something Melanie couldn't hear over the sounds of war.

Melanie saw a woman with a bad head wound staggering toward her and hurried over to offer what aid she could.

Killing or capturing the mercenaries—the d'Alençons seemed convinced now that they were mercenaries— would've been a hell of a lot easier if Bastien didn't constantly have to dodge bullets fired from the helicopter that hovered above them. He had hoped one of the dumbasses in the Humvees would hurl a grenade at him so he could lob it into the second helo and eliminate it like the first, but no such luck.

Bastien swore when another dart stuck him in the neck. That was the fifth one and, so far, Melanie's antidote was working splendidly. Bullets peppered his body as he plowed through a cluster of soldiers. Grunting, he swung his blades and savored their screams.

Leaping up onto the Sisu, he slit another soldier's throat and took possession of the machine gun. *Finally*. He'd take out the Black Hawk and—

As he aimed the heavy weapon at the chopper, what looked like a huge martial eagle with a ten- or twelve-foot wingspan swooped out of the lightening sky and dove through the helicopter, in one door and out the other. Soldiers, weapons, and ammo tumbled out and fell to the ground.

The helicopter wobbled erratically as the pilots panicked.

The raptor wheeled around and dove straight for the nose of the copter. At the last second the eagle spread its wings and extended its legs forward. Its talons drove through the front windows, shattering glass and bending metal, and clutched the two pilots.

The engine whined as the helicopter began to spin. Deftly avoiding the blades, the eagle yanked the pilots through the shattered windows and dropped them like stones.

What. The. Hell.

Bastien barely noticed the helicopter crash and burn. His gaze followed the eagle as it swooped down and ducked into the forest.

Bullets struck Bastien.

Swearing, he turned the machine gun on the soldiers firing at him. When that bunch had fallen, he looked back at the forest, searching for the raptor.

David stepped from the trees.

Shit. David could shape-shift? Nobody had told him immortals could shape-shift.

The elder immortal was garbed all in black. As he strode into the melee, his long dreadlocks wove themselves into a braid and knotted at the base. His eyes flashed bright amber. He reached over his head and drew two drool-worthy Masamune swords.

I know Ami is here.

A chill accompanied that deep voice in Bastien's head.

If anything happens to her, you're dead.

David's large form blurred. More screams joined the chorus of others already splitting the night.

A bullet ripped through Bastien's thigh.

Shaking off the distractions, he leapt down and raced for the nearest soldier. The soldier's companions yelped when Bastien yanked him from their midst and ducked into the forest to feed on him.

As warm blood entered his veins, the virus swiftly began

to repair the many wounds Bastien had suffered, pushing bullets from his flesh, closing the holes, and stopping the bleeding.

The sun would crest the horizon soon. The towering trees around them would offer some protection, but all needed to be at full strength.

Dropping the soldier, Bastien returned to the battle.

Stuart did one more sweep of Sublevel 3. When he found no more survivors, he headed for the elevator shaft.

Two forms shot past in a blur. The other vampires.

Stuart liked Cliff. But didn't really know what to think about Joe. The blond vamp was throwing off some eerie vibes.

Since those two headed into Sublevel 2, Stuart leapfrogged up to the first basement level.

This floor was all shot to shit. Huge, gaping holes in the ceiling let him see a sky brightening with approaching dawn. If this didn't end soon, whoever was left up here would die here, because he wasn't going to fry in the sun for anyone.

He had almost fried once right after he was turned. He hadn't understood what had happened to him and . . .

Stuart shuddered, remembering.

Fear trickled in. Or rather *more* fear. That immortal down on Sublevel 5 was freaking him out, staring at him with those fury-filled eyes every time Stuart delivered another walking wounded.

What the hell was *he* so pissed about? Stuart hadn't meant to bring all of this down on their heads. How was he supposed to know that tracking thing had been stuck in his head? He hadn't felt anything. The stupid drug the mercenaries had given him must have slowed the virus's ability to repair enough to keep the virus from pushing the damned thing out. Or maybe they did something to keep it in there.

If he had known it was there, he would have cut it out himself. Probably. That shit had hurt. But the knowledge that someone was tracking him or stalking him was creepy. And irritating. Like the time his parents had secretly tracked him using a GPS device and busted him for going to a party that had had drugs and alcohol at it.

So it's not like he had *wanted* that thing in his head. Or *wanted* to help those human pricks.

And wasn't Stuart helping the immortals and their human friends now to make up for it?

He was doing his part. Making up for his mistake.

Yet that ass avenger on Sublevel 5 kept glaring at him as if he wanted to cut Stuart into little pieces.

Whatever.

Stuart studied every dusty, dirty lump and peered between chunks of ceiling and whatever the hell used to be upstairs, looking for an arm or leg or any body part belonging to someone who might be trapped.

Beneath the screams and weapons fire outside (What the hell was going on up there? It sounded like the fucking Band of Brothers!), a moan sounded.

Stuart traced it to a pile of granite tile beneath another hole in the ceiling. He started tossing rubble aside.

A woman. It was a woman. He grimaced when he saw the bone protruding from the pudgy arm he uncovered. *Ugh! Nasty!* Her leg was even worse. He really wasn't cut out for this crap.

Her face, reddish-brown hair, and clothes were nearly white with dust. "Thank you," she huffed. "Thank you."

She raised her eyes, met his, and screamed.

"No-no!" Stuart held up his hands. "It's okay! It's cool. I'm here to help you."

The screaming stopped, thankfully, because this chick had a set of lungs.

She still looked scared as hell though.

"It's okay," Stuart repeated and leaned down.

Debris shifted behind him.

Stuart swung around. A dozen human soldiers stalked toward him.

Oh shit. Okay. What should he do? He didn't have a weapon and these guys were armed out the ass.

Grabbing huge hunks of cement and stone, he started hurling them at the soldiers at preternatural speeds.

He scored a lot of hits before the bullets started flying. Some struck him. Some missed. He thought one might have hit the woman at his feet because she screamed again and started crying.

Pissed off now, Stuart zipped around and came up behind the soldiers. He'd never broken someone's neck before. It was disturbingly easy.

Only three or four soldiers remained when Stuart had to dodge the first tranquilizer dart. If one of those hit him, he was a goner.

He had to go on the defensive then, dodging the deadly drug. Something hit him in the stomach and bounced to the ground. Ducking another dart, Stuart glanced down.

Oh shit! A grenade!

He leaped away.

Fire. Pain. Deafening noise.

He knew nothing else for he wasn't sure how long.

He was down. Something heavy was on top of him. He tried to move. One arm, two. One leg, two. He nearly wept he was so relieved. No missing limbs at least.

The woman continued to cry. He almost couldn't hear her for the ringing in his ears.

Stuart dug his way out of the rubble. The soldiers huddled around the woman. It looked like they were trying to fasten a harness or something around her. Were they going to take her prisoner?

A little wobbly on his feet, Stuart crept up behind them and snapped their necks.

The woman thanked him again and again as he lifted her into his arms and staggered back toward the elevator shaft.

Weird. She felt heavy. He should have been able to carry her above his head with one hand and twirl her like a pizza. But she felt heavy. And he felt tired. And thirsty.

He paused at the edge. "It's gonna be okay," he murmured and stepped off into air.

Instead of landing smoothly, he hit what was left of the elevator roof hard. Pain shot up his legs as he stumbled and nearly fell through the opening.

The woman screamed again and clung tightly to him.

"'s okay." Stuart dropped through into the elevator and started making his way through the throng down the long, seemingly endless hallway.

The human doctor—what was her name?—saw him coming. Face creased with concern, she waved two of the guards over to take the woman.

"Stuart?" the doctor said. "What happened?" She took his arm.

"Explosion." His vision was all wonky. The color was off or something.

"Come with me."

He trudged after her. His body hurt all over. Cramped. He felt like something was trying to eat him from the inside out. Like . . . like he had when he had first been transformed.

His fangs cut his lip. Salty blood hit his tongue. He needed to feed.

The doctor led him out of the hallway and into . . . He didn't know. He couldn't concentrate. He hurt too much.

She said something as she left him and opened a cabinet. Cold air rushed out and danced around his legs. A refrigerator?

She walked back toward him, held something out. ". . . losing a lot of blood . . . not healing . . . need to feed."

Yes, he did need to feed.

Knocking whatever she held aside, he grabbed her arm, yanked her close, and sank his fangs into her neck.

Sweet, sweet relief.

He nearly wept with it as the cramping ceased and the pain began to recede.

Cliff waited while Joe handed off another wounded employee to the guards in the tunnel. "We're both pretty banged up," he told his friend. "Let's stop off and get some blood before we go back."

Joe nodded.

Cliff didn't need the blood so much himself. But Joe was looking a little ragged. He'd been injured. The scent of blood was every-freaking-where. And they'd had to take out some human soldiers who had infiltrated the upper floors. Cliff worried that the strain of everything might send Joe over the edge. If he replenished what he'd lost, maybe it would help him maintain control.

Cliff nodded to the immortal by the tunnel, unsurprised when the large warrior didn't nod back. Marcus, he'd heard one of the guards call him.

Marcus looked pissed and ready to rip everyone to shreds as he stood sentinel in front of a pretty, petite woman with red hair. Her eyes were closed, her brow furrowed as if she were concentrating very hard on something. Maybe she was an immortal with one of those cool gifts.

Joe made his silent way to the lab they both had frequented so many times. Dr. Lipton kept a special refrigerator stocked with blood in there.

Cliff followed. The crowd in the hallway began to thin. There were still a hell of a lot of explosions overhead, though, and quite a few humans trapped on Sublevel 2, so he thought this thing was far from over.

A few steps inside the lab, Joe stopped short.

Cliff bumped into his back. "What is it?"

Joe didn't answer.

Cliff stepped around him and felt his heart drop into his stomach.

The new vampire was down on the floor with Dr. Lipton in his lap, his fangs buried deep in her neck.

"What the fuck are you doing?" Cliff bellowed and rushed forward.

Stuart raised his head and snarled something.

Dr. Lipton lay still, eyes closed, blood trailing down her neck.

Cliff lifted her with care, then backhanded Stuart, sending him flying across the room to shatter the already cracked sheetrock on the far wall. "Dr. Lipton?" He placed his hand on her neck to try to stanch the flow of blood. "Melanie?"

Joe watched with wild eyes. "I can't hear a heartbeat."

Neither could Cliff. He'd like to think it was because there was so damned much other noise going on, but . . .

She was pale. Her lips were blue.

"What happened?" Stuart asked, slumped across the room.

Joe turned blazing eyes on the vampire. "You killed her! You fucking killed her!"

"Wait!" Cliff shifted his warm, bloody fingers on her neck. "I-I-I think I found a pulse. She's not dead yet."

"Yet," Joe repeated and began backing toward the doorway.

"Joe? What are you doing? Get help."

Joe just kept moving, his head rocking back and forth. "I can't do it."

"What?"

"I can't do this. Not without Dr. Lipton. Not without Melanie. I can't be here."

"She isn't—"

"You know what they'll do to us! They hate us! They'll blame us! They'll kill us!"

Cliff gaped as his friend sped through the doorway. He looked over at Stuart, whose wide-eyed gaze was fixed on Dr. Lipton.

Crimson liquid trailed from the corner of his mouth. "I did that?"

"Yes!"

"I didn't mean to!"

Cliff could believe it, but . . . *shit!* Joe was on the run. Dr. Lipton's heartbeat was faltering. "If you didn't mean it, get your ass over here."

Stuart scrambled forward.

Cliff passed him Dr. Lipton, praying he was doing the right thing. "Keep pressure on her neck. I'm gonna go for help."

Stuart nodded. He should be flushed from feeding, but his face was pale as death.

Cliff took one last look at Melanie, then raced from the room. Down the hallway toward the elevator he went, moving so fast he would kill the humans if he bumped into any of them. *"Bastien!"* he shouted.

Up through the roof of the elevator he went.

What? Bastien called back from somewhere outside.

Cliff leapt up two floors, grabbed the edge, and propelled himself up two more. *"Melanie needs you! She's hurt real bad!"*

One more leap and he ran smack into Bastien on the ground floor . . . or what was left of it.

"What happened?" he demanded.

"Stuart drained her."

Bastien's eyes flared with panic as he turned to the elevator shaft.

Cliff grabbed his arm. "Joe's gone. He saw Dr. Lipton and freaked out. I have to go after him."

"The sun's coming up."

"He can't be alone. He's too close to losing it."

Bastien nodded and pulled him into a rough hug. "Be careful. If you don't make it back by sunrise, I'll find you."

Cliff nodded and watched Bastien drop through the opening and free-fall to the bottom, where he landed smoothly in a crouch.

Cliff eyed the chaos around him. There was fire everywhere. Bullets whipped past. Immortals . . .

He swallowed. *Holy crap.* No wonder Bastien's vampire army had fallen beneath the immortals' swords. They were terrifying in their speed and strength and intensity.

Cliff's heart began to pound. His chest felt tight. He felt exposed. Terrified. He hadn't been outside by himself in over two years. Had he become agoraphobic as a result? Because his feet felt frozen to the pitted floor.

Until a freaking missile shot past.

Cliff ducked behind what was left of a desk. The ceiling was gone, the roof mixed with the other rubble beneath his feet.

Where the hell was Joe?

Smoke stung his eyes as he peered around, trying to find the blond vampire.

There! Diving into the trees.

Cliff took off after him. He leaped over a pile of mercenary bodies and dodged as many bullets as he could. The damned things were flying everywhere. A blurred form sailed past, eyes flashing bright amber.

Terror cut through him like a blade.

Would the immortals think he was trying to escape and kill him?

When the dark as midnight figure kept going, Cliff allowed himself to breathe again.

Apparently he wasn't their highest priority.

Relieved, he headed for the trees, intent on finding Joe.

Something stung his neck.

Reaching up, he slapped at it and came away with a tranquilizer dart. His vision wavered. His knees buckled.

The ground lurched up and hit him hard.

A shadow fell over him.

Cliff squinted up at two soldiers. "Ah shi—"

Bastien raced through the hallway, unable to breathe, panic closing his throat.

Melanie.

He saw nothing. Saw no one. Only the door to Melanie's office.

He rushed inside.

Empty.

Stepping out into the hallway, he met Marcus's gaze. "Where is she?"

Stone-faced, Marcus pointed to the lab.

Bastien burst through the doorway.

Stuart was bent over Melanie on the floor.

Bastien roared with fury.

Stuart spun around, eyes frantic. "I didn't mean to! I swear I didn't mean to do it!"

Bastien sent the vampire flying across the room. "What did you do?" he bellowed.

Melanie's eyes were closed.

Bastien knelt beside her and gathered her limp form into his arms. "Melanie?" He brushed her hair back from her face. It was littered with powder and fragments of sheetrock. "Melanie, sweetheart?"

Cliff had made it sound as though she were dying, but . . . her skin was warm to the touch. Her heartbeat sounded strong. Blood stained her pale neck. Perhaps Cliff and Joe had seen that and assumed the worst?

"I was injured," Stuart said and approached with caution.

His pants were soaked with blood. His shirt bore a large stain and was scorched in places.

Bastien couldn't tell if the blood was Stuart's or that of the men and women he had helped. It wasn't Melanie's. The scent of her blood rose from her throat and did not match that on Stuart's clothing. Only that on his face. ·

Bastien hugged her tight, terrified by how close he had come to losing her.

"I was hurt," Stuart babbled on. "I didn't know I'd lost that much blood and . . . I don't know what happened. I just . . . I didn't realize I was feeding on her until those other vampires came in and . . . I didn't mean to drain her."

"You didn't drain her," Bastien murmured and buried his face in her hair. Why wasn't she waking up? Had she hit her head? He should kill the vampire for this. Accident or not—

"Yeah, I did," Stuart said with trepidation.

Bastien raised his head. "No, you—" He broke off, inhaled deeply. He stared down at Melanie, bent, and drew in her scent. Swearing, he looked up at Stuart. "What the hell did you do?"

Stuart halted and began to backtrack. "She was dying. I didn't know what else to do. Her pulse . . . She barely had a pulse. She wouldn't have made it if I hadn't . . ."

"You gave her your blood?" Bastien demanded.

"Yes."

"How much?" Had it just been a little, she wouldn't be so warm. She'd be going into shock and—

"A lot," Stuart admitted in a small voice. "She was nice to me. I didn't want her to die."

"You *infected* her?"

Chris burst through the doorway. "What's going on? Marcus said something was up."

"Stuart infected her."

Chris drew a tranquilizer pistol and shot Stuart.

The vampire looked down at the dart in his chest and swayed. His eyes rolled back. His legs buckled.

Bastien felt nothing but guilt and regret as the young vamp dropped to the floor. He looked up at Chris. "Can you help her? Can you stop it?"

Melanie had talked about being transformed *later on* in life. Not now. Not unless it was absolutely necessary. If they could undo it while the infection was still fresh . . .

Chris leaned his head back and shouted, "David!"

Seconds later, David stood in the room with them. "Yes?"

"She's infected," Bastien said. "Can you stop it?"

David shook his head. "My healing gift has no affect on the virus."

"Richart!" Chris whipped out his phone and dialed. "Are we up and running yet? . . . Okay."

Richart appeared in the doorway. "Yes?" His brow furrowed with concern when his gaze found Melanie.

Chris hung up. "The new network headquarters is ready. Richart, would you teleport Melanie there? Maybe if we remove as much of the infected blood as possible and replace it we can halt the transformation."

Bastien stood with Melanie in his arms.

Richart held out his own.

Handing her over was one of the hardest things Bastien had ever done.

Richart met his eyes as he cradled Melanie in his arms. "I'll take good care of her."

Bastien's throat was too thick to respond.

The two vanished.

The explosions overhead ceased. As did the automatic weapons fire. For one moment, all was silent, as if the entire world—not just Bastien—waited with bated breath to see how Melanie would fare.

Lisette entered. Étienne. Roland and Sarah. Yuri and

Stanislov, whom Bastien hadn't even realized had entered the fray. Ethan and Edward. Marcus and Ami entered last.

All formed a semicircle in front of Bastien, faces somber.

"Is it over?" Bastien asked.

Étienne nodded. "The sun has risen. A handful of mercenaries escaped."

Good. "Then Ami should be able to track them to their base."

"There's more," Lisette said.

They all looked at each other as though none of them wanted to be the one to break the bad news.

How bad could it be? Melanie had just been drained almost to the point of death and infused with the virus in massive amounts by a vampire. Surely they couldn't tell him anything that could even come *close* to that.

"What is it?"

Again Lisette spoke. "We believe they have Cliff."

Bastien shook his head. "Joe panicked when he saw Melanie and took off. Cliff went to bring him back. They probably sought shelter when the sun rose and will return tonight."

Étienne shook his head. "I saw Cliff felled by a dart. I was busy dropping a grenade I confiscated down into one of the armored personnel carriers and had to look away. When I looked back, he was gone."

Alarm shook Bastien. "Are you sure?" What if he had only ducked into the trees. If Cliff was still up there, he could die when the angle of the sun changed.

"I searched the trees," Étienne said. "He was nowhere to be found."

"Are any of the vehicles missing?" David asked. "The mercenaries would not have gone on foot."

They all shrugged.

"I was the first one on the ground," Richart said, "but

couldn't say how many there were to begin with because they were already bombing the building."

David sheathed his weapons. "I'll see if I can find them."

Étienne shook his head. "The sun is up."

"I know. I can withstand a few hours of daylight."

That long? Really?

As David strode past, Bastien grabbed his arm. "Why didn't you tell me you could shape-shift?"

"Because you didn't ask."

The others shared a look.

"You can shape-shift?" Lisette asked.

"Yes. And no, I won't show you. It isn't a parlor trick."

Bastien tightened his grip when David would have moved on. "There was no need to bring Ami here. With your shape-shifting ability, we didn't need her."

"I didn't bring Ami here," David replied, expression darkening. "I would never have put her in such danger and you shouldn't have either."

"Because I didn't know!"

Étienne gripped Bastien's arm and slowly pulled him backward.

Bastien released David. "All you have to do is change into a bird and follow the soldiers home. If I'd known that, I wouldn't have told Marcus we needed her."

David stepped up close, eyes flashing amber. "Whether you needed her or not, you should not have brought her here. You risked her life by doing so. Was my hanging up on you not indication enough that it was a phenomenally bad idea? Was there any doubt in your mind as to my disapproval of such a plan?"

"If you had—"

"Do not mistake my friendly complaisance for weakness, Sebastien. Nor for ignorance. I have walked this earth for thousands of years. I am more powerful than every immortal in this room combined. And I hold a wisdom and patience you may never acquire. The only immortal who holds more authority than I do is Seth. The next time you do something I have forbidden, you will not like the consequences. *If*, that is, Seth lets you live. You may very well have forfeited your life tonight when you risked Ami's. Seth will be furious."

David stalked from the room. A moment later, the sound of wings flapping carried to them from the elevator shaft.

Bastien met the somber gazes of the others.

"Damn," Ethan said. "You really know how to push people's buttons."

Yes. The question was: How far had he pushed Seth's?

Chapter 13

Seth stared at the slender figure on the bed. Straight, shoulder-length raven hair, as shiny as it was soft, formed a fan on the pillow beneath her head. Her nose was small, her chin impertinent. He didn't doubt she had thrust that chin out often in her lifetime.

Dark, sightless eyes stared back at him, as though even in death she beseeched him to help her. Free her. Save her.

But he had arrived too late.

The dread that had been burning his stomach like acid for days began to recede, replaced by numbness. Regret.

Bending, Seth picked a shirt up off the floor—all that remained of the vampire who had worn it—and wiped his weapons clean. He sheathed them, forced his feet to carry him forward. With a wave of his hand, he sent the ropes that bound her wrists and ankles racing to untie themselves. They fell to the covers. One slithered off and hit the floor with a thump.

Her slender arms were purple with bruises and polka dotted with bites and dried specks and trails of blood. Her legs, bare save for the small skirt she wore, bore the same. Her delicate hands were bloodstained and curled into claws that continued to grip the sheets beneath her though no breath filled her body.

Seth left to perform a quick search of her small rural home. He found what he sought in the bathroom and returned to the bedroom.

Lifting the slight form, he supported her with one arm while he ripped the bloody sheets from the bed and shook a clean white one over it. He laid the young woman down and closed those long-lashed, sightless, accusing eyes.

He had searched for her every chance he could, narrowing her location down a little more each day. It was a big damned planet. And so much was going on in North Carolina right now.

Excuses. For the inexcusable.

He turned to the crib a few feet away. Anguish pierced him as he approached it.

The body within was so tiny. He lifted the babe and placed him in his mother's arms, then tucked the sheet around them like a cocoon.

Two *gifted ones* lost.

There were three phenomena Seth always felt internally, no matter how far away they took place: the birth of a *gifted one*, the death of either a *gifted one* or an immortal, and the transformation of a *gifted one* into an immortal. The first triggered a sort of breathless tingle in his chest, as this babe's birth had three months earlier. It had been a single bright moment among a host of dark ones.

The second spawned a feeling of emptiness. Seth had thought the emptiness created by the babe's death an extension of the loneliness that had besieged him ever since he had assigned Ami to be Marcus's Second. Had he realized it was the result of a *gifted one* dying, perhaps he could have found these two sooner. Soon enough, perhaps, to save the mother.

The third, the transformation of a *gifted one* into an immortal, spawned a sick feeling of dread within him. So heavy he could follow it like a scent in the wind. But such took time.

Time this woman, the victim of the half-dozen vampires whose blood now painted the walls, had lacked.

The vampires had tried to turn her. But, as often happened, their bloodlust had thwarted their desire, driving them to drain her before the transformation could conclude. It was the only reason there were two bodies to enshroud and bury instead of one.

He lifted the bundle into his arms. They were so light. Somehow that made it all the worse.

Outside, a brisk wind bearing the scent of snow lashed him. He almost wished it carried with it the punishing sting of sleet.

The beautiful countryside outside Gyeongju, South Korea, bore a white blanket that seemed to dampen sound like cotton balls. Thunder rumbled overhead, spawned not by any meteorological disturbance, but by Seth's grief.

He would have to find a shovel.

"Here."

Seth spun around.

As always, the figure that stepped from the shadows the house cast in the moonlight reminded him of a buff Jim Morrison. His dark, wavy hair lifted and fell with the breeze, tumbling past his shoulders. His chest was bare, hairless. Soft leather pants hung low on his hips.

Seth hadn't heard his arrival and wondered if the noise the vampires had made as he had slaughtered them had drowned it out, or if he had simply been so distracted he had missed it.

The leather pants rustled slightly as the other strolled forward. Snow and ice crunched beneath his boots. One large hand clasped the handle of a shovel he held out to Seth.

Seth glanced down at the burden in his arms. He didn't want to lay them on the ground even long enough to dig the grave. Yet he didn't want to return them inside to the blood-spattered room in which both had died.

"Never mind," his visitor said. "I'll do it."

Seth would have been unable to suppress his shock if he hadn't been so numb.

"Did you know them?" the other asked as he stuck the shovel deep into the frozen earth and removed a hunk of soil.

"Not really. I knew they were *gifted ones*. I looked in on her over the years as I do to all of the *gifted ones*. But . . ."

"They didn't know *you*."

Seth nodded.

The sound of the metal blade stabbing the ground seemed obscenely loud.

Neither spoke as the grave took shape.

When it was long and deep enough, Seth lowered the bodies into it with care.

His companion abandoned the shovel and joined Seth in singing a prayer for mother and son in an ancient language none currently living had ever heard spoken.

When silence reigned once more, Seth picked up the shovel and started returning the soil to its home. "Could we maybe do this another time?" he asked without looking up at the other, who was taller than himself by a couple of inches.

"Do what?"

"Whatever it is you're here to do. Or say. I really have no interest in your threats tonight. If you and the others did more than sit on your precious asses and observe, perhaps I wouldn't be doing this right now."

"I'll issue no threats tonight, cousin."

"Well, whoop-dee-fucking-doo. Are you going to tell me you're here because you missed me?"

"No," he said simply.

From the corner of his eye, Seth watched him pace away a few yards, pause, pace back. Cross his arms. Uncross them. Pace away again.

He seemed . . . off.

Unsettled.

Something.

"What's with you tonight?"

"Nothing."

Finished filling the grave, Seth set the shovel aside and turned to the house. He closed his eyes, pictured the kitchen. The gas pipe behind the stove sprang a leak. A small spark and it ignited. He would visit her family and plant the memory of an explosion, of mother and child being killed instantly, then given a lovely funeral.

No one would see the bodies. No eyebrows would be raised by the bites. No inquiries would be made. No sensational headlines would proclaim their deaths vampire kills. No one would know the truth. Only Seth and . . .

"Are you going to tell me why you're here?"

Tense silence.

"Zach—"

"Your phone is broken."

Seth frowned. "What?"

"Your phone is broken," Zach repeated. Seth pulled his cell from a back pocket and gave it a look. No wonder things had been so quiet. The device had been shattered by a vampire strike.

Seth looked at Zach. Why would he care if Seth's phone . . .

Alarm struck him. "What's happened?" It must be bad for this one to risk the wrath of the others to interfere and bring it to Seth's attention. "Who's been trying to reach me?"

Zach's jaw flexed as he clenched his teeth.

Seth knew what this would cost him and wondered if he would—

"Your people in North Carolina."

"Which ones?"

"All of them."

Seth swore and prepared to teleport to David's place.

"Seth."

"What?"

Zach met his gaze. "You're battling a mythological beast there."

Seth shook his head. "I don't know what you're—"

"Hydra," Zach clarified. "You're fighting the Lernaean Hydra."

"The Greek mythological creature Hercules was sent to slay that had all the heads?"

Zach nodded shortly. "Cut off one head and it grows two more. Your immortal black sheep didn't know what he was breeding when he undertook his uprising."

"I assume you mean Sebastien."

"You can't defeat it. Every head poses a threat. To you. To us. The more heads, the greater the threat. They can't know who you are. And they can't know who *we* are. The others won't stand for it. Already there have been rumblings."

They had cut off Sebastien's "head" and Montrose Keegan and the Vampire King had replaced him. They had cut off those two's heads and . . . were still trying to find out who had taken their place. Was Zach saying Emrys wasn't working alone? That whomever they fought now would conquer them?

"You're forgetting one thing," Seth said.

"What?"

"Hercules defeated Hydra . . . with Iolaus's help."

"I'm no Iolaus."

Seth raised his eyebrows. "Did I say you were?" He bowed. "Thank you for the tip."

Wondering what disaster he would face next, Seth teleported to the States.

Quiet fell in Seth's absence, broken by the crackling flames that devoured the small house. The scent of disturbed earth wafted on the breeze.

Zach hadn't told Seth why he had come, why he had alerted him to the fact that he was needed, because Zach really didn't know. It had been a dumb-ass thing to do. He would gain nothing from it. And would lose much.

Sighing, he flexed his shoulders. A pair of nearly translucent wings burst from his back. Matching the tan color of his skin at their base, they gradually darkened to black at their tips. The fragile feathers fluttered a bit as wind ruffled them.

He lacked even the time to stretch them their full span before figures began to step from the shadows.

Matching him and Seth in height, they strode forward with purpose, surrounding him on all sides.

He smiled grimly.

Had they feared he wouldn't return? That they wouldn't have the chance to exact their punishment?

He tucked his wings away, hoping to protect them from what he knew would come.

"You were warned," one stated.

"So I was."

"You know what we must do."

He decided now wasn't the time to debate the word *must*.

Zach spread his arms wide and borrowed a phrase from Seth's black sheep. "So be it."

While Bastien counted every second that passed and silently castigated himself on what would be Cliff's sofa, Richart lounged in a chair near the apartment's door.

"Does Melanie know you love her?" he asked softly.

"No." Bastien kept his face buried in his hands, his elbows planted on his knees. "What the hell do I know about love? The last two people I loved were my sister Cat and her husband Blaise. Cat's been dead for two centuries, killed by Blaise, and—genius that I am—I believed him when he blamed someone else."

"What's your point?"

"My point is . . ." He shook his head. "It's been so long . . . I don't know how to love anymore."

"Well, you must be doing something right, because Melanie lights up whenever you walk into the room. And we both know you make her heart pound."

"I've brought nothing but chaos and pain into her life."

"This isn't your fault."

Bastien laughed mirthlessly. "Yes, it is. Everything I touch turns to shit. Every life I enter goes to hell." Knowing Cliff and Joe were likely being tortured by Emrys just made everything worse.

Sebastien, he heard Linda say in the OR, *you can see her now.*

Richart stopped him at the door. "You will have to fight your way through the guards if you burst through it the way I know you want to. Just let me exit first and walk with me at a brisk human pace. If Melanie is conscious, it will upset her to see you full of holes or being dragged away in titanium chains by Chris's men. She doesn't need that right now."

Bastien wanted to tell Richart that in the time it had taken him to say all of that he could have just teleported them there, but knew the Frenchman had elected not to so Chris's men would know where they were and there would be no confusion.

"Fine. Just open the damn door."

The guards out in the hallway were the same ones Bastien had plowed through last night. All stiffened at his appearance and fingered their weapons, ready to shoot him at the slightest provocation. Had he been alone and had the circumstances not been so fucked up, Bastien may have been tempted to mess with them a little, sure that even a cough would set them off. But he wasn't alone. Richart would be hit by stray bullets. And Melanie would not so much be upset as pissed when she saw the grisly results.

Linda must have warned the others she was summoning

him because the room to which her voice led him was empty save for her and Melanie.

Melanie's face was nearly as pale as the white sheet upon which she lay. Her eyelids were closed and remained so when they entered. She showed no response to their presence at all, even after Linda welcomed them.

Bastien couldn't seem to speak, couldn't bring himself to ask.

So Richart did it for him. "What's her condition?"

"We transfused her with fresh blood, removed all of the infected blood we could, but . . . the virus worked swiftly. She was infected on a large enough scale for a long enough time that her immune system has been completely compromised. The damage is irreparable."

Richart cleared his throat. "Are you saying she's going to die?"

"Yes."

Bastien stared at Melanie.

This was their greatest dilemma with the damned virus. Even if they found a cure, something to kill it, to make immortals and vampires mortal again, the mortals would be left with no immune system and would die, because the first thing the virus did was conquer, then replace the immune system.

Bastien forced his feet to carry him forward, stopped beside the bed. A needle was taped to one of Melanie's hands and led to an IV drip. But the one closest to him was bare.

He took it in his own. Her soft skin was cold, her long, graceful fingers limp. "Richart."

"Yes?"

"Bring Roland."

"What?"

"Roland can't help her, Sebastien," Linda said gently. "Seth and David can't either. No healer can. That's the nature of the virus. That's one of the many things that make it different from any other on the planet."

Bastien met Richart's gaze. "Get Roland and bring him here. Now."

Richart shared a look with Linda, then vanished.

Neither Bastien nor Linda said a word while they waited.

Moments later, Richart appeared with both Roland and Sarah. Removing his hands from their shoulders, he staggered a step to the side.

Bastien caught his gaze. "Now Étienne and Lisette."

Richart studied him, then nodded and disappeared.

Roland scowled and opened his mouth to blast him with some bullshit or other, but Bastien cut him off by turning to Linda. "I'm going to have to ask you to leave."

Her nervous gaze went from him to Roland to Sarah and back. "I respectfully decline."

"I'm afraid that option isn't available to you."

She raised her chin. "Lanie is my friend. I'm not going to leave her."

"You needn't fear," Roland vowed, that familiar scowl creasing his forehead. "We won't let him harm her."

Sarah smiled reassuringly. "We just need to talk for a moment. We'll bring you back in as soon as we're finished."

Linda looked at Roland. "Please call me back in if you're going to try to heal her."

"As you will."

Her reluctance obvious, Linda left and closed the door behind her.

Richart returned with Lisette, then vanished again.

Lisette gave Sarah a faint smile and nodded at Roland.

Roland didn't notice. He was already blistering Bastien's ears with his bitching.

"First of all," he snarled, "don't *ever* send Richart to my home without warning. I nearly killed him! And don't ever *summon* me. If *you* require my healing skills, you can kiss my arse. If someone *else* needs my skills, pick up the fucking phone and call me. If there isn't time for me to get to you by car, *then* you can send Richart to my home. But don't *ever*—"

"I get it," Bastien interrupted just as Richart reappeared with his twin.

Étienne caught his brother by the arm and steadied him as he listed to one side. "Richart told us Dr. Lipton is dying."

"I'm so sorry, Bastien," Sarah said.

"She isn't going to die," he told them.

Roland lost some of his fury. "You know I can't heal her." He actually looked sympathetic. "I can't cure the virus and I can't reverse the damage it does."

"I don't want you to heal her. I want you to transform her."

Shock rippled through the room like a jolt of electricity. Eyes widened. Looks were exchanged.

"No," Roland said finally.

"She won't turn vampire."

"Yes, she will. You may not want her to, but—"

"She's a *gifted one*."

"Bollocks."

"I wouldn't lie about this."

"You'd lie about anything if it suited your purpose."

"Not this. I wouldn't want her to turn vampire."

"Why not? You love vampires."

Bastien's nerves began to wear thin. "Richart?"

"I don't think he would lie about this. He cares for her too much."

Lisette spoke. "His thoughts match his words. He's telling the truth."

"Even if he is," Sarah said, "as Roland once told me, the fact that she *can* be transformed doesn't mean that she *wants* to be transformed."

"She wants to," he insisted. "She told me she did."

"Bollocks," Roland said again.

Sarah looked up at Lisette. "Is it true?"

"It is."

Sarah's hazel eyes met his. "Then what are you waiting for? Go ahead and transform her."

Bastien pointed at Roland. "I want *him* to do it."

"I don't give a fuck what you want. I'm not transforming her. I don't want to be the one she guts if she changes her mind afterward. You're the one who cares for her. You do it."

Bastien met Étienne's gaze. *For once, I need you to trust me. Read my mind, read my intent, and do as I ask. Tell Richart to help you restrain Roland and ask Lisette to keep Chris and his men out when the shit hits the fan.*

Are you out of your mind? Roland will destroy *you.*

Not if you restrain him. Just do it. You know actions speak louder than words with him. This is the only way. We're wasting valuable time.

Étienne glanced at his twin.

After a moment, Richart looked at Bastien as if he were nuts, shook his head, then moved closer to Roland. Étienne surreptitiously approached Roland's other side as Lisette frowned and eased backward toward the door.

Bastien drew two daggers. "Transform her . . . or I'll destroy you."

Roland laughed. "You couldn't if you tried."

Sarah did just as Bastien had hoped. She stepped in front of Roland. "What are you doing, Bastien?" She always tried to keep the peace between the two of them.

"Only what I have to." Without warning, he leapt forward, swinging his blades.

Sarah's eyes flashed green as she drew two sais in a blur of phenomenal speed and met him head-on.

From the corner of his eye, he saw Richart and Étienne fight like hell to hold Roland back as that one released a roar of fury that would rival a grizzly bear's.

After that, Bastien had to focus all of his attention on keeping Sarah from slicing and dicing him. The newest immortal was a foot shorter than he was and half his weight, yet Bastien knew there was a good chance he wouldn't come out of this intact.

Sarah was incredibly fast. And so strong. Quite a bit stronger than he was.

One of her blades sank deep into Bastien's chest, and he was reminded of the night he had kidnapped her. Even as a mortal she had been a force to be reckoned with. And now she thought he intended to kill the man she loved?

Pounding erupted on the door.

Sarah tossed Bastien across the room, where he knocked over rolling trays of surgical instruments, slid two yards, and hit the wall, cracking the sheetrock.

Leaping up, he charged her again, swinging his daggers, confident she could fend them off without suffering an injury. And fend them off she did. Every blade he drew, she sent sailing. Every kick she blocked. Every punch she ducked and countered.

Those tiny hands of hers were like rocks, pummeling his face and torso.

Shit!

No bodies swarmed into the room, ready to fill him full of bullets, so Lisette must be succeeding in keeping the door closed. Likewise, Roland wasn't removing Bastien's head from his body, so Richart and Étienne must be holding their own against the older immortal.

Sarah kicked Bastien in the chest, breaking several ribs and puncturing a lung. The wall behind him buckled and broke in a cloud of dust and sheetrock shrapnel as he went right through it, tumbled over a counter on the other side, and hit the floor.

Across what appeared to be a small break room, Linda sat at a small round table. Eyes the size of saucers, she gaped at him, a bagel poised halfway to her mouth.

Bastien staggered to his feet and shook some of the dust from his hair. "Don't let anyone come through here."

Dropping the bagel, she swallowed and nodded.

"I'm doing this for Melanie," he panted.

She rose and sidled over to the door to close and lock it.

"And stay away from this wall," he added. "You might be seeing me again." Struggling to breathe, Bastien dove through the large hole in the wall and confronted Sarah once more.

"Why are you doing this?" she demanded furiously.

"Because I have to," Bastien rasped and attacked.

A slew of curses and dire promises of vengeance steadily spilled from Roland's lips, encompassing pretty much everyone in the room except his wife and Melanie.

Bastien began to lose speed and strength as blood oozed from the dozens of wounds Sarah inflicted.

Damn, she could fight.

Blocking another thrust, she knocked the dagger from his grip and—in a heartbeat—broke his arm. More cuts. More punctures.

Another of those powerhouse kicks sent him sailing across the room to plow into a floor-to-ceiling cabinet full of medical supplies. Before he could regroup, she zipped over to his side, tore the built-in cabinet from the wall and toppled it onto him.

Bastien grunted. *Done.*

It took real effort to drag his ass out from under that cabinet and stand. His ribs hurt so much he couldn't straighten all of the way. But he did what he could and squinted at Sarah through bleary eyes.

Her clothes were damp in places. He hoped that was *his* blood. The tiny hands that clutched sais were bloody, the knuckles swollen and split. Thankfully, those minor wounds healed while he watched. Her pretty face was flushed. Her chest rose and fell with deep breaths. Flyaway strands of long, brown hair stood out around her face and poked out of her braid.

"Stop!" she said, part command and part plea. "I don't want to kill you."

"Do it!" Roland snarled. "Kill the fucker! You can do it, Sarah!"

"Yes," Bastien wheezed and swiped a damp sleeve across his face to wipe the blood from one of his eyes. The other eye was nearly swollen shut and the virus was taking its time healing the damage. "She can. That was my point."

Sarah's brow furrowed. Relaxing her fighting stance, she glanced over her shoulder at Roland.

"Don't turn your back on him!" her husband shouted.

Sarah spun around and faced Bastien, ready to fight.

Bastien shook his head and held up the hand on his unbroken arm in surrender. "I don't want to fight anymore."

A gleam of pride entered Roland's glowing amber eyes. "Because she just wiped the floor with your ass and you know she can do it again."

"Which, as I said, was my point."

"I don't give a f—"

"Wait a minute, sweetie," Sarah said, eyeing Bastien thoughtfully as she halted her husband's tirade. "I want to hear what he has to say."

"He can't be trusted."

"He can tonight," Étienne volunteered.

Roland speared him with a glare. "You think I'm going to take *your* word for it? Fuck you! You just allowed him to attack my wife."

"Look at her," Richart said. "She doesn't have a scratch on her."

"Because she's stronger than he is!"

Bastien's sigh turned into a grunt of pain. "Do I really have to say it again? That was my point."

Sarah backed over to her husband with caution as Bastien shuffled toward Roland.

Bastien hadn't experienced this much agony since the night

he had been captured by the immortals. "That's why it has to be you. That's why *you* have to be the one who transforms Melanie. Sarah is two centuries younger than I am. She's only been immortal for going on two years. I should have easily been able to overpower and defeat her. But she kicked my ass."

Bastien paused, gritting his teeth against the pain as the bone in his arm shifted back into place and began to mend. "If Richart, Étienne, and I all attacked her together, there's a damned good chance she would still come out on top because she's as strong as you are. As fast as you are. And heals almost as quickly as you do. Such has never happened before. Newer immortals are *always* weaker than older ones."

Though Roland's eyes continued to glow brightly with rage, he seemed to be listening. "It's probably because she was transformed by an immortal instead of a vampire. *Any* immortal could have transformed her with the same results."

"You don't know that. None of us do. You've stubbornly refused to let Melanie or anyone else at the network run tests on you and Sarah to see what they can learn. It could be your healing ability. Or something unique in your DNA."

"Or it could be something unique in Sarah's DNA," Roland pointed out.

"That's less likely, I think, considering her bloodline has had centuries more of being diluted with ordinary human DNA than yours has."

Sarah sheathed her weapons. "So you're hoping if he transforms Melanie, she'll be strong like me? Why didn't you just say that, Bastien? Why did you make me hurt you?"

Bastien wanted to laugh. The boys he had sparred with in his mortal youth would've never let him forget he had been *bested by a girl*. "Roland wouldn't have listened." He motioned to the two telepaths. "They wouldn't have either if they couldn't hear my thoughts. They all look at me," he said with no self-pity, "and see nothing but the murderer of a friend.

The leader of vampires, of your enemy. An outsider who can't be trusted."

Sarah looked at the others, who offered no denials. "I don't know that that's true. They listened to you at the meeting."

"Because Melanie, Seth, and David backed me." Enough talk. Bastien looked to Roland. "Our existence has never been as treacherous as it is now. I want Melanie to be as strong as possible. As safe as possible. I want her to have a greater tolerance for sunlight and the tranquilizers. I want her to have more speed and strength than I do. I want vampires to pose no threat to her in small numbers. Wouldn't you want the same for Sarah?"

Roland moved his shoulders and arms. "You can release me now."

Richart and Étienne glanced at each other uneasily, then released their hold on him.

"Will you do it?" Bastien asked. He would beg if he had to. This was for Melanie.

Roland cupped Sarah's face in one of his hands. "I would want the same for you."

"I know," she said softly.

"Would it trouble you if I transformed her?"

Her brow furrowed as her gaze slid to Melanie. Resting her hands on Roland's hips she drew him closer and looked up at him. "Would it . . . bind the two of you in some way?"

"No."

"It bound us."

He shook his head. "Our love bound us, not my transforming you."

"So you won't . . . feel her emotions or . . . develop an attraction to her?"

"No, sweetling. My heart is yours and yours alone. My desire only for you. And it will remain so always."

Her forehead smoothed out. "Then I think you should do

it. And, after this, I think we should let Melanie run those tests."

He kissed her lightly on the lips. "As you will."

When he would have pulled away, she grabbed his belt loops and stopped him. "Wait. Could you maybe bite her on her wrist or arm instead of her neck?"

He smiled. "I intended to."

Sarah rose up onto her toes and kissed him. "I love you."

"I love you, too."

She released him.

Roland lost his faint smile as he turned away. So quickly Bastien almost missed it, he slammed his fist into Richart's, then Étienne's faces. Both immortals flew backward, hit the floor, and skidded away several feet. "Don't *ever* restrain me again!"

Neither answered. They were too busy groaning and cupping their mouths and noses with their hands.

Lisette tilted her head to one side and raised one eyebrow, daring Roland to do the same to her.

Roland settled for a glare. "I'll let you off with a warning."

She grinned cheekily. "Chicken."

That almost made the dour immortal smile again. Until the door shook.

Lisette grimaced and braced her feet. "Now they've gone and gotten a battering ram. How rude."

Roland crossed to her, planted a hand on the door beside her head, and motioned her aside.

She straightened cautiously, as though she expected the guards to burst through if she abandoned her post.

Six centuries older and stronger, Roland held the door effortlessly while she moved to stand over her brothers, who remained where they had fallen.

Roland yanked the door open and bellowed *"What?"*

As one, the soldiers recoiled and stood in the hallway, eyes wide, fingers on the triggers of the automatic weapons they carried.

While the soldiers here at the network disliked Bastien, they outright *feared* Roland.

The one Bastien recognized as Todd cleared his throat. "Um . . . we know Bastien is in there and . . . we heard noises, sir, and just wanted to make sure—"

"Everything's fine. Bugger off." Roland slammed the door and turned back to the room.

A *tap tap tap* sounded.

Scowl deepening, Roland yanked the door open again. "I said—"

"With all due respect, sir," Todd stated bravely, "when Mr. Reordon gets back, he isn't going to settle for 'It's all good.' I need to know that Bastien is in custody and I need to know what's going on."

"Immortal business that's none of yours."

When Roland would have shut the door, Todd stuck his foot in the gap to stop him.

"Do you *want* to piss me off?" Roland asked him, voice soft and deadly.

The men behind Todd looked terrified, but stood their ground. Chris had chosen well.

"Sir, my job is to protect the men and women who work in this facility. Men and women, I might add, whose work has proven invaluable to you and the other immortals. Mr. Reordon believes Bastien poses a threat and . . . if whatever is happening in there will endanger *any* of the network employees—"

Sarah stepped up beside her husband. "We appreciate your loyalty, Todd, but there's no danger to anyone outside of this room. We were just . . . taking care of a little personal business." So saying, she opened the door wide enough for those in the hallway to get a good look at Bastien.

Their shock was obvious. As was the gleam of satisfaction that entered their eyes when they saw Bastien had had his ass handed to him by at least one of the other immortals present.

Yeah. They hated him.

Todd nodded and offered Sarah a smile. "No problem. Thanks for clearing that up for us, ma'am. I'll let Mr. Reordon know that everything is under control."

"Thank you." Sarah closed the door and stared up at her husband. "You see? That's all you had to do."

"Scaring them is more fun."

She grinned and kissed his chin.

Bedding rustled as Melanie shifted. Though her head rolled on the pillow, her eyes remained closed. "Bastien?"

Bastien moved toward the bed.

Sarah darted across the room and yanked the privacy curtain forward, hiding them from Melanie's view. She frowned at the others and hissed, "She can't see him like this."

Everyone in the room looked at Bastien.

"What?" he asked. Did he look that bad? The bone in his arm was no longer protruding from the skin.

Lisette pursed her lips. "You're right. Étienne, switch clothes with him."

Étienne frowned. "No way."

She rolled her eyes. "Just do it. You're the same size and Richart can teleport you home to change when we're done here."

"Fine," he grumbled and, in seconds, stripped down to his boxer shorts. He wadded his clothes up into a ball and held them out to Bastien. "Well?"

Okay. This was . . . strange.

Bastien stripped down to his skivvies, handed over his torn, sticky bundle, and donned Étienne's clothes.

Scrabbling sounds drew Bastien's attention to the hole in the wall as he zipped up the pants.

Linda awkwardly clambered through it with something

white in her hands. Once her feet were firmly planted on the floor, she straightened and blew ruffled bangs out of her eyes. "You're done fighting, right?"

"Yes," Sarah assured her.

Linda smiled. "Good." She strode toward Bastien. "Here. This should help." She held out a couple of large hand towels, both damp.

He took them, wondering why she was smiling at him. "Thank you."

Lisette snatched one of the towels from him, gripped his chin in one deadly feminine hand, and began to wipe his face clean. And she wasn't rough.

Sarah took the other towel and tossed it over his head. Rising onto her toes, she rubbed it over his hair, luring some of the blood and dust and other debris onto the towel and out of his thick locks.

Bastien stood there, feet rooted to the floor.

Yeah, this was *really* strange.

Everyone in this room scorned him. And yet they were doing their damnedest to make him presentable for Melanie. He knew it was for *her*, not him, but . . .

Was this what it felt like?

Sarah turned to Roland. "Sweetie, do you have a comb?"

Was this what it felt like to be one of them? To have friends who always had your back and were always there to help you with anything you needed? To be part of the immortal family in truth, not just in name?

Roland reached into his back pocket and drew out a comb.

"You carry a comb around with you?" Bastien couldn't resist asking around the towel Lisette was using to wipe the blood from his nose and chin. The envy that stole its way into him left him uncomfortable.

"It's for Sarah, asshole."

The towel Sarah discarded was surprisingly filthy. She

settled back on her heels. "Let's switch, Lisette. I'm too short for this."

Lisette, several inches taller than Sarah's five feet, exchanged the towel—now soiled with pink blotches—for the comb and shifted to Bastien's side.

Sarah ducked under Lisette's arm and examined Bastien's face. Her soft lips turned up in a small smile. "How's the head?"

Bastien chuckled at the question he usually presented to her. "Pounding."

Sarah wiped his face a couple of times, then drew the cloth down his neck. "I feel sort of bad now that I know why you picked the fight."

"Don't."

Her smile widened. "That's it? Just don't?"

He nodded, wincing when Lisette tried to tug the comb through his tangled hair. "You would've done the same damage had we been sparring."

She and Lisette finished spiffying him up and stepped back. Both grimaced.

"Roland, sweetie, come heal him."

"Hell, no."

"At least heal his face. It's all swollen and gross."

Well, hell.

"It's for Dr. Lipton," Lisette threw in.

Roland sighed. "Fine. But I reserve the right to bloody it up again after she recovers." Nudging his wife aside, he palmed Bastien's face with little care for the pain it spawned in the bruised flesh and broken bones.

Roland's hand heated. The aches and pains faded as the many injuries on Bastien's face healed, the tightness vanishing as swelling decreased. When Roland withdrew his hand (giving Bastien's head a shove in the process), Bastien's face felt normal again.

The rest of him still hurt like hell. But at least his other wounds weren't visible.

"So?" he asked the women.

"Good enough," Lisette said.

Sarah and Linda nodded their agreement.

"Bastien," Melanie whispered again on the other side of the curtain.

He eyed the others, feeling awkward as hell. "Thank you."

Roland shook his head. "It wasn't for you."

Right.

Chapter 14

Seth materialized in David's home and followed the sounds of voices to David's study.

Darnell was talking on the phone while typing furiously on the computer keyboard.

"What's happened?"

Darnell jumped and spun around, dropping the phone. No relief swept his countenance as he hurried to pick it up. "The network was attacked."

"By vampires?" How the hell had vampires found them?

"No, by Emrys's men. No estimates yet on how many are dead."

Seth teleported to the network . . . and had difficulty believing what he saw. Bright golden sunlight illuminated the destruction. Almost everything above ground had been obliterated. Even the paved parking lot bore large craters. A few jagged chunks of wall still stood, weary reminders of the building's dimensions. Charcoal smoke stretched to the sky and formed dark, wispy clouds.

Seth could see the first sublevel through gaping holes in the foundation. Surrounding the building's skeleton were two downed helicopters, several armored personnel carriers, and four Humvees. Bodies of the mercenaries formed piles around the places immortals had stood their ground. Damned near everything present bore scorch marks or bullet holes. *Large* bullet holes.

The scent of death clung to every surface.

A war had been fought here. With all of the casualties that went with it.

Sirens wailed in the distance.

Seth swore. A hasty inspection of the various vehicles revealed a few that were salvageable. Seth held his hand out and sent them to the field bordering the building Chris—if he lived—was no doubt already setting up as the new network headquarters. Teleporting something or someone without touching or accompanying it took a lot more energy (no other immortal could do it), but he had little choice with fire engines speeding toward him.

The other vehicles he sent to the bottom of the Mariana Trench, the deepest part of the world's oceans. The dead soldiers he sent to the morgue at the new headquarters. Perhaps network employees could identify them.

A wave of his hand produced a breeze that scattered and dispersed the smoke.

Then Seth sped into the lower levels of the network.

The scents of blood and smoke burned his nostrils. Broken bodies lay amid the rubble. Seth listened hard for a heartbeat and found none. Not on Sublevel 1. On Sublevel 2. Nor on the remaining three. The damage Emrys's men had done astounded him, reaching all the way down to the fifth basement level.

The wall at the end of the hallway had been blown, opening the escape tunnel for survivors.

The tunnel was a long one that led up to the basement of a single story home with no neighbors and no outward connection to the larger building.

How many had escaped through it?

The floor was red with blood that had dripped from the

injured as they were helped to safety. He could smell the fear and pain of those who had passed through here.

The sirens grew louder, then stopped above his head. Seth raced up to deal with them, ready to erase memories and plant new ones. His strength was flagging, not from his battle earlier with the vampires in South Korea, but from the teleporting he had done to clean up some of the mess topside. By the time he finished dealing with the firemen and policemen who would likely follow, he would barely be able to put one foot in front of the other.

Three fire engines awaited him, parked, motors idling, lights flashing, sirens off. Seth strode forward as several firemen emerged and walked toward him.

"Mr. Seth?" one said.

Hmm. "Just Seth."

The man nodded. "Mr. Reordon sent us, sir."

Seth sent a big *Thank you* Chris's way. Even when all hell broke loose around him, Chris managed to get shit done. He was a good man.

"Did he have a particular explanation in mind?" Seth asked. Chris had a knack for making just about anyone believe anything.

"Gas leak."

Tried and true.

The men made their careful way through the wreckage.

"Any chance you could block the view of the elevator shaft? This'll go down easier if we don't have to explain all of the floors below ground."

Seth nodded.

It took some doing, but he managed to cover the shaft with large portions of toppled wall and other debris. It probably wouldn't hold if some idiot jumped up and down on it, but lookers wouldn't be able to tell there were five floors underground.

More firemen arrived, legitimate ones this time. Policemen followed. Seth discarded his coat and altered their memories of speaking with him so they wouldn't remember the blood-stains on his clothing. He also removed any doubt they possessed regarding the cause of the fire and explosions some nearby claimed they had heard. When a news helicopter rumbled overhead, Seth directed the pilot and news crew away.

He didn't know how much time passed before he succeeded in clearing the scene of anyone who wasn't on the network's payroll.

Fatigued pulled at him. He hadn't slept in a couple of days and the various and assorted stunts he'd had to pull here to cover their asses had cost him a lot of energy.

"Sir?"

Seth turned.

The same mock-fireman who had spoken to him earlier approached, tucking a cell phone into his back pocket. "Something's going on over at the new network headquarters. Something to do with Sebastien Newcomb. Mr. Reordon could use your help."

Of course. Sebastien couldn't seem to go a single day without spawning chaos somewhere. Seth was beginning to lose patience with him.

Thanking the faux fireman, he teleported to the new network building to see what Sebastien had done now.

Melanie had never felt so exhausted in her life. Just opening her eyes seemed a chore. "Bastien?"

The stark whiteness of the infirmary's ceiling, floor, and walls met her gaze. What she could see of it. The privacy curtain had been drawn, blocking her view of half the room.

Confused, she took in the IV, the machines monitoring her. Felt the weakness that suffused seemingly every cell of her body.

Had she been injured again? She could think of no other explanation. But how? Had she gone hunting with Bastien and Richart? The last thing she remembered was Bastien bringing Stuart to the network.

She sensed movement on the other side of the curtain and could've sworn she heard someone call someone else an asshole.

"Bastien?"

The curtain slid back.

Melanie stared at Bastien as he stepped up to her bedside. His hair was slicked back. Behind him Linda, Richart, Étienne, Lisette, Sarah, and Roland stood. Étienne's clothes were cut and torn and bloody as though he had been fighting. And he kept shifting uncomfortably as if he had sand in his underwear.

Sarah seemed to have some blood splatter on her face. And her knuckles were crusted over with drying blood.

They must have just returned from hunting.

Bastien took her hand, rubbed his thumb across her skin in soothing circles. His warmth infused her icy flesh and traveled up her arm to fill her chest.

Her gaze strayed to Roland. Why was *he* here? Roland and Bastien in the same room usually spelled disaster.

Wait. Was that a hole in the wall back there? It was hard to see around the towering men.

Bastien didn't possess any visible injuries, though. Neither did Roland. So . . . what had damaged the wall and why was Roland here? Had he healed her again?

"What happened?" she asked Bastien. "Did I go hunting with you again?"

He shook his head. "Stuart was a pawn. Emrys got his hands on him before our rendezvous and injected a tiny electronic device beneath Stuart's skin that allowed Emrys and his mercenaries to track him anywhere he went."

They could track him? Alarm rushed through her. "Then they know he's here. They'll find him. They'll find *us*, the network."

He touched a hand to her shoulder to keep her from rising. "They already did. They attacked in force just before dawn."

She took in the grave expressions of the others. That explained the hole in the wall. "You held them off? Is it safe here? Won't they return?"

"We defeated them, but they were heavily armed."

Richart nodded. "And their numbers were such that we could not begin to estimate them."

"The network's headquarters was reduced to rubble," Bastien finished.

"I don't understand." She looked around the familiar infirmary. "We're *in* the network's headquarters."

Linda stepped up beside Bastien and patted Melanie's knee. "No, honey. This is another building. You know how Mr. Reordon takes every freaking precaution imaginable to the nth degree to ensure all of our safety?"

"Yes."

"Well, one of those precautions included constructing an identical headquarters building in Greensboro."

"This isn't the building we worked in every day?"

"No. It looks exactly like it, doesn't it? Just . . . newer and cleaner. There are even apartments across the hall for the vampires."

The vampires.

Melanie met Bastien's brown gaze. "Are Cliff and Joe okay?"

His grip tightened. "They're gone. Everything was utter chaos. Joe chose to escape in the middle of it all."

"And Cliff?"

"The mercenaries got him. We think they might have Joe, too."

Horror filled her. Emrys would torture them. To learn about the virus. To get information. He would dissect them while they were still living and breathing. And the madness she had worked so hard to help Cliff and Joe stave off would claim them wholly as a result.

Her eyes began to burn. Tears spilled over her lashes. "We have to get them back."

"We will," Bastien said. "*I* will. I vow it. But . . . there's more." He sat on the edge of her bed.

Her heart began to pound painfully in her chest. "What? What is it?"

"At my urging, Chris let the vampires out to help evacuate the injured and fight off the mercenaries who infiltrated the building." A muscle in his jaw twitched. His eyes began to glow, revealing the inner turmoil roiling within him. "Stuart was wounded. Pretty seriously apparently and . . . he bit you."

"One bite won't—"

"He infected you, Melanie. He claims he bit you to heal his wounds, then panicked when he realized he had unintentionally drained you and you were dying. He transfused you, infecting you on a massive scale. Dr. Whetsman and the others worked fast to replace the infected blood with human blood. But . . . the damage has been done. Your immune system has been compromised and they have no hope that it will recover."

"Are you saying I have no immune system?"

"Yes."

"I'm dying." Their expressions told her they already knew that. But she needed to say it out loud to wrap her mind around it. She had no immune system. At all. She wouldn't live another twenty-four hours.

Bastien looked over his shoulder.

Roland stepped forward. "Bastien has asked me to transform you, Dr. Lipton, if you so desire it."

Transform her. Make her an immortal. Like Bastien.

She had always known the option was there for her and had intended to take advantage of it. She was a *gifted one*, after all. It just had always seemed like something that would happen in the distant future. Not now.

She focused on Bastien. "Why Roland? Why don't *you* want to transform me?" It hurt that he would rather someone else do it.

Leaning forward, he stroked her face in a loving gesture she was surprised he would let the others witness. "I want you to be strong like Sarah. I want you to have every advantage over our enemies. I want you to be able to kick my ass when you get tired of my bullshit."

She covered his hand with hers, understanding now why such seemed to take so much effort.

Roland nodded somberly. "We all want you to be able to kick Bastien's ass. And you don't have to wait to get tired of his bullshit."

Melanie smiled. "I admit, there were times I would've already done so if I could."

Everyone laughed.

Except for Bastien. His brow remained furrowed with concern. "Will you do it? Will you let Roland transform you? I'll be right here. I won't leave you."

She found enough strength to squeeze his hand. "I will. But I don't want you to stay." Yes, she did. She really, really did. "I'm going to be out of commission for a few days and—"

"You'll do it? You'll become an immortal?"

"Yes."

The relief that swept his handsome features was heart-rending. For a moment she thought he would weep with it. "Thank you." He pressed a kiss to her hand. "As I said, I won't leave you. I'll stay with you and help you through the transformation."

She shook her head. "As much as I would like you to stay with me, finding Cliff and Joe is more important than holding my hair for me while I vomit."

"I don't want you to go through this alone."

Linda rested a hand on his shoulder. "I could watch over her at night while you hunt. Then you could take over during the day."

Bastien seemed surprised by the offer. "Thank you." He looked at Melanie. "Is that what you want?"

"Sounds good." Melanie drew in a deep breath and let it out slowly, nervous butterflies fluttering in her belly. "Okay then, can we go ahead and do this? The sooner we get it done, the sooner I'll stop feeling like this."

Bastien started to rise. Roland cupped his shoulder and eased him back down, then walked around to the other side of the bed.

Melanie searched out Sarah's gaze. "You're okay with this?"

Smiling, Sarah nodded. "It won't bind the two of you together or anything."

Jeeze. She hadn't even thought of that. That was good to know. "Does it hurt?"

"I don't remember Roland biting me."

Of course she didn't. Melanie had forgotten the GHB-like chemical the glands above their fangs produced and released under the pressure of a bite.

"What about the rest of it?"

"It's like having the worst case of the flu ever. You'll be miserable as hell for about three days. But, if you're like me, you won't remember most of it."

Melanie nodded. "It's worth it."

Sarah smiled at her husband. "It really is."

Roland winked at Sarah and carefully removed the IV, needle, and tape.

Melanie's heart slammed against her ribs. Her eyes sought and clung to Bastien's. "I'm nervous." She needn't say it. Everyone but Linda could hear the physical manifestations of it. "Were you nervous?"

He smiled. "My transformation took several weeks. Definitely not the way I would recommend being transformed, by the way. And when I realized what was happening, I was terrified."

Roland lifted her free arm off the mattress. "Do you want a warning, or should I do it on the sly?"

"Warning."

"Then consider this your warning."

She nodded.

His lips parted. His fangs descended. Bending his head, he sank his teeth into her arm at the bend of her elbow where she had donated blood so often.

She gritted her teeth. It felt like twin needles piercing her.

Where was the erotic ecstasy vampire bites inspired in movies and novels and TV shows? Not that she wanted to feel that for Roland.

Bastien brushed his hand over her hair. "Okay?"

"Yes." She smiled up at him, feeling very mellow all of a sudden. "You're cute with your hair slicked back like that."

Someone snickered.

Bastien's smile widened. "Thank you. Shall I wear it like this more often?"

"Absolutely. It makes me want to run my fingers through it and muss it up."

His eyes flared amber.

"I like that, too," she said. Were her words beginning to slur? "I like it when your eyes glow. You're so beautiful."

"I don't know about her," Étienne murmured, "but I'm beginning to feel rather nauseated."

Melanie laughed. "He's just jealous because you're hotter than he is."

Bastien gave her a rueful smile. "Perhaps it would be best if you rested and didn't speak."

"Why? I feel . . . I feel great. So relaxed and . . ."

The lights went out. No. No, wait. She had just closed her eyes.

Opening them, she examined Bastien with a grin. "You look like those women in the old Star Trek TV show episodes."

Someone guffawed in the background.

Bastien smiled and frowned at the same time. "I don't know how to take that."

"It's like I'm seeing you through a soft focus camera. You're all blurry and pretty."

More male laughter.

"Jackasses," a woman with a French accent said. "Stop laughing. She can't help it."

"We're not laughing at her. We're laughing at him."

"Ignore them," Bastien said, leaning forward to stroke her hair again.

Melanie practically purred with pleasure. "You know what I want to do when I'm immortal?"

"What's that?"

She licked her lips. "I want to make love with you again." His eyes flared brighter. "I want to know what your bare body will feel like against mine when all of my senses are heightened."

A throat cleared. "Okay. This is starting to get personal. I'm thinking maybe you should get us out of here, Richart."

"Good idea. Lisette, are you coming with us?"

"Oui."

Bastien leaned in close, still holding her hand. "You shouldn't say such things, sweetheart."

She tried to move her other arm, but couldn't. Someone was holding it.

"Don't move your arm, love," Bastien instructed softly.

A winter chill seemed to settle into her body. "I'm cold," she said, shivering.

Bastien turned away. "Do you have another blanket?" Releasing her hand, he shook out a blanket and draped it over her. "Better?"

When he leaned down again, she touched his face, stroked his jaw. "It isn't true."

"What isn't?"

Her eyelids felt so heavy. "Not too good for you."

"Yes, you are."

"If . . . were . . . wouldn't be . . . falling in love with . . ."

Bastien stared at Melanie, his heart jackhammering in his chest.

She was falling in love with him?

Just the possibility of it left him feeling as euphoric as if he were himself a mortal who had been bitten.

He had known she was attracted to him, that she had tender feelings for him. Hell, he had used any damned excuse he could find to brush up against her so he could let those emotions wash over him. But he hadn't realized . . .

He knew he loved her. His desire to spend every moment he could with her, his need to protect her, and the happiness that filled him whenever she smiled at him could be nothing less.

But Melanie . . .

How could she love him? How could she think he was good enough for her? He would never be worthy of her.

He looked at Roland, who watched him closely, lips locked on Melanie's arm.

He looked at Linda.

"I'm pretty sure she would've preferred to tell you that in private," she murmured.

"You don't think it's just the influence of the bite confusing her?"

"No. She talks about you all the time. Has for weeks." She clamped her lips shut. "And now I feel guilty as hell for telling you that. Crap. Forget I said anything."

Melanie talked about him to Linda?

He opted to look at the woman who had the most reason to hate him last.

"You're an empath, Bastien," Sarah said, voice kind. "Surely you knew."

Melanie's cold hand grew warm as Roland began to infuse her with the blood he had taken from her. Blood that now carried the virus in large enough amounts to effect a swift transformation.

Bastien said nothing more.

The infirmary door opened and Chris strode in. "What's going on?" He stopped short when he saw the damage done to the room. "Damn it! We haven't been here twenty-four hours and you've already wrecked the place? At least tell me you destroyed—" He looked over, caught sight of Bastien, and swore.

His eyes widened when he saw Roland standing beside Melanie's bed with his fangs buried deeply in her arm. "You're transforming her?"

Bastien nodded and prepared to fight the human if Chris tried to stop them.

"Please, tell me you got her permission first."

Sarah stepped forward. "We did."

He relaxed. "Make a list of everything she'll need during the transformation and I'll get it."

Though Bastien believed him, he would feel better if Melanie endured the illness that would soon assault her at David's place, where the elder immortal would be on hand to aid her if something went wrong. "She'll have everything she needs at David's."

Chris studied the others.

Bastien caught Sarah's eye and willed her to defend his decision. Chris would never let them take her otherwise.

Sarah produced a smile. "She might be more comfortable in a home environment than she would here. And David will be right there if she should need him. He helped me through *my* transformation."

Chris nodded. "All right. If you'd like me to arrange to have a doctor stationed in David's infirmary for the duration, let me know."

"I'll do it," Linda jumped in.

Chris drew his cell phone from his pocket. "I'll—"

Seth abruptly appeared. His eyes surveyed the room, went to Roland and Melanie, and flashed a brilliant gold.

Oh. Shit.

"Did you gain her permission?"

"Yes," they all hastened to declare.

The luminescence faded, leaving his eyes a brown so dark they were nearly black.

Roland completed the transfusion. As his fangs retracted, he touched his fingers to the bite marks and healed them, then lowered Melanie's arm gently to the covers. "I thought I would never transform a mortal. Now I've transformed two."

Sarah joined him and leaned into his side, wrapping an arm around his waist.

Seth crossed to stand beside Bastien. Reaching down, he rested his hand atop Melanie's hair.

How well did he know her?

"We should take her to David's," Seth said. "She'll be more comfortable there. And safe." He gave the damage to the other part of the room a quick once-over and sighed. "I'm not even going to ask."

Melanie wondered how many times she would have to hang her head over the damned toilet before her stomach got the message that there wasn't anything left to come up.

When the latest bout of retching finally ceased, she sat on the floor and leaned back against the huge whirlpool tub, too weary to rise. She was nearing the end of day two of her transformation and *so* wanted it to be over with already.

Sarah had warned her it would be like this, that it would feel as if she had contracted the worst case of the flu ever. Fever, aches, majorly unsettled stomach, a fluctuating migraine. Her muscles felt like she imagined they would if she had never exercised a day in her life, then spent a week working out for hours every day with heavy weights. She was hot. And cold. Her body shivered while heat flayed her just beneath the skin and poured out of her eye sockets.

Melanie grimaced at the image that evoked and told herself to get up and drag her weak ass back into the bedroom.

Minutes passed and she didn't move.

Oh well. She'd just have to come back in here and gag her head off in half an hour anyway. May as well stick around.

She contemplated her new sumptuous accommodations. Glass tile in soothing green tones. Dark wood cabinets. Bright white sink and tub. Shiny chrome fixtures. Bamboo plants. Fluffy white towels. It was like being in an expensive spa.

Closing her eyes, she rested her head back against the tub.

"Dr. Lipton?"

Frowning, Melanie pried her eyes open. Had she fallen asleep?

Peering up at the small figure leaning over her, she tried to get her eyes to focus. "Ami?"

"Yes. Are you all right?"

"Sure." She couldn't seem to get Ami and the rest of the room to quit swirling around.

"Where's Linda?"

Something about an emergency at the network? Or a Second being injured? Melanie couldn't remember.

"Can I help you back to bed?"

"Okay."

Decked out in hunting garb, Ami crouched down in front of her and pulled Melanie's arms around her neck.

"I'm sorry."

"For what?" Ami locked her hands behind Melanie's back, then hoisted her to her feet.

Melanie's knees buckled. "I don't know."

Though smaller than her, Ami shifted Melanie to one side and pretty much carried her into the bedroom. "Why were you on the bathroom floor?"

"Whatever they're eating upstairs keeps making me sick."

"You can smell that down here?"

"You can't?" The scent was so strong they may as well have been cooking it in the damn room with her.

Ami helped her into bed and pressed a hand to Melanie's forehead. "You're burning up."

The sheets felt cold against her skin, inspiring a tidal wave of shivers.

Ami arranged Melanie's limp body comfortably and drew the covers up to her chin. "She's burning up," she said softly.

Bastien loomed over the bed. "Melanie?" His hand was cool against her fiery forehead. His hair was windblown. His clothes were wet in places. His skin smelled of sweet North Carolina nights and something metallic. He must have just returned from hunting. "Melanie? Can you hear me, sweetheart?" Then lower: "How long has she been like this?"

"I don't know. I just found her."

"Where's Linda?"

"I don't know. I asked Dr. Lipton, but she didn't answer."

"Let's get the blankets off her."

Cold air embraced Melanie when he yanked the covers back.

"I'm sorry," Ami said. "I've never been sick before and didn't know what to do for a fever. She was shivering, so I thought—"

"I know, Ami. It's okay. Would you see if you can track down David while I try Roland?"

Melanie couldn't hold her eyes open any longer. The

sounds of Bastien retrieving, then dialing his phone seemed magnified.

"Roland? Melanie is spiking a fever . . . I don't know, but you don't even have to touch her to feel the heat coming off her skin . . ."

Darkness.

Quiet.

Hands shaking, Bastien stripped off everything but his boxers at preternatural speeds.

Ami and Darnell hurried past, arms full of towels they took into the bathroom. Roland, Sarah, and Richart flew past in a blur, scuffling as they hit the doorway at the same time.

Pulling the oversized shirt he had leant Melanie down over her pale pink bikini panties, Bastien found himself silently offering up a prayer for the first time in decades. Or was it centuries?

Fire radiated from Melanie's skin as he lifted her limp form into his arms.

It terrified him. As did her total lack of response.

He hurried into the bathroom, which thankfully was spacious. Ami and Darnell were lining the edges of the oversized bathtub with thick fluffy towels. The three immortals were pouring several large bags of ice into the water that filled it.

"You'll have to get into the tub with her," Roland said. "Lucid or nay, she'll do her damnedest to get out of there once the cold hits her."

Sarah twined the fingers of one hand through Roland's. "Roland did it for me. That's one of the few things I remember from my transformation."

As soon as everyone moved back, Bastien stepped into the water. Small, rectangular cubes bobbed on the surface and bounced against his shins as others beneath them tried to fight their way to the top. Extreme cold cut through him like shards of glass.

Bastien gritted his teeth. With a little concentration, he could regulate his body temperature so efficiently that steam would rise from his skin. But the whole point of this was to cool Melanie down, so his body temperature needed to match that of the water.

Taking a deep breath (he was *not* looking forward to that frigid water hitting his family jewels), he sat with Melanie reclining in his lap, her back to his chest.

A split second later, she awoke with a roar. Lunging away from him, she struggled to leave the water and escape the cold that pierced her skin like needles.

Bastien locked his arms around her and murmured reassuring nonsense as he gently eased her back against him. Her arms and legs flailed and fought, striking the edge of the tub he was glad Ami and Darnell had thought to pad with towels.

Weak from the virus wreaking havoc within her, Melanie swiftly fell still, panting and shivering against him.

"Just a little longer," he whispered, chest aching as tears silently leaked from the corners of her closed eyes. "Just a little longer, sweetheart. Then you'll never be ill again."

Every second lasted an hour. The tiny rectangular icebergs dwindled in size as Melanie's warmth reached them. And, with every second, the pain wracking his body multiplied.

But he voiced no complaints. He merely held Melanie's shivering form close and hoped this would work.

Awkward, anxious silence filled the room.

Teeth chattering, he bent his head, pressed his cheek to hers, and closed his eyes.

Chapter 15

Melanie awoke not knowing where she was or how she had come to be there. The lights were off. No windows provided ambient light. Soft sheets cushioned her back. Others were drawn up to her neck.

Habit left her squinting at her surroundings until she realized she could see them clearly in the darkness *without* squinting.

Raising her head, she examined the bedroom. It was odd, seeing it this way. In pitch blackness, much of the color had been leeched from the walls, bedding, and other decor.

Was this how immortals saw things? Was this how cats and dogs and nocturnal creatures saw things at night? Because this was very cool.

Lowering her head to the pillow, she decided the toothache plaguing her, on the other hand, was *not* cool. Nor was the throbbing headache.

At least the nausea was better.

She tried to raise one hand to rub her pounding temples and couldn't. The large fingers twined through hers tightened and drew her arm up against a hard chest.

Melanie slowly turned her head on the pillow.

Bastien slept beside her on his side, her hand and forearm

now tucked against his chest. The stubble on his chin abraded her knuckles.

His eyes were closed, his brow furrowed in sleep. She had never noticed how long his eyelashes were. Those warm, beautiful brown eyes of his always distracted her, particularly when they burned with amber flames.

She rolled onto her side, facing him.

He looked tired. He must not have been feeding.

How long had he been caring for her and watching over her?

His lashes lifted. Those chestnut eyes met hers.

Melanie reached up with her free hand and drew her fingers down the side of his handsome face.

His eyes began to glow. "Don't leave me," he whispered.

Her own eyes pricked with tears at the stark plea. "I won't. I'm better now."

He brought her hand to his lips and kissed it fervently. "Can I get you anything?"

"No. Just rest," she murmured and scooted closer.

His lids lowered. A long sigh brushed her knuckles. His brow smoothed out as his breathing deepened.

His grip on her hand, however, never lessened.

Smiling despite the headache and toothache, Melanie closed her eyes and let sleep claim her.

Bastien jerked awake when a hand clamped around his throat. Golden eyes blazing with fury met his in the darkness.

Seth. *Oh shit.*

Bastien glanced to the side where Melanie slept.

If Seth intended to kill him, Bastien hoped he would do it elsewhere.

"As you will," the immortal leader snarled.

The two of them teleported to the training room. Edward

and Ethan were there, training with Étienne and Lisette, while Tracy sparred with Sheldon.

All movement ceased when the others got a gander at their leader slowly choking the life out of Bastien, who wore only sweatpants.

"Out," Seth snapped.

Weapons slid into sheaths. The immortals exited as slowly as the humans did, feet shuffling, necks craning, reluctant to miss the action.

"Now!"

That got them moving, leaving only Bastien and his executioner.

Bastien thought fleetingly that Seth should have teleported them to his castle in England instead. Then they would have come full circle, having acted this scene out before.

Seth yanked him closer. "Ah, but that time I let you live." What felt like a fist tightened around Bastien's heart. Pain streaked through his chest.

"Oh, hell no!" Marcus entered, scowling darkly as he stomped toward the duo. "If anyone's going to kill that asshole, it's going to be me."

In his dreams. No way in hell would Bastien let Marcus be the implement of his demise. The bastard had nearly gotten Ami killed on at least two occasions.

Seth dropped him like a stone. "Are you kidding me? That's why I'm going to kill *you*! You put Ami in danger!"

Bastien coughed and choked and sucked in air. The pressure in his chest vanished.

"You're really going to kill him?" Yet another new voice.

All three turned to see David lounging in the doorway.

"Yes," Seth and Marcus both answered, then scowled at each other.

"Well, try not to make too much of a mess. I'm tired of all of the blame-it-on-Bastien shit wrecking my home."

Bastien's throat finally expanded enough for him to speak. "I thought you wanted to kill me, too," he wheezed.

David shook his head. "I just planned to kick your ass."

"Gee, thanks." Any way it went, he was screwed. His big battle with Roland a couple of years ago had shown him quite clearly that any immortal hundreds of years older than him could pretty much wipe the floor with him. Sure, he'd get some hits in and do some damage of his own, but that's about all he would do.

He looked from one to the next to the last and thought of Melanie curled up in his bed, still ill from the transformation.

You know what? Fuck that defeatist crap. Melanie needed him. He'd fight every immortal and Second in this house if he had to. He wasn't going to let her down.

David groaned and rolled his eyes.

Seth swore.

Marcus looked confused. "What?"

"Had you shown as much concern for Ami," Seth said, "I wouldn't wish to reduce you to ashes right now."

"You think that decision was easy for me?" Bastien demanded. "You think I *wanted* Ami there? I've known her for almost as long as you have and love her just as much as you all do."

David ambled forward. "Seth and I *removed* Ami from Emrys's clutches. You put her directly in his path."

"Emrys wasn't there."

"But if he had been—"

"Marcus would have ripped him limb from limb and I would've had Marcus's back. I want Emrys dead. The longer it takes us to locate him, the more opportunity he has to share his discovery with others. Chris isn't making any headway through his contacts. The whole vampire recruitment thing turned around and bit me on the ass."

"Stuart didn't betray you," David mentioned. "From what

I could glean from the mercenaries' thoughts while we fought them—"

"They're definitely mercenaries?"

"Yes," David confirmed, then continued. "The men Stuart encountered at Duke listened in on his conversation with the other vampire, observed their attack on the students they fed from, then tranqed them. They knew Stuart intended to meet with an immortal—he was trying to convince Paul to go with him—and decided to use that to their advantage, implanting the tracking device, then leaving him where he might wake up and think he had escaped. They tranqed the other vamp twice by accident and destroyed him."

Well, at least Stuart didn't screw him over like certain other vampires had.

"Stuart's behavior isn't at issue here. Yours is," Seth reminded him.

"I couldn't reach you," Bastien said. "And I knew Ami had the ability to find any of those soldiers again if we could just get her near them."

"David could track them without detection."

This again? Really? "I didn't know he could shape-shift!"

"What's going on?" Ami entered the training room. "My ears are burning." She looked to Marcus. "That's a saying, isn't it? My ears are burning? Because someone's talking about me?"

"Yes, love."

"Well, Lisette, Étienne, and the others came upstairs, then everyone started looking at me funny. Marcus, you didn't punch Seth again, did you?"

"No, sweetling. We were just . . . having a little discussion."

She pursed her lips and eyed them with skepticism. "You're picking on Bastien for inviting me to the battle, aren't you?"

Seth moved toward her. "Ami—"

"It was a smart move," she defended, thrusting out her chin.

"David was fully capable of tracking the soldiers who escaped without detection."

"Yes, David can tell you where they went. But David can't tell you if they stayed there or where they went if they didn't. I can."

"Ami—"

She held up a hand, craning her neck to look up at the eldest immortal. "I already told you I want to play an active role in bringing Emrys to justice and David agreed that I have that right. Marcus did, too." She caught and held her husband's gaze. "Didn't you?"

Marcus sighed heavily. "Yes."

"Then we don't have a problem, do we? Now, let Bastien get back to Melanie. He's been worried sick about her."

Bastien waited a full minute. When no one objected, he cautiously exited the room and headed down the hallway to the second of two quiet rooms David had added recently.

Seth appeared in front of the closed door.

Bastien stopped in front of him and waited.

Seth reached out and gripped Bastien's shoulder.

Bastien stiffened as the hallway around them fell away and was replaced by visions Seth implanted in his mind. Pain accompanied the visions. Hours of agony as men in scrubs and surgical masks cut him, burned him, removed bits of flesh. Over and over again. Hundreds of slices. Thousands of samples taken. Organs removed. Fingers and toes cut off. White hot bolts of electricity delivered to his head, his heart. A live dissection.

He had never experienced such suffering and opened his mouth to shout with it.

Seth released him. The visions vanished. The hallway resurfaced.

A cry died in Bastien's throat before he could free it. The strength left his knees. Panting, he sank to the floor and waited for the pain to recede.

"What the hell was that?" he gasped. Bracing a hand against the wall, he struggled to regain his feet.

"That," Seth said, "was a *fraction* of what you risked Ami being subjected to again when you called her to the battle."

Horror suffused him. He had known that whatever had happened to her had been bad, but . . . "That's what they did to her?"

"That and more. They spent six months torturing her and dissecting her without sedating her or giving her anything to numb the pain."

Seth was right to want to kill him.

"I won't make the same mistake twice," Bastien vowed. Even if Ami hadn't been the closest thing he'd had to a sister since Cat had died two centuries earlier, he wouldn't risk her being caught and subjected to such atrocities again. He hadn't wanted to risk it when he *hadn't* known what she had suffered. If her safety had been threatened at the network and Marcus had failed to protect her, Bastien would not have hesitated to give his life to protect her himself, but . . .

Now that just didn't seem like enough.

Seth moved away from the door and slapped Bastien on the back. "I knew you were worth saving."

Bastien stared at him. "You said you wanted to kill me!"

The elder immortal shrugged. "Ask Roland how many times I've wanted to kill *him*. It's a family thing."

Bastien frowned. Did he really want to be a part of that kind of crazy-ass family?

"Yes, you do. Trust me."

"I'd have an easier time doing that if you didn't keep trying to choke me."

"You pissed me off. I suggest you think twice about doing so again. As long as you always place Ami's safety first, you and I will be good. She's precious to me. If your stupidity should cause her death, you shall swiftly follow her into the afterlife."

Which raised another question. "How precious *is* she to you?" Bastien had never seen any romantic moments pass between the two. But Seth was extremely protective of her.

Seth cuffed him on the side of the head. "Don't be impertinent. Ami is in love with Marcus."

"And that doesn't really answer my question."

"She's like a daughter to me. Is that clear enough?"

Bastien nodded. "That'll do."

"Then we're finished here. Keep me posted on Melanie's transformation." Seth smiled suddenly and waved at someone down the hallway.

Bastien glanced over his shoulder and saw Ami standing just outside the training room. Marcus loomed in the doorway behind her.

Ami squinted her eyes at Seth and crossed her arms over her chest.

Seth held his hands out to the sides, palms up with a *What'd-I-do?* expression.

Marcus grinned.

Ami shook her head, rolled her eyes, and headed upstairs.

Bastien decided he had had enough from his surrogate family and ducked into the room he now shared with Melanie.

Standing beside the bed, Melanie nearly wilted with relief when Bastien entered. "Are you okay?" Even though she wore nothing but one of Bastien's large, black T-shirts, she had been prepared to leave the room in search of him.

"Yes." He hurried to her side, his handsome brow creased with concern. "What are you doing out of bed?"

"Seth woke me when he said, 'As you will.' I opened my eyes just in time to see him teleport you away." And she had not liked the murderous gleam in those luminescent, golden eyes.

"I'm fine. We were just . . ."

"Don't tell me you were shooting the breeze."

His eyebrows rose.

"I guessed right, didn't I? That's what you were going to say?"

"Yes. And it's scary that you know me so well."

She almost smiled. "He had his hand wrapped around your neck, Bastien."

Bending, he swept her up into his arms. Melanie looped an arm around his neck as he turned to deposit her on the mattress.

"He was pissed about Ami."

"What happened to Ami? She wasn't captured, was she?"

"No. None of the soldiers got near her. But I was the reason she was there. I was the one who put her in harm's way. I convinced Marcus to let Richart teleport them in so she could learn the mercenaries' energy signatures."

"That was smart." Melanie patted the mattress.

"Seth didn't think so." Bastien sank down beside her. "How do you feel? Is your stomach still upset? Would you like me to get you some club soda?"

"No. I want you to stay here and snuggle with me."

He smiled. "I can do that."

He scooted closer and stretched out.

Melanie cuddled up against his side and rested her head on his chest.

Much better.

Curling her arm around his torso, she raised one knee and draped her leg across his groin. She smiled when his body reacted to the contact. "I can hear your heartbeat," she murmured.

He brushed a hand over her hair. "Your ear is right above it."

"I could hear it from across the room when you entered. And I could hear Seth's out in the hallway before you closed the door."

"You've almost finished transforming then."

"I could hear Lisette and the others talking upstairs. They were betting on which immortal would kill you."

"Yeah. I heard. Since you're one of them now, you may as well know that those guys will wager on anything."

She rolled onto her stomach, folded her hands on his chest, and propped her chin on them. "You're one of them, too, Bastien."

"I'll never be one of them. My past won't allow it."

"Have they all had such perfect pasts, then?"

"As far as I know, I'm the only immortal who has ever killed another immortal. You may be able to get them to forgive that, but they'll never forget it. I'll always be the one who lived as a vampire. I'll always be the outsider. They'll never trust me."

"Seth seems to trust you."

He snorted. "Not anymore. Not after I endangered Ami."

Melanie hoped he was wrong about that. He really needed Seth as an ally.

She studied Bastien's face, the tightness around his mouth. "You seem tired."

He gave her a weary smile. "I am."

She drew a circle on his chest with her index finger and sent him a flirty look. *"How* tired?"

Some of the tightness in his features eased as his smile broadened. "What did you have in mind?"

"Well, now that my stomach is settled and my fever is down . . ."

"Yes?"

She drew in a deep breath. "You smell really good."

His eyes began to glow. "So do you."

"And I admit I'm curious about something."

He wrapped his arms around her and shifted her so that she was stretched out on top of him. "What's that?"

She slid up his body, creating as much friction as she could, and leaned over him, her weight propped on the hands she planted on either side of his head. Her hair fell down around them, forming a curtain around his beautiful face. Her lips hovered inches above his. She lowered herself until they were only a breath apart. "What's it like to make love as an immortal?"

"With another immortal? I wouldn't know," he admitted, voice low. "I've never done it before." He settled his hands on her hips. "But I wouldn't mind finding out. Care to educate me?"

Melanie smiled and kissed him. His lips were soft. Warm. Aggressive as they took control and claimed her with the same rising passion she felt for him.

"Mmmm," she hummed her approval. "I thought you tasted good before. Now you taste so good it's ridiculous." Almost good enough to make her forget the toothache still plaguing her.

His chuckle turned into a moan as she leaned back and straddled his hips. Only the loose material of his sweatpants separated them.

"I wonder if all of you tastes so good." She rolled her hips, ground her core against his erection. Pleasure shot through her.

Every muscle in Bastien's body tensed as he clamped his hands on her hips and held her still. "Are you sure you're up for this?"

Her heart pounded in her chest. "You can feel what I feel, can't you?" Again she rolled her hips.

He groaned. "Yes."

"Then there's your answer."

Because she could feel . . . everything. And hear everything. His heart raced, thudding against his broad chest as he slid his hands up her sides beneath her shirt and closed them over her breasts. Sizzling lightning zigzagged through her.

Could he feel that? The sparks that burned her as his

thumbs found her nipples? Could he feel her arousal through his gift? This vividly?

He lunged upward, slid his arms around her, eyes bright with desire that more than matched hers.

Oh, yeah. He could feel it.

He yanked the shirt she had borrowed over her head.

Melanie smiled what she hoped was a siren's smile.

Bastien growled and lowered his head. His lips hovered before her breast. Every breath was like a touch, the brush of warm fingers.

She moaned. "You don't play fair."

The low chuckle with which he responded was so full of sensual promise she nearly climaxed then and there. "I've only begun to play."

His lips closed on the hard, tight bud. Sensation shot through her as he drew on it, laved it with his tongue, teased it with his teeth.

Melanie cried out and buried her fingers in his hair. His long, soft, beautiful hair.

She hadn't realized immortals' sense of touch could be so acute. Every nerve ending in her body tingled. By the time this night was over, she may very well become the screamer Sheldon had accused Bastien of being.

He palmed her other breast, drew his thumb over the taut peak.

Her head fell back. She rocked against him.

Bastien had never felt anything so good in his long existence.

Until Melanie leaned forward and urged him down onto his back.

Her eyes glowed a bright amber. Her dark brown hair fell down around her flushed face as she leaned over him with the smile of a temptress. Her lips, swollen from their kisses, parted, revealing the tips of her new fangs.

She was more beautiful than ever.

He surged up against her, felt the answering flare of passion that claimed her.

Her head dipped. She touched her lips to his chest, explored. When those dainty teeth closed on his nipple, he groaned. And felt the shock of pain that struck her.

Abandoning his nipple, she continued her exploration, trailing a searing path of licks and kisses down his stomach. But every nip that sent fire roaring through his veins also caused her discomfort.

He curled his hands around her arms. "Melanie."

"Hmm?"

He bit back another groan. "Melanie, honey, as much as I love where you're going with this"—just the thought of her warm, wet mouth closing over his cock nearly made him come—"you need to stop."

She raised her head and frowned. "Why?"

"Because I can feel how much your teeth and gums are hurting and know that any pressure at all makes it worse."

Frustration shadowed her pretty face as she sat up. "I'm sorry."

"Don't be. We have eternity to explore each other, remember?"

That wrung a smile from her. "We do. I just wish my damned fangs would come in so my mouth would stop throbbing."

"They already have." Which was another good reason to stop her, now that he thought about it. Until she gained control over her fangs, she probably should steer clear of his—

"I have fangs?" she blurted. Eyes wide, she brought both hands up to her mouth and gingerly felt her teeth. She sucked in a breath.

Scrambling off the bed, she raced for the bathroom.

Bastien groaned and grinned at the same time, thrilled by the view of her bare body as she hurried away.

"Holy crap! My eyes!"

Stripping off his sweatpants, he joined her in the bathroom, as bare as she was.

"Look!" She leaned forward to peer into the large mirror above the sink. "They're glowing like yours."

Frankly, he was more interested in the view of her bare bottom as she bent over the sink. Damn, that was tempting.

"And my teeth!" Wrinkling her face up in a snarl, she hissed at her reflection.

Bastien laughed, utterly charmed.

She spun around. "What do you think?"

"Beautiful and fierce," he declared.

Grinning, she looped her arms around his neck and jumped up, wrapping her long, lovely legs around his waist.

Bastien caught her against him with a groan.

Face glowing, she pressed her mouth to his for an exuberant kiss. "Ow!" She drew back with a frown and touched the fingers of one hand to her lips again. "Damn it! This sucks! I can't even kiss you!"

"It doesn't suck," he said, carrying her back into the bedroom, breath shortening and body burning as she rubbed against him with every step.

"It doesn't?"

"Nope."

"Why?"

He tossed her onto the bed and gave her a wicked grin. "Because *my* mouth works just fine." So saying, he knelt on the bed, grabbed her ankles and parted her thighs.

He heard her heart skip a beat.

His own did the same as he leaned down and claimed her with his mouth.

Pleasure careened through Melanie.

Moaning, she buried her hands in Bastien's hair and held him to her as his tongue swept across her clit, then returned for another taste.

He slid a finger inside her.

So good. So damned good she couldn't catch her breath, panting as he bit and licked and sucked and stroked.

"Bastien."

"Come for me," he coaxed, his breathing as labored as hers.

Did he feel *everything* she felt?

He slipped a second finger inside her, stroked her in time with those long draws of his mouth.

Melanie gasped.

Bastien moaned.

Every muscle in her body stiffened as an orgasm shook her. "Bastien!"

On and on it went, prolonged by the eager flicks of his tongue and magnified by her heightened senses. She collapsed against the sheets.

Bastien fisted his hands in the covers and fought for control. Melanie's orgasm had nearly sent him over the edge. And her shouting his name in ecstasy . . .

He needed to be inside her. Needed to feel her inner muscles squeezing him. Needed to experience the same ecstasy he had just felt consume her.

Every muscle trembling, he kissed a path up her pale abdomen, paused to delight in her lovely breasts, then stared down at her.

"Melanie?"

He loved the satisfied smile that graced her face as much as the purring rumble that drifted from her throat as she opened glowing amber eyes and stared up at him.

"That was unbelievable," she murmured and combed her fingers through his hair.

"How do you feel?" he asked. His own emotions were clamoring so loudly now he really didn't know. If she felt sick again . . .

Abandoning his hair, she dropped her hands to his hips, slid them down over his ass, and drew him down to her. "Eager for more." Leaning up, she gingerly captured his lips and stroked them with her tongue. "Are *you* going to come for *me* now?"

Hell, yes!

He opened his mouth over hers, careful not to apply too much pressure, and settled his lower body in the cradle of her thighs. Melanie reached between them, curled her fingers around his sensitive cock, and guided him to her entrance.

Bastien didn't hesitate to plunge inside. So warm and wet, squeezing him tight. He felt the same pleasure that engulfed him blaze through Melanie.

"More," she begged.

He drew back and plunged again. And again. The friction too good.

She gripped his ass and urged him on. "Harder."

Oh, yeah.

Melanie met him thrust for thrust, loving the feel of him inside her. Looming over her. His hair falling down and caressing her breasts with every stroke as he drove himself into her over and over again. Her breath shortened.

Weight supported by one strong arm, Bastien reached between them and teased her clit. A brush. A stroke. A tug.

Another hard climax rippled through her.

Bastien shouted as Melanie's muscles clamped down around him. Pleasure seared him as an orgasm swept over him.

Both gasped for breath, bodies bathed in a fine sheen of perspiration.

Bastien had never known the like.

Utterly sated, he withdrew and lay beside her.

Melanie rolled onto her side and snuggled up against him.

A peace he hadn't known since his sister's murder enveloped him as he soaked in Melanie's warmth and contentment. Her breathing deepened, evened.

Closing his eyes, Bastien let sleep claim him.

* * *

The voices of the immortals and their mortal friends wafted up to Zach. Sitting quietly above their heads, his butt parked on the icy roof, he carefully modulated his body temperature so shivers wouldn't jar his wounds.

Damn, they stung.

The moon peered down at him through wispy clouds. All the usual nocturnal culprits moved about in the darkness below and beyond his line of sight.

Laughter erupted in David's home. How easy it sounded. How free.

Zach tried to remember if he had ever laughed like that and couldn't.

The back door opened and closed. Footsteps crossed the deck, tapped down the stairs and swished through the dormant grasses on the side of the house. Metal clanked, a hollow sound.

Zach looked to his right.

The top of an aluminum ladder swung into view and gently came to rest against the edge of the sloping roof.

He sighed. What new hell was this?

No one should know he was up here. Even Seth didn't seem to have registered his presence. That poor bastard had so much on his plate Zach didn't know why he didn't throw in the towel and join Zach and the others out of sheer exhaustion.

Feet scaled the ladder's treads. Hands slid up the sides.

He released his wings, preparing to leave, and lost his breath. Pain cut through him like buckshot. He curled his hands into fists, waited for it to ease.

Are you okay?

The voice was female. Soft, low, and such a shock it actually helped him weather the storm.

Zach looked toward the ladder.

A head full of fiery orange curls popped into view as bright green eyes peered at him over the edge of the roof.

Zach stared at her. It was the woman Seth and David had rescued from the mercenaries two or three years ago.

The woman from another planet.

When he made no move to leave, she must have taken it as an invitation, because she finished scaling the ladder and clambered up onto the roof.

Zach braced himself to dive after her if she should lose her footing. Seth would blame *him* if she fell, and Zach really wasn't up for whatever Seth would want to dish out in retribution.

She was amazingly sure-footed for a mortal, her small, sneaker-clad feet carrying her up the rise with ease, then across the peak to his side.

I like your wings.

So she was telepathic. *Thank you?*

She smiled and seated herself next to him. *May I join you?*

He noticed she didn't ask until she had already done so. It *almost* made him smile. Perhaps if he hadn't been in so much pain . . . *Okay.*

Do you mind if we talk like this instead of out loud? I get the feeling you don't want the others to know you're here and they'll come running—well, Marcus and Seth will at least— if they hear us talking.

I would rather not have company, so this will do.

Good.

How did you know I was here?

I felt your pain. Are you all right? Is there anything I can do?

Damn. No wonder Seth and everyone else adored her. She didn't even know him and was up here offering to help him.

I'm all right.

Why don't you ask Seth or David to heal you?

He shook his head. *That would blow the whole* I'm not really here *thing.*

She nodded.

Don't you fear me? With her history, he would've thought she would be terrified of him. He was, after all, aware of the anxiety that struck her whenever she encountered strangers.

And he was as strange a stranger as she would meet.

No.

Why?

She shrugged. *You remind me of Seth.*

Well, hell.

I suppose I should ask . . . Are you friend or foe?

That was a head-scratcher. *Neither?*

If you're not one, you're the other.

If only things were that simple.

She shivered. The cold must be creeping in through her jacket.

Gritting his teeth, he spread his wings, then drew them in close to form a shield that insulated her from the wintery wind.

She glanced at him from the corner of her eye. *I knew you were a friend.*

He swore silently, then apologized when he remembered she could hear it.

She grinned. Opening up the front of her jacket, she reached inside.

Was she going for a weapon? Immortals and their Seconds *did* lean toward violence.

Plastic rattled.

When she withdrew her hand, she clutched two lollipops.

He drew in a breath. One was blueberry. One was strawberry.

Which do you prefer? Strawberryyyyyy? She waved the pink candy under his nose. *Or blueberry? Strawberryyyyyyyy?* Again she waved it just beneath his nose. *Or blueberry?*

Hmmm. Let me think. Strawberry?

Perfect! She handed him the pink one.

He smiled. It felt . . . peculiar . . . almost as if he were trying out a foreign language for the first time.

She unwrapped her blueberry lollipop and slipped it between her lips.

Zach unwrapped the strawberry lollipop and stuck it in his mouth. Sweet strawberry flavor flooded his taste buds.

She smiled. *They're good, right?*

He nodded and smoothed his tongue over the tasty candy.

Quiet enfolded them. Night creatures occasionally broke it, as did the various conversations and sparring sounds from the house, though he supposed Ami couldn't hear those.

The wispy clouds parted. Moonlight glinted off the solar panels below them. Fog hovered above David's tidy lawn, shifting and swirling with the breeze.

So? she said at length. *You know what I am.*

Yes. Curiosity drove him to ask, *Do you know what I am?*

She tilted her head to one side and studied him. *I suspect I do.*

Interesting. How much had Seth confided in her?

Minutes passed while they whittled down their lollipops. When both were left with only sticks, she drew out two more.

Which one do I prefer this time? he asked.

She grinned. *Orange mango.*

He held out his hand and accepted the yellow/orange lollipop. She unwrapped a pink one that carried a delicious watermelon scent for herself.

It took him until the end of the second candy to realize that some of his pain had ebbed. He heard Marcus asking someone below if they had seen Ami.

Your husband is looking for you.

She rose and made her way over to the ladder.

Zach watched her carefully until she planted her feet on a rung. *What will you tell him?*

She descended a few rungs until only her eyes and fiery hair were visible. *The truth. That I needed some fresh air.*

Thank you.

Her eyes smiled. *You're welcome.*

He listened to her descent. The ladder swung away from the house and disappeared. Her small feet swished through the grass again, then scaled the few steps to the deck. The back door opened, then closed.

Various immortals and mortals called greetings to her as she walked through the house and down the basement stairs.

"Hi, sweetie."

"Hi, babe. Hey, you're cold. Have you been outside?"

"Yes. I needed some fresh air."

He heard them share a quick kiss. "Mmm. You taste like blueberries and watermelon."

"I stole some of your lollipops."

"Really. Well, if you're in the mood to lick something . . ."

She laughed.

"We can hear you," Seth called.

"So?" Marcus countered and kissed his wife again.

"So she's like a daughter to me, jackass."

"Yeah," David seconded. "There's a reason I poured thousands of dollars into soundproofing your bedroom."

"Hmm." Marcus sounded thoughtful. "I do believe your family is trying to tell me I should take you to bed."

"That isn't what I—oh screw it," Seth muttered.

Marcus laughed. "Let's go warm you up."

Ami chuckled.

A moment later a door closed.

Zach's feathers fluttered in the biting wind.

He looked down at the short white sticks he twirled between his fingers, all that remained of the two lollipops.

They were the only gifts he had ever received in his long existence.

Conversations started and stopped, overlapped and interrupted, down in the house.

Zach rose stiffly. Again, he was forced to hold his breath until the agony the movement had spawned eased. His fingers continued to toy with the white sticks.

Shaking his head at himself, he tucked them into one of the pockets of his leather pants.

Utterly pathetic.

Gritting his teeth, he bent his knees, leapt up, swept his powerful wings down, and lost himself amid the night sky.

Chapter 16

Dappled sunlight tumbled down, dodging the barren branches of deciduous trees and bouncing off the leaves of evergreens until it could fall in clumsy polka dot patterns on the two men below.

Quieter than mice, the tall, dark figures made their way through the brush.

"This isn't right," David announced.

Seth eyed David's grim countenance. "I know. But it's necessary."

"We promised her we wouldn't deny her vengeance."

"Actually we didn't. You said we *couldn't* deny her vengeance, not that we *wouldn't*."

"You're splitting hairs."

"I would rather Ami be pissed at me than risk losing her, physically or mentally, if something should go awry that allowed Emrys to get his hands on her."

They had told no one of their intentions. David's house had been quiet, save the sounds of slumber, when they had teleported away without a word.

No words spoken aloud, that is.

We're getting close, David told him.

Seth knew David saw the wisdom of their handling this

alone. That battle at network headquarters had been too close. Humans had died. Dr. Lipton had been forced to transform. At least one of the vampires had been captured by the mercenaries and was now most likely suffering the same torture Ami had.

Seth wasn't willing to risk that happening again.

They were going to meet Emrys on his home turf. The fire- and manpower the mercenaries had brought to the network would likely be nothing compared to what they possessed at their base. But Seth and David had breeched Emrys's compound in Texas. Had, in fact, burned it to the ground.

They would do the same today.

Just the two of them.

No Seconds or immortals would be killed. Ami would remain safe, tucked in the protective arms of her husband. And the threat the Immortal Guardians faced from the human world would be destroyed.

Almost there, David said. He had followed a couple of soldiers from the attack on the network to their base, but told only Seth its location.

I'm going to do a little recon, Seth announced.

David nodded.

Wings sprang from Seth's back and his clothing fell away as he shifted forms and took to the air. The tips of his feathers brushed branches as he found a break wide enough to allow him freedom from the trees.

Once he flew high above the earth, he saw exactly what David had described: two buildings in the center of a clearing. One was a two-story brick building with few windows. The other was a steel hangar. The open door of the latter revealed a solitary vehicle—what appeared to be a broken-down Humvee.

A pool of asphalt formed a small parking lot beside the main building. Weeds slain by winter's chill dotted the ground around it. A fence strung with razor wire circled all. But that fence boasted no guards. Nor did the gate—closed and padlocked—at the sole entrance.

Seth sailed past, then swooped around to backtrack. Surveillance cameras clung to the corners of the building, but he could detect no hum of electricity that would indicate they were functioning.

He listened carefully for a moment longer, then returned to David, who waited patiently in the shadows of the nearby forest.

"We have a problem," he announced as he regained and clothed his form with a thought.

"What's wrong?"

"No one is manning the gate. And I detected no heartbeats within the building."

David frowned. "There were men there last night. Many of them."

"Did you see them or did you hear their heartbeats?"

"Both."

"So there's no chance they could be blocking us?"

"No. Not unless they've developed a method of doing so within the past few hours. And I have no idea what they could do to block *you*."

Seth hated surprises. He really did. They were so rarely good. "Well, let's go ahead and see what happens."

"Do you want to take the Texas approach?"

Seth thought about it. He just wasn't sensing anything. "No. What do you say we simply take a stroll?"

David smiled. "It's a nice blustery day for it."

Laughing, Seth walked through the forest to the break in the trees with David by his side.

They paused as though by prior agreement.

"I don't sense anything either," David murmured. "The place has a totally different feel to it than when I was here before."

They strode to the fence and climbed it like humans,

careful to avoid the sharp razor wire. If anyone *did* keep
watch through those surveillance cameras, all they would
see is two unusually tall men trespassing.

Across the field, then over the blacktop they ambled. No
mercenaries raced out to meet them. No bullets struck from
concealed snipers. No guard dogs charged, barking and
frothing at the mouth. No challenges were issued.

Instead birds chirped. Squirrels scuttled about in the detri-
tus littering the nearby forest floor. A hawk forged a leisurely
path through the blue sky above, its shadow scampering
across the ground beneath it.

The front double doors of the building were glass, but not
of the usual grade. Should someone aim an automatic weapon
at them, the bullets would bounce off without so much as
cracking it.

Seth and David each grasped a door handle and opened the
doors. Unlocked.

David grimaced. "You smell that?"

Seth nodded. Death was not a subtle scent.

They stepped inside. The doors shushed closed behind them.

The heavy-duty white linoleum floor was streaked with
dried blood and black boot scuffs. Two hallways were divided
by a vacant desk topped with a bank of surveillance monitors,
all dark.

Seth took the hallway on the left, David the one on the
right. The thud of their boots hitting the floor echoed loudly
in the silence. There seemed to be no electricity. The fluores-
cents overhead were dark. No heater droned. The temperature
within the building nearly matched that outside. No heartbeat
thumped, speeding at Seth's approach. No breath stirred. No
clothing rustled or weapons rattled.

His way dimly lit by the light streaming through the front
doors, Seth reached an open doorway and peered inside.

A classroom?

The next doorway exposed a boardroom with a long table

and cushy chairs. The next a clinic, blood-spattered and chaotic. Instruments and red-stained first aid materials were strewn across the floor and every other surface. Flies buzzed around the mess left behind.

The last room was a weight room.

On the opposite side of the hallway, a quartet of identical locked doors with what looked like mail slots gave beneath his strength. Reinforced steel walls. Titanium chains as big as his arms. Clearly, these were rooms meant to hold any vampires or immortals they captured. Two of the rooms were pristinely clean and showed no indication that they had ever been occupied.

The third and fourth . . .

Bastien's vampires must have been held in there. Based on his visits with them, Seth guessed Joe had been in the third room. There were bloodstains on one wall that indicated the incarcerated vamp had repeatedly slammed his head into it. Bloody stripes marked the other walls where he had clawed them so hard his fingernails had ripped off. A pool of dried blood on the floor smelled of the virus.

It was a large stain. Large enough that Seth wondered if the vampire had bled out, finally finding peace in his own destruction.

The fourth room bore many bloodstains as well. But he didn't think enough had been lost to kill Cliff.

You need to see this, David said.

Seth retraced his steps up the hallway and headed down the other. Open doors revealed an office, sleeping quarters, a cafeteria, and a lounge with games and a television.

David waited at the end of the hallway, just outside the last doorway.

The scent of death grew to stifling proportions as Seth approached.

He stepped inside.

The bodies of a dozen or so soldiers, all shot in the head, had been tossed into a pile in the center of the room.

Seth stared down into their unseeing eyes. "Why the hell would Emrys kill his own men?"

David stepped up beside him. "I recognize a few of them from the battle. That one there. Those two. I think this one, too."

"The vampire king killed any of his followers who sowed dissent or spread doubt amongst the ranks. Perhaps these men rethought the wisdom of working for Emrys after coming face-to-face with immortals in battle."

"Such is my guess."

"Let's search the rest of the building, then check the hangar."

David nodded. "I'll take the basement."

"I'll head upstairs."

Whatever had filled the rooms upstairs had been removed. Only dust bunnies remained.

Seth heard David curse.

You'd better come down here, the other said.

David met Seth at the bottom of the stairs. The basement was as large as the other floors. Death floated on the stale air down here, too.

David motioned to the first open doorway.

Seth looked inside and felt as though he had stepped back in time to the day he had rescued Ami. A first glance revealed an operating room. A second uncovered the manacles and leather strap that would immobilize anyone unwillingly placed on the steel table's surface. Whatever tools of torture the butchers had utilized had been removed, leaving only discarded scrubs, a few soiled towels, and a half-empty bottle of rubbing alcohol turned on its side.

"There are three more like this one," David said and led Seth from the room.

Offices robbed of everything save battered desks and crappy chairs followed the torture chambers. Past those . . .

Seth stared at the bodies, shot execution style like the ones above, in the first cell. "These are civilians."

"Yes. There are more."

The dead in the basement included women and children. Some of the women still clutched their daughters or sons, their bodies curled around the little ones in an eternal gesture of protection.

"Let's check the hangar."

Aside from the disabled Humvee, the hangar boasted only oil stains and discarded lug nuts.

Seth took out his cell phone. "How are you doing with the daylight?"

David shrugged. "I can take another couple hours or so, more if I stay in the shade as much as possible."

Seth nodded and dialed.

"Reordon," a sleepy voice answered.

"I need to show you something."

"Give me a second to throw on some clothes."

Seth returned his phone to his back pocket.

"Think his men will be able to lift any prints?" David asked.

"They should. It looks like the mercenaries cleared out in a hurry. Hell, they didn't even lock the front door."

"While you go get Chris, I think I'll search the place for trip wires or explosives. It seems odd that they would leave these bodies here for anyone to find."

"Think they're bait?"

"Could be. I'd hate for any of the network employees to lose a life or a limb when they arrive."

"I'll join you when we return. We can sweep the entire compound. If anything is here, you and I will find it."

* * *

Chris was pulling on a peacoat when Seth teleported to his living room.

Seth glanced around. Chris's home was the antithesis of David's. While David's was pristinely neat, Chris's was all chaos, greasy pizza boxes, discarded clothes, and dirty dishes. Since Chris always kept his office neat, Seth wondered if the man wasn't simply too damned busy to do housework.

"So . . ."

Chris moved some crap around on the coffee table and dug out a pile of small, brand-new spiral notebooks. "Yeah?"

"You ever consider having someone from the network's cleaning crew come out here to tidy things up a bit?"

Chris grinned. "The clutter aggravating your OCD?"

Seth nodded. "It's making me feel guilty as hell, too. Is it that you're too busy to clean or too tired when you finally make it home?"

"A little of both."

"You're welcome to put it on the network's dime."

Chris shook his head. "This place may look like shit, but at least I know where everything is. If someone comes in and starts cleaning, I'll have to waste time looking for things."

"Just tell whoever does it to only worry about the dishes, the trash, and the clothes. Because . . . damn."

Chris laughed. "If you think this is bad, don't look in the kitchen."

"I don't have to. I can smell the fungus and the dried-up, crusted food from here."

Still grinning, Chris stuck the pads in his coat pocket and added a couple of short, stubby pencils.

"At least think about it," Seth requested.

"I will. Okay, let's book."

Seth teleported them both to the entrance of the compound's main building.

David's blurred form raced toward them from the vicinity of the hangar. "Nothing so far."

While Chris and David exchanged greetings, Seth opened one of the front doors and motioned for them to enter.

They showed him the dead soldiers first. Out came the first notepad and pencil. Chris didn't enter the room. He merely studied it, taking in every detail and scribbling down notes.

"Which ones do you recognize, David?"

David pointed out the ones he had seen at the network.

"Okay. What's next?"

They showed him the rooms Seth believed had temporarily housed the vampires.

"You think they still have both of them?"

"Joe may have been destroyed by the blood loss."

"I don't think so. They probably wouldn't have bothered to pick up his clothes if he had expired and there aren't any lying around."

Good point.

Chris exhibited no emotion until they showed him the first pair of the civilian bodies downstairs.

Seth cast David a questioning glance when Chris's face lost all color.

"Do you know them?" David asked.

Chris swallowed. "The man is one of my contacts. I think . . . I think the woman is his wife."

Or what was left of her. Emrys and his men must have tortured her to extract information from her husband.

Chris left the room, walked to the next and halted in the doorway. "Shit!" He strode to the next room. And the next. And the next. Spun around. "They're my contacts!" He turned and continued on to the next. "They're my fucking contacts. All of them!" Judging by the moan of regret that hummed in his throat, he had caught sight of the children in that one. "And their families! Why the fuck did they kill their families? Their children?"

"Leverage," Seth stated.

David sighed. "What better way to make a man talk than by threatening to harm those he loves the most?"

Chris paced furiously for a moment.

Seth didn't have to read his friend's mind to know guilt was eating him up inside.

Pausing, Chris closed his eyes and pinched the bridge of his nose as if he were trying very hard to erase those images from his mind. "Why leave them here like this?"

"Only two reasons come to mind," Seth said. "A message, warning you not to use such resources again to search for the mercenaries in the future."

"Or bait," David added. "Seth and I are going to scour the place for explosives or other booby traps that may have been set to take us out while we were distracted by the bodies so we can be sure no harm will come to the cleaners when they arrive."

Chris nodded.

"This wasn't your fault, Chris," Seth told him.

"I recruited them," he said, unconsoled.

"At my instruction."

"You aren't going to make me feel better about this."

Seth nodded. He could relate.

"So how are we going to locate Emrys and the remainder of his men now? This was our biggest lead to date."

Seth met David's gaze, knowing they had both come to the same conclusion.

"I don't see that we have any choice," David said.

Seth sighed. "We'll have to let Ami lead us to them."

Chris stared. "Is there no other way?" He had read the files. He may not have *seen* what Emrys and his butchers had done to Ami, but he knew all of the details.

"I think the one thing we can bank on is Emrys being wherever the vampires are. Since Ami was in close proximity to the vampires on numerous occasions during the attack on the network, she should be able to lead us to them."

Somber silence enfolded them, made worse by the sickening stench that constantly assaulted them.

"Tell me something," Chris said. "Have you guys ever dealt with a situation this . . . dark . . . before?"

"Yes," they answered simultaneously. Seth and David had seen trials the others would never believe.

"Okay. Pity party is over. You guys go ahead and do your thing. I'll start making calls."

"Make them outside." Seth didn't want the man to stay down here and stare at the bodies he felt he had placed in these rooms.

"Is he dead?"

Emrys, Donald, and Nelson stood in the observation room that overlooked one operating room on one side and a second on the opposite. Both of the rooms below looked very much like the ORs one might find in a hospital. Except the table in the center rested atop a titanium pedestal and was bolted to the floor with titanium screws coated in heavy concrete.

The *patient* they currently studied was held immobile by steel manacles it would take a blow torch hours to cut through. Two at the wrists. Two just above the elbows. Two across the thighs. And two more at his ankles. A ninth steel manacle, covered in a strip of leather, kept him from moving his head.

The short stubs of his dreadlocks poked out above it.

A narrow sheet had been draped across his groin to spare the partners' delicate feelings.

Delicate my ass, Emrys thought, eyeing Donald resentfully. The man acted like he shit diamonds.

He returned his gaze to the captive. "No. He's sleeping." Sedated actually, but that was need-to-know.

Both vampires had been in pretty bad shape after their *examination* by Emrys's medical team. The other one had left half his damn brain on the wall and hadn't cleaned up as well, so Emrys had shown Donald and his yes-man this one first.

"Why is he restrained?"

Because he's fucking Charles Manson times a thousand. They both were. "The torture the immortals subjected them to has driven them insane." He had not yet confided that the virus tended to have that effect on any humans infected with it. He had removed that little tidbit from any and all information he had handed over to Donald, who may have wondered how exactly they would command an army of supersoldiers who were totally off their rockers.

Emrys would figure out the whole insanity thing later. *After* he made his first billion.

He pressed a button on the wall beside him. "Proceed, Nate."

A man in scrubs and gloves stepped into view. A blue surgical mask hid his face. A cap the same color covered most of his light brown hair.

Rolling a cart full of instruments along with him, he stopped beside the vampire.

"Check this out," Emrys said, smiling in anticipation.

Picking up a scalpel, Nate pressed it to the vampire's waist on the far side and carved a deep path across the vamp's abdomen.

Blood welled and spilled out of the wound that, on the battlefield, would have required the attention of a medic and taken a human soldier out of play. As they watched, the wound narrowed, the gaping sides drawing together as though magnetized, then sealing. Scar tissue formed, then faded. All in a matter of minutes.

Donald stepped closer to the glass. "Holy shit."

Even that little pissant, suck-up Nelson moved closer to the glass and stared with wide eyes.

Again, Emrys depressed the button. "Demonstration number two, please, Nate."

Nodding, Nate left their line of sight for a few seconds.

When he returned, he wore protective ear phones and carried a Smith & Wesson M&P. He raised the semiautomatic pistol and aimed it at the vampire's torso.

Donald and Nelson both stuck their fingers in their ears.

Pussies.

"Fire in the hole," Nate called and squeezed the trigger. Emrys had told him to leave the silencer off for effect.

The vampire's body jerked as a hole sprang open in his chest.

Blood welled and spilled from the wound in thin rivulets that wound their way down the vampire's sides to drip onto the table. Moments passed. A misshapen lump of metal slowly rose to the entrance of the wound and tumbled out.

The ass-kisser gaped. "You are shitting me!"

The hole closed, sealed itself, and began to scar over. It took longer than Emrys would've liked because the vampire was drugged (and would have taken longer if they hadn't pumped him full of extra blood), but the men beside him were no less astonished.

Donald turned to Emrys. "He's still alive?"

"Yes. After what he endured in the immortal's compound, we thought it kinder to sedate him."

"I want a closer look."

"I thought you might. Follow me."

Emrys led them down to the room they kept the Black vampire in, glad Donald hadn't asked to see the other one. The White vampire's wounds weren't healing as quickly because they had nearly OD'd him on the tranquilizer, so he was still in pretty rough shape. They'd slapped some makeup on him to hide the worst of it, but that wouldn't fly up close and personal.

Emrys waited while both men donned scrubs over their suits.

Nate nodded to each of them in turn as they entered.

Donald leaned over the recumbent form on the table. The

vampire's medium brown skin was smooth and free of wounds, the blood that had not yet dried and the expelled bullet the only evidence left that he had been cut and shot.

Donald held his hand out for the scalpel. "May I?"

Nate met Emrys's gaze.

Emrys nodded.

When Nate handed over the blade, Donald sliced a deep gash across the vampire's thigh.

Like the others, the wound welled with blood, then closed and healed.

"See?" Emrys said. "No special effects."

"Are they really as fast and as strong as you say they are?"

"You saw the video. Did your analysts find anything to indicate the footage had been altered in any way or sped up?"

Donald shook his head.

"We are going to be so rich," Nelson said, his expression full of awe as he stared down at the vampire.

For once, Emrys agreed with him.

And so did Donald, who at last met Emrys's gaze. "Let's talk."

Melanie felt strange in her new vampire-hunting togs. Almost as if she were playing dress-up. Instead of her usual jeans and Chuck Taylors, she wore boots and black cargo pants with a butt-load of pockets. A black turtleneck hugged her torso. A gun belt hung on each hip, sporting Sig Sauer P220s. Her breasts were flattened by a Kevlar vest. A bandolier sporting a dozen daggers draped across her chest. Several auto-injectors full of the antidote filled one hip pocket. Extra clips and auto-injectors containing a human dose of tranquilizer filled the other.

Bastien paced the bedroom they shared, throwing off a real caged tiger vibe.

"Is it that you're pissed?" she asked finally. "Or are you just worried?"

"Just worried?" he repeated. "We're heading into the den of the men who shot you three times in the chest. Men who tortured Ami. Men who left piles of bodies behind at the compound Seth and David found. *Just worried* doesn't cover it."

"I'm immortal now, Bastien. I'm also wearing a vest. *And* I've already been trained, so it's not like I'm going into this blind or unprepared."

"Immortal doesn't mean immortal. It means *almost* immortal."

"You're going up against the same people," she pointed out. "Why—"

"I didn't nearly die *twice* in recent weeks."

"If I've cheated death twice, I can cheat it again."

"Don't joke about this."

She sighed. "I'm sorry. I don't want you to think I'm not taking all of this seriously. I'm taking it *very* seriously. I know any of us could be killed tonight. I also know that having me around to both kick ass *and* serve as a medic will be to your advantage. And if, when we find Cliff and Joe, either one of them has gone over the edge, I know that I'm most likely the only one who will be able to talk them down and bring them back under control without hurting them."

"You think I can't? I talked Vince down."

"I know. But his psychosis was different than that afflicting Joe. Joe's is infused with a lot more paranoia. At times it makes him view *everyone*—even you—as the enemy. Everyone but me. Which is why it's so important that I'm there when you find him."

Bastien ran a hand through his hair. "No wonder he took off when he thought you were dead."

She twisted and bent and walked around, trying to acquaint herself with the feel of the weapons and ammo and the slight shifting of the holsters and belts and weighted pockets. Were she still human, it would have taken her time to get used to it.

The ammo alone was surprisingly heavy. But her increased strength made it a breeze.

Bastien continued to pace restively.

"Bastien?"

He glanced over. "Yes?"

When his eyes flared, she forgot whatever she had intended to say. "What is it?" she asked, uncertain what emotion had struck him.

He raised his brows in question, his luminous gaze piercing as it traveled over her.

"Your eyes are glowing," she said.

He shook his head. "I shouldn't tell you."

"You can tell me anything."

"It'll just encourage you," he said and smiled wryly. "You look hot all geared up for a fight."

A momentary brightness entered her being. "I do?"

He laughed and shook his head. "Yes, damn it." He closed the distance between them and rested his hands on her hips. "Incredibly hot." He drew her close until their noses touched. "I-want-to-rip-your-clothes-off-with-my-teeth hot."

Shivers of arousal rippled through her at those husky words. Their doorbell rang, squelching any notion of engaging in a quickie.

So much soundproofing had been used to create this and the other quiet room that anyone inside—save Seth—couldn't hear the knock of someone out in the hallway, so David had installed doorbells.

"To be continued?" Melanie suggested.

His hands tightened on her hips. "Are you sure you're up to this? I'm not asking because you're a woman, or a doctor, or an egghead."

She grinned. He made egghead sound like an endearment.

"I'm asking because you're fresh from your transformation." He pressed his forehead to hers. "And because I don't want anything to happen to you."

"I'm up for it," she assured him.

Dipping his head, he took her lips in a warm passionate kiss that carried with it his fear that it may be their last.

"It won't be our last," she promised. "Can you feel my certainty of that?"

"I can. How did you know what I was thinking?"

Reaching up, she stroked his face. "I just know you."

The bell rang again.

Bastien sighed. Backing away, he released her and crossed to the bedroom door.

Tanner stood out in the hallway. "It's time."

Bastien's Second was garbed in typical vampire-hunting togs like Melanie, but with fewer blades.

Something about him looked different, though.

Melanie studied him. Same lean form. Same broad shoulders. Hair still cut as short as an accountant's. *Oh!* "Did you get contacts?"

He smiled, blue eyes no longer hidden behind spectacles. "No. David corrected my vision."

"Really?" That was so cool.

He nodded. "He was worried that glasses or contacts would hinder me when I'm fighting, so he put his hand over my eyes, it got warm for a minute, then I could see perfectly."

Melanie looked up at Bastien. "Why couldn't I have been given that gift?"

He rubbed a hand up and down her back. "Even though you weren't, you're still a born healer." He ushered her through the door. "Will you and the other Seconds be accompanying us?"

"To a point," Tanner said. "We're going to monitor things from a distance."

Melanie wondered if that was wise. The humans at the network had pretty much gotten their asses kicked the last time.

Bastien shook his head. "I think the humans should stay out of it. You're too vulnerable."

"Not with the armored vehicles Chris and Seth commandeered for us."

"Do you even know how to drive one of those things?"

"Hell, no. I've never driven anything with more than two doors. But Chris and Seth have apparently recruited a *lot* of military veterans over the years."

A little twinge of nerves made Melanie's stomach jump.

Bastien removed his hand from her back and twined his fingers through hers.

"How are you getting along with the other Seconds, Tanner?" she asked, needing a diversion.

"Fine." His jaw tightened as he looked at Bastien. *"Someone let my tragic past be known, so now everyone feels fucking sorry for me. Too sorry for me to condemn me for allying with vampires and this asshole."*

"It wasn't me," Bastien denied. "Your past is your business."

Melanie didn't know exactly what Tanner's tragic past entailed, just that it had something to do with his son.

"I don't even like any of those guys," Bastien went on, not caring that *those guys* could hear him. "You think I sit around drinking tea and gossiping with them?"

"No, but if you thought them knowing about my son would soften them toward me and keep them from giving me shit, I doubt your FU attitude would prevent you from blabbing."

Melanie pursed her lips. "Tanner, Bastien wouldn't even clear up misconceptions about his *own* past. And doing so might keep the other immortals' contempt from spilling over onto *me* when I defend him."

Bastien squeezed her hand. "I thought it would be easier to just kick their asses if they said anything to you."

Melanie gave Tanner a *See what I'm saying?* look.

Tanner frowned. "Well, who else could it have been? No one else knows."

Bastien shrugged. "It must have been one of the telepaths. Those nosy bastards can dig around in your head and uncover *anything*."

"Can you teach me how to keep them out?"

"I can try."

"Great. Thanks."

Bastien followed Melanie up the stairs and down the hall-way to the large living room. A sea of black met them. Black shirts. Black pants. Black coats. Black Kevlar vests. Black weapons. Black hair.

The only spots of color were Ami's and Sheldon's red hair and Tracy and Chris's blond locks.

So far the uneasy truce between Bastien and Reordon was holding. *Uneasy* being the key word.

The immortals turned as Bastien, Melanie, and Tanner entered. All bowed gallantly and smiled at Melanie, bidding her a good evening.

She smiled back. "Hi."

As they had with Sarah, the immortals wanted her to feel welcome so strongly Bastien didn't even have to touch them to feel it. No *gifted one* had willingly been transformed . . . ever . . . until Sarah and Melanie. Not that Melanie had had much of a choice. Transformation or death. She'd chosen the former. But an alarming number of *gifted ones* who had come before her had chosen the latter.

Bastien's worry that their scorn for *him* would suck the warmth right out of any welcome they gave *her* appeared unfounded. Everyone in the room, including the Seconds, seemed determined to prevent her from regretting her decision.

He did a quick count of those present. Seth, David, and

Darnell. Marcus and Ami. Roland and Sarah. Reordon. Richart and Sheldon. Lisette and her Second, Tracy. Étienne and his Second, Cameron. Ethan, Edward, Yuri, Stanislov, and their Seconds.

Seth greeted Melanie and asked how she was feeling.

"Good, thank you."

"Dr. Lipton—"

"Melanie," she corrected with a smile he returned.

"Melanie, no one here will think less of you should you not wish to join us tonight. Your combat experience is limited and the humans we'll face have proven to be very dangerous foes."

"I'm going," she stated, voice firm, expression confident, though Bastien could feel anxiety pulsing through her.

He didn't fault her for it. He had been nervous as hell the first time he had seen combat as a mortal.

"There will be other battles," David added.

Sarah's entrance to the Immortal Guardians' world had been a harrowing one. Bastien supposed the two elders would prefer that Melanie's be a little less so.

But Melanie was having none of it. "I've spent more time with Cliff and Joe in the past two years than anyone else here. I want to be there when you find them. Knowing what I do about Emrys, I think they'll *need* me to be there. Especially Joe. If their mental state has declined, I'll likely be the only one they won't view as a threat."

"As you will. We're grateful you'll be joining us." Seth addressed the group. "For those of you who don't know, I've been taking Ami out every day in search of the missing vampires and we were finally able to pinpoint an approximate location this afternoon. When we leave in a few moments, we will travel together, Seconds included, to an area a few miles distant. The immortals will then move in under my command."

Heads nodded.

"Let no one at the compound escape. And whatever happens, Emrys cannot be allowed to get his hands on Ami. I don't care what you must do to prevent this. Just do it."

Ami bit her lip and looked up at Marcus.

Bastien resolved to stay near her and back her and Marcus up whenever he could.

"Everyone know the plan? First we take out the humans. Next we ensure there are no traps or land mines like the few we found at the smaller compound. Then we bring in the Seconds. Should we require the assistance of those manning the armored vehicles, I will call them in."

David spoke next. "Tread carefully if you locate the imprisoned vampires. As Melanie said, whatever torture they have endured may have spurred their decline into madness and she's likely the only one capable of calming them."

Melanie stepped forward. "That reminds me . . ." She tucked her hand into a thigh pocket, withdrew a fistful of auto-injectors with green caps, and started handing them out to the immortals. "If any of you are tranqed, flip the cap off and press this against your skin for three seconds. It will keep you from losing consciousness."

Ethan turned his over and over in his hands, then tucked it in a pocket. "Do we need extras for when we're tranqed again?" He must not have had to use it the night the network was attacked.

"No. I'm unclear why, but once you inject it, it seems to have a prophylactic effect, protecting you from further sedation. It may simply stay in your system longer than the other drug. But whatever the reason, one dose will do it."

She looked so fragile surrounded by the tall, hulking male immortals.

"Once the compound is under our control," Seth continued, "Darnell will go to work hacking and track down any of the mercenaries' allies or connections, find out where they're backing up their data offsite. Then we'll confiscate their computers, hard drives, etcetera, and torch the place. Should something happen that causes us to deviate from this plan, know this: If we accomplish nothing more, Emrys must die. Understood?"

"Understood."

"Any questions?"

The heavily muscled human standing beside Yuri said, "Tell me again why we're doing this at night? Won't they be expecting us? Wouldn't it be better to do it during the day when they think you guys can't go out?"

Seth shook his head. "In recent years, that has become our MO. We descended upon Bastien's lair in daylight. The vampire king's, too. David and I destroyed Emrys's Texas facility at dawn. I think at this point they're more likely to expect us during daylight hours than at night, so we may as well strike when we're all at our strongest."

The man nodded. "Makes sense."

"Any more questions?"

Silence.

"Good. Let's book."

Bastien reclaimed Melanie's hand and joined the river of black flowing out the front door.

Lisette hung back as the others filed outside. When Bastien's Second drew even with her, she caught his arm and gently held him back.

His eyebrows rose.

She hadn't spoken to him alone since she had tied him up at Bastien's lair the day they had overthrown Bastien's vampire army.

"I told them," she admitted.

He started to shake his head, then frowned. "About my son?"

"Yes." She had read his mind that night to determine

whether or not he was worth saving and had discovered tragedy.

His face tightened. "You had no right."

She nodded. "I know. I meant no harm. I just . . . Bastien was right. I could hear the thoughts of the other Seconds and the immortals, knew the hostility they felt toward you, and thought it unfair. I thought if they knew how you served Bastien—in what capacity—and what had driven you to do so . . ."

No forgiveness lit his handsome face. "I'm not a child. I can handle scorn. Sticks and stones and all that shit. And I don't regret one minute of the time I spent aiding Bastien so anything anyone says to condemn that period of my life will roll off me like water."

"I know, but . . . I like you. I wanted them to welcome you," she finished lamely.

He sighed. "You realize you sound just like Bastien, don't you?"

She grimaced, appalled.

Tanner laughed. "All right. You're forgiven, as long as you stay out of my head and don't reveal any more of the secrets I keep up there. Now let's go before we hold things up."

She nodded and stepped out into the cold.

Tanner set the alarm and closed the door behind them. "So, I hear you like sports."

"I love it," she said. Football. Basketball. Baseball. She liked it all.

"Want to watch a game together sometime?"

She smiled. "I'd love to."

Chapter 17

Ami led Seth, David, and Marcus through dense forest, following the unique energy signatures of Cliff and Joe.

"It's different," she murmured. "The energy. Not as strong. But it's them. I'm sure of it. I think they've been drugged."

"Can you still find them?" Marcus asked.

"Yes. It's just taking me longer."

"Don't worry about time," Seth told her. "We have plenty of that."

She took off again, leading them through the trees and naked brush. Above their heads, branches, whose leaves had been stolen by winter, clacked together as they swayed with the wind.

Seth followed close behind Ami, David at his side. Marcus clung to Ami's hand and observed everything in front of them with eagle eyes.

Ami paused, drew her weapon and sighted down the barrel, tapping her arm with three fingers and pointing ahead and to the right.

They slowed their approach.

David raised a thermal scope to his right eye and scanned the trees and ground ahead.

Marcus halted and stopped Ami. Eyes on the ground, he took two steps forward and crouched down.

Seth and the others looked where he pointed and saw the trip wire of a land mine poking up through the dead leaves.

They were close.

Wait here, Seth instructed.

He strode ahead, eyes sharp, until he reached a big enough break in the trees for him to shift and launch into the air.

Only a mile away, the compound was eerily similar to the one he and David had destroyed in Texas. A three-story brick and mortar structure, nearly devoid of windows, rested in the center of a sizable clearing. A large parking lot peppered with vehicles painted the ground in front of it black with white stripes.

Behind the building, narrow wooden structures he'd heard some call pigeon coops or shacks formed two rows. Barracks for his mercenaries?

Those without families anyway. Those *with* families probably lived in nearby towns. Darnell would have to uncover all of their names so Seth could either eliminate them or wipe their memories, depending on what he found housed in their thoughts.

Near the back of the clearing lay two hangars of roughly the same height with domed roofs. The doors of both were open, allowing Seth to see a couple of Black Hawk helicopters within one. The other brightly lit interior housed a few armored vehicles, being serviced by industrious mercenaries, and a lot of empty space where the vehicles they had lost in the skirmish at the network probably used to reside.

A similar structure had just been erected at Chris's behest not far from the new network headquarters and housed the vehicles Seth had salvaged from the battle. Chris's mechanical geniuses had been working furiously on them while the network's soldiers who were military veterans practically salivated as each awaited his chance to *get behind the wheel*.

Which they did tonight. Three armored personnel carriers hid among the trees five miles distant. Should they be needed, they would have to take the main road and come right up the drive in order to avoid any other land mines the mercenaries might have placed along the compound's perimeter.

The drive leading to the compound from the highway was a two-lane road the same black as the parking lot and parted dormant vegetation, allowing all visitors one way in and out after they passed through a gate guarded by men carrying automatic weapons. Those guards walked stiffly in the cold, shoulders high, hands tucked into the pockets of their thick jackets, asses no doubt as frozen as the ground beneath their boots or the breath that frosted the air in front of their mouths.

Other guards manned a fence strung with razor wire that circled the compound.

Seth flew past, looped around, and doubled back. One of the guards along the fence looked up and marveled at the *big-ass* owl soaring overhead.

Surveillance cameras clung to the corner of every roof and some of the fence poles, all with red lights and the faint hum of electricity indicating they were operational.

Seth rejoined Ami, David, and Marcus. Then they made their way to the immortals and Chris Reordon, who waited not-very-patiently for him amid the trees. Borrowing one of Chris's ever-present notepads and pencils, Seth sketched a quick map that included placement of the guards and the land mines he had spotted.

Ami, Sarah, Melanie, and Lisette were maneuvered into the front, then the men peered over their shoulders at the drawing.

"Based on the heartbeats, I believe the vampires are being held in this area." Seth indicated an area of the main building with his pencil.

Chris took the pencil and pad back when all had memorized the hasty schematic. "I'm sorry I couldn't get you real-time satellite surveillance images, but my contacts in the agencies that could supply them are too new. I didn't think this would be a good way to break them in and . . . we don't know how closely Emrys might be watching for such things. His tentacles are far-reaching, so getting the satellite images could tip him off."

"Understood," Seth said. "David and I will enter the main building first. Bastien, you and Melanie follow and take out as many as you can, but focus on reaching the vampires as quickly as possible. Marcus, you and Ami enter next. Ami, I want you to concentrate on feeling the presence of *anyone* you remember from the Texas compound. The moment you find Emrys, summon me."

Marcus's eyes flared with fury and promised pain.

"Marcus, do *not* deliver a swift death to Emrys. Disarm and disable him, then summon me."

When Marcus didn't agree fast enough, Seth told him telepathically, *I want him to suffer for what he has done.*

Marcus gave an abrupt nod.

"Yuri and Stanislov, disable the helicopters."

Chris held up a finger. "If you could do that without destroying them, I would appreciate it. Those things aren't easy to come by without sparking scrutiny."

"Won't be as fun," Stanislov grumbled, "but we'll try."

Seth smiled. "When you're done with the helos, do the same with the armored vehicles in the next hangar. Ethan, you and Edward take out the guards on the grounds and make sure no one enters or exits. Lisette and Étienne, take the barracks. Scan the minds of the mercenaries before you kill them. If you think any are good men, knock them out and restrain them. Perhaps we can recruit them ourselves. If not, I'll erase their memories."

The siblings nodded.

"Richart, do your thing. You cause more chaos and fear than any of the others."

Richart grinned and gave him a cocky salute.

Roland grunted. "You forgot us."

Seth shook his head. "You and Sarah are free to wreak havoc where you will, though I'd prefer to have you in the building with us. There were a lot of heartbeats in there when I flew over, so the bulk of Emrys's troops are likely there."

Roland and Sarah nodded.

Chris held up a finger again. "My tech team will begin blocking outgoing cell signals on my mark, but they can't block satellite phones. If you hear a call going out, take out the caller without damaging the phone so we can find out who the hell they're calling."

More nods.

"Okay," Seth said. "We clear on our assignments?"

Everyone nodded.

"Then I'll mention one more time that everyone here is to do everything in your power to ensure Ami is not taken by Emrys."

Ami's brow furrowed as she glanced at the warriors around her. "I'm sorry."

Several large hands clapped her on the shoulders and patted her on the back with rough affection.

"You're our sister," Étienne said. "We protect our family."

Her eyes shimmered suspiciously when she smiled at them.

Seth knew she must be terrified. She was about to enter the den of the monsters who had tortured her for six months and nearly robbed her of her sanity.

He nodded at Chris. "Make your call."

Chris called his tech people. As soon as he disconnected the call, Seth led the immortals forward.

Melanie's heart pounded so loudly she expected it to burst from her chest.

Seth and David moved phenomenally fast. Roland and

Sarah were right on their heels. Melanie put on a burst of speed and kept up . . . until she realized she was leaving Bastien and the others behind. He had been right. Having Roland transform her had leant her the same strength and speed of a millennium-old immortal.

She fell back to run alongside Bastien and the d'Alençons. Ethan and Edward followed next, with Marcus and Ami bringing up the rear.

Ami ran just a bit faster than a human. Marcus could have carried her and kept up with Seth, but Melanie guessed he was hoping the others would clear a path for them and reduce the danger to her.

Over the fence the immortals bounded.

Even though she was scared as hell, Melanie couldn't help but smile as she leaped easily over the twenty-foot fence. Her heart raced with excitement as she sailed through the air and landed smoothly on the other side. Barely a bend of the knees. No jostling of the joints. Then she was racing forward.

Seth and David plowed through the front doors of the main building before the mercenaries patrolling the grounds and manning the front gate even knew they were under attack. And they plowed through them literally. Neither stopped to open a door. They just burst through the heavy glass, bending back the metal frame as they went so that it looked as though it had imploded.

Melanie followed and paused just inside the door, shards of glass crackling under her boots. Bastien halted beside her.

There were three hallways. Seth raced down the one on the right. David took the left. Shouts erupted. Then howls of pain as the elder immortals' weapons delivered death to their enemies. Gunshots ensued. Crashes. More of the same arose outside.

"Which way?" she asked.

Based on Seth's drawing, it could be either the middle or the left.

"Cliff! Joe!" Bastien shouted.

Melanie heard nothing but the panicked bursts of speech spewing from the mercenaries' mouths.

"Let's try the middle," he said, face grim, and took off.

She knew what he was thinking, because she thought the same thing: If the vampires hadn't been sedated, the lack of response meant they were dead.

Humans in camouflage poured into the hallway, weapons raised. Bastien ducked this way and that as bullets and darts flew at them. Melanie tried to do the same as she drew her weapons, but was not yet as experienced. Two bullets hit her in the chest and were stopped by the vest. A dart hit the vest, too. Then another hit her in the arm.

Holstering one of her Sigs, she shoved her hand into her thigh pocket and withdrew one of the green-capped auto-injectors. Lethargy began to seep through her as she flipped open the cap. Raising her other Sig, she fired at the soldiers and shoved the auto-injector into her thigh.

Bodies fell. So many she lost count. Had the men not been doing their damnedest to kill her, she didn't know if she would've been able to hurt them. She was a doctor. A healer. She *repaired* wounds. She didn't inflict them.

At least not until now.

Energy flowed into her, extinguishing the sluggishness. Fortified, she dropped the other Sig in its holster and drew out the auto-injectors she had filled with the weaker human dose of the sedative.

With a burst of speed, she dashed from human to human, hitting them with the tranquilizer instead of killing them. She told herself it was so Seth could read their minds and unearth information, but she really just needed more time to grow accustomed to taking another person's life. Some of these men could be innocent dupes. Some may relish the violence Emrys ordered them to perpetrate, the pain he told them to inflict. She couldn't tell one from the other and didn't like the idea of executing the first just to ensure they got the second.

Each man she sedated struggled. Melanie was shocked at how easily she disarmed and restrained them.

She could feel Bastien's gaze and knew he was keeping an eye on her. "I'm fine," she called, then remembered she didn't have to raise her voice. Even over the gunfire and the explosion that just shattered the rest of the front windows, they both could hear normal speech.

"I'm fine," she repeated. Ducking bullets, she dropped another unconscious soldier and chased down the next.

Bastien had never been so afraid in his life. He wanted to tell Melanie to stop tranqing the fuckers and just kill them. It was a hell of a lot faster and half as risky.

But he knew her. And he knew, though she had said nothing of it, that killing was difficult for her.

Hell, it had been difficult for him, too, in the beginning. It had been difficult when he had been a mortal and fought Napoleon's—

He swore as two bullets struck him in the arm and shoulder. Knocking the gun that had fired them out of its owner's hand, he struck out twice with his daggers and moved on as the shooter's body thudded to the floor behind him.

No, killing wasn't something that came easily. Hell, he'd heard that Sarah still shook like a leaf after she took out vampires, even though she did so with astounding expediency. And Sarah had been hunting for a couple of years now.

He saw Melanie jerk as blood spurted from her thigh.

Pain was something else she would have to grow accustomed to. He hated that. He never wanted her to have so much as a paper cut for the rest of her long—and it had better be damned long—existence.

Curses spilled from her lips.

Bastien smiled.

He rarely heard her curse and laughed as she now turned the air blue.

She glanced over at the sound, caught his expression, and smiled. "This shit hurts!"

"I'll kiss it and make it better later," he promised.

Her lovely lips stretched in a wide grin as she tranqed another mercenary.

Dropping the empty auto-injector, she drew her Sigs.

That must have been her last.

More men poured into the hallway.

What, was the fucking cafeteria down this way or something?

He and Melanie formed a united front. He sliced and diced with his daggers. She cut men down with her 9mms.

A second explosion rent the night outside. Then a third. And a fourth.

Bastien and Melanie stepped over bodies, forcing their way forward until they finally reached the first door.

Bastien looked inside. Unbelievable. It *was* a cafeteria.

They made their way to a door on the other side.

Melanie peeked inside. "Training room," she announced. *Great.*

Were there even any men left out in the barracks for Lisette and Étienne to worry about?

Melanie jerked again. Two holes appeared in her clothes, one in her hip and one above it at her waist, just beneath the lower edge of the damned vest. Blood quickly began to moisten her cargo pants.

Bastien swore.

"That's *my* line," she gritted and, eyes blazing amber with pain and fury, shot her assailant in the head.

Bastien eased closer to her.

"I'm fine," she growled.

No, she wasn't. Multiple wounds always slowed the healing. She was limping badly.

The mercenaries, like sharks drawn by chum in the water, all turned on her, sensing weakness.

"Richart!" Bastien called and dove in front of her as the men fired.

Half a dozen bullets hit him as he dropped his daggers, then drew and swung his katanas in sweeping arcs, severing heads, limbs, and arteries.

Richart appeared in the midst of the mercenaries, blades flashing. As soon as those he *didn't* kill noticed him, he vanished and reappeared farther down.

Again and again he teleported, instilling fear and delivering death while Melanie's guns and Bastien's swords continued to claim lives.

The last man fell.

All three immortals swung around to face the entrance of the hallway.

No mercenaries rushed forward to save their comrades. All seemed to be occupied in battles in the other hallways.

Bastien let his shoulders slump. His torso riddled with bullet wounds, he turned to Melanie.

Breath ragged, she leaned against the wall. She nodded to him that she was okay. "It's just going to take some getting used to," she said through clenched teeth. "The pain. I'm not used to it."

Richart shook some of the blood off his blades. "It took me a century to get used to it. You should feed."

Melanie shook her head. Since her transformation, she had only sunk her new fangs into bagged blood, allowing them to draw it directly into her veins. She had not yet fed from a person. And, even though she wouldn't actually be drinking it, she couldn't help but feel a bit nauseated at the thought of it.

Or was the nausea simply a result of her wounds?

Either way . . . "We need to find Cliff and Joe. I'll feed after that." On bagged blood, back at David's place.

Richart looked to Bastien.

That grated a little. It was *her* decision, after all.

Bastien nodded.

Melanie frowned, eyeing the holes in the front of his shirt. "Do *you* need to feed?"

"Later. Let's find Cliff and Joe."

The foundation of the building suddenly shook as thunder rumbled outside. The walls vibrated. Cracked.

All three fought for balance and dodged pieces of ceiling that fell down around them.

"Was that a bomb?" she asked, peering toward the front of the building. She had seen no flash of light.

Bastien shook his head. "I think Seth just found Emrys."

Ami's heart pounded so erratically she had difficulty breathing. Standing in the doorway, she stared inside. Not at the vampire manacled to the table, but at the two men standing over him.

Her feet glued themselves to the floor. Her body began to tremble.

"Ami?" Marcus crowded her side and rested a hand on her back.

She couldn't speak. Couldn't pry her tongue from the roof of her mouth. Or silence the screams that erupted in her head.

Marcus's hand clenched, tugging her shirt tight.

Fear and hatred and remembered pain must have tumbled the barriers of her mind, allowing the screams to batter him through the mental channel she used to communicate with him.

The foundation of the building suddenly shook beneath their feet. Thunder rumbled outside.

Seth must have heard, too. And David. Somewhere in the building the latter emitted a roar of rage.

Wind buffeted her as two presences loomed behind her.

"Is that him?" Seth asked.

Yes.

"Which one?" Marcus demanded.

Both of them were there. In Texas. Both of these men tortured me.

Seth growled and shoved Marcus aside. In a blink, he was across the room, the older of the two humans shoved up against the wall two or three feet off the floor, a dagger at his throat. "Emrys, I presume?"

Marcus shot forward and claimed the other before David could. His prey tried to swing a bone saw at him. Marcus knocked it out of his hands, grabbed him by the throat, and spun him around so his back was pressed to Marcus's chest. A dagger appeared in Marcus's hand and pricked the man's throat.

David touched Ami's back.

Forcing herself to breathe, she took a jerky step forward. Then another. Then another until she stared up into the eyes of the man Marcus held. He was only a few inches taller than her. Paunchy. Pale.

"Remember me?" she asked, infusing the words with all of the loathing she felt for him.

"No," he lied, voice high and tense.

"You will," she promised.

Bastien followed Melanie, cursing the fact that she was faster than him. He skidded to halt beside her just inside the door of what appeared to be an operating room with an observation gallery overlooking it.

Seth was choking one human and applying enough pressure with his dagger to make him wet himself.

Marcus held another man against his chest while Ami addressed him.

Melanie made a sound of distress and hurried over to the form on the *operating table*. Dried blood from countless wounds covered Cliff's bare flesh. A couple dozen of them hadn't healed and oozed blood. His eyes were closed.

Melanie leaned over him, drew a hand over his dreadlocks. Tears welled in her eyes and spilled onto Cliff's forehead and cheek. "Cliff?"

"How do we free him?" Bastien asked the humans

Seth rammed his victim against the wall. "Answer him."

The man clamped his lips shut.

Seth offered him a sinister smile.

The man grimaced in agony, abandoned trying to pry Seth's hand loose, and started to claw at his own head.

Seth turned to Melanie. "There are several buttons on the underside of the table that open and close the cuffs."

Bastien found the buttons for her and pressed them.

"It's okay, Cliff," she whispered. "We're going to take you home."

Bastien lifted the young vampire into his arms. As Melanie headed for the doorway, Bastien looked down at his friend.

Cliff's eyelids raised a fraction. Just enough to expose sleepy, glowing eyes devoid of recognition.

And brimming with madness.

Unconsciousness reclaimed him.

Bastien swallowed hard, fought the grief and fear that rose within him. The madness couldn't vanquish Cliff. It was too soon. They needed more time. And would have had it if he hadn't been tortured.

Bastien swung toward Seth with a snarl.

We've got it covered, Seth promised, dark anticipation in the glowing golden gaze that met his.

Bastien nodded and followed Melanie out into the hallway.

Seth spun around and slammed Emrys back-first onto the table hard enough to knock the wind out of him at the very least.

Emrys cried out.

David waved his hand. The manacles clamped down on the mercenary leader's limbs.

"I can make you rich!" Emrys screeched. "I can make you all rich!"

Seth's lips stretched in a smile that nearly made *Bastien* shiver. "I can make you scream."

The man began to shout for help.

None would come.

Ami stepped away from the man Marcus held and approached the table.

As the door swung closed without visual assistance, Bastien saw her reach for a scalpel.

"Dr. Lipton."

Melanie turned away from the door behind which screams arose.

The French immortals all faced her, expressions somber.

"Melanie," she corrected mechanically. Pain still rode her hard and she was feeling a little shell-shocked by the night's events.

"We've found Joe," Richart announced. And the gentle way he spoke warned her of what would follow.

Lisette came forward and touched her arm. "He's conscious. But . . . there is only madness in his thoughts."

Étienne nodded, face full of regret. "Only the ravings of a lunatic."

Melanie stared through them. She couldn't do this. All the pain and death and . . .

She couldn't lose Joe tonight. Couldn't stand quietly by

while Bastien drew his katana and swung it. Couldn't watch Joe's head leave his body and tumble to the floor. See his body shrivel up until nothing of him remained.

Tears welled in her eyes and spilled over her lashes as she turned to Bastien. She shook her head. "Please . . . Not tonight. Not here. Not . . . like this. Not without even trying to bring him back to us. Please."

His eyes glowed a vibrant amber that illuminated the moisture shimmering in them. These were his friends. She knew she was making it harder on him by asking him to delay the inevitable, but . . .

The relief she felt when he nodded weakened her knees and nearly landed her on the floor.

The siblings motioned to a doorway down the hall.

Melanie limped forward and passed through it.

Joe lay still on a table identical to the one that had restrained Cliff. Manacles, coated with blood from his struggles and the wounds the butchers had inflicted, held his arms, legs, and head down. His chest rose and fell in quick bursts.

As Melanie crossed to his side, his eyes opened and rolled her way. Luminous blue, they speared her with hatred. Spittle flew from his lips as he shouted words so slurred she couldn't understand them.

"Joe?" she said softly. "It's Dr. Lipton. It's Melanie."

Nothing. No change.

She reached under the table and pressed the button that would open the manacle holding his head immobile.

The heavy metal clamp sprang open and slid apart.

Joe instantly raised his head and snapped at her like a feral animal.

"Joe." She struggled to speak soothingly around the lump in her throat. "It's okay, Joe. You're safe now. Cliff is here. And Bastien. We're going to take you home."

He started to slam his head back against the table over and

over again. His arms and legs flexed. The manacles dug deeper with every movement.

Melanie reached into her back pocket and withdrew one of the two auto-injectors she had loaded with the vampires' dose. She flipped the yellow cap open.

"Everything will be okay," she lied and pressed the pen to his shoulder.

His struggles slowed. His head fell still. His muscles relaxed.

She drew her hand over his tangled blond hair and met those burning eyes. "You're with friends now."

His lids drooped, then closed.

She circled the table to press the buttons on the other side. Bastien hovered in the doorway with Cliff in his arms.

As she raised her head and met his gaze, her chest hitched with a sob.

Both knew what the morrow would bring.

Chapter 18

As immortals, Seconds, and Chris gathered around David's impressive dining table, conversation abounded. Seth and David took their usual places at either end of the table. The others filled in the chairs along the sides.

Bastien found himself seated between Melanie and Richart, with Richart's siblings across from them.

Almost a month had passed since they had descended upon Emrys's compound, though it seemed only days had instead. The time since had been a roller coaster of ups and downs, leaving Bastien feeling as if he had no control over anything in his life.

Joe had been beyond their help. Melanie had tried to reach him . . . tried so hard it broke Bastien's heart. And made him love her all the more. But the young vampire had been lost to them, all sanity devoured by the virus.

In accordance with the living will Joe had created when he had moved into network headquarters, he had been sedated. Then Melanie had drained his blood. All of it. And he had . . . gone. Just like that. Leaving nothing of himself behind to bury.

Dr. Whetsman had argued and fought, trying to convince

Chris to let him throw out the will and extract the vampire's organs and brain for study.

Chris had held firm.

And Bastien had not antagonized the network leader once since.

The two had finally found common ground. Chris had lost his contacts. Bastien had lost his friend. Both held themselves responsible.

Cliff had bounced back. Bastien had not thought such would be possible. Nor had Melanie. But Cliff was still succeeding in staving off the madness that had claimed both of his friends. He was also mentoring Stuart, who—every day—sought new ways to make amends for the attack his entrance into their lives had instigated.

Food platters circulated the table on large hands. The scents suffusing the air were mouthwatering. Water, tea, and sparkling grape juice flowed freely. As did laughter and teasing.

Melanie rested a hand on Bastien's thigh.

He glanced down at her.

"You okay?" she asked.

He nodded, clasped her hand, and brought it to his lips for a kiss.

The two of them were closer than ever. Though she could have returned to her cozy home, Melanie had spent every day here with him. Every night she continued her research at the network, given leave to do so by Seth, who thought her research more important than having her in the field, hunting vampires.

Across the table, Richart cleared his throat. "How is Cliff?"

Bastien felt Melanie's surprise as she answered.

"He's good. He hasn't had any episodes since the day after we rescued him."

Richart pushed his food around on his plate. "I was thinking of visiting him."

She glanced at Bastien.

He was as shocked as she was. "I think he'd like that," Bastien said slowly. "I'm sure he's tired of seeing the same faces day after day."

Étienne spoke up. "Perhaps I will visit him as well."

Both Frenchmen had met Cliff while monitoring Bastien. Had they seen what he had seen? Someone worth saving? Worth fighting for?

Melanie smiled. "That would be wonderful."

"Does he like sports?" Lisette asked, face hopeful.

"Yes."

"Perhaps I could catch a game with him."

Tanner nodded beside her. "I'd be up for that, too. We should catch a Lakers game. If I remember correctly from our days serving Bastien, Cliff's a pretty big Lakers fan."

"Excellent," Lisette proclaimed. "I'll bring the peanuts and popcorn."

The rest of the meal passed in a blur. Bastien may not be as hated as he had been before, but he wasn't yet welcomed into many conversations. Not that he really noticed. He was too busy wondering if Hell had frozen over.

Immortals making friends with a vampire? What the hell would happen next?

He and Melanie made their escape shortly after dinner, which technically was their breakfast or brunch since it was their first meal of the night.

Holding hands, they slipped down into the basement, dodged Marcus's partially bald cat, Slim, and headed for their quiet room, where they would make love before Melanie headed for the network and Bastien left to hunt and possibly recruit more vampires.

Emrys was dead. What was left of his shadow army had been disbanded with no memory of how they had spent recent months. And Seth had erased Donald and Nelson's memories.

But the vampire population in the area continued to flourish and grow.

The whole situation sort of reminded Bastien of newspapers and scandal sheets. Accusations of this or that would be splashed across the front page in large letters. Then, if they proved unfounded, apologies and retractions would be offered in tiny print on the bottom of page thirty-seven, where few would notice them.

Well, news of the uprisings and wars being waged in North Carolina had circled the globe. Word that those uprisings and wars had ended with Immortal Guardians the victors, however, had garnered little attention.

"Bastien. Melanie."

They turned at the sound of Chris's voice.

"Seth meant to catch you before he left, but got called away early."

"Did he need something?" Bastien asked.

"No. He wanted you to have this." Strolling forward, Chris held out a set of keys.

Melanie took them and turned them over in her hand. "What are these for?"

"Your new home. Seth thought you two might like to have a place of your own, but Melanie's house isn't secure."

Bastien stared.

Chris pulled out his trusty notepad, flipped through it, and tore off a sheet. "Here's the address and directions to it. It's fully furnished, but you're welcome to make any changes you want. I knew you guys wouldn't have a lot of time to shop and just thought I'd get you started. The house is in a suitably isolated location. The kitchen is fully stocked. There's blood in the fridge. Toiletries in the bathroom. An escape tunnel in the basement. And I dropped by there on my way here and turned on the heater, so if you want to go check it out or spend the day there after work, you're good to go."

Feeling Melanie's stare, Bastien glanced down at her.

"We have our own house?" she asked. "Just the two of us?"

Uncertainty rose. "If you don't want to live with me . . ."

She frowned, then hit him hard in the shoulder. "Of course I want to live with you. I love you, Bastien. And I fully intend to marry you whenever you get off your ass and ask me."

All conversation in the house ceased.

His mouth fell open.

Chris's did, too.

"Seriously?" they both asked at the same time.

Melanie rolled her eyes. Tilting her head back, she told the ceiling. "Yes. Seriously. I am in love with Sebastien Newcombe. I intend to spend all of eternity with him. If any of you don't like it, get over it."

Bastien grinned. He had known she cared about him. He felt it every time he touched her. He supposed he had just thought that might change if she spent more time with him and . . .

Well, she pretty much knew all of his secrets. So maybe it wouldn't change?

Dipping his head, he kissed her lips. "Will you marry me, Melanie?"

"Hell, yes. Now let's get out of here and go check out our new home so I can talk dirty to you without all of *them* listening."

Laughing, he reclaimed her hand and headed back upstairs. By the time they reached the front door, they were practically running, eager to embrace their future.

And damned if some of the other immortals didn't hoot and cheer.

Ami gritted her teeth as her stomach churned and turned and threatened to eject her dinner.

A large, warm body pressed up against her back. Marcus

dipped his head and kissed her neck as he slipped his arms around her middle.

Relaxing back against him, she closed her eyes.

The room they now shared at David's place held a tropical feel, the humidity from their shared shower lingering in the air.

"Your heart is racing," Marcus murmured between kisses.

Ami forced a smile. "You tend to have that effect on me."

Turning her in his arms, he brushed his lips against hers, trailed them across her cheek, skipped to her forehead. "You feel warm."

"You do that to me, too," she teased. "Well, you *and* the shower. That's a powerful combination."

He laughed, low and husky. "I wish we could spend all night in that shower."

She nipped his chin and stepped away. "Me, too. Unfortunately, those vampires aren't going to hunt themselves."

Groaning, he went to work buttoning his shirt.

As soon as he finished, Ami draped the bandolier carrying his throwing knives across his chest.

"Is something wrong, love?" he asked, studying her a little too intently.

Avoiding his gaze, she reached for his short swords and slid them into their sheaths. "I'm worried about the mercenaries. What if we didn't get them all? What if there are others?"

"Chris seems to think we've neutralized the human threat."

She met his gaze. "We didn't expect Keegan to cause any real problems and look what happened with that."

"That little weasel *did* catch us off guard, but Emrys was the true threat. Now that he's dead, he can't hurt us anymore."

Ami nodded. She had helped them make sure of that and still wasn't sure how she felt about her part in the violence that had taken place that night.

Sitting on the edge of the bed, Marcus pulled on one of his boots and laced it up.

Ami crossed her arms over her chest and tried to ignore her stomach when it lurched again.

"You didn't eat very much at dinner," Marcus commented, watching her shrewdly.

Damn, he knew her well. "Tracy's perfume was driving me crazy," she admitted. "I couldn't smell the food for it."

Marcus frowned. "You could smell that?"

"How could I not? It was so strong it overpowered the room."

He shook his head. "Tracy doesn't wear perfume, love. That was her deodorant."

Ami stared at him. A sickening feeling that had nothing to do with whatever was going on with her dinner entered her stomach. "It was?"

"Yes. I didn't realize humans . . ." he smiled "or you could smell it."

"We can. She needs to start using a scentless deodorant stone. If she ever has to go to Lisette's aid, the vampires will smell her coming a mile away."

"Well," he said and took the other boot she handed him, "I'll let *you* be the one to tell her that."

I don't think so.

"Is that all it was?" he asked, eyeing her as though he were trying to figure out what had changed, if she had cut her hair or wore it differently . . .

"What do you mean?" She knew he saw through the words. She couldn't lie worth a damn, especially to him or Seth.

He shoved his big foot in the boot, then paused. "There's been a lot of coming and going around here lately . . . a lot of traffic."

More immortals and Seconds than usual had been taking advantage of David's open door policy and making use of his home, dropping by for meals, sometimes staying through the day.

"Do you need a break, honey?" Marcus asked, voice soft

with concern. "I understand the network owns a number of safe houses. We could make arrangements with Chris to use one and get away for a while."

Ami blinked back tears. Marcus knew how difficult it was for her to meet new people and spend time with men and women she didn't know, an unfortunate consequence of the capture and subsequent months of torture she had endured at the hands of Emrys and his fellow monsters.

She shook her head. "No, we can't. You know I'm the reason David's home has been inundated with twice as many visitors as usual. They all knew Emrys was determined to capture me again and have been lingering here to protect me. How can I reject that?"

He laced his boot, then rose. "Just say the word and I'll reject it for you. We don't even have to stay in the area. I could take you to England or France. Italy. Australia. Somewhere we can truly be alone."

Closing the distance between them, she wrapped her arms around him and leaned into his strong chest. "My family is here. *Our* family is here. So here we'll stay."

He hugged her close, kissed the top of her head. "Whatever makes you happy."

Ami squeezed him tight and swallowed hard against the lump in her throat. "You'd better get going."

Marcus drew back, took her lips in a deep, pulse-spiking kiss, then headed for the door. "Oh, by the way. I heard Sheldon will be training with Darnell tonight."

Sheldon had once landed Marcus in such a vampire muck that Ami had raced to Marcus's rescue and ended up with a knife sticking out of her back.

Even as she frowned, Marcus tossed her a grin and winked at her. "Try not to terrorize the boy too much."

Ami actually managed to find a smile and hold it . . . until he ducked out into the hallway and closed the door behind him. Clamping a hand over her mouth, she bolted for the bathroom, bent over the toilet, and lost what little dinner she had managed to consume earlier.

When at last the retching ended, she rinsed her mouth out and brushed her teeth, splashed some cold water on her face for good measure. Her hands shook as she drew a towel down over her eyes and cheeks.

Ami studied her pallid reflection in the mirror. Large tears welled in her eyes and spilled down her cheeks.

She couldn't ignore what was happening to her any longer. For days she had felt that something was wrong, but had hoped it was simply anxiety. Being around so many strangers and hunting Emrys really had been stressful for her, but . . . anxiety didn't enhance one's sense of smell. Anxiety didn't make one run a fever. It might make one lose one's appetite, but would that escalate to vomiting?

Returning to the bedroom, she picked up her cell phone and dialed Darnell's number.

"Hey, Ami," he answered jovially. "You ought to join us in the training room. I'm about to kick Sheldon's ass."

"Oh, ha freaking ha," Sheldon said in the background. "Wait, did you say Ami?"

Darnell laughed. "He is *so* afraid of you. What did you do to him?"

Aside from telling him in explicit detail how she would maim him if he ever endangered Marcus's life again . . . nothing.

"I need to talk to you," she said in lieu of a reply.

"Sure," Darnell said, voice sobering. "Where are you?"

"Our bedroom." One of the two quiet rooms that would afford them privacy.

"On my way."

Mere seconds passed before the door opened. Darnell slipped inside and closed it behind him. Six feet tall, he wore the standard garb of a Second, his broad-muscled shoulders stretching the fabric of the black shirt. His bald, brown head gleamed beneath the overhead light.

Ami tossed her phone on the bed.

Darnell took one look at her face and said, "Oh shit. What happened? What's wrong?"

Her breath hitched in a sob. "I'm infected," she announced, then burst into tears.

If Darnell's face could have blanched, it would have. "What?"

"I'm infected with the virus. I'm transforming," Ami cried.

Swearing again, he hurried across the room and drew her into his arms. "Are you sure?"

She nodded. Because she was neither human nor *gifted one*, none of them knew whether she would become vampire or immortal if infected. Or if she would survive the transformation at all.

"Does Marcus know?"

She shook her head, sobbing too hard to speak. She couldn't bare to tell Marcus. He would blame himself and . . . if she died or turned vampire . . .

She just couldn't tell him yet.

Darnell shifted and withdrew one arm. She heard him dial his cell phone. "Yeah, it's me. We have a situation. Ami needs you in the quiet room stat. Bring David."

There was a hardness to his voice that she had never heard before. Darnell was a happy-go-lucky kind of guy. One who did not anger easily. Even Bastien couldn't piss him off, which always succeeded in pissing *Bastien* off whenever he tried and failed.

A ripple of energy filled the room. Seth and David appeared just inside the door. Ami drew back enough to meet their concerned gazes.

"What happened?" Seth asked without preamble.

"Marcus fucking bit her and now she's infected," Darnell growled with such venom Ami was shocked speechless.

Seth's eyes flashed a bright gold. David's flashed amber. A rumbling sound arose as floor, wall, and ceiling began to vibrate.

"I'll kill him," Seth snarled.

"No!" Ami shouted above the racket. "It isn't what you think!"

"You would lie for him? You would protect him?" he demanded furiously.

"Because he didn't bite me! Darnell misunderstood. He didn't bite me." She looked to David. "Marcus didn't bite me!"

Eyes still glowing with anger, David placed a restraining hand on Seth's shoulder and looked to Darnell.

Darnell frowned down at Ami. "You said you were infected, that you're transforming."

"I am," she said. "But—"

Seth shrugged off David's hand with a roar and vanished. The rumbling and quaking ceased.

Panic ripped through Ami. "Where is he going?"

"To find Marcus would be my guess," David said, voice tight.

"Well, call him back!" she pleaded. "He'll kill him!" When David merely stared back, she looked up at Darnell. "Marcus didn't bite me, Darnell. Please! You can't let Seth kill him!"

Uncertainty entered Darnell's deep brown eyes. "How the hell am I supposed to stop him?"

"I don't know! Get on your damned phone and—"

Seth reappeared, one hand closed around Marcus's throat, holding him a foot above the ground. The house once more began to shake with Seth's fury.

Marcus's hands pried futilely at Seth's fingers. Face reddening, he looked with wide eyes at Ami, silently asking her what the hell was going on.

He thinks you bit me, she told him telepathically.

What? He looked at Seth. *I didn't bite her! I swear it to you! I love her! I would give my life to protect her! Why the hell would I infect her with the virus when I know what it might do to her? That it might hurt her? That it might take her from me?*

Seth's brows drew down into a deep V. Opening his fingers, he let Marcus drop.

Seth could read one's thoughts, feel one's emotions, see one's past. All would have confirmed that Marcus had never bitten her.

Marcus stumbled when his boots hit the ground, but managed to remain upright. He did not, however, begin to breathe again. Seth's grip had wrought too much damage.

"David," Ami begged, *"please."*

David didn't look at Seth as he wrapped midnight fingers around Marcus's throat to heal him.

Air whooshed into Marcus's mouth and filled his lungs.

When David withdrew his touch, Marcus bent over and breathed deeply for a long moment. In and out. In and out.

The bedroom's doorbell rang.

Darnell crossed to the door and opened it a crack.

Étienne, Lisette, Tracy, Sheldon, Yuri, Stanislov, Ethan, and Edward all stood out in the hallway, expressions uncertain.

Étienne cleared his throat. "Everything all right in there?"

"Yes," Darnell said, deadpan. "Why do you ask?"

Étienne pointed to the ceiling. "Because the house is about to collapse around us."

Everyone in the quiet room looked to Seth.

Seth closed his eyes and drew in several deep, calming breaths.

The rumbling quieted. The quaking ceased.

Darnell addressed the others. "We're fine. Thanks."

Étienne was opening his mouth to speak when Darnell closed the door in their faces and leaned back against it.

"Would someone please tell me what the hell is going on?" Marcus demanded and turned to Seth. "Who told you I bit Ami?"

"I did," Darnell said.

"It was a misunderstanding," she interjected, her body beginning to tremble. Marcus would be devastated when she told him.

Marcus looked around, face full of confusion. "A misunderstanding? What kind of misunderstanding?" He drew in another deep breath. "And what the hell is that smell? Did someone vomit in here or something?"

"I did," Ami admitted.

Brow furrowing, Marcus moved to stand in front of her and cupped her face in his big hands. "I *knew* something was off earlier. What's the matter, honey? Are you sick?"

"Ami doesn't get sick," David pronounced.

Marcus gave him an irritated glance. "Clearly, she does."

"No," Seth added, "she doesn't."

Marcus met Ami's gaze, not yet understanding.

"Tell him," Darnell murmured.

"I'm infected," she whispered, tears again welling and spilling over her lashes.

Marcus stilled, his face draining of color. "What?"

"I'm transforming."

"That's impossible. You can't be. I've never bitten you."

"Was it a vampire?" Darnell asked.

Marcus's eyes flashed amber. "A vampire bit you? When?"

"No. No vampire bit me."

"Then who infected you?"

Ami stared up at him, saying nothing.

David suddenly swore, then Seth.

"What?" Darnell asked, frowning at them.

Seth dragged a hand down over his face. "Please tell me you use condoms, Marcus."

"Of course I don't," he said, confusion crinkling his forehead. "Why would I need to? Our sperm die as soon as we ejaculate and the virus dies with them."

"In a human female, yes," David said. "But Ami isn't

human and her body possesses remarkable regenerative properties. If her body kept the sperm from dying, then . . ."

"I infected her?" Marcus concluded, his horrified gaze returning to Ami. "I infected you?"

She bit her lip. "It was an accident."

"Do you think that matters to me?" he nearly shouted. Yanking her to him, he wrapped his arms around her in a crushing embrace fraught with fear. "Why didn't you tell me?"

"I just put it together today and—"

"You knew when I left."

"I wasn't completely sure until I threw up. I've never done that before. And I'm running a fever and . . . I didn't know my sense of smell had become so acute until you told me you were surprised I could smell Tracy's deodorant," she told him, hugging him back. "I didn't want to believe it."

"You idiot!" Darnell shouted at Marcus. "How could you be so fucking stupid?"

"Darnell!" Ami bit out. "I said it was an accident!"

"Stepping on your toe is an accident, Ami," Darnell protested. "Spilling your tea is an accident. This is fucking stupidity!" he bellowed, his fear for her plain.

Not wanting Marcus to condemn himself even more, Ami jumped to his defense, bickering with Darnell while Marcus silently held her, face buried in the crook of her neck, squeezing her tighter and tighter until his grip bordered on pain.

"Wait," Seth said suddenly.

Ami and Darnell fell silent.

"Ami, what are your symptoms again?"

She saw a look pass between him and David.

"Fever. Nausea. Vomiting. Fatigue. A heightened sense of smell."

Again, he and David shared a look.

"Everyone be quiet for a moment," Seth commanded.

No one said a word.

A minute passed, during which Seth didn't move.

David suddenly sucked in a breath. His eyes widened.

"You hear it?" Seth asked him.

"Yes."

Marcus straightened. Keeping one arm around Ami, he faced the elder immortals. "Hear what?"

"Ami," Seth said, "you aren't infected with the virus."

"I'm not?" Relief suffused her . . . until she realized they did *not* look relieved. "Then, what is it?"

David drew her gaze. "You're pregnant."

For the first time in a month, Melanie felt only happiness. She adored Bastien and felt *so* loved in return. They grew closer every day. They were going to marry.

And now they had their own home. No more watching every word spoken outside their bedroom because *anyone* could be listening. And would.

As Bastien guided her Chevy up the last stretch of a very long drive, the headlights fell upon a lovely one-story home. Melanie was still getting used to the way color appeared at night with her newly enhanced vision, but thought it was tan or some similar pale earth tone with white trim and dark shutters. Solar panels on the roof reflected the light of the moon overhead. A quaint front porch . . . was occupied.

Seth sat on the steps leading up to it.

Bastien pulled the car up close to the garage and parked.

As they exited the car and crunched their way up the gravel path, Seth rose.

He seemed . . . very somber. Or upset. His eyes were glowing a faint, entrancing gold.

"What's up?" Bastien asked. He touched a hand to Melanie's back.

Melanie leaned into his side.

"We have a situation."

Oh, no. Not Cliff, she thought. *Please, not Cliff. He's been doing so well.*

"It isn't Cliff," Seth told her.

"Then what is it?" Bastien asked.

Seth hesitated. His long hair, usually neatly combed and confined by a leather tie, was loose and disheveled as if he had run his hands through it repeatedly. "I'm betraying a confidence here. But I need your help."

Melanie glanced up at Bastien. Judging by his puckered brow, he was picking up on their leader's anxiety, too. "We'll do whatever we can," she said.

Bastien seconded her vow. "What is it? What's happened?"

Seth drew in a deep breath. "Ami is pregnant."

The stark declaration sent shock rippling through Melanie. Beside her, Bastien stopped breathing.

"I thought immortals were incapable of impregnating a mortal," she said slowly.

Seth's lips stretched in a tight smile that held no amusement. "Ami isn't your ordinary mortal."

"That moron!" Bastien blurted, face darkening with fury. "Of all the half-witted, imbecilic, numbnutted things to do! Didn't he use condoms?"

"No. He thought it unnecessary because technically she's mortal."

"She isn't human!" Bastien bellowed. "She heals at an accelerated rate! Did he never think that—"

Seth held up a hand. "He didn't."

Melanie studied the men. "Are you worried that Ami has become infected with the virus? Or are you worried that the fetus is infected?"

"Both," Seth confided. "I can't smell the virus on her, but . . . because her physiology is different . . . on her I may not be able to."

Melanie understood their concern. There was no way of anticipating what the virus would do to her, if it would transform her or kill her. Make her vampire or immortal. And an infant . . .

Would the virus keep it from developing properly? From aging?

And what of Ami's origins? Would a fetus that resulted from *gifted one* DNA and alien DNA combining be . . . healthy?

"How are they taking it?" she asked.

Seth shook his head. "Marcus is devastated and is doing his damnedest to hide it because Ami is thrilled. The primary reason she came here was because a virus used as a bioweapon by people from another solar system has rendered an overwhelming majority of the women on her planet either infertile or unable to carry a baby to term. Births are extremely rare on her home world, so . . . yeah. She's excited."

Bastien swore. "She doesn't understand."

"No," Seth agreed, "she doesn't."

"You have to tell her," Melanie said. "She deserves to know the truth."

Seth met her gaze. "Would you talk to her? Examine her?"

"I don't think she'll—"

"She wants you to. I told her that, because difficult pregnancies are the norm now for her people, she would need nearly constant medical supervision by immortal healers *and* human physicians. David and I may have both delivered babies in the past—"

Bastien's eyebrows rose. "You have?"

"But our overall knowledge of gestation and the various problems that can arise is limited. Unless her health is threatened, I'm not sure we would know what was normal and what wasn't. I told her as much and . . . she asked that *you* examine her, Melanie, and guide her through her pregnancy."

Melanie would be happy to do so. Ami must have lost her fear of Melanie while caring for her during her transformation.

And, because Melanie had spent so much time studying the intricate differences in physiology between vampires and immortals, she was the most qualified to monitor the fetus—and Ami—for signs of infection.

"My specialty isn't obstetrics, but I can read a lot faster now and can learn everything I need to know in very little time. I'll get started tonight if you'd like."

"Tomorrow will be soon enough. Tell Chris what books and other materials you need and he'll have them here by sunrise."

"Great. I'll do that."

"I was also thinking of bringing in an immortal from Germany who has been doing his own research on the virus. He might know more about its effect on babies."

"I'd welcome his knowledge."

"David and I discussed it and . . . either he or I will remain here at his home in case anything goes wrong or she should need our healing abilities to help her carry the baby to term."

Bastien said, "I know nothing about any of this, but I'll do whatever I can to help, too. Anything you need, just say the word."

Melanie knew he thought of Ami as a sister and was very protective of her.

Melanie felt protective of her, too. Ami had been the first in the Immortal Guardians' world to offer Bastien friendship without strings attached. And Melanie had been one of the few people who had been told Ami's true origins. Most believed her a *gifted one*.

"So," Bastien broached hesitantly, "how are you going to keep this quiet?"

"I don't think we can. We all missed the fetus's heartbeat because the pregnancy is so new and babies just aren't part of our world. I realize now that I heard it at dinner. I just assumed it was Slim. But, that heartbeat will grow stronger."

"And Ami will get bigger," Bastien added.

"What will you tell the others?" Melanie asked.

"I don't know. We haven't gotten that far. Hell, we just found out she's pregnant twenty minutes ago." He sighed and ran his hands down his face. "I'm sorry to lay this on you two. And on tonight of all nights. Congratulations on your engagement."

Surprised, Melanie smiled. "Thank you. Although I think I kind of pushed him into it."

Seth smiled. "No, you didn't. He's wanted to spend the rest of his life with you since before the network was attacked."

Melanie looked up at Bastien. "Really?"

Bastien frowned at Seth. "If you're as busy as you claim you are, how do you manage to spend so much time in my head?"

"It's *because* I'm so busy that I *spend* time in your head. If I know what you're thinking, I don't have to worry about what you'll do next. I already know it."

Melanie took Bastien's hand and spoke quickly to prevent him from pursuing the subject further. "Thank you for the house, Seth. We really appreciate it."

"You're welcome. I hope it will be to your liking."

"What about Tanner?" Bastien asked. "Is he still going to be my Second?"

"Yes. The two of you work well together and he's fervently loyal to you. There's a small guesthouse in back for Tanner. That way he'll be near enough to be here when you need him and far enough away to give you privacy."

"Perfect." Melanie looked forward to getting to know Bastien's friend better.

Seth continued to look anxious. Somehow she thought that wasn't a look he wore very often.

"Is there anything we can do for *you*?"

Much to her surprise, Bastien nodded. "Would you like to

come in? Have something to eat? Chris said the kitchen is fully stocked."

At last, Seth's lips tilted up in a small smile. "Careful there. I might think you're actually starting to like me."

Bastien flipped him the bird.

Seth shook his head. "If I told you just how alike you and Roland are you would crap your pants."

"Please, don't," Melanie quipped with a smile.

Both men laughed.

"Thank you for your gracious offer, but I need to check on something in Denmark. I just . . . needed to . . ."

"Talk?" she suggested softly.

He nodded. "Yes. Why don't the two of you take the night off? Get a feel for the house. See what you'd like to change."

"Make love in every room?" Bastien added with a teasing leer at Melanie.

She laughed.

As did Seth. "That would be my choice were I you. In fact, take tomorrow night off as well." He drew out a pocket watch, flipped it open, and consulted the face. "I'm sorry. I have to go. Thank you both."

"Stay safe," Melanie told him.

Smiling, he nodded.

"Seth," Bastien said suddenly.

Seth met his gaze.

Melanie waited for Bastien to speak. When he didn't, she wondered if he might not be *thinking* what he wanted to say instead.

Seth smiled and clapped Bastien on the shoulder, then vanished.

"What did you say?" she asked curiously.

"Nothing," he disclosed with a faint frown. "I wasn't sure how to say it."

"Well, what did you *want* to say?"

"I wanted to thank him." Facing her, he reached out and toyed with the hair she had left loose. "If he hadn't ignored all of the calls for my execution and taken me under his wing, I never would have found you."

Smiling, Melanie leaned into him and kissed his chin. "I think he heard you."

He hugged her close.

"So . . ." she said.

Bastien quirked an eyebrow. "So?"

"Every room, huh?"

A slow smile spread across his handsome features. "Every room." He lifted her into his arms and started up the steps.

She wrapped her own arms around his neck. "Did you really know before the network was attacked that you wanted to spend the rest of your life with me?"

"I may have fantasized about it a time or two. Or twenty. I just couldn't let myself believe that you would want to spend the rest of yours with me. Especially after you were transformed. Eternity is a long time."

She pressed her lips to his in a tender kiss. "Then I'll have plenty of time to convince you I love you."

He kissed her hard. "I don't know what the hell you see in me, Melanie, but I am *so* glad you see it. I never thought I would be happy again."

"Are you happy?"

"Yes. With you."

She claimed his lips once more, stroked them with her tongue, heard his heartbeat pick up its pace.

He groaned. "I'd be happier if I could get the front door open without splintering it. Where the hell are those keys?"

Grinning, she dangled them in front of his face, then unlocked the front door. "Which room do you want to break in first?"

He opened the door and stepped inside.

Melanie flipped on the light switch just inside the door, illuminating a lovely living room.

Bastien grinned. "How about the living room?"

Melanie laughed as he kicked the door shut and headed for a nice, long, cushy sofa.

Did you miss the other books in the Immortal Guardians series?

DARKNESS DAWNS

In this dazzling, sensual novel, Dianne Duvall beckons readers into a world of vampires, immortals, and humans with extraordinary gifts . . . where passion can last forever, if you're willing to pay the price . . .

Once, Sarah Bingham's biggest challenge was making her students pay attention in class. Now, after rescuing a wounded stranger, she's landed in the middle of a battle between corrupt vampires and powerful immortals who also need blood to survive. Roland Warbrook is the most compelling man Sarah has ever laid hands on. But his desire for her is mingled with a hunger he can barely control . . .

In his nine centuries of immortal existence, no woman has tempted Roland as much as Sarah. But asking her to love him is impossible—when it means forfeiting the world she's always known, and the life he would do anything to protect . . .

NIGHT REIGNS

Dianne Duvall portrays a world of temptation, loyalty, and heartbreak . . . a world where danger and desire walk hand in hand . . .

Ami isn't much for trusting strangers. She has a hard time trusting anyone. But she's no coward, and she's no pushover in the protection department either. So when she comes across a mysterious warrior taking on eight deranged vampires on his own, she doesn't hesitate to save his bacon. Of course, that was before she realized what one little rescue would get her into . . .

Marcus Graden has been an Immortal protector of humanity for eight hundred years, and he's not interested in backup. From the moment Ami arrives in his life, he can't deny that she's strong, smart, and extremely skilled at watching his back. But she's also destroying his protective solitude and stirring desires he can't bear to awaken. After all, whatever her secrets—how can she defeat death itself?

Romantic Suspense from
Lisa Jackson

See How She Dies	0-8217-7605-3	$6.99US/$9.99CAN
Final Scream	0-8217-7712-2	$7.99US/$10.99CAN
Wishes	0-8217-6309-1	$5.99US/$7.99CAN
Whispers	0-8217-7603-7	$6.99US/$9.99CAN
Twice Kissed	0-8217-6038-6	$5.99US/$7.99CAN
Unspoken	0-8217-6402-0	$6.50US/$8.50CAN
If She Only Knew	0-8217-6708-9	$6.50US/$8.50CAN
Hot Blooded	0-8217-6841-7	$6.99US/$9.99CAN
Cold Blooded	0-8217-6934-0	$6.99US/$9.99CAN
The Night Before	0-8217-6936-7	$6.99US/$9.99CAN
The Morning After	0-8217-7295-3	$6.99US/$9.99CAN
Deep Freeze	0-8217-7296-1	$7.99US/$10.99CAN
Fatal Burn	0-8217-7577-4	$7.99US/$10.99CAN
Shiver	0-8217-7578-2	$7.99US/$10.99CAN
Most Likely to Die	0-8217-7576-6	$7.99US/$10.99CAN
Absolute Fear	0-8217-7936-2	$7.99US/$9.49CAN
Almost Dead	0-8217-7579-0	$7.99US/$10.99CAN
Lost Souls	0-8217-7938-9	$7.99US/$10.99CAN
Left to Die	1-4201-0276-1	$7.99US/$10.99CAN
Wicked Game	1-4201-0338-5	$7.99US/$9.99CAN
Malice	0-8217-7940-0	$7.99US/$9.49CAN